Lyn Andrews was born in Liverpool in September 1943. Her father was killed on D-Day when Lyn was just nine months old. When Lyn was three her mother Monica married Frank Moore, who became 'Dad' to the little girl. Lyn was brought up in Liverpool and became a secretary before marrying policeman Bob Andrews. In 1970 Lyn gave birth to triplets – two sons and a daughter – who kept her busy for the next few years. Once they'd gone to school Lyn began writing, and her first novel was quickly accepted for publication. She has since written a further thirty-five novels.

Lyn lived for eleven years in Ireland and is now resident on the Isle of Man, but spends as much time as possible back on Merseyside, seeing her children and four grandchildren.

Lyn Andrews

Liverpool Angels

headline

First published in Great Britain in 2013 by
HEADLINE PUBLISHING GROUP

First published in paperback in Great Britain in 2014 by
HEADLINE PUBLISHING GROUP

2

Cataloguing in Publication Data is available from the British Library

ISBN 978 0 7553 9971 0

Typeset in Janson by Avon DataSet Ltd, Bidford-on-Avon, Warwickshire

Printed and bound in Great Britain by Clays Ltd, St Ives plc

Headline's policy is to use papers that are natural, renewable and
recyclable products and made from wood grown in sustainable forests.
The logging and manufacturing processes are expected to conform
to the environmental regulations of the country of origin.

HEADLINE PUBLISHING GROUP
An Hachette UK Company
338 Euston Road
London NW1 3BH

www.headline.co.uk
www.hachette.co.uk

For Margaret Harry, owner of The House Beauty Spa, Liverpool, a lady whose generosity of spirit, enthusiasm, organisation and loyalty I greatly admire, who has worked tirelessly raising thousands of pounds for charities, particularly The Variety Club of Great Britain. Thank you, Margaret, for a wonderful evening at the Hope St Hotel.

Part One

Chapter One

Liverpool, May 1898

'MAGGIE, I...I DON'T think there's much hope for her. I'm afraid she's sinking fast,' the midwife whispered.

Her words dropped like stones into the anxiety-laden atmosphere of the stuffy bedroom at the back of the small terraced house in Albion Street. And, like pebbles cast into a mill pond, ripples of fear and anguish washed over the two young women who now clung together, trembling with fatigue and shock. The flaxen-haired girl lying on sweat-stained sheets in the bed was beyond their help. Beth Strickland was dying, but she did not know it.

Maggie McEvoy felt tears pricking her eyes. Beth, her sister-in-law, was too young to die! Pretty, sweet-natured Beth had endured eighteen hours of agonising labour to bring her first child into the world. A daughter with soft, pale-blond hair and blue eyes like herself, a child for whom Beth it now appeared

3

had sacrificed her own life. Maggie's shoulders heaved as a sob welled up. Her brother John's wife was the very opposite in looks and temperament to herself and yet they'd become so close. Dark-haired where Beth was fair, plump and buxom where Beth was slight and slim, Maggie knew she was inclined to be brash and outspoken whereas her sister-in-law was quiet and gentle. She herself was twenty-three; Beth had only just turned twenty.

'Can't we get a doctor?' she begged the midwife. 'Can't we get her across to the hospital? The John Bagot isn't far. We have to do *something*!' She just couldn't stand here and watch Beth's life ebbing away.

The older woman frowned, creasing her heavily lined face even further, and shook her head. 'Too late for that now I'm afraid, Maggie, luv. She had a bad time of it and she wasn't as robust as the pair of you. These things happen; there's nothing anyone can do once the fever takes hold. All we can do now is make her as comfortable as possible and . . . and let nature take its course.'

Agnes Mercer, Maggie's close friend and neighbour who, at Maggie's urgent summons, had hurried across from her mam's corner shop, nodded slowly. Her mam had said more or less the same thing. Very few women recovered from the dreaded fever. Her heart went out to Maggie whom she'd known all her life: Maggie was close to John's wife and would miss her terribly.

Maggie felt the weight of grief and despair settle on her shoulders as she crossed to the bed and bent and gently stroked the strands of hair, dark with sweat, from her sister-in-law's fevered cheeks. She'd sat beside her all through the night, helplessly watching her toss and turn and cry out in her pain and delirium for John and her baby.

The tiny girl who, because she'd finally arrived on the first of the month, Beth had said should be called 'Mae', was asleep in her makeshift crib downstairs. There was no possibility of John getting home in time to either welcome his little daughter or say goodbye to his young wife for the *Campania* wasn't due back in Liverpool for another four days. Finally, overwhelmed with exhaustion and sorrow, Maggie broke down. 'Oh, Beth, luv, I'm sorry! I'm so, so sorry!'

'Now, Maggie, there's no use laying any blame on yourself. There's nothing anyone could have done,' Lizzie Kemp stated firmly, rearranging her hair beneath its creased and grubby linen cap and wiping her hands on her apron, which was still heavily stained with blood from a birth she had attended last night. She'd delivered more babies than she'd had hot dinners and women frequently succumbed to childbed fever. It was a tragic fact of life. Childbirth was a dangerous time for mother and baby and Beth Strickland was a slight girl with narrow hips and the baby hadn't been small. She didn't hold with the practice of women going into the lying-in hospital with all their rules and regulations: the place for a baby to be born was at home and at least the child seemed to be thriving. 'Now, if you two will give me a hand, we'll tidy her up and straighten these covers,' she instructed briskly.

'She . . . she'll . . . go in some comfort. We'll sponge her down and change the sheets,' Maggie replied, fighting down the sobs.

The midwife shrugged but made no comment. If they wanted to give themselves the extra work of washing all that bed linen that was their affair. She was tired; she'd been up all night with a woman in York Terrace who'd had a difficult labour and now this. She was beginning to feel she was too old for this work.

They worked quickly, in silence and with infinite care, though both girls were still in shock. When Beth was gently eased down between clean sheets, clad in a fresh nightgown, with her hair brushed free of its tangles, the midwife left.

'She's barely breathing and she's as pale as the sheet that's covering her,' Agnes whispered, thinking that Beth looked as if every drop of blood had been drained from her body. Oh, neither she nor Maggie were strangers to death; it seemed to stalk these narrow streets of closely packed terraced houses that ran down from St George's Hill to the docks, but not since her da's death three years ago had it come so close.

The air in the room was foetid and she rose and crossed to the small window and managed to force it open a crack, the wood being warped and the sash stiff. A waft of fresh air penetrated the room, filled with the warmth of the spring morning but tinged with the smell of the soot that enveloped everything in the city. Slowly she came back to Maggie's side and took her hand. 'I can't believe that only a few days ago she was sitting up, holding little Mae in her arms and smiling.'

Maggie nodded sadly and brushed away the tears with the back of her hand. 'Neither can I, Agnes. Oh, how am I going to break this to our John?' Her big strapping brother had been delighted that he was going to be a father, but anxious that he'd be halfway across the Atlantic Ocean shovelling tons of coal into a furnace in the stokehold of the *Campania* when Beth's time arrived. Maggie had told him not to worry, that she would see to everything. Hadn't Mrs Kemp assured them all that Beth would be fine, and she'd spoken from years of experience? She wondered bitterly now if she should have ignored the woman and encouraged Beth to go into the lying-in hospital where at least there would have been a doctor on hand. Guilt and regret added to her misery.

Agnes shook her head. 'Big John Strickland', as he was known, would be devastated. He'd idolised his pretty wife and always brought her some little bit of finery from New York each time he returned. He didn't spend his few hours' leisure time ashore getting drunk as most of them did; he'd go off to the cheaper stores looking for some little gift for his wife and usually Maggie too. There were few men in this neighbourhood who were foolish enough to deliberately antagonise him – six years of the brutal conditions of the stokehold had hardened him – but with his family he was always gentle and considerate. And she felt heartily sorry for Maggie too. Her parents had both succumbed to an epidemic of diphtheria when she'd been in her teens; John was her only sibling but he was away for most of the time. It was no wonder she'd fallen for the charms of Billy McEvoy and, despite John's misgivings, had married him. In Agnes's opinion he wasn't good enough for her friend. He was too glib, too fond of wanting his own way and far too fond of a drink. He was what her mam called 'a waster' and she was thankful her Albert was of a steadier nature. He also had a regular job, in Ogden's Tobacco factory, whereas Billy was a dock labourer and that was far from what could be termed 'steady' work.

She sighed as her thoughts turned to her friend's predicament. Not only did Maggie have to bear the pain of the grief that now engulfed them both but she had to run a home and care for little Eddie who was two years old. It would fall on Maggie to rear Mae too, she reflected.

Her gaze rested on Beth's ashen features and she realised that there was very little time left now. 'Maggie, luv, will I go and fetch Mam? She'll be of more help to you now than me. I'll take Eddie and the baby with me. I'll put a notice on the shop door – people will understand – and the kids will be better off in our kitchen.' She wondered briefly how her mam was managing having to serve in the shop and keep her eye on her own two boys, the twins Harry and Jimmy, who were the same age as Eddie and a handful at the best of times. She now heartily thanked God that both her own and Maggie's pregnancies hadn't ended like poor Beth's.

When Agnes had gone, Maggie took Beth's hand and held it against her cheek. She wasn't even sure if her sister-in-law was still breathing. 'Beth, don't you worry about little Mae. I'll take care of her, I promise,' she said steadily. 'I'll love and care for her as if she were my own and . . . and John and I will see she never goes without. He loves you so much, Beth. We . . . we all do.' She paused; the room seemed very still: even the noises from the surrounding streets were distant and muffled. 'I . . . I'll tell her . . . about you. I'll not let her forget you.' Her voice cracked with emotion and she bit her lip, wishing Agnes's mam would hurry; she felt so alone, helpless and, in the light of what she was about to announce, a little afraid. She didn't know if Beth could even hear her. 'I . . . I want to tell you something. Something I've told no one else yet, Beth. I know – I hope you'll understand and be . . . happy for me. I'm expecting again. So, please God, in time Mae will have a new cousin to play with.'

There was no response to her words. Beth's eyes were closed and although her hand was still warm Maggie felt that her soul had already departed. She broke down and sobbed helplessly; the last hours had been traumatic and had taken their toll. 'How am I going to tell our John?' she whispered to herself, praying that when the time came she would somehow find the strength.

Maggie felt as though she were walking in a dream world as the day passed. Agnes had brought little Eddie and Mae back home after the women had been to lay Beth out. Then the neighbours had called in to offer condolences and help and one of them, who had a young baby herself, had offered to nurse Mae too. 'It's the least I can do, Maggie, for poor Beth,' she'd said, taking the wailing child who was obviously hungry. Now, both Eddie and the baby were asleep.

'I just feel so lost! I can't seem to think straight,' Maggie said wearily as she took yet another cup of tea from her friend.

'You'll be better in the morning. You're worn out. You need a good night's kip and at least after Annie Taylor has been down to feed the baby last thing she should sleep. I'll have Eddie tomorrow morning – he can play with the twins and Mam will keep her eye on them all while I serve in the shop. There's bound to be things you'll have to attend to.' She glanced at the clock on the mantel above the range. 'Shouldn't your Billy be in by now? Albert's putting the kids to bed.'

Maggie sighed; she never knew exactly when Billy would get home. It always depended on whether he'd got any work that day, how much money he had in his pocket and how many pubs he had to pass on his way home. Like all their neighbours they never had enough money at the best of times; even though she considered herself to be a good manager, it was so hard to make ends meet. Few women went out to work for families were large and suitable jobs almost impossible to find. If a woman was really desperate she might take in washing or go out cleaning offices in the evening when someone was in to mind the kids. All Maggie had each week was what Billy didn't spend, the small but regular amount old Isaac Ziegler paid her each Saturday morning for doing some chores and of course what John left her.

She'd known the Zieglers for years; they were Jewish and the late Mrs Ziegler had been good to her when she was growing up. Rachel Ziegler had died in the same epidemic that had taken her parents; Isaac, a tailor, lived with his son – who was also his business partner – above their shop on the corner of Albion Street. She enjoyed going there on Saturday mornings. Isaac always had a cheery word for her and their kitchen was so quiet and peaceful, but she doubted she'd be able to go this week. She hoped Billy wouldn't be long. She didn't want to have to sit here alone and Agnes couldn't stay for much longer.

It was half an hour later when she heard him come in through the scullery, whistling. He obviously hadn't heard, she thought dully, though he'd known Beth was very ill and that she'd sat up all night with her. She hadn't been able to contact him all day – she hadn't known where he would be – but couldn't he at least show some concern?

He knew instantly by her expression that something was very wrong. He took off his jacket and cap and ran his hands through his mop of thick curly dark hair. 'Maggie, what's wrong? Is she worse? I'd have been home the sooner hadn't I chanced to fall in with a feller I knew back in Belfast and we went for a wee drop or two.'

Maggie thought bitterly of the long grief-filled hours she'd endured. 'She . . . she died this afternoon, Billy. There wasn't anything anyone could do.'

'Jaysus! I'd have come straight home, Maggie, if I'd known! The Lord have mercy on her.' He was shocked. He'd realised Beth was desperately ill but women often were after giving birth and he'd not thought she would die. 'Did ye get a doctor?'

Maggie shook her head. 'I told you there wasn't anything . . . Agnes and her mam have been very good and so have the neighbours. The women came to lay her out . . .' She dissolved into tears and Billy came and put his arms around her.

'Ah, don't fret so, darlin'. Isn't she in a better place now?'

'But she was so young, Billy!'

'I know, I know,' he soothed, wondering how Big John Strickland would take it. 'When's Himself due home?'

Maggie calmed down a little and wiped her eyes. 'In four days and God only knows how I'm going to break the news to him. He has a baby daughter but he no longer has a wife.'

Billy nodded as he glanced around the kitchen, which was more untidy than usual, with dirty dishes still on the table and Eddie's clothes hanging to air over the fender although the fire was almost out. There might be little in the way of furniture but the kitchen was usually neat and tidy with a good fire burning by the time he got home. 'Where is the bairn?'

'In our bedroom with little Eddie, both asleep. She . . . Beth . . . is in the back bedroom.'

Billy nodded. 'What's going to happen to the bairn now?' he wondered aloud.

Maggie raised her tear-stained face from his shoulder. 'We'll look after her. I promised Beth.'

Billy frowned. 'Isn't that your John's responsibility?'

Maggie was confused; she didn't understand. 'How can he bring her up when he's away so much?'

Billy didn't reply. He was certain that John Strickland wouldn't want to give up a steady job with a fairly decent regular wage to stay at home and mind a baby, not that slaving away in that pit of hell known as a stokehold was any kind of a picnic, but it was better than the few bits of jobs he managed to get, and John always had money in his pocket. His brother-in-law would be devastated by the loss of his young wife but he was sure that he would be quite happy to leave Maggie to care for Mae. The thought didn't please him one bit. Why should they be responsible for Beth's child? John Strickland was her father. But hadn't Maggie already gone and promised the dying woman? She would be sure to inform her brother of the fact. The more he thought about it, the more annoyed he became. Couldn't she have waited and discussed it with him first? John would be away at sea; it would be himself who would have to cope with the child on a day-to-day basis as she got older, as well as being responsible for Eddie. Well, for now he'd let the matter rest, he thought, but he certainly wasn't going to just let it go.

He wasn't at all happy with the way life was working out, he thought irritably. Jobs were hard come by, they were short of space in this decrepit old house and Maggie had changed lately. Where had the easy-going, cheerful girl he'd married gone? Oh, to be sure she was upset by Beth's death but it wasn't just that. She'd become sharp-tongued of late, always complaining and comparing him – unfavourably – to that Bertie Mercer who was married to Agnes. Didn't she make *him* out to be some kind of paragon who didn't drink or smoke or have the occasional bet on a game of pitch and toss? Who never seemed to put a foot wrong or say a thing out of place? No, this wasn't the life he'd envisaged when he'd left Belfast. Lately he'd begun to realise that Liverpool, with its grand buildings and docks crammed with ships, wasn't the Promised Land of his dreams and now it looked as if he was going to be saddled with someone else's child too. He wished he'd stayed longer in the pub.

Chapter Two

B ILLY DIDN'T GO to look for work the following day. There was never very much going on at the docks on a Saturday and he intended to call into the pub later to meet his mate from Belfast, for the atmosphere in the house was dark and depressing. He wasn't very pleased when Maggie asked him would he go down to see old Mr Ziegler today as she had so much to do that morning and she felt far from well. Apart from the shock, regret and grief, she was also suffering the nausea of early pregnancy. She hoped he would offer to help with the formalities that had to be undertaken today too.

'Agnes has promised to have our Eddie this morning even though it's their busiest day and you know I always go down and light the fire and put their meal on to cook and do whatever else needs to be done. It's their Sabbath and they can't do things like that,' she reminded him.

'Both he and Harold manage to work just the same – Sabbath or no Sabbath!' Billy retorted but grudgingly put on his jacket;

it wouldn't take him long to complete the tasks that Maggie usually carried out. She said she did it to help the old man, but he knew Isaac paid her for her time. At least he'd have a few more coppers in his pocket to spend when he finally arrived at the Alexandra.

'I'd be very grateful, Billy, if later you could go and . . . register poor Beth's death. They close after dinner and I've to see the undertaker and the vicar and then I'll have Eddie as well as the baby to see to this afternoon.'

Billy frowned, his annoyance increasing. At this rate he wouldn't get to see his mate at all. By the time he'd finished at Ziegler's and been to register the death, Nick MacNally would have given up hope of seeing him and moved on. John Strickland should be doing all this running around, not him. 'Didn't Himself pick a fine time to be away,' he muttered as he went out.

Maggie stared after him bleakly, too sick and heartsore to demand to know just what he meant, as she would have done ordinarily. He'd obviously had plans that would now have to be disrupted. But it surely wasn't too much to ask that he give her some support? She wasn't looking forward to the visits she must make this morning either and Agnes couldn't be of assistance. She could hear the baby beginning to wake and murmur, she'd soon be wailing to be fed so she'd have to call into Mrs Taylor's on her way to the undertakers. Yes, she thought wearily, as another wave of nausea overtook her, she had a full day ahead of her.

Both Isaac and his son Harold were working when Billy entered the shop. The garments and materials here were way beyond his means, he deduced as he glanced around. Harold Ziegler was about his own age, tall and slim, but his black hair, brown eyes and rather swarthy complexion betrayed his origins. Old Isaac was stooped now, his hair snow-white, his face lined with age but his dark eyes were bright and questioning.

'Maggie isn't able to come this morning, so I've come instead. If you'll show me what needs to be done I'll be after making a start. I've to go on to the register office afterwards,' Billy informed them.

'We heard about poor Beth. Ah, such a tragedy – so young. We both offer our deepest condolences. We prayed for her when we attended *shul* – synagogue. How is Maggie? She was fond of John's wife,' Isaac asked, shaking his head sadly. Maggie was a good girl, kind, hard-working and generous, his Rachel had always said so. Maggie was clean, tidy and organised and a thrifty housekeeper too, and he knew that wasn't easy on what little she had. She had suffered such loss in her own young life and now this.

'She's upset – it was a terrible shock – but isn't that only natural? And hasn't she been left to see to the bairn, with Beth dead and Himself away.'

Isaac nodded his agreement. 'Poor little Mae. The world is a hard place for a child without its parents, that I know. I came to this country as a small boy with my *zayde* – my grandfather – for my parents had been killed. It was not a good time to be Jewish – the pogroms? Persecution,' he added, noting Billy's mystified expression.

'Ah, don't we understand all about persecution in Ireland,' Billy agreed, thinking of his own country's troubled past.

'But we have no wish to be involved in politics or rebellions, we just want to live and work and practise our religion in peace,' Harold added quietly, 'and perhaps this is not the time to be talking of such things,' he gently reminded them both.

Billy certainly had no wish to continue this discussion either; he just wanted to be away as soon as he could.

'You will tell Maggie that our thoughts are with her and that she is not to trouble herself about us, and if she has need of anything she must come to me and I will do all I can to be of help, ' Isaac instructed Billy as he showed him through into the kitchen at the back of the shop. 'She is a good woman and a good wife, Billy, and they are more precious than diamonds. You must cherish her always – as I did my Rachel. I have great admiration for Maggie.'

Billy nodded but made no further comment as the old man pressed some coins into his hand. Maybe the old feller meant what he said about help but he doubted that it would extend to anything of a financial nature. The general consensus in the neighbourhood was that old Isaac wasn't short of a few pounds by any means, even though he lived very frugally and seemed to have worn the same suit for decades. But, Billy thought sourly, there wasn't much likelihood of him giving any of it away.

Maggie was physically and emotionally drained when she called into Webster's corner shop to pick up little Eddie. Agnes finished serving and then resolutely put the 'Closed' sign on the door.

'They can wait for half an hour for their sugar or flour or whatever else is on the shopping list while we all have a cup of tea. You look as if you need one and Mam will be worn out with the antics of those three,' she said as she guided her friend through to the kitchen, taking the sleeping baby from Maggie's arms.

Maggie was relieved to see that Eddie, Jimmy and Harry were sitting quietly at the table with a slice of bread and jam each. Agnes had a better standard of living than herself with Bertie in regular work and with what they made in the shop. She rarely had jam; usually Eddie only got dripping on his bread and sometimes not even that.

'Sit down, girl, you look terrible,' Edith instructed, reaching for the kettle.

'I feel terrible,' Maggie agreed, 'although everyone was very kind and considerate.'

'So everything is all arranged?' Agnes asked, taking the cups from the dresser and wiping the excess of jam from Harry's face with a damp cloth at the same time.

Maggie nodded. 'I . . . I didn't think it would be right for her to be . . . buried before our John gets home.'

'When is he expected?' Edith asked.

'Tuesday – late afternoon I think, according to the *Journal of Commerce*.'

Agnes and her mother exchanged glances. It was going to be hard on Maggie having poor Beth in the house for another three, possibly four more days; it wouldn't be healthy either, Edith thought. Especially not with those young children. She handed the girl a cup of tea. 'Did Mr Thompson make any . . . suggestions?' she asked.

Maggie sipped her tea gratefully. 'He did. He said that that being the case it would be better if he moved Beth to his Chapel of Rest later on today. It would be better for John to . . . see her there, rather than in the room they shared. Less painful, less upsetting. And then the funeral could take place on Thursday, the vicar being amenable, and he is.'

Agnes placed a hand on her shoulder. 'That will all be for the best, luv.'

'He's due to sail again on Friday, Agnes, you know they only have two days in port,' Maggie reminded her. 'It's not very long to . . . to try to come to terms with it all, if he ever does.'

'Will he go back, Maggie, do you think? Or will he want to stay at home longer?' Mrs Webster asked.

Maggie shrugged. She really hadn't thought about that; how she would break the news to him had been her only concern.

'Drink your tea, luv, while I wipe the hands and faces of these other two and then we'd better open up or they'll be hammering on the shop door,' Agnes's mam stated.

'At least you've got all the arrangements sorted out, that's something to be grateful for,' Agnes reminded her friend. She only hoped Billy had been to the register office and would be at home when Mr Thompson arrived with the hearse. She didn't want her friend to have to cope with that all alone.

Nick MacNally had waited for Billy and they'd had a few drinks and a great chat – in fact he'd have stayed longer but they'd both spent up and the landlord had a strict 'no tick' policy. On the way home Billy greeted the women gossiping on their doorsteps cheerfully and joked with those kids still playing in the street about being 'mucky bairns' and so was in a far better mood when he arrived. However, it didn't last long. Both the baby and Eddie were fractious and Maggie was tired, harassed and tearful as she took his meal from the oven.

'It's dried up: I've been trying to keep it warm for an hour, we've had ours,' she informed him as she put it on the table in front of him. 'And I wanted to get the meal over with before Mr Thompson comes. He thinks it best if he takes Beth to his Chapel of Rest. The funeral is arranged for next Thursday.'

Billy looked disdainfully at the dried gravy, fatty brisket and shrivelled potatoes before pushing the plate away. 'I've lost me appetite. Can't you keep those two quiet? I can't hear meself think. What time is this Thompson feller coming?' He'd expected to come home to a hot meal and a comfortable evening sitting reading his newspaper and dozing; instead of that his dinner looked disgusting, the kids were whining, Maggie was in a temper and the undertaker and his cronies would shortly be arriving and tramping up and down the stairs.

Maggie snatched the plate away, her nerves stretched to breaking point. 'Well, there's nothing else!' she snapped. 'And Mr Thompson will be here any minute now so I'd be obliged if you could let him in and be civil to him while I see to the baby and meladdo here.' She picked Mae up and instructed Eddie to be a big lad and stop crying while they took Mae up to Mrs Taylor to be fed. 'And you might at least show more respect and a bit of consideration for me – maybe even some grief. Haven't I enough to contend with as it is, without being in the family way again?' she cried before slamming out.

Billy stared hard at the door. There was no need for her to go carrying on like that, he fumed, she was getting more and more short-tempered these days. But as the meaning of her final words dawned on him he dropped his head in his hands and groaned. Ah, God, another bairn! He felt as though he was slowly sinking deeper into a bog of hardship and penury, disillusionment and despair, and he could see no way out. Life looked even bleaker now, but there just had to be something he could do about it, he thought in desperation. Things had to be better than *this!*

Chapter Three

T HAT BRIGHT MAY morning the waterfront's familiar forest of masts, spars and rigging, broken by the occasional smokestack of a steamship, held no fascination for John Strickland. His only thought was to get home to Beth and his family. As trips went it had been an easy one with no rough weather to speak of but he'd been anxious throughout the passage. Time after time as he'd laboured in the fierce heat of the stokehold, the sweat trickling down his bare torso, his thoughts had turned to Beth. Thankfully, now he was back; he couldn't wait to get to Albion Street.

He waved cheerfully, bidding farewell to the group of men now heading purposefully towards the nearest pub, thinking there wouldn't be much left of their pay by the time they got home. But he didn't blame them. The 'Black Gang', as the stokers, trimmers and firemen were collectively known, endured some of the worst working conditions at sea, slaving away in shifts of twelve hours on and four off in searing, dust-laden heat, tending the *Campania*'s thirteen boilers and hundred furnaces. She was Cunard's first real steamship, with two smokestacks and a top speed of twenty-two knots. Sail had at last been abandoned by the company but the twenty tons of coal those boilers used per hour all had to be manhandled from the bunkers. The work was relentless and brutal, the heat intense and accidents frequent for they had little protection from the burning coals and white-hot cinders that spilled out from the furnace if the door wasn't slammed shut before the ship's bow rose. They were well fed and reasonably well paid by seafaring standards but were allowed no alcohol at all whilst at sea. Fights could and did erupt frequently between members of the Black Gang even without the inflammatory effects of liquor – and no officer was ever fool enough to intervene – so when the men were paid off they headed immediately for the pub or, if they were in New York, to the nearest dockside bar.

The spring sun was warm on his face as he headed towards the tram stop, his kitbag, containing amongst other things the little gifts he always brought for Beth and Maggie, slung over his broad shoulder. He'd scrubbed the coal dust from his skin as best he could but it was impossible to get rid of it completely; it became ingrained and needed to be soaked away in a hot bath, a luxury he always looked forward to even though the tin tub had to be dragged in from the yard and filled with kettles of hot water. He grinned to himself. Beth always declared in mock horror that she'd never known water could instantly turn black.

He boarded the tram, paid his fare and settled down on a wooden slatted seat by the door, wishing the vehicle could move as fast as his ship as it slowly trundled its way through the city streets. Had she had the baby yet? Was she all right? Was the baby perfect and thriving? The questions chased through his mind. He'd given up wondering if it would be a boy or a girl, all that mattered was that it was healthy. Of course he would like a son but he wouldn't be overly disappointed with a daughter.

He trudged the last few yards towards Albion Street panting a little for all the streets on Everton Ridge were very steep – some even had handrails to aid pedestrians – but as he rounded the corner he thought that it was quieter than usual. At this time of the day usually there were kids playing football on its cobbled surface with a makeshift ball of rags, or swinging on a rope tied to an arm of a streetlamp, or playing marbles in the gutter. In warm weather like this the doors usually stood wide open, the women inside preparing whatever they'd managed to scrape together for the evening meal – which was never very much, although Maggie and Beth usually managed better than most on the money he left and whatever wages Billy hadn't spent on drink.

Webster's corner shop was still open and busy, he noted, but as soon as he drew level with the house a feeling of foreboding crept over him. Something was wrong. The door was firmly shut, the windows closed and the bleached sacking that served as curtains were pulled tightly across them.

Maggie was waiting for him in the dark narrow lobby. She'd gone up to the top of St George's Hill earlier and had watched the *Campania* steam up the river, come alongside and tie up. She'd known he would be home soon. 'John . . .' she started as he opened the door, and then the words failed her.

He dropped the kitbag and headed for the stairs, his heart hammering sickeningly against his ribs.

Instantly she ran and grabbed his arm. 'John! She . . . she's not . . . Beth isn't . . .' The tears were pouring unheeded down her cheeks.

Suddenly he felt sick and dizzy and clung to the banister rail for support, fear as cold as ice creeping over him. 'No! Oh, God, no! Maggie . . . tell me!'

Maggie fought for control of her emotions. 'There was nothing anyone could do, John. It . . . She took the fever, the childbed fever. She was fine at first, exhausted . . . it was a long, hard labour but we thought she . . . she would soon recover but then . . .'

John sank down on the stairs, his legs unable to support him any longer. She was telling him that Beth was dead. He covered his face with his hands and sobbed like a child. His Beth, his beautiful, gentle Beth . . . He'd never see her smile again, never hold her in his arms, feel the softness of her hair against his cheek, the sweetness of her lips; she'd never again hold out her arms to welcome him home.

Her brother's grief broke Maggie's heart. It was so terrible to see her big, strong, amiable bear of a brother huddled on the stairs, devastated by grief. She put her arms around him and held him tightly and he clung to her. 'She went peacefully in the end . . .' she would never tell him of the hours Beth had spent thrashing in agony and delirium '. . . on Friday afternoon. Agnes's mam was with me. I – I couldn't . . . *wouldn't* let her be buried until you . . . Oh, John, I'm so sorry!'

His sobs were slowly diminishing but he felt numb, completely numb, his mind refusing to accept the immensity of the tragedy that had overtaken him.

Maggie helped him to his feet, drawing on the depths of her

courage to give him all the facts so that maybe . . . maybe *somehow* he would feel a little easier in his mind. 'Billy went to the register office and everything is arranged for Thursday. I've seen the vicar and Mr Thompson has been very helpful. He . . . he's taken her to his chapel. I'll come with you now, if you want me to, to see her. She looks so . . . peaceful.' She did, she thought brokenly, but she also looked so cold and unlike the Beth he'd loved.

He didn't reply so she guided him into the kitchen.

'Ah, John, what can I say except that we're all so desperately sorry,' Billy said, getting to his feet and thrusting his hands deep into the pockets of his trousers, feeling both embarrassed and shocked. He'd never really got on well with his brother-in-law. If the truth were told he was a little afraid of him, but he was away more often than he was at home so they rubbed along well enough. But to see him now looking so . . . broken was disturbing. 'Will I go down to the pub and get him a drop of something?' he muttered sotto voce to Maggie.

'No, but thanks. Sweet tea is best for shock,' she replied. She took a deep breath as she gently pushed her brother down into the armchair Billy had just vacated. 'But the baby is well. You have a daughter, John.'

He just stared into the fire in the range. He hadn't thought about the child and now he didn't even want to. He got to his feet again. 'I'm going out, Maggie. I . . . I have to walk. I have to try to . . . think . . .'

'No! John, please!' Maggie cried, but Billy laid a hand on her arm.

'Let him be, Maggie. He needs time, luv. Time on his own, away from this house.'

She couldn't stop him but she was frantic with worry about him and knew she wouldn't rest until he returned – safely – to the house.

In later years he could never remember how long he'd walked or what streets he'd stumbled along that night, or maybe he'd just blanked it from his mind. Eventually he'd made his way back and had found his sister waiting up for him, her face drawn and anxious. He'd slumped down on the sofa and fallen into a deep sleep, a sleep of utter mental and physical exhaustion. She'd brought a blanket and covered him before she'd finally gone to bed.

The next days passed in a blur. He didn't want to eat; he didn't want to see or speak to the neighbours, not even Agnes, with whom he'd grown up. He realised that there was a baby in the house but he hadn't been able to bring himself even to ask about her, never mind go to look at her. He'd made up his mind that he would go back to sea on Friday – for what would be the point of staying here now? Maybe hours engrossed in the repetitious, physically demanding work of shovelling coal into a furnace would block out the memory of Beth's pale, cold face and the pain of his loss. He could only hope.

He was as much in control of himself as could possibly be expected when Beth was buried. Beside him Maggie had dabbed at her eyes, sobs shaking her, but he'd remained dry-eyed. It had been a moment of darkest despair when on that bright sunny morning he'd watched his beloved wife's body being lowered into the dark earth. There had been a decent crowd in the church, which had touched him, and the vicar had been very sympathetic, but he'd never been much of a believer and was even less so now. There were so many truly bad people in the world: why had one of them not been struck down with a fever? Why someone as gentle and good as Beth? he'd thought bitterly.

After the burial the family went back to the house, accompanied by Agnes and Bertie and some of the neighbours for the traditional 'funeral tea', although John had excused himself, saying he needed some time alone. Mrs Webster had taken Eddie over to the shop with the twins.

At length Agnes and Bertie went home to put all three boys to bed. Eddie was too young to understand what had happened to Aunty Beth but Agnes felt the child sensed there was something wrong. He'd been quieter of late, and when she'd mentioned it to her mam she'd concurred and agreed that it would be better if the little boy stayed the night. John would sail tomorrow and then maybe some sense of normality would return.

When John returned Billy looked at him hopefully. 'Will you come down for a drink with me, John?' he enquired. 'It's been a desperate day altogether and you'll be away again tomorrow.' Billy hadn't had a drink for days and he thought the atmosphere in the pub would help to cheer them both up. He didn't fancy sitting here for the rest of the evening; the gloom was almost palpable.

John shook his head but thanked him. 'Thanks, but I've never been one for the drink, Billy, you know that. And I've an early start tomorrow.'

Maggie sighed, seeing her husband was anxious to get away. 'Oh, get off with you, Billy. Go and have a drink. You're right, it's been a desperate day.' Even though she was bone-tired she wanted to talk to her brother about Mae and she didn't want Billy chipping in.

'I've your clothes washed and dried and ready to put in your bag,' she said to her brother. 'You are sure this will be the best thing to do? Go back to sea?' she asked again.

John nodded. 'I . . . I can't stay, Maggie, I just *can't*! Maybe filling my days with sheer hard slog might help me to . . . to get through.'

'At least I'll know you're being well fed,' she replied. He'd hardly eaten at all since he'd been home but the gruelling physical work would bring back his appetite and the long hours would ensure he slept. She prayed that when he returned home next time his raw grief would be less acute.

'I'll leave you the usual amount of money, Maggie. You still have bills to pay and I don't suppose you can rely entirely on what Billy earns.' He'd had a bit saved up but that had gone on the funeral expenses – not that he'd begrudged it.

Maggie nodded her thanks and got up and gently took the sleeping baby from her crib, a deep drawer lined with a blanket. 'It's about time you held her, John. You've barely looked at her and her mam was so . . . so proud of her, she told me so the evening before the fever took hold.'

At first he hesitated but, thinking that Beth would have been upset if she'd known, he took her gingerly from his sister. She was so tiny, he thought. Her head was covered with a soft down of silvery blond hair and her mouth was like a miniature rosebud. Gently she stirred in his arms, slowly opening her eyes and looking up at him with a wide deep blue gaze. A ghost of a smile hovered on his lips. She was so like her mother it was uncanny, he marvelled, feeling the first stirrings of affection.

Beth would never be truly gone from his life, he realised, for each time this little one looked at him he would see his wife. Tentatively he reached out to touch her soft little cheek with his index finger and her tiny fingers curled around it, callused and rough as it was. The smile grew and slowly spread across his face. 'Mae. What a pretty name. You're just as beautiful as my Beth too.'

Maggie smiled too, relief surging through her. It was the first time he'd spoken Beth's name and she'd feared that he would totally reject his daughter. 'I promised Beth I'd bring her up, John. That I'd love her every bit as much as Eddie and try to make sure she never wanted for anything.'

'Thank you for that, Maggie, but I'll do whatever I can to help. She is my child and I . . . I do love her.'

'I know you do. We'll both do our best for her, John, for Beth's sake.'

Chapter Four

———◆◆◆———

SOME SEMBLANCE OF normality did return to Maggie's life as the days passed. She was constantly busy for her time was taken up with the household tasks, the shopping, the cooking, the washing, but it all seemed harder now, for Beth had always done her fair share of the chores and there was Mae to look after now too. She was struggling with morning sickness and although she remembered how she'd blurted out the news of her pregnancy to Billy he'd not made any mention of it at all. She decided that she would confide in Agnes before Mrs Webster's sharp eyes detected her increasing girth.

'I thought you've not been looking at all well lately, Maggie, but I put it down to everything that's happened and all the stress and strain and the broken nights with Mae,' Agnes said as the two friends were sitting beside the range in Maggie's kitchen that evening, nursing a mug of tea each. 'I'm amazed Mam hasn't already guessed; she always says there is a certain "look" about a pregnant woman's face,' she mused. 'Are you pleased?'

Maggie nodded and managed a smile. 'Of course I am. I wouldn't mind a girl this time.'

'I'd like a daughter too. Make a nice change from those two little hooligans of mine, but I've told Bertie not for a few years yet. I've enough to do as it is,' Agnes confided, a note of firmness in her voice.

'And what did he say to that?' Maggie asked, raising an eyebrow.

Agnes grimaced. 'Not a lot. I was adamant though. I'm determined I'm not going to be like some women in this street, ending up with hordes of kids and worn out by the time I'm forty.'

They both fell silent, thinking of the recent tragedy: child-birth was dangerous and Beth wasn't the first woman in this street to lose her life. Maggie felt a frisson of anxiety pass over her. She might consider going into hospital this time, for her confidence in Mrs Kemp had been seriously undermined.

'Have you told Billy?' Agnes asked, watching her friend's face closely and wondering just what reaction Maggie would have had from him at the news.

'I blurted it out when we had a bit of a row, the night Mr Thompson came.'

'And?'

Maggie sighed and frowned. 'He just hasn't mentioned a word about it since, Agnes. I sometimes wonder if he's even realised. He'd had a few drinks when I told him.'

Agnes raised her eyes to the ceiling. That was typical of him. 'Was he very drunk?'

'No, just merry, but that mood didn't last long.'

'Then he *must* realise. Do you think he's keeping quiet

because . . . well, because he's not pleased?' If he was displeased then he had no right to be, he'd had no small part in the matter, Agnes thought.

Maggie bit her lip and gazed into the fire. There was very little she and Agnes didn't share. They'd always confided their hopes, dreams and anxieties to each other. 'Lately he doesn't seem to be very happy about *anything* and it's got nothing to do with Beth. In fact I don't think he was too upset over her death at all.'

Agnes pursed her lips and refrained from saying that in her opinion the only person Billy McEvoy really did care about was himself. 'Is it because he often can't get regular work?' she asked. It was depressing but he wasn't the only man in this city who didn't have a steady job – far from it.

'That and he . . . he just seems sort of offhand with me now. He never wants to stay at home with me and Eddie. He never offers to take Eddie out anywhere. Oh, I know he doesn't have the money to spend on the child but he could take him down to the river to see the ships or for a trip on that new overhead railway, or even on the ferry now the weather's getting warmer.' Billy seemed different lately from the cheerful, easy-going lad she'd married. She wasn't sure just when he'd started to change and she really didn't know what was wrong with him; she sometimes wondered if it was something she'd done or said. Times were hard but she didn't complain. Had *she* changed? She didn't think so.

Agnes understood only too well how there was never enough money for treats for the kids. It was hard enough to feed and clothe them but at least Bertie did spend time with the twins when he got home from work. Billy McEvoy was just selfish in her opinion. 'So, will you tell him again that he's going to be a father or will you wait until you're showing and he won't be able to ignore the fact?'

Maggie reached for the teapot to refill their mugs. Now that she had told Agnes of Billy's silence on the matter she felt hurt, as if talking about it had made her face the fact that he didn't seem to have any interest at all in the baby. 'I don't know. I suppose I'll tell him again, Agnes, just to make sure he did understand when I yelled at him.'

Agnes decided it was time to change the subject for she could see by Maggie's face that it was upsetting her to talk about it. 'Did you hear that Nancy Ellis from number sixteen is going to marry that lad, Tommy Farraday, from Northumberland Terrace? Her mam was in the shop today, jangling with my mam. She's not very pleased about it at all.'

'Is she "having" to get married?' Maggie asked, thinking that Nancy had always appeared to her to be a bit on the flighty side.

'No, although she was always a one for chasing after the lads. It's the "intended" that her mam's objecting to. He's on the same ship as your John. Apparently he's a trimmer.' Agnes rolled her eyes.

'God help her then. I think our John is the only one of that lot who doesn't get blind drunk, spend his wages and end up in a fight at the end of each trip. They work damned hard but you know what kind of a reputation they've all got.'

Agnes nodded. 'That's just what her mam said. That she'd never have a penny to her name, she'd have no guarantee that he'd treat her well, might even belt her when he's had a drink, probably leave her struggling with a gang of kids. But apparently

Nancy won't be told, says he loves her and doesn't he bring her fancy trinkets and things.'

Maggie sighed. Nancy wasn't the first or the last who would make a big mistake by marrying the 'wrong' man.

When John returned home two weeks later Maggie could see that he was more himself and she was relieved. There was still a look of pain in his eyes, a note of sorrow in his voice when he spoke of Beth, but overall he was brighter and he'd brought a beautiful shawl from New York for Mae to be christened in.

'It's so delicate!' Maggie exclaimed, fingering it carefully and thinking that it was far too fine for everyday use. She'd wrap it in tissue paper and store it away after the visit to the church on Saturday.

'She's grown in the short time I've been away. How have you been managing, Maggie?' he asked as he sat cuddling the baby, who was waving her little fists in the air.

'Fine. Oh, babies are always hard work but well worth it,' she said, thinking of her baby who had quickened only yesterday. 'Do you know a lad called Tommy Farraday?'

John frowned and nodded. 'I do, he's a trimmer. Why?'

'Oh, it's just that he's going to marry Nancy Ellis from down the street and her mam's not very pleased about it.'

'I can't say I blame her. I certainly wouldn't allow my Mae to get involved with the likes of him. If there's a fight, and there usually is, he's always in the thick of it. No, I want far better for her – when the time comes, of course.' He managed a smile.

Maggie smiled back – he was clearly so proud of the baby.

'Has Billy been able to get work?' he asked, for there was no sign of his brother-in-law.

Maggie shrugged. 'On and off. He's been very down lately but he went out early enough this morning; I was just getting up. He hasn't come back so I suppose he's been taken on somewhere.'

'He knows I'm home today?'

'Yes, I reminded him last night. Now, pass her over to me, she's due a feed so she'll start yelling any minute now. I need to get her down to Annie's.'

'I really must go and see her, to thank her,' John said, carefully handing his daughter back to her aunt.

'Come up with me now. You don't have to stay long. It's always bedlam in their house but she's so easy-going and it doesn't seem to affect Mae. I've a cottage pie in the oven; we'll have it when I get back and Billy should be in by then.'

John got to his feet. She was right, he wouldn't need to stay long but he had to thank Annie Taylor. Without her help the Lord alone knew what would have happened to his little girl.

John wasn't surprised that there was still no sign of Billy when he got back from Annie Taylor's house, so he busied himself unpacking his kitbag and putting his bundle of filthy working clothes in the scullery, then settled down with the early edition of the *Mercury* that he'd bought from the news vendor at the waterfront. When Maggie came back with Mae and Eddie he put the paper aside and got up.

'She's asleep so I'll put her down, if you don't mind,' Maggie said. 'I know you love cuddling her but you'll spoil her and then when you've gone I won't be able to do a thing with her. Believe me, they learn very quickly about things, tiny though they are. Is there no sign of Billy?' she asked, feeling annoyed. At least he could have made an effort, knowing John was coming home.

'Well, I'm not going to have another meal ruined. We'll have ours now.'

By nine o'clock she was getting worried but at the same time increasingly angry. There would be precious little left of whatever he'd earned today. 'He should be in by now,' she commented sharply, glancing at the clock.

'Do you want me to go and look for him?' John asked. It wouldn't be the first time he'd had to drag his brother-in-law out of some pub.

'No. I'll give him another hour or so then I'm going to lock the door,' she snapped. 'He seems to be totally incapable of passing a pub when he has a few bob in his pocket.' It was about time he took his responsibilities more seriously – especially now that there was another child on the way, although she had no intention of informing her brother of the fact this trip, given she'd not fully discussed it with Billy. John would be able to see for himself next time. She'd be showing by then.

Half an hour later Eddie awoke and started to cry and Maggie went up to see to him.

'He's probably had a bit of a bad dream,' she said to John, who nodded in agreement. It hadn't been an easy time for the little lad either, he thought.

When Maggie came downstairs she looked pale and distraught.

'What's wrong? Is he ill?'

She shook her head. 'No, just a bad dream, but I went to get him an extra blanket from the chest and . . . and everything has gone! All Billy's things! Gone! The wardrobe is half-empty. Just my few clothes are left.'

John's expression changed. He jumped up, shocked, and,

walking over to his shaking sister, put his arm around her. 'You're sure?'

'Everything. He . . . he's gone, he's . . . left us!'

John felt fury rising in him. The bastard. The cowardly, selfish, pathetic bastard! 'Sit down, Maggie. I'm going out to find him and bring him back here if I have to break every bone in his miserable body. He can't desert you like this.'

Maggie had to sit down now as the full realisation began to dawn on her that Billy had gone for good.

John had rammed his cap on his head and was shrugging into his jacket. 'Have you any idea where he'd make for, Maggie? Think, luv!'

'He . . . he had a drink with a feller he knew from home recently,' she remembered.

'From Belfast?'

She nodded.

'Right, I'll go first of all to the Landing Stage.'

'But he went out early this morning, John. If . . . if he intended to go back to Belfast the ferry will have sailed hours ago.'

'Then I'll bloody well take the next one!' he vowed. If he had to sail to Belfast and scour the city for Billy he'd do it. Maggie hadn't seen him so furious for a long time.

After he'd gone she sat hugging her misery to herself. What had she done that had made Billy desert her? And even if John found him and dragged him back, what good would it do? Would he only leave again when her brother had gone back to sea? She felt as though she had been dealt a physical blow. He didn't want her. He didn't want little Eddie or the baby she was carrying.

Chapter Five

———◆———

ON HIS WAY INTO the city John's anger increased even more. He'd never really taken to Billy; like Agnes he thought Maggie deserved better. She was right, of course; if Billy had left early that morning he was more than likely disembarking from the ferry now, but he'd sworn he'd follow him and so he would.

The waterfront was crowded with the usual assortment of drunks, thieves, pimps and Maggie Mays – prostitutes – but none of them accosted him, the expression on his face making them turn aside. He asked in various pubs what time the Belfast ferry had sailed and was told it had gone on time at noon. He also enquired, without much hope, if anyone had seen a man fitting Billy's description either boarding it or waiting to board. He was disappointed – no one appeared to have noticed one man amongst many. He was about to make his way back towards the tram stop when he noticed the old man he'd bought his newspaper from earlier that day packing up to go home.

'Wait a minute, mate!' he called, hurrying across the cobbles towards him. 'It's all right, I'm not about to rob you or knock you on the head and I'm not drunk,' he assured him. 'I bought a paper from you earlier. I'd just come off the *Campania*. I'm looking for my brother-in-law. He's scarpered, run out on my sister and her little lad. I think he got the Belfast ferry.'

'What's he look like?' the old man asked.

John described Billy, saying he was probably carrying a large bag of some sort, seeing as he'd taken all his belongings.

The news vendor thought and then shook his head. 'Didn't get that ferry. I was watching them all going up the gangway, wondering what Belfast is like. Never been out of the 'Pool in me life but I like watching people who do go.'

John thrust his hands deeper into his jacket pockets. 'If he wasn't going to Belfast then where the hell is he?' he wondered aloud. 'Thanks, mate.' He nodded to the newspaper seller. 'I'll probably have to search every pub in the city for him now.'

The old man turned away and then he turned back. 'Hang on, lad. I do remember seeing someone like him. Remember now he looked sort of . . . scared, as if the scuffers were after him. Kept looking over his shoulder and I wondered why.'

'Where did you see him?' John felt slightly relieved. It would help if he had some idea of where to start to look for Billy.

'He was going aboard one of them old trampers, the sort that will carry any cargo anywhere for a price.'

'And ask no questions about who they take on as crew,' John added to himself. 'I take it that it's already sailed?'

'Left about three o'clock, headed out into the river about the same time as you were coming up it on that big Cunard steamship.'

John sighed. They would be well out to sea by now and could be going anywhere. It was hopeless. They'd never see Billy McEvoy again, he was almost certain of that. He'd have to go home and break the news to Maggie and he wasn't looking forward to it one bit.

'Thanks for your help, mate. Goodnight and take care,' he said tiredly as he turned away. Fate was being exceptionally cruel to both himself and his sister of late, he mused grimly, but there was no use letting it grind you down. That wasn't the way people in this city behaved; they gritted their teeth and got on with it.

Maggie just nodded when he told her. She hadn't held out much hope that he would find Billy and she'd already decided, reluctantly and bitterly, that she didn't want John going on a wild-goose chase to Belfast to look for him. Billy had made his decision and in the circumstances she felt that she really didn't want him back.

'I just wish you'd never married him, Maggie,' John said wearily as he sat down to the tea she'd made.

'I know. You warned me, Agnes warned me, but like Nancy Ellis I wouldn't listen. You know he could charm the birds off the trees with that blarney of his.' She'd fallen for his easy charm the moment she'd met him, she mused; then she sighed. 'I'll manage, John. I'll get over it.' She smiled sadly. 'As Mrs Webster is always saying, "Time is a great healer," but I feel so . . . utterly humiliated!'

He nodded, understanding her pain at such a public rejection. 'Don't be worrying about not being able to manage, luv. You know I'll do whatever I can for both you and little Eddie.'

'I know you will and I'm grateful,' she replied, but it made her feel even worse. She could do nothing to help herself, not pregnant and with a young child. Without her brother's help the alternative was the workhouse and that didn't bear thinking about. She couldn't even contemplate telling him now that in time there would be another mouth to feed. The feelings of hurt and humiliation were beginning to harden into anger and contempt for her husband. She'd never forgive Billy for this – never!

When she told Agnes the following day what had happened, she expected her friend to say 'I tried to warn you' or words to that effect. Instead Agnes's hazel eyes darkened.

'Maggie, you're better off without him! I mean that. Times are going to be damned hard for you, luv, but at least you'll not spend your life having to watch him become more and more addicted to the drink – and he will. We've all seen fellers like him. Oh, they start off with just a few pints after work, but in the end it gets to the stage where every last penny is spent in the pub. You'd have had a life of terrible poverty and the shame of having to drag him out of the gutter every day.'

'I've the shame of having everyone know he's run out on me. That he couldn't stand the thought of spending his life with me,' Maggie replied, for that was what hurt her so deeply. 'Am I that bad, Agnes?'

'Of course not! You're a good-looking woman, you keep the place clean and tidy, you're thrifty and hard-working and I think you've stayed cheerful despite everything. He's a fool who doesn't appreciate how fortunate he was. You know I'll do whatever I can to help you. Even if he came back you'd never be able to trust him again and you can't live like that, Maggie.'

Maggie knew she was right, that everything Agnes had said was true. Hadn't she begun to realise that Billy couldn't pass a pub lately? She'd said it often enough. Yes, she told herself, she was probably better off without him. He was a weak man who would only get weaker, and that was the top and bottom of Billy McEvoy.

Both she and John were very surprised when, the day before John was due to sail again, old Isaac Ziegler called at the house.

Maggie ushered him into the kitchen, wondering what had brought him here. She had said nothing about Billy's leaving when she'd gone to carry out the usual Saturday tasks; she was still trying to come to terms with his desertion and the bitter hurt she felt.

'Maggie, I hope you won't think I have come to pry, but I have heard how Billy has . . . treated you and I am sorry. It makes me feel ashamed to be a man. I want to help.'

Maggie twisted her hands together and bit her lip. It must be all over the neighbourhood then, but you couldn't keep something like that quiet for very long.

John frowned at what Mr Ziegler seemed to be offering. John himself had told Maggie that she was not to worry about money, and if the truth were told Billy hadn't contributed much to running the home.

'Harold and I . . . we are so very sorry such a thing has happened. I have discussed this with my son and we agreed we will help you. So I am here.'

'That's good of you, Isaac, to offer but I have a steady job . . .' John started but the old man held up his hand.

'You also have a child, John. You will need to look to her future – she was precious to her mother – and Maggie must have some means of earning a living of her own, not only for Eddie but so that she can hold up her head.'

'But how can I earn my own living? I can't go out to work with Eddie and Mae to look after,' Maggie reminded him. She hadn't been able to bring herself to admit that the fact she was pregnant again had probably proved to be the last straw where Billy was concerned. That was the reason why he had avoided mentioning it. She wondered if the old man had taken leave of his senses to think about her going out to work.

'That is where I can help, Maggie. Always you have been a hard worker, always my Rachel said you were a good girl with much common sense, and it is for her sake that I come with this offer of help.'

John was as bemused as his sister. 'Help how, Isaac?'

The old man raised his index finger and moved it slowly up and down in her direction. 'I will lend to you some money, Maggie, which you in turn will lend out in small amounts to people who ask. When they pay you back you will charge them interest on the loan and so you will earn a little each time.'

Maggie couldn't quite grasp what he was saying. 'But . . . but how will I pay you back?'

He smiled. 'A little at a time and I will waive the interest. I will not charge you. It will only be a very small profit to start with, Maggie, but it will grow and then you will be able to lend more and so increase your profits. It will be your own business, yes?'

Maggie was shaking her head in confusion but John had instantly grasped what the old man was saying. 'You mean you'll lend her the money so she can become . . . a proper moneylender?'

Isaac nodded.

'But they charge extortionate rates of interest,' John stated, thinking he wasn't sure about all this.

'Not necessarily and there are those who would say that "business is business", that it is only fair to charge; after all, it is your own money you are risking. It is the old situation of supply and demand. If people have urgent need of money, you will have it to lend them and they must pay for the service.'

'But what if . . . if people can't . . . or won't pay it back?' Maggie asked.

The old man looked meaningfully at John. 'I am sure that wouldn't often be the case. Think about it, Maggie. It would mean a little money of your own, a little bit of independence. Oh, I do not wish to offend you, John, you will provide as best you can, I know, but surely she should have this chance that I am offering?'

Maggie didn't know what to say. Having some money of her own was something she'd never envisaged and he'd said it would be a business, her business. Oh, it wasn't the conventional type of business such as Mrs Webster's shop but he was right, it would help her to put behind her the humiliation of Billy's desertion and she wouldn't be dependent on John for the rest of her life. She had no experience but she knew a lot of people who she was sure would be only too glad to come to her for the loan of a few shillings and no, she wouldn't charge them an exorbitant rate of interest and she'd always been good at arithmetic. She smiled. 'Thank you, Isaac. I'd be very grateful for the chance of having my own business and I can promise you that I'll pay you back as quickly as I can.'

John nodded. He could see she was determined to get on with her life now and he'd try to help her pay back whatever Isaac agreed to lend her. At least if anything were to happen to him, she'd have something to fall back on. And he appreciated Isaac's generosity. There were very few people round here who had money and if they did, they'd think twice about lending some of it to help a woman who'd been left virtually destitute by a faithless husband to get on her feet again financially. Just as he was determined that he would work himself into the ground so that Mae would have a decent life, he knew Maggie was prepared to do the same for her family.

Part Two

Chapter Six

Liverpool, 1907

'EDDIE, GO AND SEE if our Alice and Mae are ready,' Maggie instructed her son as she adjusted her hat in front of the mirror in the small parlour. 'I'll have Agnes and the family over here in a minute and I can hear your Uncle John mooching around in the kitchen, a sure sign he's getting impatient.' Today they were going out as a family – which was in itself a rarity – but this was a very special day indeed.

Rays of strong August sunlight filtered through the cotton lace curtains that now adorned her windows, backed by a pair of dark blue chenille drapes – the bleached sacking had long gone. The room was well furnished, there was a rug on the floor and her two treasured Staffordshire dogs reposed on the mantelpiece either side of the clock. She smiled at her reflection. She was still quite a good-looking woman, she thought, although she'd grown plumper and was now approaching middle age. The years had been kind to her: there were no grey hairs amongst the dark ones, no deep lines of anxiety etched on her face, but then, apart from the welfare of the children and that of her brother, she had few worries. Agnes had been right all those years ago when she'd said she was better off without Billy. She barely gave him a thought these days.

She certainly didn't have to worry about relying on him for anything any more. From tiny beginnings her business had grown. She'd quickly had a steady stream of customers seeking loans when the word had got around, and they did not complain or grumble too much about the rate of interest she charged; desperate times needed desperate remedies and they expected no charity. As she always said, she hoped she was fair. They knew her; they knew she had not had an easy life and that every penny was hard come by, and that she'd sold some of her small number of possessions, including her wedding ring, to get started. She had never told anyone that it had been Isaac Ziegler who had lent her the initial sum, apart from Agnes whom she trusted implicitly, and she'd paid off Isaac's loan with John's help and the sale of a few items to a local pawnbroker.

Her expression hardened a little. There had been one unpleasant incident at the beginning when someone in the same line of business had violently objected to her rates and had come to the house and threatened her, but it had come to nothing. She'd heard that he'd fallen foul of a group of ruffians in a back alley one night although very few people, including herself, believed that. As he'd left the house on that particular night John Strickland's expression had spoken volumes.

Their standard of living had greatly improved although she didn't indulge in ostentation; ever thrifty, she was saving for what she termed 'the kids' futures'. Eddie was a bright lad and she wanted him to go to the Mechanics Institute when he left school to learn a proper trade, which would stand him in good stead for the rest of his life.

Yes, she would be eternally grateful to Isaac and she still made sure that one of the girls went down to his house each Saturday morning and she wouldn't hear of him paying them. She smiled. Even Isaac and his son and daughter-in-law were going out today.

She raised her eyes to the ceiling as Eddie bawled up the stairs demanding to know if his sister and his cousin were going to keep them all waiting much longer. 'I told you to go and *see*, not bawl up the stairs like a barrow boy! You'll be the death of me, Eddie McEvoy. Go into the kitchen and tell your Uncle John that we're ready to go, here's Agnes now.' She shoved eleven-year-old Eddie towards the kitchen as Agnes and Bertie, accompanied by their children, arrived on the doorstep.

'It's hot out there already – it will be sweltering by noon! Mam's decided that she's not up to coming, she'll have a rest and keep her eye on the shop, not that there'll be many customers today. By, that colour does suit you, Maggie,' Agnes announced, nodding approvingly at her friend's burgundy skirt, which finished just on the ankle, showing neat, high, black buttoned boots. The white cotton blouse, its high neck and leg-o'-mutton sleeves intricately pintucked and trimmed with burgundy ribbon, looked crisp and smart. The small cameo brooch Maggie had pinned to the neck set it off to perfection and her wide-brimmed hat, fashionably trimmed with a big artificial flower, completed the outfit.

'You look very smart yourself, Agnes, luv. In fact, you *all* do,' she said firmly, looking pointedly at the twins whose faces showed signs of recent scrubbing, their hair plastered down into neatness with a wet comb. They looked every bit as uncomfortable as Eddie in their Sunday suits, complete with starched Eton collars, even though it was only Saturday. Eddie had been complaining all morning that the collar was choking him but she'd deliberately ignored him.

'Well, now, don't you two look like a pair of angels!' Agnes exclaimed as nine-year-old Mae and her eight-year-old cousin Alice finally came downstairs.

Maggie beamed at them both, feeling a sense of pride welling up in her. Mae had grown into a lovely, fair-haired, blue-eyed miniature of her mother, and her own daughter Alice, born long after Billy's disappearance, had his dark curly hair, brown eyes and vivacity, although thankfully she had very few of his other traits. Both girls wore their hair long and loose, Alice's falling in thick ringlets over her shoulders, while Mae's looked like a curtain of pale silk cascading down her back, almost to her waist. They both wore straw boater hats and summer dresses of pale blue and white striped cotton with starched white petticoats beneath. Their buttoned buckskin boots had been whitened with Blanco that morning by John, who had remarked that he doubted they'd stay that colour for very long when they got in amongst the crowds.

Eddie, accompanied by his uncle, in his good suit and wearing a clean shirt and starched collar and a tie, joined them.

'Do I look pretty, Da?' Mae asked, tugging at his sleeve, excitement dancing in her eyes.

John smiled fondly down at her. She was the light of his life, his reason for living and he was so proud of her. She had the best he could afford and he was saving hard so she could go to learn to use one of those newfangled typewriting machines when she left school. His Mae wasn't destined for a factory or a shop. No, she would work in an office where she would mix with a better class of person and hopefully marry well. It had been Maggie's idea, of course; she had determined that Alice would also learn and she too was saving hard for the fees.

'Do I look pretty too, Uncle John?' Alice begged. 'Do I?'

John grinned at them both. 'You both look as pretty as pictures! And so do you, Lucy,' he added, noting the petulant expression on the face of Agnes's five-year-old daughter, who he knew was the bane of her brothers' lives.

'Right then, we'd better get a move on or we'll not get a decent place to see everything from, never mind a seat in the grandstand,' Maggie announced, ushering her family towards the door.

It seemed as though the entire population of the city was on the move towards Wavertree Park, John thought as they mingled with the crowds thronging the city streets, and by every conceivable means of transport. Trams, omnibuses, motor cars, bicycles, horse, pony, dog carts, or on foot, but then it wasn't every day that the City of Liverpool celebrated being seven hundred years old.

'It's hard to think that back when King John granted the city its charter it was just a little place with a castle and a few houses by a muddy pool on the river,' Bertie Mercer commented – he'd been reading up on it all at the library. 'The Liverpool Pageant' it was being called and there were to be all kinds of balls and parties for the civic dignitaries as well as events for ordinary citizens such as themselves. Nothing like it had ever happened before.

'It said in the newspaper that there's going to be a display with floats depicting all the centuries and the important events with people dressed up in costumes,' Maggie added. 'I'm really looking forward to seeing them.'

'I'm not half glad we weren't chosen to do all those Swedish exercise things! Having to get dressed up in that daft outfit and you'd be worn out and sweating like a pig in this sun,' young Jimmy muttered thankfully to Eddie.

Agnes heard him and cuffed him smartly. 'Stop showing us all up, saying things like that! It might have done the three of you lads some good.' Thousands of schoolchildren from all over the city had been drilled for weeks in what was going to be a spectacle of 'physical excellence' as they demonstrated – in unison, it was sincerely hoped – a series of Swedish exercises. Only a handful had been chosen from St George's and neither Harry, Jimmy nor Eddie had been amongst them, much to their relief.

'When we've seen all these "float" things, can we go down to the river, Mam, to see the ships?' Eddie asked. Anchored in the Mersey and stretching five miles from the pier at New Brighton to the training ship *Conway* were the fourteen battleships and three cruisers of the Channel Fleet, which had arrived to celebrate the Liverpool Pageant and Eddie viewed these as a far more interesting spectacle than a parade of floats depicting history.

'I thought we'd make our way towards Stanley Park for the fireworks. It will get very packed later on,' Maggie replied.

'But they're not until Monday night, Mam!' Eddie protested. He wanted to see the battleships and he'd heard that all kinds of small boats would be on the river, ready to take sightseers for a closer view.

'He's right, Maggie. It definitely said in the paper the fireworks are on Monday night. I'll miss them, I'm afraid,' John added a little regretfully, for he was sailing on Monday morning. 'I suggest that Bertie and I take the lads down to the waterfront to see the fleet after the displays are over and you, Agnes and the girls go back home. You don't want to be standing in this heat all day and it will take a while to get back home because of the crowds.' He was looking forward to seeing the ships of the fleet himself, all of which were bigger than the *Campania*. Still, he wouldn't be making many more trips on her, he mused. She was an old ship now and Cunard's latest and biggest ship had been launched on the Clyde in June and he'd been notified that he'd been transferred and was to sail on the new ship's maiden voyage from Liverpool early next month.

'He's got a point, Maggie,' Agnes agreed; already she could feel beads of perspiration forming on her forehead and was glad of the shade afforded by the brim of her hat. 'We can't go hours without a cup of tea and a bite to eat, we'd all be fainting and you'd never get served in a café – those that will be open, and I bet there won't be many.'

'What about you two and the lads? Won't you be parched?' Maggie asked her brother.

'I'm sure Bertie and I can manage to find the coppers for a bottle of ginger beer for us all,' John replied, winking at Agnes's husband, who grinned back, looking forward to spending an hour with the lads on the waterfront and maybe even taking a trip on a sightseeing boat. It wasn't every day you got to see the ships of the finest Navy in the world at close hand.

When they at last reached the park it was already very crowded but all the children were hugely excited to see the funfair and the stalls selling sweets and ice cream that had been set up in one area, well away from the grandstand where the main events would take place.

'Mam, can we have an ice cream, please? It's so hot!' Alice begged.

'Mam, can Jimmy, Harry and me have a go on that stall over there! They've got real rifles to shoot and you can win prizes!' Eddie begged, his eyes wide with excitement. Mae and the Mercer twins added their pleas for ice cream and turns on the various rides.

'Would you just listen to them, Agnes! Do they think we're made of money? You bring them on a day out and they're not satisfied with that!' Maggie protested.

John laughed as he exchanged glances with Bertie. 'Oh, go on, Maggie. It's a special occasion and I don't mind giving them a few pence to spend on treats. Why don't you and Agnes go and see if you can get us seats in the grandstand?'

'And leave this lot to their own devices and with money to spend? For a start they'll get lost in this crowd and we'll never find them, and I dread to think what damage our Eddie could do with a rifle,' Maggie shuddered.

'What if Bertie and I stayed with them, kept our eye on them? We'll come and find you when they've spent up, which won't be long as they're only getting pennies,' John offered.

Maggie looked enquiringly at Agnes and then nodded. 'All right, as long as you don't mind and you don't let them run riot. I doubt we'll get seats though so we'd better pick a spot to meet up,' she said, looking across to the already packed raised grandstand on the other side of the park.

'How about over there by the bandstand?' John suggested, and Agnes and his sister agreed.

'Right, what do you want to do first? Rides or ice cream?' John asked the over-excited little group.

'We want a go on that rifle range!' Eddie and Jimmy instantly replied in unison.

'Da, can we go on that ride with the painted horses?' Mae pleaded and Alice nodded enthusiastically.

'I wouldn't mind going on that too,' Harry added. He was quieter than his twin and wasn't at all sure that he wanted to try the rifle range; it looked a bit dangerous. But the ride with the horses was going round really quite fast too.

'Don't be daft, that's a ride for girls!' Eddie scoffed while Jimmy sneered at his brother.

Seeing an argument brewing, John intervened. 'I think you'll find that you've got to be a certain age before they'll let you have a go on the rifle range, lads, and I'd say you're too young. So why don't you all have a turn on the carousel, or those swinging boats, and then ice cream? By then it will be almost time for the big events and we certainly don't want to miss them.'

Eddie was disappointed. 'That carousel thing doesn't look very exciting,' he muttered.

'There seems to be just girls on it,' Jimmy added gloomily.

'Uncle John, do we have to have them with us?' Alice demanded, glaring at her brother and Jimmy Mercer. 'They'll only go showing us up, won't they, Mae?'

Mae supposed Alice had a point although she didn't mind

Harry Mercer: he at least was quieter than the other two.

'We'd sooner go on those swinging-boat things, anyway. They look more exciting than those soppy wooden horses,' Jimmy stated, frowning at Alice.

'See what I mean, Uncle John?' Alice retorted smugly.

'Right! You lads all come with me to the swinging boats. Mae, Alice and Lucy, you go with Mr Mercer to the carousel, then we'll meet up when the rides finish for ice cream – and no more arguments! We're all supposed to be enjoying ourselves,' John stated firmly before shepherding the boys in the direction of their chosen ride.

Bertie Mercer grinned at him. 'Kids! You can never please them!'

When Maggie, Agnes and the girls got home later that afternoon they all agreed that it had been well worth standing in the hot sun to see the spectacle, even if they hadn't been able to get seats in the grandstand.

'You girls go up and take off those hats and dresses. I see you managed to get ice cream all down the front of yours, Alice; you never seem to stay tidy for long. I'll put the kettle on,' Maggie told them, removing her own hat and unbuttoning the neck of her blouse, which was sticking to her with perspiration.

Agnes did the same as she got out Maggie's cups and saucers, instructing Lucy to take off her hat and not scuff her boots against the stretcher of the bench. 'It must have taken hours and hours to decorate some of those floats – and didn't the Mayoress and Lady Derby look elegant? I wish we'd had one of those lacy parasol things to keep the sun off us.'

'I'd like to see the style tonight at the ball; it will be silks, satins and diamonds and pearls,' Maggie added.

'I liked the float with the Rose Queen best,' Mae remarked dreamily as both she and Alice, now changed into their everyday dresses, sat beside Lucy on the bench next to the table with a mug of buttermilk each.

'Now that's one that must have taken ages to dress,' Agnes stated. 'All those pink tissue-paper roses and green leaves: it was a blessing the weather is so fine – a shower of rain would have absolutely ruined all that work.'

'And don't forget the horses, Aunty Agnes, they had pink and silver ribbons plaited into their manes and tails,' Mae reminded her. 'And we had a great time on the carousel. I'm glad Da was home.'

'You're spoiled, all of you! Well, I hope they don't stay down on the waterfront for very much longer or we'll do no good with those lads for the rest of the day; they'll be over-excited seeing so many battleships and no doubt start going on about joining the Navy,' Agnes said, looking meaningfully at Maggie.

'Our Eddie can get any ideas like that right out of his head. Having John away at sea is enough, isn't it, Mae?'

Mae nodded as she sipped her drink. She wished her da wasn't away so much, she always missed him. It was a shame he wouldn't see the firework display in the park, but at least he'd been home today and it *had* been a very special day.

Chapter Seven

⸺◆⸺

THE HEAT OF August had given way to the cooler but still fine days of early September as John prepared to take his next trip, which for once he was looking forward to.

'I won't be away for as long this time, Maggie. That service speed of twenty-five knots'll cut a day off the trip. I shouldn't wonder if we take the record for the fastest crossing of the Atlantic – the Blue Riband.'

Maggie was folding his laundered work clothes prior to putting them into his kitbag. Both the girls had gone to bed although neither were asleep and Eddie was over at Agnes's.

She smiled at his enthusiasm. Even as a young boy he'd always wanted to go to sea; he'd always pointed out to her the different types of ships in the river when they'd gone down to the waterfront as children. 'I'm looking forward to going down to see you off tomorrow. It looks as if it's going to be a great occasion; they're expecting thousands of people to turn out for it and there'll be a band and everything.'

'I won't see any of that, we'll be hard at it getting the boilers fired up. At least on this ship the bunkers are lined up against the stokehold bulkheads,' he informed her, 'so the lads won't have to cart the coal as far as they do on older ships. That's a big improvement.' There were other more technical innovations too which she wouldn't understand and he wouldn't bore her with.

'It's still damned hard work, John, and I bet they haven't improved the conditions *that* much. You know, you're not getting any younger and work like that takes its toll. Do you never think of looking for a job ashore?'

Although he knew she was right he shook his head. Years of working in that heat and dust-laden atmosphere played havoc with men's bodies, particularly their lungs, but he'd become used to life at sea. 'I don't know if I could settle to anything else now, luv, even if I could get a steady job that paid me the same wage. The sea sort of gets into your blood – and don't forget that while I'm away, bed and board are included.' He grinned. 'We're well fed *and* we get to see the world.'

'Not much of it, and most of that lot only get as far as the docks whichever side of the Atlantic they're on. You must have seen far more of New York than the rest of the Black Gang put together.'

'I have and it's a fine city. I bet we get a great welcome when we sail up the Hudson at the end of this trip – especially if we've managed to break the record.'

She sighed, wondering if he would ever give up the sea. 'I do worry about you though, especially during the winter in all that atrocious weather. You've been lucky so far to escape with just minor injuries. You know as well as I do that men have been seriously hurt, even killed.'

He got up and placed the last few items in the bag before pulling the drawstring tight. 'Aye, it can be bad and I'm not saying the weather doesn't affect us in the stokehold. You can be flung off your feet, pitched against the side of a boiler and burned, and it's far harder to get the furnace door shut with the ship rolling. I've known us go through three blizzards in one day in winter – not that we ever get to see with our own eyes just what the weather is doing.' He grinned at her and pulled a face of mock-horror. 'Can't have the likes of us loose on the decks, we'd frighten the daylights out of the paying passengers – and some of them pay a small fortune. Can you imagine if you were taking a stroll on deck after dinner in all your finery and came face to face with one of us covered from head to foot in coal dust? You'd think you'd come across one of the fiends from hell!'

She smiled although she thought it little more than barbarous that they were imprisoned the way they were. 'You'd better go on up and say goodnight to Mae and Alice now, you know they'll not settle until you do – especially Mae. She does miss you, John.'

Both girls were sitting up expectantly waiting for him.

'Now, you're to go to sleep both of you,' he instructed, 'or you'll be too tired tomorrow to go to see us off.' All three of the children were accompanying Maggie as it was a Saturday and they had no school. Agnes and Bertie were going too as Mrs Webster had agreed to mind the shop.

'But I won't *see* you, Da! You'll be working; I won't be able to wave to you,' Mae reminded him.

'But there will be plenty of people you *can* wave to – even if you don't know them. All the passengers and some of the crew will be at the ship's rails: they love people waving to them. And your Aunty Maggie says there's to be a band playing as well. It will be a great sight.'

She looked up at him, excitement replacing regret in her blue eyes. 'As good as the pageant and the fireworks?'

He nodded enthusiastically. 'Every bit as good and maybe even better. Now, give your old da a kiss and a hug because I have to be away early in the morning. But I won't be away as long this time: that's good news, isn't it? This is a very fast ship so the trip will be quicker. And of course I'll bring you both something,' he promised.

Mae reached up and put her arms around his neck and kissed his cheek. She was looking forward to going to see the spectacle but she wished he could have been on deck so she could actually *see* him. 'I'll miss you, Da. Come home soon.'

All the estimates about the size of the crowds had been right, Maggie thought as the following morning they got the tram to the Pier Head.

'In the name of God, where have all these people come from?' Agnes exclaimed, looking round. 'Hang on to me and your da. Whatever you do don't let go or we'll never find you again in this crowd,' she instructed her brood.

The closer they drew, the more the crowds and activity increased. Passengers were ascending the gangways or queuing to have their tickets checked by officials on the dockside from where luggage was being loaded. The last few stragglers from the crew were being hurried aboard with threats of deducted pay by harassed officers, and the boat train had arrived at the Riverside Station so there were porters with luggage trolleys, passengers and Cunard officials and clerks adding to the confusion. On the waterfront the City of Liverpool Police Band was assembling and overall a carnival atmosphere of chaos and good humour prevailed. Even though it was a special occasion Maggie thought that for her it held a deeper significance than just a day out. She was here primarily to see her brother off on his new ship.

At last they managed by sheer determination and a good deal of ruthless pushing and shoving to get quite close to the front of the crowd, finding themselves near to the first-class gangway.

'Would you just look at the style, Maggie!' Agnes cried, noting the women in furs and expensive costumes and hats being courteously escorted aboard by men in beautifully tailored suits and overcoats.

Maggie nodded and then gazed upwards at the enormous black hull that towered above them. There were no fewer than four smokestacks, all painted in that distinctive vermilion favoured by Cunard and banded with black, which seemed to soar far into the sky, each emitting a thin ribbon of greyish smoke. Already there were crowds lining the ship's rails high above them, waving and throwing down thin coloured paper streamers. The rigging that stretched between the two masts was decked with flags, the company flag with its rampant golden lion and globe on a red background taking prominent place, while from the stern the red ensign fluttered in the breeze coming off the river.

'I heard a feller say it's the biggest and fastest ship in the whole world. It can beat *anything*!' Eddie cried excitedly, craning his neck to get a better view. 'And it's one of ours! See, it's got

"LIVERPOOL" painted in big white letters. Everyone will know where it's come from.'

'I can well believe it,' Maggie answered. It was *huge*! Her gaze ran over the fresh white paint of the lettering on the bows which stood out against the black hull and proudly proclaimed the name of this leviathan, the Royal Mail Ship 'RMS *Lusitania*.'

The police band launched into a rousing version of 'A Life on the Ocean Wave' but was almost drowned out by the first deep, ear-splitting blast of the ship's steam whistle, which resounded across the waters of the Mersey, making some people cover their ears in anticipation of the following two blasts, proclaiming the *Lusitania*'s imminent departure from her home port. As the last reverberations died away cheers erupted from the huge crowds lining the waterfront, cheering which continued as the lines were slipped, the hawsers pulled in and with the aid of the tugs the ship slowly began to edge away from the Landing Stage.

'It's certainly a sight to remember,' Maggie pronounced with a note of pride in her voice, a sentiment echoed by the other two hundred thousand people gathered to cheer and wave the vessel off that day.

Chapter Eight

———————

'HURRY UP, ALICE! Give me your hand and we'll run!' Mae instructed her cousin as they ran out of the school yard and up the steep incline of St George's Hill. The December dusk was falling rapidly as the two girls laboured up the slope, and in the maze of streets below them the lamplighters were already at work.

Panting a little, they finally stopped as they reached the top and Mae's eyes lit up as excitement filled her. In the distance and despite the gloom she could make out the wide, flat, dark ribbon of water that was the River Mersey. Intermittently, small slow-moving lights could be discerned as the ferries and dredgers plied their way across the waters, but just abreast of the Clarence Dock power station was a much bigger ship – ablaze with light from bow to stern – making her way upriver towards the Landing Stage.

Excitedly, Mae pointed towards it. 'There she is, Alice! There's the *Lucy*! Da's on his way in and it's going to be the best

Christmas we've ever had!' she cried.

Alice nodded joyfully as she peered into the distance. 'Let's run and tell Mam and Eddie – he's been dying for Uncle John to get home.'

'Only because he knows Da's going to bring him one of those toy guns that fires real caps for Christmas and all his mates will be dead jealous!' Mae laughed as they broke into a trot, heading downhill now towards Albion Street. She was delighted that for the first time that she could remember her father would be home for the entire holiday. The *Lucy* wouldn't sail again until the evening of Boxing Day. The two new ships *Lusitania* and *Mauretania*, together with the older *Aquitania*, provided a regular service between Liverpool and America, but the new 'sisters' were known as the '*Lucy*' and the '*Maury*', such was the affection in which the people of Liverpool held them.

Maggie was up to her eyes with the preparations for the holiday and wasn't amused that Eddie had brought Agnes's boys, plus two more of his mates from school, to view the Christmas tree which Bertie Mercer had anchored in a pot and stood on a stool for her under the window. Alice and Mae had spent last evening decorating it. It did look splendid, though, and Maggie was quietly proud that it was the biggest tree they'd ever had, despite the fact that it was only three feet high. However, its position now looked rather precarious and she wondered if it should be moved into the parlour, otherwise it might not survive the holiday at all, never mind last as long as Twelfth Night.

'Don't go poking at it or you'll have it over and then you'll be for it, Eddie!' she warned, deftly manoeuvring between the group of over-excited lads, the tree and the range on top of which the pudding was gently steaming in a pan. Suddenly the kitchen seemed overcrowded, she thought, and she'd have the girls in as well any minute now. Mae had told her that after school they were going to see if they could sight the *Lucy* and before long she'd have John home too and no meal ready. A nice homecoming that would be, she fretted, but then smiled as she thought of her brother's return; this was going to be a really great Christmas.

Of course tomorrow, Christmas Eve, would be very busy, for like all her neighbours she went to St John's Market where bargains could be obtained later on and there was always plenty of good-natured banter between the stallholders and customers. She only needed vegetables and fruit for she already had the goose. She'd picked that up this morning and it now sat on the marble slab in the pantry, plucked, dressed and ready for the stuffing. Oh yes, there was still plenty of work to be done tomorrow but the two girls would help.

Over these last weeks she had seen an increase in the number of people wanting to borrow money to provide a bit of Christmas cheer. She didn't need to hear their reasons for wanting a loan, she knew them already and counted herself fortunate that she didn't have to wrest every penny from a reluctant husband who was more interested in celebrating with his mates in the pub. Not that she was well off by any means, something she frequently impressed upon the kids. They knew they were very fortunate that they got far more than many children in this street but she was determined they were not going to be spoiled. She had small gifts for each of them plus a shiny new penny, an orange and some nuts, and John was bringing a doll each for the girls and this gun that fired caps that

Eddie had set his heart on. He'd no doubt persecute them all and succeed in breaking it before very long. Still, this year it would be good to spend the holiday as a family.

'We saw the *Lucy*, Mam,' Alice informed her mother as she followed Mae into the kitchen and unwound her knitted scarf from around her neck.

'She was just off the Three Ugly Sisters, Aunty Maggie, so Da won't be very long,' Mae added, using the local name for the power station and its three chimneys. She took off her coat and hung it up on the peg behind the door.

'What's our Eddie brought half the street in here for?' Alice demanded, glaring at her brother and his mates, particularly Jimmy Mercer, who had managed to dislodge one of the silver stars she'd made from cardboard and covered with the silver paper from the inside of a cigarette packet. 'Trust you, Jimmy, to go ruining our decorations! It took Mae and me hours and hours to make those things. And you've got a tree of your own, I know you have, so it's not *that* much of a novelty!'

'Right, off you go home, the lot of you! You heard Mae, the *Lucy*'s docking and her da will be home and he'll be wanting his dinner in peace,' Maggie told them all, ushering the group of lads towards the door while glaring at her daughter, who had stuck out her tongue in Jimmy's direction. 'And that will do from you, miss!'

Mae, who had retrieved the silver star and was fastening it back on the branch, grinned at Eddie. 'Bet you can't wait to see what Da's got you, Eddie.'

Eddie nodded enthusiastically but before he had a chance to speak, his mother shook her head. 'Whatever it is, you're not having it until Christmas morning!'

'Ah, Mam!' he protested.

'You'll all wait until then for your presents, so don't you go mithering John the minute he sets foot in the door. Now, you girls set the table while I have a look at this pudding and then make a start on the meal. Eddie, go and fill the coal bucket up. It's freezing hard outside and I want this kitchen as warm as toast when John gets in.'

Reluctantly Eddie picked up the old battered bucket they used as a scuttle while the two girls got out the dishes and cutlery and Maggie prodded the pudding in its muslin cloth and decided it needed another hour.

'I wonder if we'll find any money in it this year?' Alice pondered aloud, thinking that if she were lucky enough she'd spend it on sweets, which were a luxury they only ever had at Christmas.

Mae smiled at her. 'Who knows?' she replied, but she was more excited by having her da home for Christmas than by the prospect of money in the pudding.

The kitchen was warm and looked bright and festive with the tree and the crêpe-paper strips that had been twisted and pinned across the ceiling. Bunches of holly decorated the top of the dresser and the mantel over the range.

The door was flung open and John's big frame filled the aperture. 'I'm home! Something smells good, Maggie!' he announced.

Mae flung herself at him and hugged him, her cheeks flushed and her eyes sparkling. 'Da! Oh, I'm so glad you're home. I knew you wouldn't be long – Alice and I saw the *Lucy* coming in – we ran up the hill after school!'

John laughed. 'I had a feeling you would. Now, let me get my things off and put my bag down.' He winked at Maggie, having noted Eddie's barely suppressed excitement. The Wyandotte toy pistol was safely stowed in his bag. 'And I hope you've all been behaving yourselves or Santa won't be very pleased.'

Maggie bustled about, smiling. 'They haven't been too bad but I've already told them: no presents until Christmas morning. Now, sit down and get this meal while it's hot,' she instructed.

When she'd at last got all three over-excited children to bed she settled down before the fire with John. 'Was it a good trip?'

He nodded, thinking he would relish this holiday – it was such a rarity to be home. 'Not bad, but I don't think young Nancy Ellis – or Farraday as she is now – is going to have much of a "festive" time.'

Maggie frowned. 'Why not? What's happened to meladdo? He hasn't been locked up, has he?' she asked.

'No, that wouldn't be as bad. He's had an accident. It was rough on the way back and he slipped on the deck and missed getting the furnace door shut – and the whole damned lot spilled out on him. He's badly burned all over his lower body and legs. The screams were unmerciful. They don't know if he'll ever work again or even walk. They were taking him straight to hospital. Had an ambulance waiting.'

Maggie shook her head sadly, thinking how easily it could have been John. 'I wish you'd look for a job ashore, John. It's so dangerous down in that stokehold.'

He shrugged. 'Jobs ashore have their dangers too, Maggie. How many men are killed and injured on the docks, the railways or down the mines?' He paused and smiled at her. 'Well, let's not let it put a damper on things. I got the kids the presents they wanted. I bet Eddie's had you demented?'

Maggie rolled her eyes. 'That's a bit of an understatement but I hope you didn't spend too much on them.'

'It's a hard world, Maggie. Let them enjoy their childhood: it doesn't last long. In a couple of years Eddie will be leaving school. I don't begrudge what I spent and it's good to be home to be able to see their faces. That's a real treat for me.'

She smiled at him. 'I know and we're all really looking forward to Christmas Day. Mind you, I've plenty to do tomorrow.'

'Well, I'll be here to keep my eye on them all, particularly Eddie,' he promised as he stoked up the fire, thinking wryly that tending fires and furnaces was something he was indeed expert at.

It was bitterly cold the following morning. A slight dusting of snow had fallen during the night and had been covered by a layer of hoar frost, making the cobbles of the steep streets on Everton Ridge lethal underfoot to man and beast alike. Pedestrians clung tightly to the handrails whilst the carters put down cinders and sacking for their horses, knowing that a broken leg meant not only the loss of the animal but the loss of livelihood too.

'You'll have to be careful when you're out and about today, Maggie, it's easy to slip and fall,' John warned as he looked at the frost and snow covering the yard.

'Don't I know it and haven't I already had words with our Eddie over it! He was out there in the street with Agnes's two lads making a *slide*! I ask you! Did he want half the neighbourhood falling and breaking arms and legs and ending up in hospital for Christmas? I asked him. I sometimes wonder what he's got for brains but those Mercer twins are as bad. Jimmy had even brought out a shelf from the oven to slide on until Agnes came out and belted him and took it back inside.'

John smothered a grin. It was something he'd done himself as a lad and he'd not given a thought to folk's safety any more than Eddie and his mates had. 'I'll go out and put the cinders from the fire on it, Maggie. They'll give people a bit more grip.'

'And I want the girls to go down to Isaac's. He's very partial to mince pies, so I've made him a dozen,' Maggie informed him.

'I didn't think they celebrated Christmas,' John mused aloud.

'They don't, they have something called Han . . . Hanukkah or something like that instead. I think it means the "Festival of the Lights". Oh, but he's getting very frail now and his eyesight is ruined with all those years of sewing.' She sighed. 'I feel sorry for him – he's been good to me. Still, that wife of Harold's is very good to him and he likes to see our Alice and Mae and they're fond of him too. They call him "Uncle Isaac". I suppose they look on him as a sort of grandfather figure, seeing as they never knew one of their own.'

'It must be very . . . odd, Maggie, seeing everyone celebrating Christmas and not being part of it all. Not even believing in it.'

Maggie pondered this; she'd never really given it much thought before. 'I suppose they've got used to it. It must have seemed very . . . strange to him when he was a little lad just come to this country. I expect *everything* was odd and unfamiliar to him then, but he's been here so long now that I for one forget he wasn't born here. And I never think of him as being "foreign".' Her expression softened. 'Mrs Ziegler was a lovely woman. She used to give me little cakes that were very sweet and we never ever had cake in our house, you know that. And he was so thoughtful after Beth died. He was fond of her too, you know. He often says how like her Mae is growing.'

John nodded, smiling sadly. His beautiful Beth was a fading memory but she would never be completely erased from his mind while he had Mae. 'I'll walk down with the girls, Maggie. Wish him Happy . . . Hanukkah! He's a nice old man.'

They'd had one of the best Christmases she could remember, Maggie thought as on Boxing Day she prepared to bid farewell to her brother. It would have been the icing on the cake if he could have been home just a day longer, she mused as she folded his clean work clothes and put them into his bag. The kids had all been delighted with their gifts, Eddie particularly so with the pistol. The girls had begged to be allowed to go and show 'Uncle Isaac' the dolls they'd received, which were dressed in very fancy clothes, complete with stiffened organza bonnets. 'You never see dolls dressed like this in the shops here, Mam!' Alice had marvelled.

'You are both very, very lucky and make sure you take care of them. No dressing and undressing them constantly or those dresses and bonnets will look like rags in no time,' she'd warned. But she had said they could go down to Ziegler's for half an hour to show Isaac their gifts, providing they were back in time to say goodbye to John.

Both Isaac and Esther, Harold's wife, had exclaimed over how beautifully the dolls were dressed.

'Look how neat the stitching is, Father, even on the petticoats,' Esther cried, lifting the organza skirt.

Isaac examined it closely and nodded. 'You are indeed both very lucky girls and you must take special care of such gifts. They must have cost your father a good deal of money and he works so hard for it.'

'Oh, we intend to,' Mae replied gravely as the doll was handed back.

Isaac smiled at them both.

'Thank your mother for the pies, Alice. It was good of her and I know it has been a very busy time for her,' Esther urged.

'I will, Mrs Ziegler,' Alice promised.

'We have a little gift for you both,' Esther said, crossing to the table and picking up two small cloth bags. 'One each.'

'Thank you. We really didn't expect anything, with you not really . . . well . . . believing in Christmas,' Alice replied in some confusion.

Esther smiled at her. 'For us this is Hanukkah, a time when we also give gifts and we light a candle every day for the eight days of the festival. These are called *gelt* and we hope you will enjoy them.'

Tentatively Alice opened the little bag; inside were some small coins made of chocolate. 'Oh, thanks. Chocolate!'

'Can we eat some now?' Mae asked, intrigued by the designs on the surface of the sweets.

'First you must have some *latkes* with us,' Isaac instructed, nodding to his daughter-in-law.

'Crispy pancakes made from potatoes. It is also a tradition,' Esther enlightened them as she passed around the small plates.

Mae mumbled her thanks, her mouth full, although she decided she would have preferred the chocolate.

'And you have enjoyed having your father home this year for the celebrations, Mae?' Isaac asked.

'Oh yes! We've all had a really great time but . . .' Mae paused. 'But it would have been better if he could have sailed tomorrow morning.'

The old man nodded. 'Ah, there is never a good time to say goodbye.'

Alice was becoming impatient, wanting to show her mam the little coins. 'We'd better be getting back now, Mae, we don't want to miss waving him off,' she reminded her cousin and Esther showed them out as the winter dusk was falling.

Clutching their dolls carefully the girls walked up the street towards home but as they drew level with Webster's shop a scruffy-looking lad came hurtling around the corner and collided with them, knocking Alice to the ground. She screamed as the precious toy dropped from her arms on to the cobbles and into a puddle of muddy water left by the melted snow.

'Why don't yer look where yer goin'!' he yelled at them as Mae bent down to help Alice up.

'Why don't you look where *you're* going! You're the one who came charging round the corner!' Mae cried, glaring at him. 'If you've ruined her doll you'll pay for it!'

He peered closely at them both. He knew who they were, everyone did round here, and spoiled little madams they were, both of them. 'Oh, shurrup! There's nothin' wrong with 'er flamin' doll! Yer lucky to 'ave dolls – me sisters 'aven't. None of us kids gor anythin' – as usual.'

'Her clothes are all wet, dirty and spoiled now!' Alice cried, holding up the toy. 'Just see what you've gone and done, Davy Hardcastle. She's *ruined*!'

He glared back at her. 'Yer mam can afford ter buy yer a new one, with all the money she's got,' he jeered. Maggie McEvoy was a moneylender and had a better home, food and clothes than his own family. Look at the get-up of the pair of them, he thought jealously. They had good winter coats and woollen scarves and hats, thick stockings and shiny black buttoned boots while he shivered in his old threadbare jacket, cut-down trousers and patched boots. 'Me mam says she's nothing but a leech, a bloodsucker, takin' advantage of poor folk's misery by charging them over the odds. Nothin' short of daylight robbery, what she charges. No wonder yer don't go short of anythin'.'

'She doesn't charge over the odds!' Alice shot back angrily.

'Course she does, yer stupid little tart! 'Ow do yer think she pays fer all the stuff you've got? By robbin' poor folk, that's 'ow!'

'Don't you call me a "tart", Davy Hardcastle! You wait until I tell me mam what you called me!' Alice yelled at him. Calling her that name was a terrible insult, as bad as swearing at her.

He laughed at her. 'What's she goin' ter do, then?'

'She'll go and see your mam,' Alice said.

'An' me mam'll chase 'er. She 'ates 'er because she's so thick with them dirty Jews . . .'

Mae had said nothing during this tirade but she was angry – and even though he was as old as Eddie and bigger than her, she lashed out furiously, catching him a hefty swipe across the cheek. 'Don't you dare say such things about Aunty Maggie or Uncle Isaac! I'm not going to let you call nice, kind people horrible names, Davy Hardcastle . . .'

He yelled and clutched his stinging cheek. 'Yer little bitch! I'll teach yer to mess with me!' He lunged forward towards

Mae, trying to wrench the doll from her, but she backed away.

'They're not "dirty Jews". I hate you! I hate you!' she cried.

'It's you who's the "dirty" one, Davy Hardcastle! Look at the cut of you, I bet you haven't had a wash all week! I bet you could grow potatoes in your ears!' Alice taunted him.

The lad was now furious, humiliated and smarting at being belted and jeered at by girls both younger than himself. His manner became far more menacing and he lunged out and caught Mae by her long hair that tumbled from under her hat. 'I'll twist yer head off! See 'ow yer like that!'

Mae screamed more in fear than pain and Alice began to yell at him to stop.

'I wouldn't do that if I were you, lad. It would make me very angry and you wouldn't want to see me when I'm angry. Now let her go or I'll knock you into next week!' John Strickland hadn't raised his voice but at the sound of her da's voice May let out a cry of relief.

'Da! He . . . he was calling Aunty Maggie names and said Uncle Isaac was a "dirty Jew", so I belted him!'

'And he started it, Uncle John! He knocked me over and he called me a "stupid little tart". Look what he's done to my dolly,' Alice added.

Confronted by this giant of a man whose reputation as a long-serving member of the Black Gang was legendary in the neighbourhood, Davy had had enough. He turned on his heels and ran.

'He's horrible! He's really, really hateful!' Mae cried.

'Are you both all right?' John asked. As there had been no sign of the girls returning he'd gone out into the street to look for them and had seen some of what happened.

They both nodded.

'Ah well, I wouldn't take too much notice of the likes of him. He's just repeating what he's heard others say and they're bigoted and ignorant people. Don't let him spoil your day. Come on inside now, the pair of you. I'm sure your mam will be able to do something to spruce your doll up, Alice,' he urged. There was always someone who wanted to ruin things for others, he thought sadly as he ushered them across the road.

Chapter Nine

Liverpool, 1912

MAGGIE HAD MADE up her mind. She had decided to hold what she termed a 'get-together' for a number of reasons. The first was to celebrate Eddie's sixteenth birthday and his apparently satisfactorily progressing apprenticeship at Cammell Laird's shipyard, and the second being Mae having just commenced a course on shorthand and typewriting at the quite prestigious Havering Lloyd College of Office Procedures in the city centre.

'You mean you're going to have a bit of a "do"?' Agnes remarked when she was informed.

'Not really what you'd call a party, Agnes. I mean I don't intend to go inviting half the street. Just a few friends.'

'So, who will you invite?' Agnes asked, thinking that it wasn't usual to celebrate a sixteenth birthday, a twenty-first was more normal, but still she supposed both Eddie and Mae were doing well.

'You and the family, of course, the Zieglers, our John will be home and I thought I'd ask Eddie if he'd like to invite a couple of his mates.'

Agnes had nodded her agreement; sixteen people, she deduced. More than enough in a house this size.

They'd then spent the rest of the evening working out how much food they would need, bearing in mind the fact that Isaac and his family did not eat pork or ham, and what should be provided in the way of drink. Maggie decided that she would write formally to invite Isaac, Harold and Esther. 'It looks better, Agnes, more polite,' she'd stated.

Both Eddie and Mae were quite delighted when they heard the news.

'It's very good of you, Aunty Maggie,' Mae said, glancing at Alice to see if she was in any way disappointed, but her cousin was looking quite happy about the little celebration.

'And I can invite a couple of my mates?' Eddie pressed, not quite sure if he'd understood properly. Usually his mam classed his mates under the general heading of 'young hooligans', or she had done in the past, but he supposed that now she looked on him as being more grown up and sensible; indeed he had begun to feel so.

'I said you could, as long as they're respectable. It goes without saying that Jimmy and Harry will be coming, but of course we've known them for years,' Maggie replied, frowning over the lists of groceries.

'Then I'll ask Alfie and Derek. They're apprentices like me,' Eddie announced.

'Where do they live?' Alice asked, wondering why her mam hadn't asked this. She usually wanted to know everything about their friends.

'Birkenhead – well, Alfie does. I think Derek lives further out – more Prenton way,' Eddie replied, beginning to feel quite important.

'There's some posh parts on that side of the river,' Alice commented.

'Birkenhead's not posh!' Eddie retorted.

'Oh, don't you two start arguing, it'll spoil everything,' Mae intervened, heading off one of their frequent bickering matches.

'How will they get home then?' Alice asked, not quite ready to give up on the discussion regarding the distinctions between Liverpool and its neighbours on the Wirral peninsula.

'I don't intend this get-together to go on that late, Alice. They'll be in plenty of time to get a tram and then the ferry,' Maggie stated firmly, putting an end to the discussion.

The following evening after supper Mae was struggling with the rudiments of Pitman's shorthand while Alice was half-heartedly trying to memorise the major rivers of Europe for her geography class next day.

'I can't see the point of learning about the Rhine or the Danube – I'm never going to get to see them, am I? Who do we know who's got the money to go travelling to Germany or Hungary or any other country for that matter? Uncle John, of course, but that's part of his job, he's not sightseeing,' she said, chewing the end of her pencil.

'You should try having to learn all these dots and dashes and strokes which are supposed to represent sounds and letters,' Mae complained.

Alice grimaced. 'Don't forget I'm going to have to when I leave school and join you at that college. Is it really *that* hard?'

Mae nodded gloomily but she felt she had to try her best as

it was costing her da a lot of money and she didn't want him to think her ungrateful. She wanted him to be as proud of her as she was of him – John Strickland was greatly respected in Albion Street. 'We'll both manage it in the end, Alice, I'm sure.' She paused. 'You don't mind about this get-together? You don't feel . . . left out?'

Alice shook her head. 'No, why should I? I think it's mainly because our Eddie's sixteen and he seems to be doing well,' she replied, thinking that her brother would be starting evening classes soon at the Mechanics Institute to learn the more technical side of engineering. He was bright, was Eddie, much brighter than she was, but she wasn't jealous of him. Then she grinned. 'And besides, I think Mam really wants to show off the new piano.'

Mae grinned back. The piano that resided in pride of place in the parlour was a very recent acquisition. Her aunt dusted it meticulously every day and every Saturday it was polished vigorously. When Maggie had announced that she'd purchased it Eddie had demanded to know why as none of them could play. His mother had replied that that was irrelevant. Every decently furnished parlour had a piano.

'Maybe one of Eddie's mates can play,' Mae mused. 'I wonder what they're like, this Alfie and Derek?'

'Probably the same as our Eddie and Jimmy and Harry. Football mad, I'd say; it's all they ever seem to talk and argue about,' Alice replied without much interest. Lads of her brother's age she considered very boring.

Mae nodded her agreement although she knew Harry Mercer was just as interested in cricket despite the fact none of them played that game.

When John arrived home he was mildly amused to learn of the forthcoming get-together, although he agreed with his sister that it was a good time to mark Eddie's birthday and both his and Mae's achievements. 'They're growing up, Maggie,' he'd said. 'We'll have to start looking towards their futures.'

'Thanks to you and me they'll both have the skills to earn a decent living. Mind you, it's not been easy to keep our Eddie's nose to the grindstone and I've a lot to thank Isaac for on the matter of the apprenticeship. He had a word with a foreman he knows who works there, so that's a very good reason to invite him and Harold and Esther for a bit of supper,' she'd concluded.

She had decided to hold the little party on the Sunday evening, knowing that both Friday and Saturday were rather inconvenient for the Zieglers and besides, as she confided to Agnes, as everyone had work or college or school on Monday morning she didn't expect it to go on much later than eleven o'clock.

Both girls had helped her to lay the table in the kitchen with her best cloth and dishes and set out the plates of sandwiches, cakes and other delicacies that had been purchased for the occasion. On the dresser were set out glasses and the bottle of whiskey she had bought for Bertie, Isaac and Harold and the bottle of cream sherry for Agnes, Mrs Webster, Esther and herself. There had been a bit of a heated discussion as to whether or not some bottles of pale ale should be purchased for the lads but she had been firmly against it, declaring that they were far too young to start drinking beer and what would Alfie and Derek's parents think of her if they went home reeking of ale? No, lemonade would be provided. John had finally persuaded her to at least let them have shandies; that would make them feel more grown up and if plenty of lemonade was used to dilute the beer they wouldn't be very alcoholic at all. This was something to which Eddie eventually agreed, feeling that to invite his mates to drink lemonade or tea was a bit humiliating.

Gradually the guests arrived and as the parlour became rather overcrowded, the young ones retreated to the kitchen, leaving Agnes, her mother and husband, Isaac and his family and Maggie and John to chat.

'We'd all be bored stiff if we'd stayed in there listening to them going on about the "good old days"!' Eddie snorted as he poured the drinks.

'Go easy on the pale ale, Eddie, there's only six bottles and it's got to last all night, and there's five of us, remember,' Jimmy instructed.

'Perhaps Mae and Alice might like to try a shandy too,' Harry suggested, thinking it only polite to include the girls, although he didn't include his little sister Lucy.

'No thanks, the smell of ale is enough to turn your stomach,' Alice protested, pulling a face.

At that Jimmy, who thought his brother was being a bit too free with what was after all Eddie's hospitality, muttered, 'Good.'

'It's not that bad when you get used to it. I've sampled a couple of pints lately,' Alfie Duggan boasted. He was a tall, gangly lad with a shock of unruly brown hair and a mild outbreak of acne.

'How did you manage to get served in a pub?' Alice asked pointedly but without waiting for a reply shook her head. 'I don't want to get used to it. Besides, if Mam came in and caught us there would be holy murder and you'd be in dead trouble, Eddie,' she stated.

'I don't think my da would be very pleased either if he saw me drinking anything alcoholic,' Mae added.

Derek Schofield, Eddie's other mate, was quieter than Alfie and seemed quite taken with Mae. 'Are you really learning to use a typewriter? They look quite complicated machines to me,' he asked earnestly, sitting beside her.

Mae nodded, sipping her glass of lemonade. 'That's the fairly easy part. I've only been at the college three weeks. We're not allowed to look at the keys, we have to memorise them and use different fingers for each one. It's the shorthand I'm finding terribly . . . complicated.'

'And will you get a good job in an office when you've finished?' he continued.

'I certainly hope so. What about you? Are you finding engineering hard?' she asked politely, noticing that Alice was grinning at her.

'So far there's not been much "engineering", has there, Derek?' Alfie interrupted.

'We're more like "can lads" and "gofers". "Go fer this, go fer that!"'

'"Get the can, lad, and make the tea." That's mainly what we seem to do all day,' Alfie enlightened them. The tea was made in a billycan, with the tea, sugar, condensed milk and hot water all mixed together.

'Well, it should start to get better soon, Alfie, we begin at the Mechanics Institute next week,' Eddie reminded them, not wishing for what was always referred to in reverent tones as their 'apprenticeships' to be viewed in such an unfavourable light. He turned to Jimmy. 'Mind you, I might have to miss a few midweek games,' he added a bit ruefully.

Alice was totally bored with this conversation, which she had known would eventually include the dreaded football. 'This is supposed to be a celebration, Eddie. Can either of you two play the piano?'

Derek and Alfie looked at each other and shook their heads. 'You never said anything about there being music, Eddie,' Alfie commented.

'There won't be, seeing as no one can play,' Alice said flatly.

'Shame that, I don't mind a good sing-song,' Alfie replied.

A silence fell during which Mae looked hopefully at Harry Mercer, willing him to introduce a fresh topic of conversation, but he seemed lost for words, sipping his drink in an awkward manner, although he was finding it tasted quite pleasant.

Alice was about to say she'd sooner sit in the parlour with the old ones and listen to stories of when the old queen was alive than sit here in silence when her mother appeared, frowning.

'You're all very quiet in here! I thought you'd be nattering away ten to the dozen. Usually I can't shut you up, our Alice.' She beamed at them all. 'Well, come on into the parlour. Mrs Ziegler is going to play for us,' she announced delightedly.

'I never knew she could play,' Alice responded, stung by her mother's description of her as a chatterbox.

'Well, apparently she can and Harold has nipped home for her music. She's got all the popular songs. We'll have a great evening,' Maggie said firmly, ushering them out of the kitchen and away from the food and drink, which she noted was rather depleted already.

They started with 'Happy Birthday to You' in honour of

Eddie, which everyone sang heartily while Eddie felt his cheeks growing pink with embarrassment, then progressed to 'Shine On, Harvest Moon' followed by 'Down by the Old Mill Stream'. John gave a solo of 'Has Anyone Here Seen Kelly?' in a surprisingly good baritone while Harold Ziegler's rendition of 'Let Me Call You Sweetheart' had his wife's cheeks pink with pleasure. After this Maggie decided it was time Esther had a break and urged everyone to go and help themselves to the food.

'Your da's got a great voice, Mae,' Derek said admiringly.

Mae smiled politely, aware that the attention he was paying her was causing some amusement to both Alice and Jimmy.

'I don't see what you and Jimmy Mercer are finding so funny,' she commented sotto voce to her cousin as she helped herself to a cold beef sandwich.

'He's been giving you the eye all night, Mae, and Jimmy said every time he gazes into your eyes you look as though you're sucking a lemon!' Alice giggled.

'I thought I was smiling! I'm just trying to be polite, Alice.'

Alice helped herself to an iced cake. 'Jimmy also said their Harry doesn't like the way that feller was looking at you when Harold Ziegler was singing.'

Mae was exasperated. 'Oh, honestly, Alice, I don't care what either Harry or that Derek think. Stop teasing me! Although it certainly makes a change for you and Jimmy to agree on something.'

Alice decided to let the matter drop. 'Well, having a singsong has livened up the evening – it was getting a bit dire to say the least. Mam's idea of a party hasn't been much fun up to now.'

Mae's good humour was restored. 'I wonder who we can persuade to sing next? What about you? You know the words to "By the Light of the Silvery Moon", I've heard you singing it often enough.'

Alice looked horrified. 'That was only when there was just us! I'm not singing in front of everyone – especially Jimmy Mercer. He'd skit me something shocking for months!'

Mae laughed. 'Maybe I can get that Derek to sing something.'

'Oh, don't do that, Mae, please. He's bound to sing something soppy like "I Wonder Who's Kissing Her Now?" while gazing at you.'

'I don't think he would; Da wouldn't be very happy about that,' Mae replied.

The soirée resumed with first Maggie, then Agnes being persuaded to sing. Then Bertie launched into a lively, if not altogether tuneful version of 'Alexander's Ragtime Band' to which everyone joined in and finally Isaac's haunting 'My Yiddishe Momme' brought the evening's entertainment to a close and Maggie and Agnes went to put the kettle on.

When Eddie bade his friends farewell Mae was relieved to see them go for she'd found Derek's undisguised admiration a bit embarrassing.

'If we ever have another one, I hope he doesn't invite those two,' Alice confided as they cleared away the dishes. 'That Alfie is a bit of a loudmouth and that Derek is just a . . . pain!'

'It wasn't a bad evening though, Alice. I never realised that Mrs Ziegler was such a good pianist. Usually she's really quiet.'

'It's a good job someone could play otherwise we'd all have ended up just chatting or having to listen to all the men going on about flaming football! You know what they're like: once one starts there's no stopping them.'

'Well, Aunty Maggie seems happy that it went off well and it did make a change,' Mae said, thinking that now they were all growing up they would no doubt get invited to more parties. She said as much to Alice.

'You and our Eddie might but I'm a bit too young for grown-up parties and too old for kids' parties – not that kids round here ever have a birthday party. We never did.'

'Well, I think that all went off very nicely,' Maggie said, pouring herself another cup of tea. 'And those two mates of our Eddie's weren't bad lads at all.'

Mae and Alice exchanged glances, which John noted and deduced that his daughter and his niece had a different opinion. He smiled to himself. They were both growing into beautiful young girls and no doubt in time they would both attract attention from the lads. Not too soon though, he thought. There was plenty of time yet for that sort of thing.

Part Three

Chapter Ten

———

Liverpool, 1914

I T WASN'T MUCH COOLER out here sitting on the step, Mae thought as she drew aside her long skirt to make room for Alice.

'It's like an oven inside that house even though Mam's got all the windows and doors open. It's no wonder she's got a headache,' Alice complained, thinking that this summer had to be the hottest she could remember and now that it was August it was bound to get even warmer.

'I had a bit of a headache myself earlier on,' Mae confided. 'But that walk by the river soon got rid of it; there's always a breeze on the waterfront.' This time she hadn't gone down to the Mersey to look for the *Lucy* for her father wasn't due home for another week. She'd gone to try to sort out in her mind her feelings for Harry Mercer. It was a week now since he'd confided bashfully that he'd been sweet on her since last Christmas. Of course she'd known him all her life, they'd grown up together, and she did like him. Now at eighteen he was a handsome lad, tall with fair hair and hazel eyes, and he'd certainly calmed down a lot too, far more so than his brother Jimmy, who was dark-haired and was the more outspoken and reckless of the two. But she wasn't at all sure that she liked him enough to walk out with him and that was the problem. She liked him the way she liked her cousin Eddie. Yet she didn't want to hurt him. She had promised to give him an answer this week and she still hadn't made up her mind. She glanced sideways at Alice. When they'd been younger Jimmy Mercer and her cousin had always been at loggerheads but they got on much better now although there was still the occasional row, for they were both stubborn and a bit outspoken. She thought that Alice was now in fact rather fond of Jimmy, although she wouldn't admit it.

'Well, it will be great to have the day off on Monday and not be stuck in that stuffy, poky office,' Alice replied, thinking of the Bank Holiday tomorrow as she tucked a few stray tendrils of curly dark hair back up into the loose chignon, a hairstyle her mother said suited her. Both she and Mae had gone to a private school to learn typewriting after they'd left St George's, paid for from hard-saved funds by her mam and Uncle John. Despite all their efforts neither of them had been able to master the Pitman's shorthand so were employed as copy typists, Mae in the elaborate, brand-new and still not fully completed offices of Cunard Steamship Company at the Pier Head – a fact of which John Strickland was inordinately proud – and Alice in the offices of a large shipping agent in Water Street. She had started work six months ago and unfortunately often found the work boring but she did admit to herself that it was far better than working in a factory where conditions were terrible and you came home covered either in flour, molasses or jute dust depending on what was processed there. And the pay was better too. They'd both get an increase when they were eighteen but for her that was still two and a half years away. 'Will we go somewhere on the Bank Holiday?' she asked her cousin. She'd been looking forward to a day off for some time.

Mae looked thoughtful. 'If it's going to be as hot as this everywhere will be crowded and after saving up for months for a new hat I don't want it getting ruined in a crush.'

Alice nodded her agreement. They both had to dress plainly but smartly for work but they liked to be fashionable too, which wasn't easy with their limited amount of spending money. In fact when they'd both turned up a percentage towards their keep, after tram fares and lunches there wasn't much left at all. 'You're right. It won't be much fun being packed on to a ferry or in a stifling railway carriage but I just hope all this talk of war won't spoil the day entirely. It's not often we get a day's holiday.'

It was Mae's turn to nod her agreement. For months it seemed as if everyone was concerned with what the Kaiser was doing and planning but during the last weeks the very real prospect of war had become the only topic of conversation everywhere. 'I saw the headline "Will Britain Fight?" in the paper this evening and everyone seems to think we should and that we will.'

Alice sighed. 'I don't know how we've got involved. I don't understand politics or tsars and emperors or foreign archdukes getting shot and the like. What's it all got to do with us? I wish someone could explain it but it's all so . . . *complicated*! But it's all everyone seems to be talking about, and they seem quite *excited* about it too, as if it's some huge adventure.'

'Eddie's full of it and so are Jimmy and Harry,' Mae said. Like her cousin, she didn't fully understand the situation. Her da had often talked gravely about the ever-increasing size of the German Navy and the threat to British superiority at sea, and also the serious implications of the situation in Europe and the Balkans, but she wondered if he in fact understood it all. Her Aunty Maggie often said the Kaiser was getting too big for his boots but the fact that the *Mauretania* had taken the Blue Riband of the Atlantic from the *Deutschland* and still held it should surely have served to take him down a peg or two. She looked down the street to where the lamps were slowly being lit, little pools of yellow light in the increasing darkness of the summer night. 'At last, here's old Ned. He's late tonight,' she remarked as the elderly lamplighter made his way towards them. 'It's nearly dark, Ned, did you get held up?' she called.

He nodded as he lit the gas light, which threw out a golden circle into which moths and other insects were instantly drawn; the glow cast shadows on Mae's blonde hair, piled high on her head, and softened Alice's rather sharp elfin features. They were both pretty lasses, he thought. 'Aye, I was. Everyone wants to stop and talk about this war, that's what delayed me, and you can't move along Lime Street for all the Navy reservists going for the trains to Chatham and Portsmouth. And you'd think they were all off to a picnic, the laughing, joking and cheering out of them! Well, they'll soon find out it's not. I had a belly full of it fighting the Boers but you can't tell them, they won't listen. It's all "King and Country" and wanting to take a pop at the Hun.' He shook his head and moved on up the street.

'Well, that certainly sounds serious if the Navy has been called up. I think we can say goodbye to a day out on Monday,' Alice pronounced gloomily.

Maggie appeared in the lobby behind them. 'I've made a pot of tea. Are you two coming in or do I have to bring it out here to you?' She frowned. What on earth were they doing, sitting on the steps of the house? They were young women now with decent jobs, not children in short petticoats and pigtails.

'We'll come in, Aunty Maggie. It's not much cooler out here. Old Ned said the Navy reservists have been called up so it looks as if there really is going to be a war,' Mae informed her.

Maggie thought of John and the thousands of miles of ocean between him and home. 'Well, I don't suppose there's much any of us can do about it. The damned Kaiser's been spoiling for a fight for months and now it looks as if he's going to get one. We'll just have to wait to see what Mr Asquith has to say about it all,' she replied stoically. She'd expected as much for things had become too serious to ignore.

The girls followed her inside to have their tea but the conversation faltered, for each of them was deep in her own thoughts.

On Tuesday 5 August the announcement that war had been officially declared was met with an outpouring of patriotism and excitement throughout the country. Overnight, recruiting posters appeared all over the city declaring 'YOUR KING AND COUNTRY NEED YOU!' and 'A CALL TO ARMS'.

That evening after work Eddie and the twins met up as usual on the corner of Albion Street. Jimmy and Harry both worked in Ogden's Tobacco factory where their father Bertie was now a foreman. Eddie was an engineering apprentice at Cammell Laird's shipyard over the water in Birkenhead where the workers' annual week's holiday had been summarily cancelled.

'Have you seen the posters?' Jimmy asked excitedly as Eddie got off the tram – he always arrived later, having the furthest to travel.

'You can't exactly miss them,' Eddie replied. 'So, what are we going to do? It says they want men aged nineteen to thirty to go and join up but I'm not going to pass up the chance of this adventure. I'm going to join up. What about you two?'

'Good idea, Eddie,' Jimmy agreed eagerly.

'We're only eighteen, they might not take us.' Harry was doubtful.

'What's the matter with you? It's the biggest opportunity of some real adventure that we'll ever have!' Eddie demanded.

'I know but we're not the right age.' Harry was still reluctant. Over the years Eddie had always been the instigator and ringleader in their escapades, which had often resulted in disaster followed by punishment of some kind.

'You're not scared, are you, Harry?' Jimmy demanded. He was as keen as Eddie about joining up.

'Of course I'm not! I'm just as eager as you are but I don't want us to look fools if they turn us away. What would . . . everyone think of us then? We'd look right idiots!'

'You mean what would Mae think of you?' Jimmy put in.

Harry ignored him.

'They won't turn us away. We won't tell them our proper age; we'll tell them we're nineteen. We will be next year anyway,' Eddie reminded them.

'There'll be thousands of other lads lying about their ages.

No one is going to miss out because of a few years,' Jimmy encouraged his brother.

'We'll go tomorrow after work,' Eddie stated firmly. 'Everyone is saying it'll be over by Christmas so we don't want to miss out on all the excitement, do we?'

'Where do we have to go to sign up?' Harry queried. Despite his misgivings, the others' enthusiasm was making him feel excited now too.

'St Anne Street at half past seven. It's the King's Liverpool Regiment, so the poster I read said,' Eddie informed them. 'We'd better not mention it to anyone. I don't think my mam will be very pleased and I bet yours won't be either; they might even try to stop us. So don't let on we'll be going out tomorrow night and, Harry, don't go saying anything about it to Mae.'

Reluctantly Harry agreed, though it was just what he wanted to tell Mae. Surely she would agree to walk out with him now? He'd be a soldier; he was certain she would be proud to be seen on his arm.

They went the following evening to St Anne Street and were astonished when they got off the tram to find crowds of men and boys waiting outside the drill hall, standing three and four deep.

'I didn't expect there'd be so many!' Eddie exclaimed.

'Most of this lot are office wallahs. Maybe they won't want us,' Harry pointed out to his companions as they joined the long line waiting to get into the hall. 'Do you think we'll have to go and sign up somewhere else? Did it say "Clerical workers only"?' he asked, looking concerned. He felt uneasy amongst all these other lads who were better dressed and obviously better educated.

Jimmy looked at his brother with some scepticism while Eddie looked irritated.

'No. Besides, your mam's got a shop, hasn't she? So say you're in "Provisions". I'll say "Finance" – Mam lends money. That's if they ask and I don't know why they should: what does it matter what kind of jobs we've got?' Eddie replied confidently.

The crowd packed into the drill hall where some officers in uniform stood on the platform. It was so crowded that the overflow spilled over into a basement. The Earl of Derby addressed the crowd, thanking them all for coming and responding so enthusiastically to the call. He gave a short speech about the honour and the spirit of Liverpool, which brought resounding cheers; along with all the rest, Eddie and the twins shouted themselves almost hoarse as they threw their caps in the air. Then they were directed to tables for attestation.

The recruiting officer scrutinised Eddie closely when he came to the head of the queue to present himself at the table. 'Name?'

'Edward McEvoy.'

'Address?'

The Albion Street address was duly recorded and he began to feel a little apprehensive under the older man's gaze.

'Age?'

Eddie took a deep breath. 'Nineteen last birthday, sir.' For a second he didn't dare breathe but then came the question 'Religion?' and he relaxed. 'Church of England, sir.'

'Right, repeat after me, "I, Edward McEvoy, do swear . . ."'

Eddie repeated the oath with great solemnity, wondering how Jimmy and Harry were getting on for they'd been directed to another table.

'Go on over to the medical officers now and good luck, lad. You're in the King's Liverpool Regiment: don't ever disgrace it.'

Pride surged through Eddie. 'I won't, sir,' he promised. He was in! He was a soldier and would be going to join his mates and they'd all soon be going to war! It was an exhilarating feeling.

The twins too had been sworn in; if anyone had doubted their age it hadn't been mentioned.

'There's plenty of lads here who aren't nineteen,' Jimmy said, nudging Eddie but looking round proudly.

'What happens now?' Harry asked, buoyed up on a cloud of patriotic excitement. He couldn't wait to get back to tell Mae that he was in, that he was now Private Henry Mercer of the 18th Battalion, the King's Liverpool Regiment.

'A bit of a let-down, I'm afraid, lads. You go home and we send for you when arrangements have been made for your training,' an officer informed them, having overheard Harry.

'No uniforms, no rifles?' Eddie asked, disappointment evident in his tone.

'In time. You'll get everything in time, don't worry.' The older man grinned at them as he ushered them towards the door.

'I just hope we get all our kit and training before it's all over,' Eddie said grimly as they left to get the tram back to Albion Street.

'In the name of God, you've done *what*?' Maggie exclaimed when the three lads arrived home later that evening, flushed with pride and bravado.

'Joined up, Mam. We're in the King's Liverpool Regiment now.' Eddie looked at Mae and his sister for approval.

'I don't believe I'm hearing this! Alice, go over and get Agnes and Bertie. I bet you two haven't told them.' Maggie sat down heavily in an armchair.

This wasn't exactly the reaction Eddie had expected. 'Mam, aren't you proud?'

'I'm shocked, that's what I am! What possessed you all? They only declared war two days ago!'

An obviously anxious and agitated Agnes and Bertie arrived, ushered in by an apprehensive Mae.

'What's going on, Maggie? What the hell have they done now?' Agnes asked.

'They've only been and gone and joined the Army – all three of them!'

Agnes clutched at her throat. 'They . . . they can't have! They're too young! What about their jobs?' She turned to her husband. 'Bertie, you've got to do something!'

'You bloody young fools! You lied to them, didn't you? How old did you tell them you were?' Bertie Mercer wanted to know.

'Nineteen,' Jimmy replied sullenly. Like Eddie, he was taken aback by the reception their news had received. Harry's enthusiasm, never as strong as the others', was beginning to falter.

'And they believed you?' Maggie was incredulous.

'There were plenty of lads down there who weren't nineteen, Mam. We weren't the only ones,' Eddie stated defiantly.

'Bertie, you'll have to go down and see them, tell them they lied, that they can't take them, they're all only eighteen. They're too young!' Agnes cried.

Bertie Mercer shook his head. 'There's nothing I can do, Agnes, luv. If they've sworn the oath, it's too late. What in the name of God possessed the three of you?' he demanded.

'We didn't want to be left out, Da!' Jimmy burst out. 'We didn't want to miss all the excitement. We didn't want to be left here when everyone else is going to fight the Hun!'

Despite his annoyance and misgivings Bertie could understand that. He nodded slowly. 'So, what happens now?'

'We have to wait to be contacted about training but they'll pay us a "living out" allowance as well as the shilling a day,' Harry replied, looking across at Mae, who smiled encouragingly at him.

'Oh, just wait until your Uncle John gets home and hears this, Eddie McEvoy, and you with an engineering apprenticeship and the opportunity of a secure future,' Maggie muttered, shaking her head in disbelief.

'Get home, the pair of you!' Agnes stormed at her sons. 'Get home and tell your granny what you've gone and done. You'll break her heart! Her brother was your age when he was killed in the Crimea. And now she's got to go through it all again with you two!'

'Well, I think they are all very brave and patriotic and we should congratulate them and be proud of them, instead of yelling at them!' Alice announced, looking at Jimmy and smiling. 'I'm proud of them and I bet Mae is too!'

This was greeted by utter silence until Mae spoke. 'I *am* proud of them too and I know Da will be. Aunty Maggie, we all have to stand together now. We can't back down. Like the posters say: "For King and Country"!' She paused and smiled at Alice. 'I've been thinking that we should do our bit too. We'll see about joining the Red Cross.'

Maggie found her voice. 'You'll give up your jobs over my dead body!'

'In our spare time, Mam!' Alice cried, thinking Mae's idea was splendid. They had to do something too.

Agnes looked at her old friend and realised she had to accept the situation. 'Oh, put the kettle on, Maggie, luv. It looks as if we're all going to be in this together.'

Before he went home Harry managed to get a quiet word with Mae, something he'd been hoping for all evening. 'I was wondering, Mae, if you've thought any more about our . . . walking out together?'

Mae had known this was what he had intended to ask her and inwardly she sighed. She liked him a great deal, she was impressed that he had volunteered and now the last thing she wanted to do was hurt or disappoint him. 'Harry, you know I really like you, but do you think now is a good time to be making decisions like this? I mean, you'll be going away somewhere soon . . .'

'Not right away, Mae. We've got to be trained first,' he reminded her. 'I'll be around for a while yet.'

'I am proud of you, Harry, but let's not rush into anything,' she begged.

He looked crestfallen and she reached out and put her hand on his arm. 'Your time is going to be devoted to the Army now, Harry, and that's only right. But you'll know that I will be thinking of you. I promise,' she said firmly.

He nodded. She was right: from now on he wouldn't have as much free time; and she hadn't actually flatly turned him down, had she? That thought cheered him.

Chapter Eleven

———

I T ALL SEEMED A bit of an anti-climax, Mae thought as in the weeks that followed, the lads went off each day to the local park to spend the day drilling, without uniforms or weapons, and she and Alice continued to go to work. Full of enthusiasm, they had gone one evening to the John Bagot Hospital, their nearest, and enrolled on a first-aid course, which seemed to be the only type of training available for 'girls from a background like yours', as the frosty-faced nursing sister had said in what Mae had considered a very patronising and dismissive manner. It was very basic but they would get a certificate at the end of it, she'd added curtly. On their way home Alice had declared bitterly that it didn't make her feel very useful at all and she'd agreed, adding, 'I hope we don't get her, she's a right old tartar!'

'Well, what did you expect?' Maggie had asked when they'd told her of the reception they'd got. 'It takes years of dedication and training to be a proper nurse and you have to have had a good education. It's not just a job, it's a vocation. Still, I suppose first aid'll be useful for burns and scalds and sprains. Agnes was saying that the vicar's wife is organising a group to provide comforts for the troops who've already gone to France. You could join that too.'

'What kind of "comforts"?' Alice had asked rather unenthusiastically.

'Knitted socks, scarves, balaclavas . . . things like that. This warm weather won't last for very much longer,' Maggie had reminded them. They'd looked at each other pointedly. A knitting class didn't sound in the least bit exciting or entertaining.

When John Strickland arrived home it was to a city buzzing with preparations for war. Each day the men and boys of the four battalions the Earl of Derby had raised arrived at the city parks to be put through their paces. The Earl had made strenuous personal efforts to obtain uniforms and weapons, instructing the Countess to purchase every yard of available khaki cloth and have it made up. All this was imparted by the conductor on the tram, who also said he'd heard that it was hoped that the new battalions would be ready for a march past in the city centre early next month. 'But if yer ask me, mate, it will be a bloody miracle if they are!' he'd added laconically. 'I've heard half of 'em don't know one end of a rifle from the next, not that they've got any yet.'

Maggie informed him of all the news as soon as he got back to Albion Street. 'I still can't get over them going off like that, John,' she said, shaking her head as she made him a cup of tea.

'I don't suppose you can blame them, Maggie. I know for a fact that we'll lose most of our crew this time home to the

Army or Navy; it's all they were talking about, joining up, and the company will be hard put to sign on a new crew. They're young—'

'Too young! Oh, when I think of the way I've struggled and saved for years to bring that lad up and see that he got an education and a job with prospects. Is it any wonder I don't want him going off with the Army? And he's always been impetuous! Constantly dragging those Mercer lads along with him in his mad schemes – not that Jimmy takes much encouraging, but I thought Harry at least would have had more sense!' Maggie interrupted.

'I know, Maggie. You've brought Eddie and the girls up almost single-handed; it's not been easy and you've done a good job. But in this matter we had no choice. We couldn't stand by and let the Kaiser march his troops into Belgium and ride roughshod over everyone. We have to fight to stop him. If we don't stop him we could well be next!' Then, seeing the look of alarm in her eyes, he continued: 'But that won't happen, not while we've got the British Army in France, all the lads here flocking to fight and the Navy and the Channel between us.'

She nodded, feeling relieved as she handed him the cup. It was comforting to think that the British Army, unbeaten in conflict for decades, with soldiers from all over the Empire, and the greatest Navy in the world stood between them and the ravaging forces of the Hun. 'What about you? What will you do?' she asked.

He smiled a little wryly. 'I'm too old to fight, luv, so I'll go on doing my bit in getting the *Lucy* backwards and forwards across the Atlantic. It's not America's war but we're going to need their help.'

'I still worry about you. What about all these battleships the Germans have been building?'

'We're too fast for them, Maggie. The *Lucy* and the *Maury* can outrun any naval ship. Battleships, destroyers and cruisers may be big and heavily armed but they're not fast,' he assured her. 'And we're now officially under the control of the Admiralty so after this trip we'll only be doing two trips a month, to save coal and money. So I'll be home for longer – less worry for you. Now, what have the girls been up to?'

Maggie informed him of how proud both girls were that Eddie and the Mercer twins had joined up and of the fact that they too had wanted to 'do something to help' and so had enrolled for a first-aid course.

'Don't worry, Maggie. It's not that bad. It will all be over by Christmas, you mark my words.' In this quiet cheerful kitchen it was hard enough to believe that the country was going to war, impossible to imagine that it would last longer than a few months.

Within a week came the terrible and almost unbelievable news that Mons had fallen, the British Expeditionary Force was in retreat and casualties were heavy.

'I can't believe it! I just can't believe it!' Eddie cried as he burst into the kitchen, waving a newspaper. 'It says here the Hun has captured Mons and Le Cateau and that hundreds have been killed. The poor Belgians are trying to hold out but it's no use. And we're still drilling in the bloody park with no uniforms and not a single rifle between us!'

'Mind your language, Eddie,' Maggie snapped, although she was shocked at the news herself.

'Calm down, Eddie. It's probably just a setback. They'll

regroup and then push forward again. And there are always casualties in a battle,' John commented, although he didn't have a great deal of confidence in his words. What had gone so terribly wrong that the German Army had swept so seemingly easily into Belgium?

'Read it for yourself,' Eddie retorted, still consumed with outrage and frustration.

John scanned the lines of newsprint. This wasn't good. The Germans had advanced into Belgium and had dug in; now they were firing huge shells from siege howitzers into the British and French lines, wreaking devastation, while thousands of terrified civilians were fleeing south with tales of the atrocities committed by the German troops. Women raped, babies bayoneted, houses burned to the ground. Limited though his knowledge was, this wasn't how he understood real battles were fought. There were cavalry charges followed by infantry charges until one side gained superiority and won the day, but it was becoming obvious that this war wasn't going to be fought like that. He handed the newspaper to his sister and looked seriously at his nephew. 'You might well be getting your kit sooner than expected now, lad.'

The day the boys received their uniforms they felt that at last they really looked like soldiers.

'It's a bit on the stiff and scratchy side,' Eddie grumbled as he buttoned up the tunic.

'And a bit tight around the neck,' Harry added, running his finger inside the collar.

'Stop moaning, it'll soon soften up,' Jimmy told him as he attempted to wind the strips of webbing known as puttees around the bottom of the uniform trousers and over the top of his boots.

'Bind it tighter than that, lad – you don't want it to come undone and trip you up,' the sergeant instructed as he viewed their efforts. 'Look a right fool then, you would. And I want to see all buttons, badges and boots polished until I can see my face in them. Let's have some pride in your appearance, pride in the regiment. His lordship's paid for those uniforms out of his own pocket.'

'Oh, we're dead proud of the regiment and we won't let his lordship down, sergeant,' Eddie had replied firmly.

The *Lusitania* had sailed again when on 5 September the troops of the Liverpool 'Pals' Battalions marched from Aigburth to St George's Hall to take the salute from General Sir Henry Mackinnon, with the three boys among them. They had their uniforms now but still no rifles; however, the battalions marched with pride. The mood of the crowds who had turned out to cheer them was still fervently patriotic but there was an underlying sense of grim determination as well. In Belgium Liège had fallen and only the desperate remnants of the Belgian Army stood between Brussels and Antwerp. The Germans had advanced into France and had overrun Rheims, burning the beautiful old Gothic cathedral, and the thousands of casualties – British, French and Belgian – were being ferried across the Channel by hundreds of ships to the hospitals along the south coast and beyond. Private hospitals were being established in country houses and village halls, anywhere the wounded could be cared for.

Soon they'd be going to train on the estate of the Earl of

Derby, Knowsley Hall near Prescot, and marching with the others Eddie felt a little disappointed that the Earl himself wasn't on the platform on St George's Plateau where the statues of Victoria and Albert on high-stepping mounts gazed down and the huge, crouching bronze lions appeared to view the multitude with proud approval, but his brother, the Countess and her daughter were. Somewhere in that crowd were his own mother and sister, he thought, and for an instant he wondered where in the world his father was or even if he was alive; then he banished the thought. He just wanted Mam to be proud of him today.

Beside him Harry and Jimmy were thinking along similar lines. Harry was filled with pride and the affection he felt for Mae: he knew she'd be in the crowd cheering him on and he did consider her to be his 'girl' even if she hadn't actually agreed to it. Jimmy was thinking of Alice and how she'd spoken up for them all the night they'd joined up when everyone else had been horrified. She might only be fifteen but she had guts, did Alice, and that was something he admired in her. The news coming in from France wasn't good but soon the tide would turn and they'd have the Hun in retreat, he was sure. He just wished they could get all the training over and done with and get out there where they were needed. It was an exciting thought although at times when he thought of the shells and bullets he would have to face he couldn't help but feel a bit fearful.

Chapter Twelve

───◆───

'I T'S VERY QUIET without all the lads, there's hardly anyone out at all,' Mae commented to Alice as they walked home from the tram stop on that bitterly cold late November evening. Usually groups of men and boys were making their way homewards too, often exchanging banter or cheerful remarks, but now the streets appeared deserted. As flurries of sleet driven by a blustery wind stung her cheeks she thought it was really no wonder there were so few people out. She'd be glad to get home herself to a good fire and a hot meal and she wondered if there would be a letter for her from Harry. He wrote regularly even though the camp at Prescot, where the boys were training, wasn't that far away.

Alice pulled the collar of her coat higher around her ears and thought that it would be even quieter if Lord Kitchener got the five hundred thousand more men he'd asked for.

Everyone was aware now that the war wasn't going to be over by Christmas. German U-boats had sunk three British cruisers off the coast of the Netherlands and the Allies had fought a bitter battle for Ypres in October, sustaining heavy losses, and now both sides were dug in in a line of trenches that stretched from the North Sea to Switzerland. It didn't appear as if either side was winning, Mae thought, and with the onset of winter conditions would be harsh for the lads in the trenches, very harsh indeed. They were all knitting in earnest now; it no longer seemed the trivial pastime she and Alice had scorned, for Queen Mary herself had urged everyone to take up their knitting needles. They'd both completed their first-aid course and received their certificates but that had been the end of it. Aunty Maggie was adamant that they were not giving up their jobs to train as nurses for it wasn't what either she or John wanted for them. They hadn't scrimped and saved to send them to that commercial school for them to give it all up.

'Oh, what's for tea, Mam? I'm freezing,' Alice declared as she held out her hands before the fire in the range, thankful to be home in the cosy kitchen at last.

'Oxtail. That'll warm you up and there's mashed potato to go with it,' Maggie replied as she sniffed appreciatively at the aroma coming from the pan on the range. 'Move out of my way, Alice, and there's a letter for you, Mae,' she announced, picking up the envelope and handing it to her niece. 'He's as regular as clockwork with his letters, which is more than can be said for our Eddie or Jimmy Mercer. Agnes says they're as different as chalk and cheese those two lads of hers and I'm beginning to think she's right. I bet our Eddie and Jimmy spend their spare time playing cards and such like. Too much trouble to pick up a pen,' she grumbled. If she had a letter from Eddie once a fortnight she counted herself lucky.

Alice nodded, feeling a little disappointed. No, Jimmy wasn't much of a letter-writer. She'd had two since he'd been at Prescot, that's all, and they'd only been what she'd call 'notes'. 'What does Harry say?' she asked as Mae scanned the lines of neat copperplate written in pencil.

'That it's freezing now getting up so early and turning out for parade but they soon warm up and the stove they have in the hut keeps the place warm. They're still training hard but there will be a certain number of passes issued for leave at Christmas.'

'I suppose it's too much to hope for that all three of them will get home,' Maggie said, ladling out the thick meaty stew.

Mae put the letter aside; she'd read it more carefully later. She hoped they would get home for she realised that some time early next year they would all be going to France and she did want to see Harry again before then. They'd only had a few minutes alone together before he'd gone to Prescot. She wanted to say a proper goodbye, at least, and she'd try and make this Christmas special for him. Her da would be home too.

The meal was over and the dishes cleared away when Maggie was surprised to hear a knock on the front door. She wasn't expecting anyone at this time of night; usually people looking for a loan or calling to pay her came during the day.

'Shall I go, Mam?' Alice asked, putting down the balaclava she was knitting, which was for her a very complicated task involving the use of four needles at the same time.

'No, I'll go, you carry on with that or you'll go dropping stitches all over the place and I'll have to unpick it – again,' Maggie replied, laying aside her own knitting.

She looked concerned when she saw Esther Ziegler on the doorstep. 'What's wrong? Is it Isaac?'

Harold's wife nodded and bit her lip.

'You'd better come in, luv,' Maggie urged, ushering her into the parlour. Isaac hadn't been at all well of late and Harold had had the doctor out to his father twice.

'Harold asked me to come for you. We think he's . . . dying.'

Maggie put a hand to her mouth and shook her head sadly. 'I'll get my coat, Esther.'

She informed the girls that the old man was gravely ill and that she was going to visit him.

'Can we come too, please, Mrs Ziegler?' Mae asked, for both she and Alice were fond of Isaac.

Maggie looked questioningly at Esther. 'Might it be too much for him?'

'No, I think he would like to see you . . . all,' Esther replied a little stiffly. She had always been a rather reserved woman who didn't mix freely with her neighbours but she knew her father-in-law didn't have long and that he held Maggie McEvoy in high esteem, as she did herself.

Maggie was shocked when she saw how thin and frail he'd become. He looked like a small child lying in the depths of the big brass bed, she thought. 'Well now, Isaac, here's a nice state you've got into,' she said quietly, smiling down at him. 'You've got us all worried.'

She could see he was having trouble breathing and his eyes were dull and sunk into his head. She knew it was probably pneumonia; it claimed so many old people, especially in winter.

He struggled to speak. 'I wanted to see you, Maggie, perhaps for a last time.'

'Now, don't be talking like that, Isaac,' Maggie gently chided.

'I am tired, so very tired of it . . . all,' he said, gazing ahead into the distance at something she couldn't see. 'That it should come to . . . this, Maggie. This war they said would soon be over. This . . . hatred. The young men . . . the boys . . .'

He was becoming distressed and Esther bent to quieten him.

'Hush now, Father. It does no good to dwell on things.' She looked at Maggie, who reached and patted the gnarled hand that clutched the sheet.

'Esther is right, Isaac. You must rest and not upset yourself. There is little we can do; we have to trust the generals and the politicians,' she soothed, thinking that so far neither were doing particularly well.

Esther beckoned the two girls to come closer and the old man smiled at them.

'Mae! Alice! You . . . you both work hard, you have a good life, you look after Maggie.'

They both promised and then Maggie got to her feet. She could see that the visit had exhausted what little strength he had left. 'We'll go and let you sleep now, Isaac.'

When they'd left the room she turned to Esther and took her hand and squeezed it sympathetically. 'I doubt he'll last the night, Esther, but we'll pray for him.'

Esther nodded. 'I know. It's as if the war has . . . taken away his will to live. He . . . he knew much suffering as a child in Germany.'

Maggie nodded. 'He told me how his parents were killed. I'm fond of him, Esther, and I'll always be grateful to him for helping me when I needed it and for helping Eddie get that apprenticeship.'

'Thank you, Maggie, for coming. Harold and I will sit with him now.'

Maggie was collecting her thoughts; their customs were different and she didn't want to say anything inappropriate. 'We will pray and give thanks for Isaac's kindness, Esther, and . . . and may your God give both you and Harold comfort and strength.'

Esther smiled. 'Thank you, Maggie.'

'Poor Uncle Isaac,' Mae said sadly as they walked home.

'He's old and he's tired, Mae, and he's had a long life. We all have to go sometime and he'll be happy to be reunited with his Rachel. Now, let's get home and say a prayer that he goes peacefully.'

Eddie leaned on his shovel and looked at the small pile of earth he'd moved in the last half-hour. Although it was bitterly cold, all around him lads in their shirtsleeves were digging away as Sergeant Dewhurst walked up and down the line, firing instructions to 'put your backs into it' and other such comments. Beyond the perimeter of the field the neat lines of wooden huts stretched away towards a line of trees – their branches bare now – that separated the training camp from the rest of the estate. Beyond them stretched the parkland and in the far distance the sweep of the wide drive that led up to the magnificent home of the Earl, Knowsley Hall, which of course was strictly out of bounds to them.

'What's up with you, Eddie?' Jimmy asked, noticing Eddie's lack of effort.

'What flaming use is all this digging?'

'It's practice for digging trenches,' Jimmy replied in a tone that he would have used explaining something to a not-very-bright child.

'But we're not digging trenches, we're just moving one pile of earth to another part of the field. What use is that going to be to us? What kind of training is that?'

Jimmy grinned at him. 'Ours not to reason why, Eddie. We just do as we're told. Now get on with it before Sergeant Dewhurst sees you slacking.'

Eddie grimaced. He supposed Jimmy was right. They just followed orders – even if it did seem a waste of time. 'Do you think we'll be lucky enough to get some leave at Christmas?'

Jimmy shrugged. 'Who knows? Although I wouldn't mind sleeping in my own bed and having a few home comforts. I don't suppose we'll know for a while yet.'

'I wouldn't mind a break from all this digging. It doesn't seem like real training to me and it won't be much fun being stuck here at Christmas without you and Harry if you get leave and I don't,' Eddie replied, driving the edge of his spade into the clay.

'We're supposed to be at war, in case you've forgotten,' Jimmy retorted, but of course he too hoped that they would all be fortunate enough to get leave for the holiday.

When John arrived home he learned that Isaac Ziegler had died in the early hours of that November morning and had been buried, as was the custom, before sunset of the same day.

'He had a good innings, Maggie, he was nearly ninety,' he commented sadly.

'I sent flowers. I wasn't sure . . . but Esther said it would be all right,' she confided. Then her thoughts turned to their own family. 'I finally had a letter from Eddie yesterday,' she went on. 'He said they should know this week if they'll be able to get home for Christmas. If they can I think we should make an effort; God knows we all need a bit of cheer in our lives and it might be a while before they get to spend another Christmas at home.'

John nodded. Things weren't looking at all good in France and the German U-boats were becoming a serious threat. But, though the situation was grave, he wasn't unduly concerned. The *Lucy* was primarily an unarmed passenger ship and her speed added to her safety; even the U-boats were slow by comparison. 'I agree, Maggie, and next trip I'll bring some tinned stuff home. Food is going to get scarcer.'

'I know and, John, do you think, if I give you the money, you could get something . . . a bit special for Eddie? Something useful that he can take with him?'

'Like what?' he queried, thinking that he might get something a bit special for Mae too; she'd be seventeen next birthday.

Maggie shrugged. 'I'm not sure. Perhaps something like a real leather wallet or maybe a writing case – that might prompt him to write home more often.'

John raised an eyebrow, thinking a writing case might be a bit too ostentatious and rather incongruous for a mere infantryman and he doubted Eddie would use it. 'I think he'd use a wallet more, and there's no need for you to be giving me money. And I'm thinking of looking for a little watch for Mae, as she doesn't have one.'

'Then will you get one for our Alice too and I *will* give you the money for that,' Maggie said determinedly. 'Agnes, the girls and I will see that Eddie and the twins have plenty of woollen socks, gloves, scarves and balaclavas – even if they might not be able to see properly out of the ones our Alice knits.' She shook her head in mock despair. 'I swear Lucy Mercer makes a better fist of knitting and she's only twelve.'

Both families were delighted when they learned that Eddie, Jimmy and Harry had all been fortunate enough to get leave for Christmas, even if it was only for forty-eight hours and they'd spend some of that travelling. Maggie was even more delighted when John arrived home with his kitbag stuffed with tins of pressed ham, tongue, corned beef, peaches and pineapple chunks.

'We'll have a real feast, Agnes!' she informed her friend. 'I want you all to come over for tea on Christmas Night, that way even if we can't get the stuff for the traditional Christmas dinner, tea will be a treat.'

'That's good of you, Maggie, but are you sure? I mean, you should save that stuff.'

'Of course I'm sure and John will be able to bring more. I know they don't do as many trips now but he'll make sure we don't go without.'

Agnes beamed at her. 'It *will* be a treat. We don't have things like peaches and pineapple anyway, they're much too expensive. I'll bring a couple of tins of evaporated milk to pour over them. It might be a bit of a squeeze getting everyone in the kitchen though,' she added, thinking of the practicalities. 'I mean these kitchens were definitely not made for eleven people to eat in.'

Maggie pondered this. 'If you ask Bertie to bring your table and some chairs over we can set up in the parlour as well.'

'Won't you mind? You've all your good furniture in there.'

Maggie shook her head. 'Not at all. You, Bertie, your mam, John and I will sit in there; the kids can eat here in the kitchen,' she said firmly.

They'd all made an effort to decorate the kitchen and parlour for the occasion and Maggie and Agnes had selected the food they would serve; and when Eddie and the twins arrived home late on Christmas Eve they were greeted with hugs and kisses by their families for they'd been away for almost three months.

'You look well, Eddie, I have to say that,' Maggie said proudly, thinking how smart he looked in his uniform.

'Plenty of fresh air, exercise and the food's not too bad either,' he replied, grinning. It was true but he, like Jimmy, was looking forward to some home comforts now.

'We've got a real feast planned for tomorrow,' Alice informed him, 'and the whole Mercer family are coming over to share it.'

'Blimey! All of them? How are we all going to fit into the kitchen? You can hardly move in here now.'

'Don't worry about that, Eddie, your mam and Agnes have got it all in hand,' John said, slapping him on the back and thinking that the lad did look older. He had an air of confidence about him now. 'You were lucky to get home.'

Eddie sat down and stretched his hands out to the welcoming warmth of the fire in the range. 'I know. Tommy Mitford's dead narked that he's had to stay behind.' They'd known Tommy Mitford from school and at fifteen he was decidedly under age, having been in the same class as Alice. His mother Nelly had been horrified that they'd believed him when he'd so blatantly lied about his age, and Maggie and Agnes had been astounded by the fact.

Alice handed him the glass of pale ale her Uncle John had poured from the jug he'd bought for the occasion from the pub on the corner. 'I still don't know how he had the bare-faced cheek to swear he was nineteen.'

'And I don't know how *they* were stupid enough to believe him!' Maggie added acidly. 'His poor mam is real cut up about it; he's her youngest.'

'See what the Earl gave us, Mam. Every single one of us got one.' Eddie held out a cap badge depicting an eagle standing on an eyrie that contained a young child. 'It's solid silver, made by Elkington's; it's their family crest and he presented each one himself and wished us luck,' he said proudly.

John nodded, weighing it in his hand. It must have cost his lordship a fortune to have had so many made. The device was well known: there were a dozen pubs in Liverpool called 'The Eagle and Child'.

'Then you take care of it and don't go losing it or getting it pinched,' Maggie instructed.

'Oh, they've given us brass ones to wear for every day; these are just for "ceremonial",' Eddie replied and then grinned. 'The lads are calling it "Derby's Duck".'

Maggie frowned. 'That's not very respectful now, is it, after his lordship's gone to all that expense and trouble?'

John grinned to himself. Scousers always managed to find a nickname for things; it was part of the culture and was usually meant as a term of affection, not disrespect. You only had to think of the *Lucy* and the *Maury* to know that.

Next morning everyone was delighted with their gifts. Eddie thought the leather wallet, or 'billfold' as his uncle said

Americans would call it, was the handsomest thing he'd ever seen. 'I'll feel like a real toff now!' he'd exclaimed. 'A real leather wallet and a solid silver cap badge.'

Mae and Alice both loved the little heart-shaped watches to be worn like a brooch on their dress or jacket. Mae's was silver enamelled with turquoise, Alice's silver and green.

'They're even made so when you turn them up to look at them the face is the right way up!' Alice exclaimed delightedly.

John laughed. 'Well, if they weren't you'd have to stand on your head!'

'Oh, thank you, Da! It's so pretty but practical too, and I'll take such good care of it,' Mae promised, hugging him. She'd treasure it always.

Later on John, helped by Eddie, brought Agnes's table across to Maggie's parlour with Jimmy and Harry bringing the chairs. Maggie, Agnes and the girls set both tables and laid out the food. For the occasion Bertie Mercer had brought a bottle of sherry for the 'ladies' as he called them and a bottle of whiskey. Maggie stipulated that Alice and Mae could have just one glass each of sherry.

'I don't know that these lads should be getting stuck into the hard stuff, Bertie. They've a very early start in the morning,' she added doubtfully.

'There's only a glass or two each, Maggie, and I reckon if they're old enough to go and fight they're old enough for a drink or two,' he replied, to which all three heartily assented.

When all the young ones were seated in the kitchen their food was served by Mae and Alice. 'And don't go making pigs of yourselves,' Alice said bossily.

'Well, it's not every day we have ham, tongue, peaches and

pineapple for tea,' Jimmy protested. 'Wait until we tell the other lads about this.'

'I bet you're glad you managed to get home,' Mae said, looking at Harry, who nodded and smiled at her. It was really good to see her and he would try to wangle a few minutes alone with her later if he could.

'What exactly do you do all day? March up and down and practise shooting?' Alice asked.

'Yes, and we have bayonet practice and route marches,' Jimmy answered, his mouth full of ham.

'And we dig,' Eddie announced grimly, helping himself to a large slice of crusty homemade bread thickly spread with butter.

'Dig? Dig what?' Mae asked, bemused.

'Trenches. We're practising digging trenches,' Harry said. 'There's a big bank of clay and we're digging it out and moving it.'

'That sounds like a bit of a waste of time,' Alice remarked scathingly.

'Aye, there's some of us that think that too,' Eddie agreed.

'We've made up a ditty and we sing it while we dig, it's to the tune of "Moonlight Bay".' Jimmy grinned and launched into song. '"We were digging all day, on Derby's clay—"'

'You were great before tunes were invented, Jimmy Mercer,' Alice interrupted, covering her ears and pulling a face.

'Do you know how long you'll stay there before you have to go to France?' Mae asked, looking directly at Harry.

'They don't tell us things like that,' he replied seriously.

'We're all hoping it won't be long now. We're getting fed up with all this "practising",' Eddie added.

'Then we'd better all enjoy the evening, hadn't we?' Alice said, thinking that it was quite amazing how much older and more grown up Jimmy looked in his uniform. And quite handsome too.

Before they went home Harry did manage to get a few moments alone with Mae, something he'd been trying to do all evening. 'When I've gone to France will you . . . miss me, Mae?' he asked shyly.

She smiled and nodded. 'Of course I will. I'll miss you all. Aunty Maggie is always saying how quiet the place is without you and she's right.' She was trying to keep the conversation light although she realised that he was hoping for something a bit more serious.

'I mean . . . especially . . . me? You know how I feel about you, Mae.'

'I know, Harry, and I really do like you a lot,' she answered. It was true but she still didn't know if her feelings went deeper than just affection.

'I don't know when I'll get to see you again, Mae. None of us know how long we'll be away or even if . . . we'll—'

'I'll write to you, Harry, I promise,' she interrupted hastily; she didn't want to think about the possibility that he might not come back. It was too awful to contemplate.

'Can I . . . kiss you, Mae? A goodbye kiss?'

She felt apprehension and confusion wash over her and yet she was curious. She'd never been kissed by a boy before and wondered what it would be like. Perhaps if she let him kiss her it would help her to make up her mind about how she really felt? Perhaps it would make her realise whether she did care deeply for him or not. She nodded and closed her eyes and felt his arms around her as he drew her close. His mouth was gentle on hers and it wasn't an unpleasant sensation, she thought, but she didn't feel any *different*. She wasn't overcome by any sweeping emotions. It was just pleasant and she felt slightly disappointed. Then he released her and she opened her eyes. He was gazing at her with an expression of love and pride and she felt guilty that she didn't feel the same way.

'You're the only girl for me, Mae. You're very special. I'll write to you as often as I can,' he promised.

She smiled at him. 'I know. Goodbye and take care of yourself, Harry,' she replied as he turned towards the door.

When he'd gone she sighed. Her feelings hadn't changed. She didn't love him, she was just fond of him and it had only been a goodbye kiss as far as she was concerned. However, she was fully aware that that wasn't how he viewed it and for that she felt sorry and more than a little guilty.

Unbeknown to them both their farewell had been watched quietly by Maggie and John. As Harry left, Maggie smiled at her brother. 'Well, that looks like a budding romance to me,' she whispered.

John frowned. 'She's too young for romance, Maggie, and even though I've nothing against the lad – I like him – I have to say that I was hoping for . . . *more* for her.'

Maggie was surprised. 'He's a good lad, John. He's steadier and more serious than their Jimmy and you know what kind of a family he comes from.'

John nodded slowly. It was difficult to put into words but he wanted something better for Mae than just being the wife of a factory worker. 'I know all that, Maggie.' He sighed heavily.

'Oh, she's still very young and who knows what the future holds for any of them?' he said.

Maggie didn't pursue the matter but she thought that Mae hadn't chosen too badly in young Harry Mercer. Surely her brother would accept that – in time?

Chapter Thirteen

———◆———

WHEN IT WAS announced in March, the appeal for women to serve their country by signing up for war service was not met with much enthusiasm by Maggie. 'I don't care what the Government says, Alice and Mae've both got decent jobs and I'm not having them working on the railways or the docks or in a munitions factory or – God forbid – in a coal yard! They're already doing a lot of the work of the men who've joined up. That's sufficient,' she stated grimly to Agnes.

'I blame a lot of it on that Pankhurst woman and those suffragettes,' Agnes added. Neither of them approved of the Women's Suffrage Movement or their activities, despite what their daughters thought. 'I read that she even said women are only "too anxious" to be recruited – I ask you! She's certainly not speaking for me!'

Maggie nodded. 'And that Mrs Fox saying women are capable of doing *any* job! It's this war, Agnes, it's . . . wreaking havoc with society and morals. Young girls filling shells and carting coal! What are things coming to? Well, those two will stay where they are. It's enough that the lads'll be going off next month,' she finished determinedly.

The *Lusitania* wasn't due to make her next trip until 17 April and so John was able to join the family when they went to see the battalions of the King's Liverpool Regiment when, early that month, they marched to Lime Street Station to board the trains that would take them to Grantham in Lincolnshire and then on to France.

The trees in St John's Gardens at the back of St George's Hall were in blossom and the spring flowers were a riot of colour in the neat beds as on that sunny April morning Maggie and her family and Agnes and hers made their way into the city. The streets were crowded, the traffic at a standstill and the police working hard to control the crowds.

'We'll never get anywhere near the station!' Maggie exclaimed as they pushed their way along the pavement outside the Empire Theatre.

'We'll do our best,' John promised, but the closest they got was outside the Washington Hotel and the police stood two deep at the station entrance.

'We won't be able to see them at all,' Mae said disappointedly. 'We won't be able to get through the police lines.'

'I'm afraid there's nothing we can do about that,' her father commiserated with her and they resigned themselves to wait with the thousands of other families.

At last they heard the sound of the regimental bands and the crowds erupted into a cheering, waving mass as the first line of khaki-clad soldiers from the 17th Battalion swung into Lime Street, their battalion colonel at their head. A token force of twelve men from the newly formed County Palatine Artillery marched behind them, the white horse of Hanover on their cap badges, an irony lost on almost everyone in the crowd. Following them were the men of the 18th Battalion and both families craned their necks to try to spot the lads within their ranks.

They were all young, strong, fresh-faced and so smart in their uniforms, Maggie thought with pride as they marched jauntily to the strains of 'Pack Up Your Troubles'.

John, who was taller than everyone else, suddenly shouted and pointed and the rest of them caught sight of Eddie, Jimmy, Harry and young Tommy Mitford marching together and grinning widely.

Then they were all shouting and laughing and yet both Mae and Alice were aware that tears were coursing down their faces. 'It's daft' – Alice dashed a hand across her wet cheeks – 'we're all so cheerful and yet we're bawling like babies.'

'It's because we're so proud of them, Alice!' Mae laughed.

When the last soldier had disappeared in to the cavernous station concourse John and Bertie, with some difficulty, ushered them all towards the tram stop.

'They were a fine sight and I'm glad I was here to see it and I know we all wish them well,' John said.

'We *are* proud of them,' Maggie agreed. 'But . . . it's a terrible worry just the same,' she went on quietly. Now that the lads had finally left she felt bereft and terribly anxious, wondering what the future held for them.

* * *

Ten days later she bade goodbye to her brother. 'You take care of yourself and don't go bringing a ton of tinned stuff back, I've still got plenty left.'

He grinned at her. 'Just the odd one then, Maggie. Look after yourself and the girls – no letting them sign up to work in a coal yard.'

'Oh, I've no intention of doing that, John,' she replied firmly; then she leaned back against the door jamb and watched him as he walked briskly down the street towards the tram stop. She'd become used to him spending longer at home and so had Mae. She wished he'd find a shore job. She felt he was getting too old for such heavy work, but he wanted to do his 'bit' too and she could understand that. Well, it would certainly be very quiet now, with just herself and the girls in the house, she thought as she turned back into the lobby.

It was Agnes who came flying into the kitchen that Saturday evening in May, still with her apron on, her face drained of all colour, her eyes brimming with tears.

'Agnes! In the name of God, what's wrong?' Maggie cried, her heart dropping like a stone, instinctively knowing something terrible had happened.

'Oh, Maggie! Oh, Maggie!' Agnes was clutching her apron and fighting down the sobs, the tears now streaming down her cheeks.

Maggie's hand went to her throat as Alice grabbed Mae's hand and clung to it tightly. 'What? Is it . . . one of the lads?'

Agnes shook her head. 'It's . . . it's . . . the *Lucy*! Oh, God, Maggie! They've sunk the *Lusitania*! There's hundreds lost!'

Mae gasped in utter disbelief. It couldn't be true! It *couldn't*!

'*NO!*' she screamed as Maggie's knees gave way and she sank, shaking, into a chair.

'John!' Maggie cried in a strangled voice. 'He . . . he wouldn't have stood a chance, not . . . down there in the stokehold!'

Agnes put her arms around her friend and held her tightly and they both sobbed uncontrollably, Maggie for a brother she had loved dearly and who had been her strength and security over the years, and Agnes for her dear old friend.

'Oh, Alice . . . Alice . . . I can't believe it,' Mae wept as she fell into her cousin's arms. Her da, her wonderful, generous, loving da . . . was never coming home again.

Their grief filled the room and was almost unbearable to witness, Bertie thought as he came into the kitchen, having followed Agnes. He was deeply shaken himself, consumed with grief and anger. He'd been in the city centre when he'd heard the cries of the news vendor and had grabbed a copy of the early edition of the paper. You could almost feel the shock and disbelief that had gripped everyone on the streets as the facts became known. The *Lusitania* had been torpedoed off the Old Head of Kinsale in County Cork as, nearing home, she'd slowed her speed to ensure she caught the tide at the Mersey Bar on Sunday morning. Two explosions had ripped through her and in barely twenty-one minutes she'd sunk; it was feared that over a thousand men, women and children had gone down with her – amongst them John Strickland. The members of the Black Gang would have been the first to die; Bertie had known that instantly.

He did his best to help Agnes comfort Maggie and the girls but at length realised he wasn't being of much use. 'I'll go back over, luv, your mam is upset too,' he said quietly.

Agnes nodded, trying to put aside her own feelings. 'I'll make us some tea, it'll help with the shock,' she said, patting Maggie on the shoulder.

Maggie nodded and dabbed at her swollen eyes, trying to calm herself for both Alice and Mae's sake. 'Thanks, Agnes. Why? Why the *Lucy*? That's what I keep asking myself. They were carrying people, not cargo.'

'They couldn't have mistaken her for another ship, they *must* have known!' Agnes concurred, then her eyes hardened. 'But maybe they just didn't care! Who knows what goes on in the minds of those . . . *fiends*! Everything we've heard about them must be true, to deliberately fire on helpless people, babies even! It defies belief. Oh, I hope our Jimmy and Harry blast every single one they come across to hell!'

Maggie didn't reply. Strangely she didn't feel angry, just overcome by a terrible sense of grief and loss. Maybe the anger would come later. She looked to where Mae, inconsolable, was sobbing quietly in Alice's arms. Oh, poor, poor Mae! Losing her mother when only a few days old and now . . . now her da. She had no one in the world except herself, Alice and Eddie – and who knew what lay ahead for Eddie on the battlefields of France.

A sombre atmosphere had prevailed in Agnes's house since Saturday. Bertie was reading out a report from the *Daily Post & Mercury* to Agnes and her mother on the Monday evening. 'It states specifically "that she was hit low down on the starboard side between the third and fourth funnels by one torpedo but survivors have said there were two explosions very close together and there is now speculation that she was carrying ammunition",' he read, 'but I don't believe a word of it. John and I had a talk about the danger of U-boats and he said they never carry explosives, just food, wood, iron bars, things like that, and I believe him. The company wouldn't put their passengers at risk by carrying munitions.'

Agnes rubbed her forehead; she seemed to have had a headache for days. 'I don't suppose they would but what good does it do for the papers to go on endlessly reporting all the facts and details? All those poor souls are dead.'

Bertie nodded but something John Strickland had said suddenly came back to him. 'Coal dust,' he said aloud.

Agnes and his mother-in-law looked at him as though he'd lost his wits. '"Coal dust"?' Agnes repeated.

'John said that coal dust is a very unstable substance; a spark from a boot on the iron deck or a shovel and it will explode. I wonder, did that cause the second explosion? She was nearly home, off the coast of Cork, when the torpedo hit. Her bunkers must have been almost empty – except for coal dust.'

Edith Webster was losing patience with her son-in-law whom she had always considered to be on the pedantic side. 'What does it matter now, Bertie, for God's sake? The *Lucy* is at the bottom of the ocean and all this debating what happened won't bring her back, or any of the poor souls who perished, so let's hear no more about it. I'll put the kettle on,' she finished firmly.

Agnes shrugged and then frowned. 'What's that noise? Can you hear it, Bertie? It sounds like shouting.'

Bertie got up and went through into the shop and opened the door, looking up the street. It *was* shouting; in fact it was more than that, it was yelling and there was a crowd of people in front of Ziegler's shop. Agnes had joined him. 'What's going on?'

Bertie looked grim. 'Looks like the riots have reached us, Agnes. There's a mob outside Ziegler's. People are so furious about the *Lucy* they're attacking anything with a German name.' Liverpudlians felt great affinity for their liners, particularly the three big Cunarders, and there were many families like Maggie's who had lost loved ones.

Agnes was astonished. 'But . . . but Harold Ziegler isn't German. He was born here; he's as British as you and me.'

'Try telling them that,' Bertie said.

'Where are the police?' Agnes cried, pushing past him and going into the street. She could see no sign of them.

'Come inside, Agnes!' Bertie called to her but she ignored him and ran across to Maggie's house.

'There's a rabble outside Ziegler's, screaming abuse and throwing stones,' she informed her friend.

Maggie looked at her in some confusion. 'Why?'

Agnes told her what had been going on all over the city in retaliation for the recent tragedy and as she listened Maggie felt anger begin to grow in her. 'So, they're taking it out on poor Harold and Esther?' She thought of Isaac and of how he'd helped her, of Rachel Ziegler who had always been kind to her and Harold and Esther who worked so hard and were so polite and inoffensive. She grabbed Agnes by the arm. 'Well, I'm not having it! They had nothing to do with sinking the *Lucy*!'

As they hurried up the street towards the tailor's shop they heard the sound of breaking glass but whereas Agnes hesitated, Maggie quickened her steps. The shop window was smashed in completely and a couple of lads were already helping themselves to whatever they could and that infuriated her even further.

She roughly shoved her way through the roaring crowd until she reached the front, and glimpsed at the back of the shop a terrified, sobbing Esther clinging to Harold, who was white-faced with fear. Maggie turned on those nearest her, bawling at the top of her voice and grabbing hold of one lad who was clutching a smart tailored waistcoat. 'You thieving little toe-rag! You're nothing but a bunch of bloody robbers and hooligans! Get out of here and leave these people alone!'

'They're bloody Germans! They sunk the *Lucy*!' a man bellowed back.

'Aye, they deserve it, they sunk the *Lucy*!' another yelled and they surged forward.

Maggie held her ground, shaking with fury for she recognised a lot of them; they lived in this neighbourhood and knew the Zieglers. 'They are no more German than I am, you know that and you all know me! I'm Maggie McEvoy and my own brother was a stoker on the *Lucy*. Would I be defending them if I believed they'd killed Big John Strickland?'

'Yer should be ashamed of yerself then! Dancin' on his grave, yer are, by stickin' up fer the likes of them!' the lad who was clutching the waistcoat howled.

Maggie grabbed hold of his ear and twisted it hard. 'I know you, Davy Hardcastle, you've been in and out of borstal and you're old enough to be in the Army!' She released him and turned on another man. 'And you, Fred Higgins, you've come to me often enough in the past for money! And you, and you . . . !' She jabbed each man hard on the shoulder. 'Well, you'll get nothing more! You can go somewhere else or damn well starve. And there's quite a few of you who should have joined up too! Why aren't you in the Army or Navy, Ted Roberts? And you, Tommy Naylor? You're nothing but cowards and thieves, the lot of you! Attacking a defenceless man and his wife who never did you any harm and using the deaths of the poor souls who drowned as an excuse! Clear off the lot of you! Go on, clear off!'

She was trembling with the force of her anger but was relieved to see that finally the police had arrived. The crowd, still muttering threats, began to draw back and move away and a very shaken Agnes caught her arm as Maggie glared up at a burly sergeant. 'It's about time you lot put in an appearance. Aren't you paid to keep the peace? You'd better go and see if the Zieglers are all right. I'm going home,' she announced, turning away. Now that her rage was dying down she felt utterly exhausted.

'God, Maggie, they might have lynched you! I dread to think what could have happened if the police hadn't arrived,' Agnes said as they walked back down the street.

'I was too bloody angry to think about that, Agnes. That Hardcastle lad is a bad lot! I'm glad poor Isaac wasn't here to suffer *that*! Our John would have been the first to agree with what I did. He liked and respected Isaac and Harold, he wouldn't have approved of what that shower of no-marks and cowards were up to. And what good will ruining people's lives and businesses do? It won't bring any of them back . . .' She began to cry softly and Agnes put her arm around her shoulder.

'Come on home, Maggie. It's been a terrible few days for you and there's poor Mae to think about now. I don't know how she's going to get over this. Stay strong for her, Maggie. That's what John would want. Stay strong for his daughter.'

Chapter Fourteen

———◆———

MAE DIDN'T THINK she would ever get over it. She would always feel so alone and *lost*, she thought as she sat in the kitchen with Alice on Saturday almost four weeks later. She didn't want to eat, she couldn't sleep, there were times when she felt so angry and others when she felt just numb. She couldn't believe that she would never see her father again, never hear his voice or see him smile. He didn't even have a grave; there could be no funeral, and that made it seem worse. Maggie had gone to see the vicar to see if there was some kind of service that could take place as a memorial.

Alice did her best to try to comfort her and for this Mae was grateful. Alice had loved her father too but not nearly as much as she had. 'Oh, Alice, I just don't know how I'm going to carry on . . .'

'You will, Mae. In a few weeks you'll be able to . . . try to accept it,' Alice replied softly. She felt totally out of her depth for this was the first death in the family she had experienced.

Mae shook her head. 'I know you mean well but you don't really know how it feels, Alice. He was my da . . . and he's gone forever.'

'I do, in a way,' Alice replied sadly. 'I never knew my da, he left before I was born. At least you had your da for all the years you were growing up, Mae. I never did. And Mam said Uncle John was devastated when your mam died but he got over it. He never forgot her and you'll never forget him but you'll get on with your life, Mae. You do have to think about the future.'

Alice had only been repeating what Maggie had already said but her words stayed with Mae. Her cousin was right; she would have to look to the future, and it was one she would have to face without her father. His death in a way had made her grow up, she thought sadly.

After her talk with Alice, she'd spent a long night pondering her future but she had at last decided what she must do, what she felt she *had* to do.

She had already returned to work for she needed to support herself now she no longer had a father to help, but she broached the subject with her aunt the following day.

'I've come to a decision, Aunty Maggie. I'm going to have to stay at my job but I'm going to see if I can train as a nurse now too.'

Maggie looked at her, horrified. 'I promised your poor da that I wouldn't let you do war work, Mae! It was the very last thing we spoke of and I'm not going back on that promise.'

'But I have to do something, Aunty Maggie!' Mae protested.

'No, you don't. You've a good job and you are already covering for men who've gone off and that's enough. There are

Regular Army nurses and auxiliaries – have been since the days of Miss Nightingale – and things aren't so bad that you have to go too. How can I let your da down by agreeing? '

'It's not the same. I want to do something . . . helpful. What use is sitting at a desk all day typing passenger manifests and bills of lading and invoices? That's not helping anyone! No, I've made up my mind,' Mae said determinedly.

Maggie got to her feet, equally determined that she was not going to break her word to John. 'Then you can just unmake it.'

'Aunty Maggie, I know . . . Da . . . would want me to do something for the war effort.'

'What your da wanted for you, Mae, was to keep on working in the offices of the company he had served for all his working life and in whose employment he . . . died. He was so proud that you had a decent job there and him a mere stoker, you know he was. He certainly didn't want you being a nurse – a kind of glorified skivvy doing all sorts of dirty and menial tasks.'

Mae felt resentment rising in her. 'How do you know that? He never said he didn't want me to train as a nurse and it can't all be skivvying.'

'What I know, milady, is that he didn't want you doing war work. Now, that's the end of it. I want to hear no more about it.'

Mae had never openly defied her aunt in her life and old habits die hard, so she pressed her lips together and stormed out of the kitchen. She wasn't going to give up, she thought. She wanted to do something worthwhile, something she was sure in her heart that her father would indeed have approved of: nursing wounded soldiers.

When she'd left, Maggie turned her attention to Alice. 'And don't you go encouraging her either, Alice. She's . . . she's still overcome by grief, she only thinks she knows what she wants and what I said was true. Our John didn't want her doing war work.'

'I never said a word to her, Mam, honestly, but it can't be all that bad. I mean, it's not working in a munitions factory or anything like that.'

'I've heard enough about this, Alice. I don't want it mentioned again,' Maggie warned.

Alice nodded but somehow she didn't think that this was the end of the matter.

Alice was right; Mae had no intention of giving up. It seemed even more important to her now. 'I've got to make her see that I want to do it for Da's sake, Alice,' she confided as they sat on the tram coming home from work.

'She'll go mad – she told me not to encourage you,' Alice replied. 'But I have to say I'm on your side, Mae.'

'Then I'll try again after supper. I saw this in the newspaper this morning and it looks as if nurses are badly needed.' Mae passed Alice the piece she had cut out of the paper.

Alice read it and nodded. 'I'll back you up, Mae, even though I'll probably get an ear-bashing for it.'

When the dishes had been washed and put away Mae passed the newspaper cutting to her aunt. 'They are recruiting girls for the Voluntary Aid Detachment at Walton Hospital tomorrow, Aunty Maggie, so I'm going to see if they'll take me. I *have* to do something. There's nothing I can do now for . . . Da, but maybe I can help wounded soldiers. Da would want me to be more . . . independent and do something I believe in and I just can't do nothing at all! You can't want me to stay mollycoddled in that office while men and boys are dying!'

'Mae, I thought I said I wanted to hear no more about this. I promised him and you know how proud he was that you had a good job . . . He wanted a better life for you, Mae, not—' Maggie started but Mae interrupted her.

'Aunty Maggie, I . . . We have to face the fact that he's . . . dead and that the world he knew has changed. He . . . he couldn't know what this war would do to people, how it would affect their feelings. When you promised him you wouldn't let me do war work, I know he meant working in munitions or on the docks or railways. In my heart I know he would have wanted me to do something useful to help the wounded. I know he would have been equally as proud of me for that. He wouldn't want me sitting in the safety and . . . comfort of that office when I could be of more use in a hospital. He'd be proud that I want to help.'

Before Maggie could answer Alice spoke. 'Mam, I think Mae is right. Sooner or later we'll both have to register for war work, we won't have any choice in the matter and nothing you can do or say will change that. When that happens we'll get no say in where they send us: a factory, the docks, the railways or trams and it could even be a coal yard! You've got to admit that nursing is better than a lot of other jobs.'

Maggie gazed grimly at the two girls but her resolve was wavering. What Alice had said about them being forced to register and go where they were sent was true and Mae's eloquence and determination had caused doubts to niggle at her. After all, John had only said not to let her sign up to work

142

in a coal yard and indeed if that was where the powers that be decided to send her, Mae would have to go, horrifying though the thought was. He hadn't mentioned nursing and Mae had said she wasn't going to give up her job, just train in the evenings.

At last she relented; Alice's words had had a very sobering effect. 'Well, you're far too young, Alice, they'll not take you. And I'll be surprised if they take you either, Mae. I saw that piece in the paper too, they're looking for girls of twenty-one and over.'

'But I can try,' Mae said determinedly, thankful that her aunt's resistance had crumbled. 'I'll go after work tomorrow.'

'I'll come with you, Mae. Even if they won't take me I can give you a bit of support,' Alice added. She knew her mam was right, that at sixteen she was far too young and she also knew that she didn't look very much older than that. But she felt she should stand by her cousin in whatever way she could.

'It's a bit grim-looking,' Alice stated as they got off the tram the following evening and gazed across at the big soot-coated building with its tall clock tower. They both knew it had once been a workhouse.

They entered the main reception area, which was half tiled in green; the remaining expanse of wall was painted in dark green and even the floor was green. 'It's for the bugs,' Alice whispered. 'It's a well-known fact that bugs don't like green.'

Mae didn't reply, her gaze sweeping around the room, which was empty except for a nurse sitting at a desk, writing.

She looked up as the two girls approached. 'Can I help you?' she asked briskly.

'I've come to see if I can join the Voluntary Aid Detachment. There was an article in the paper asking people to come here today,' Mae informed her.

'I think you're both too young,' the nurse said flatly.

'Oh, I've not come to join, I'm only sixteen,' Alice said a little dejectedly.

'But . . . but I'm definitely old enough,' Mae said firmly. The lads had lied about their ages so why shouldn't she? She was determined now to train and wasn't going to be put off so easily.

'I'll fetch Sister Forshaw then.' The nurse rose, her apron crackling with starch as she moved. 'If you'd wait here please, Miss er . . . ?'

'Strickland. Mae Strickland,' Mae said.

'I didn't like her much,' Alice remarked caustically. 'She looked at us as though we'd crawled out from under a stone.'

The nurse didn't return but a nursing sister did; Mae judged her to be in her late thirties and rather strict, the stiff white winged headdress adding to the illusion, but perhaps that was part of her job. 'Miss Strickland? I believe you wish to join the Voluntary Aid Detachment?'

'I do,' Mae replied.

'You are rather late; we've had a steady stream of people coming to register all day, until six o'clock in fact.'

'I work, ma'am. I'm a typist in the offices of the Cunard Steamship Company. I'm afraid I need to work, but I'm hoping that I can continue to work and train in my time off. We both already have a basic first-aid certificate,' she added.

'You must address me as "Sister", Miss Strickland,' the woman said, not unkindly, and then she nodded slowly. The girl was not of the usual class who had come through these doors today: they'd had no need to work for a living. It was ironic that the girls who had come to register had plenty of time on their hands yet were the very ones least likely to be used to hard, demanding and often menial work. 'I see. You have no parents?'

Mae shook her head. 'My mother died when I was a few days old from childbed fever.'

She paused as the older woman nodded and murmured, 'Puerperal sepsis. And your father?' Sister enquired.

Mae swallowed hard; it was still so painful and difficult to tell people about her da.

'He was lost when the *Lusitania* went down,' Alice put in. 'I'm her cousin; she lives with us.'

'I see.' Sister Forshaw's attitude softened a little although she glanced appraisingly at the younger girl.

'I can do nothing now for my father, Sister, there isn't even a grave I can visit, but I want to do something to help the wounded. I feel it is something he'd approve of. And my cousin Edward – Alice's brother – is serving with the Liverpool Pals.'

Sister nodded. 'I can see no problem with you training in the evenings and at weekends. It's true that the girls and women who have volunteered so far have no need to work but we do desperately need nurses.' She turned her attention to Alice. 'And how old are you, Miss . . . ?'

'Miss McEvoy. I'm sixteen, Sister. I won't be seventeen until the end of the year,' Alice supplied. 'Mam's already told me I'm too young. I just came along to support Mae,' she added.

'Indeed, nurses are required to be more mature, to have some experience of life and be able to make sensible decisions, but as you already have some first-aid training I don't see why that can't be utilised. We need every pair of hands, so would you be willing to accompany your cousin?' she asked. It wasn't usual to take a girl so young – the age stipulated was twenty-one, but she'd already shown some initiative; these were difficult times and if things didn't improve by the time the girl was fully trained, her services could prove invaluable.

'Oh yes, Sister!' Alice replied enthusiastically. Mam couldn't possibly object now.

'Good. I must impress upon you both that this is not a convalescent home; your training will be intensive and very hard work indeed. It should take years, not months, but there simply isn't the time.' Sister Forshaw looked directly at Mae. 'And you do realise, Miss Strickland, that there is a real possibility that you will have to go to France if you are needed? Would that present a problem – financially?'

'I hope not, Sister,' Mae replied truthfully. She paid her own way at home and had some small savings. 'If I have to go, what would be provided?'

'Your food and lodgings and travelling expenses; anything else you will have to pay for yourself. Could you manage that?'

'I think so, Sister.'

'Then I'll take down some details. We provide a uniform, which you will have to pay for, but not all at once. I will expect you to be here by seven o'clock tomorrow evening at the latest.'

They both nodded. 'We won't be late, Sister,' they promised.

They decided on the way home that Mae would break the news to Maggie. 'It will seem better coming from me,' Mae said firmly, although she was still not looking forward to her aunt's reaction.

* * *

'Well, how did you get on?' Maggie asked when they arrived home. Agnes was sitting with her friend, reading out a letter she'd received from Harry, which he said he'd written on behalf of both himself, his brother and Eddie as things had 'become a bit hectic over here' and they didn't know when they would find time to write again.

'We've to report for training tomorrow night, we've to be there before seven,' Mae replied calmly, taking off her hat. 'We'll have to take a sandwich or something as there won't be time to come home for a meal first and it will be late when we do get home.'

'*We?*' Maggie queried, wondering if she had heard correctly. It came as a surprise that Mae seemed to have had no difficulty enrolling and yet they'd stipulated twenty-one in the paper. She'd assured Agnes that she expected them both to come back disappointed.

'Yes, Aunty Maggie. Sister asked how old Alice was and she answered truthfully that she was sixteen, but as she's already got some basic training Sister asked her would she train too, they desperately need nurses apparently. She didn't even ask me how old I was.'

'And I said I'd like to, Mam,' Alice put in.

Maggie looked at her closely and with some suspicion. 'Are you sure you didn't tell her any lies, Alice?'

'Mam! I didn't! I told both her and the nurse we saw when we went in that I'm sixteen. What Mae said is true but I'm delighted that she wants me too. I'll feel as though I'll be doing something useful.'

'They provide a uniform,' Mae told her aunt.

'And we have to pay for that, but not all at once,' Alice added.

There was nothing Maggie could say, although she was far from happy that they'd both been accepted.

Agnes got up to return home; she'd only popped over with the letter but after Maggie had told her where the girls had gone and her misgivings on the matter, she'd decided to stay and wait for their return. 'It looks as if you'll just have to let her go and train, Maggie,' she concurred. 'Although I can't see that it will do either of them any harm and it's not as if they're giving up their jobs.'

'Even if we were, typewriting is a bit like riding a bike, you don't forget how to do it. We could always go back to it,' Alice informed them.

'Well, let's hear no more talk of giving up jobs,' Maggie said crossly. It seemed as if she'd been presented with a *fait accompli*. 'I just hope you'll still be as pleased with nursing in a month's time, Alice.'

Sister Forshaw hadn't been joking when she'd said the work would be hard, Mae thought grimly a couple of weeks later as she scrubbed a wooden draining board in the sink room. It was never-ending and quite often after a day at work in the office the last thing she felt like was travelling here by the tram, rolling up her sleeves and getting down to the very menial tasks required of her, but she was determined not to complain.

Everything in the sink room had to be scrubbed. Shelves, tables, sinks, bowls, rubber sheets, the floor, and the urinals and bedpans stacked on the shelves. The smell of carbolic mixed with antiseptic had made her feel ill at first until she'd become used to it. They'd both been disappointed in the first week when they realised that there seemed to be very little in the way of actual medical training.

'We didn't volunteer to be flaming skivvies, Mae! We had our chores at home but nothing like *this*! We volunteered to become nurses,' Alice had complained bitterly as they'd returned home that first evening. Their duties had been explained in detail by Sister Forshaw and they were to work their way through the tasks on the sheet that Sister had pinned to the wall, work that was supervised by a senior nurse and checked by Sister herself.

They weren't the only volunteers and many of the tasks required of them they all found distasteful and acutely embarrassing.

'Sister, we're a bit curious as to what that stuff in the sack is used for,' Mae had volunteered to ask for no one had any idea what it was. She and Alice had been detailed to the sink room with two other girls, both older and from a very different background. They'd looked at each other and shrugged in mystification at the sack leaning against the wall.

'I can't think of a purpose for it, unless it's used in cleaning . . . something,' Elizabeth Lawson, whose father was a solicitor, had surmised.

Alice had poked about in the sack, wrinkling her nose. 'It looks like the stuff they use to make coconut matting.'

'Surely we won't be expected to make it into mats?' Elizabeth had wondered, so Mae had said she would ask Sister.

'It's called "tow" and it's a product of hemp, Nurse Strickland,' Sister had replied curtly.

'What's it for, Sister?' Alice had asked, rubbing the coarse fibres between her fingers.

'It is used instead of toilet paper, Nurse. You take a handful and stuff it into the handle of the bedpan, so ...' She demonstrated, taking a handful of tow and a bedpan from a shelf. 'Then, when it has been used you dispose of it in that bin there to be burned. The rest of the contents of the bedpan you throw down the sluice.' She'd indicated the huge sinks with their big brass taps. 'Then you scrub the bedpan and its cover. Is all that quite clear?'

They'd all nodded, their cheeks pink with embarrassment.

'I'm sorry I asked,' Mae said, grimacing, when Sister had departed.

'I don't think we'd better say anything to Mam about that,' Alice had advised.

'Elizabeth, you've gone quite pale,' Mae had remarked.

'I ... I didn't think we'd have to do such ... personal things,' Elizabeth had replied a little faintly.

'I don't suppose any of us *really* realised just *what* we would be expected to do,' Mae added.

'I bet you have a proper bathroom in your house, Elizabeth. You don't have a privy in the yard like us, do you?' Alice had asked candidly.

'Please call me "Lizzie", and yes, we do have a proper bathroom.'

Mae had smiled kindly at her. 'We're all going to have to get used to a lot of difficult things but we'll manage it. After all, the lads in France are risking their lives.'

Lizzie had nodded and smiled back.

'You are here to work, not gossip or complain or debate social conditions,' Sister reprimanded them sharply from the other side of the door.

Alice had raised her eyes to the ceiling. 'She's got eyes in the back of her head!' she hissed as they'd hastily resumed work.

They'd discussed their duties and their companions as they walked home from the tram at the end of that first week. 'I meant it about not telling Mam we'll have to give out bedpans and wipe the behinds of . . . complete strangers,' Alice had urged.

'But she must realise that we'll have to do things like that,' Mae had replied. 'A lot of these lads will be badly injured and can't walk. It's all part of being a nurse.'

'You know what she's like, Mae. She'll go mad and say it's not "proper" for us to do things like that, us being so young and unmarried. She's not at all happy about me being here in the first place, let alone knowing I'll have to do those kinds of jobs.'

'It must be as bad for the likes of Lizzie,' Mae had mused aloud.

'Worse, I should think,' Alice had replied. 'For a start she's never had to scrub anything in her life before, let alone floors and tables and bedpans. She's probably never even seen anyone having a bath either, unlike us with the tub in the kitchen.'

'She'd never even made a cup of tea before she came here, she told me that herself,' Mae had confided. 'They have a cook and a maid.'

Alice had grinned. 'I know, but at least she brought the maid with her. I was working with her yesterday and she's very down to earth. She's used to hard work but she said Lizzie isn't and is finding it very tough-going and is complaining that her hands are ruined.'

Mae had smiled and nodded. '*Everyone's* hands are ruined, Alice, but it's a very small price we have to pay.'

As the weeks passed they became accustomed to the work and the sights and smells, and embarrassment became a thing of the past. They learned about morphine, ether and paraldehyde, which had a foul smell and was used for insomnia. They learned how to clean and dress wounds, give an enema, check a pulse and read a thermometer. It was more like 'real' nursing, Mae thought, wondering when she was going to find time to write up all the notes Sister Tutor had given them.

Between them they'd bought a second-hand edition of *Taylor's Manual of Nursing* and *Black's Medical Dictionary*, which they studied closely in any spare minute they had. Sister Tutor had a porcelain human figure with little hooks attached to it and a box of 'organs', as she called them, which could be attached to the hooks: liver, kidneys, heart and numerous bones. 'I never realised there was just so much to learn,' Alice complained.

'At least Sister Tutor's more approachable than Sister Forshaw,' Mae reminded her. 'If you don't understand something, she'll go over and over it until you do. Sister Forshaw expects you to know everything at once.'

Alice nodded her agreement. 'Mam was right about that, Mae. She said you had to have had a good education to be a nurse, not just a basic one like us. I've never come across so many long, complicated words in all my life,' she pronounced rather gloomily.

'Well, they can't be too choosy these days, Alice. Not when there are so many casualties.'

'I know. I just hope our Eddie and the twins will be all right,' Alice replied.

Mae frowned and gave a little shiver of concern. They hadn't heard from any of the boys for a few weeks now and she wondered how Harry was coping. He was by far the quietest of the boys, and she knew he felt things deeply. She was afraid he would find the fighting very hard to bear.

Chapter Fifteen

———◆———

IT WAS CERTAINLY EASIER to write now that they had been taken out of the line and stationed in the village of La Haie – or what was left of it, Harry thought. He'd felt very bad about not being able to write regularly to Mae but it had been an almost impossible task given the fact that there was little time or, on Jimmy's part, inclination for such things. All he'd managed was a couple of very brief notes to his mam to let her know they were all still safe and reasonably well.

News had reached them about the sinking of the *Lusitania* and even before he'd received the letter from his mam he'd realised that it was improbable that John Strickland would have been amongst the survivors. The news had hit Eddie hard for over the years his uncle had taken the place of the father who'd deserted him and of whom he had no recollection. They'd done what they could to bolster Eddie's spirits but none of them had been feeling particularly cheerful and now the cold and damp of autumn added to their discomfort; it seemed to have rained for most of the time they'd been stationed in France but the weather affected everyone: the British and colonial troops, French and Belgian soldiers and those of Germany and her allies, Austria and Hungary. The conditions were also sapping their strength.

He frowned and chewed the end of the pencil, trying to gather his thoughts, choosing the words he would write to her with care. He'd only had the occasional letter from Mae since her da's death but that hadn't upset him, she was obviously overcome by grief, he'd thought. Poor Mae, he'd known she would be broken-hearted but his mam had said she was bearing it bravely. She and Alice had both joined the VAD and were finding the work hard going. He knew there were VAD nurses out here and he wondered if she would be sent out too. He hoped not, he wouldn't want her to have to endure this kind of life on top of the grief and loss she was trying to cope with.

They'd had no idea what conditions were like here, he thought gloomily. They'd been eager and excited when they'd boarded the train at Boulogne. Before then, when they'd disembarked from the ship, they'd been cheered by the French citizens as they'd marched through the streets but had been exhausted by the time they'd reached the rest camp at Ostre Hove because they'd had to climb a steep hill with their heavy packs on their backs. And they'd only stayed there one night; then it had been back down to the station. But their spirits had been high and had remained so throughout the exceedingly slow and tedious journey. It had been stop, start, stop, start all the way but they'd been cheerful because at last they were going to fight.

'Are you going to write that letter or are you going to stare at the sheet of paper forever?' Jimmy Mercer asked, lighting a cigarette and drawing deeply on it. They were all muffled up against the cold in greatcoats over uniforms, scarves and gloves and with balaclavas under their helmets as they sheltered in the ruins of a shop. A burst of artillery thundered in the background but they ignored it; they'd become accustomed to the sound and it was miles away so there was very little danger.

'I'm trying to think what to say. I mean, I don't want to go upsetting her, now do I? She's starting to get over her da and if I put my big foot in it by saying the wrong thing . . .' Harry explained curtly. 'Anyway, it wouldn't hurt you to write a note to Mam, tell her our bits of news and that we're all right.'

Jimmy shrugged. 'You know I hate writing letters and anyway I don't think she'd really like to know that we're due to go back up the line again to the front before Christmas.'

Eddie appeared carrying a billycan of hot tea. 'Get your tin mugs out; it won't stay hot for very long and God knows when we'll get any more. Have you got a woodie to spare, Jimmy?'

Jimmy duly lit and handed over a cigarette as Eddie filled the mugs and Harry put aside his letter to relish the first hot drink they'd had all day.

Eddie took a gulp of tea. 'At least it's a bit better here than that place near Abbeville,' he remarked, referring to the tiny hamlet where they'd first come under fire.

'Well, there wasn't much left of that by the time we got there, was there? And those trenches were in a bloody terrible state. I know we "practised" at Prescot and Grantham but they didn't tell us that the damned trenches would be always full of water and mud.'

'And at the end of the day back in Blighty we had warm huts and a hot meal and a proper bed,' Harry added and then shuddered. 'And no rats!' When they'd first arrived they'd been attached to a Regular Army unit, albeit a greatly depleted one, who'd shown them the ropes, and it had been then that the first seeds of doubt and disillusionment had been sown.

'We've got to be thankful that this part of the line is quiet and that so far we've had no serious casualties,' Jimmy reminded them. They'd been told that a few shells came over from time to time and a few were fired back. Damaged buildings took a few more hits, there were more shell holes but there had been no one killed or badly wounded. However, they were always cold, hungry and tired.

'If they keep us stuck in these trenches all winter we'll go down with pneumonia and that won't be a very glorious end to our military service, will it? No one is going to give us a medal for that, there's nothing heroic about pneumonia,' Eddie commented bitterly.

'Where's Tommy?' Jimmy asked, glancing around as Harry resumed his task. Young Tommy Mitford had become part of their little group for he lived in the next street and had attended the same school.

'Said he was going for a scout around,' Eddie replied.

'We're not supposed to do that,' Jimmy reminded him but before Eddie could answer Tommy appeared, grinning and with something stuffed under his greatcoat.

'What have you got there? You haven't been pinching stuff – there'll be hell to pay if you have.'

'No! I didn't pinch this, she gave it me,' Tommy replied indignantly, pulling out a small flat loaf of coarse black bread.

'She?' Eddie repeated pointedly. 'You been chatting up the Mad-em-oiselles? You know we're not supposed to do that either.'

'I 'aven't been doing any "fraternising". 'Er name's Mariette, she's the baker's daughter and I think she's taken a fancy to me so she gave me this,' Tommy informed them, looking both proud and bashful at the same time. 'She said I wasn't to tell 'er Pa; she sort of mimed that. I can't understand much of what she says and seeing as I don't speak the lingo . . .'

'Well, share it out then,' Eddie instructed. 'We're starving and it's ages before mess time and even then it'll only be dry bully beef.'

'You can be certain of one thing,' Jimmy remarked, his mouth full. 'There won't be ham, tongue, peaches or anything else like that this Christmas.'

Harry nodded and then grinned. 'Still, it might not be too bad. We'll get parcels from home. That's something to look forward to.'

They did get parcels from home but by then they were back in the front-line trenches. However, the socks, soap, cigarettes, biscuits, chocolate, magazines and other small comforts were very welcome and with the parcels came the mail.

'My God! They're sending Mae over here after Christmas,' Harry informed his mates and his brother. He'd opened her letter first and had quickly scanned the lines, delighted to hear from her but rather taken aback at her news.

'What, here?' Jimmy probed.

'Well, not exactly *here*. She's going to be allocated to one of the hospital trains that take the wounded to the hospital from the Casualty Clearing Stations. There are two other girls coming out with her.'

Eddie started to wheeze for he'd developed a racking cough since they'd left La Haie. 'Christ! They're not sending our Alice out too, are they? She's just a bit of a kid,' he asked when he'd stopped coughing.

Harry shook his head. 'No, Mae says the sister knows how old she is and she's too young to be sent over. Apparently she doesn't know how old Mae is or if she does she's not letting on. There's a girl called Lizzie and one called Ethel coming over with Mae.'

'That's a relief. Mam would have created merry hell if they'd wanted to send our Alice, and if they had then I'd have been worrying about my sister – and I've enough to worry about as it is with you, Tommy.'

'Yer don't 'ave ter worry about me, Eddie. I can take care of meself!' Tommy protested indignantly. 'And yer know . . .' The rest of his words were drowned out by the loud whistling of a shell followed by an explosion and they all ducked. It was an automatic reflex now.

'I hope they're not going to start that up again, they've been quiet for the last couple of days,' Jimmy stated irritably, wiping the spattering of mud that had fallen into the trench from his face. Then he grinned wryly at Tommy. 'Stand on the fire step and stick your head over the parapet and yell over do they know it's Christmas Eve and can we all have a bit of quiet, if not peace?'

Tommy grinned back. 'I just told yer I can look after meself! Do I look soft? I'm not that daft, I'd get a bullet fer an answer! Mind you, that might not be a bad idea, at least then I'd get ter spend Christmas in a hospital bed.'

Harry frowned, thinking of Mae. How on earth would she cope with all this? Oh, she wouldn't be anywhere near the front line so she wouldn't be in any danger but tending the wounded on those interminably slow and crowded hospital trains would be no picnic, so he'd heard. He closed his eyes for a second, thinking of last Christmas and wishing fervently that he was back home in his mam's kitchen. He'd be warm, dry, clean and well fed, not cold, dirty, crawling with lice, up to his ankles in filthy freezing water and hungry. But then he thought he was lucky that he was alive, uninjured and hadn't succumbed to any of the diseases that were proving to be so prevalent in these atrocious conditions. He was worried about Eddie, though. That cough wasn't getting any better at all.

By the first week of the New Year it was obvious to them all that Eddie was seriously ill. He'd grown steadily worse as the days passed but as the bombardment had resumed and with increased ferocity they'd had little time to think of anything other than staying alive. But that afternoon Eddie was running a fever and was on the point of collapse so they'd laid him on one of the narrow wire bunks in the dugout, although that offered little in the way of comfort for there was no mattress, pillow or blankets.

'We've got to get him out of here – and soon,' Jimmy said worriedly to his brother and Tommy.

'I'll go along the trench and get Captain Dixon,' Tommy offered, shouting to make himself heard over the noise of the guns.

Jimmy nodded. 'Get a move on then.'

Harry took off his muffler and wrapped it around Eddie's neck, over the one he already wore. 'It won't help much, more's the pity.' Eddie was shivering, his skin felt clammy and his breathing was very laboured.

Tommy duly arrived back with their grim-faced superior officer and they all crowded into the tiny dugout.

'How long has he been like this, Private Mitford?' the captain demanded of Tommy.

'He's had a terrible cough for weeks now, sir, but he only took really bad like this a few hours ago,' Tommy replied.

'He's having trouble breathing, sir. We think he's got pneumonia. He's really bad,' Harry added.

'I can see that. Well, we'd better get him to the clearing station. Mitford, go and shout for a stretcher,' Captain Dixon instructed Tommy, feeling his outrage and frustration growing. It was no wonder the lad was in this state; they were all permanently cold, wet and exhausted, for they got very little sleep.

'Sir, if we can be spared we'll take him ourselves. We'll carry him if we have to,' Jimmy suggested. Eddie was his mate and you could wait for ages for the stretcher-bearers to get along the line.

The captain nodded; he understood the close comradeship these lads felt for their pals and the stretcher-bearers were already overworked with the casualties from the increased bombardment. 'Get back as soon as you can and keep your heads down,' he ordered before departing.

It seemed as though it had taken them hours to negotiate their way back through the communication trenches towards the clearing station carrying Eddie between them but finally, exhausted, they made it. There were sick and wounded men lying everywhere, Harry thought grimly, far more than he'd

161

ever seen before and some with terrible wounds.

A medical officer approached them. 'What's his name, rank and battalion? What's wrong with him? What are his symptoms?' he asked, looking harassed.

'Private Edward McEvoy, 18th King's Liverpool. We think he's got pneumonia, sir. He's got a fever, having trouble breathing and he's not really been conscious for the last half-hour. We've carried him,' Jimmy informed the man.

He nodded and sighed inwardly. Another one! Disease and the appalling conditions were killing as many of these lads as the shells and shrapnel were. 'You can leave him with us now; we'll get him to a hospital. You've done your best for him, now get back up the line,' he said before turning to issue instructions to an orderly.

Jimmy knelt down beside Eddie and touched him on the shoulder. 'You'll be all right now, mate. Soon have you in a clean, warm bed and you'll be right as rain in no time at all, lucky blighter!'

Tommy managed a grin as he nodded. 'Yer always were a lucky so and so, Eddie McEvoy. I'm green with envy. Just don't go falling fer any of them nurses now.'

Harry wondered somewhat distractedly if Mae would be one of the nurses on the train that would take Eddie to Boulogne or Le Touquet or Le Havre, whichever one had room for another casualty, although he hoped it wouldn't be Le Havre, which was the furthest away. He remembered what Eddie had said about there being no glory in succumbing to pneumonia. There was no glory in dying at all as far as he could see now, whether it was from terrible wounds or disease. He turned wearily away. It was a long trek back.

Chapter Sixteen

———◆———

M AE LOOKED AROUND her in some confusion. Ever since she had left Liverpool in the first week of the New Year with a dozen other nurses, including Lizzie Lawson and Ethel Rhodes, waved off at Lime Street Station by an anxious Maggie and a rather envious Alice, everything had seemed unfamiliar: different but a little exciting too. Now that they had finally disembarked from the Channel steamer she was for the first time in her life on foreign soil and it was unsettling. The streets were crowded with civilians and refugees – whose language she didn't understand – and soldiers. The men were all weary-looking, their uniforms crumpled and caked with mud and dirt, their faces grey with exhaustion and cold as they marched or simply moved between the mass of buildings, most of which were makeshift hospitals, supply and ammunition depots, ware-houses, stables, feed stores and rail yards. On the dockside ships were embarking wounded and sick men en route to hospitals in England, for there were too few French hospitals to cope – even the town's casino had been turned into one. The ships were unloading more supplies and disembarking yet more soldiers, and everywhere there were horses and carts, a few motorised lorries and teams of mules pulling wagons and guns.

'Where do we go now?' Ethel enquired, looking as bewildered as both Mae and Lizzie at the crowds and traffic that surged around them.

'We're to report to Sister Allinson at the Gare de Boulogne, wherever that is,' Lizzie read from a scrap of paper taken from her pocket.

'Maybe we should ask someone,' Mae suggested, and then headed towards two young men who stood nearby, peering intently into the engine of a motorised ambulance and looking perplexed. 'Excuse me, I'm sorry to trouble you, but could you help us?' she asked politely.

They both turned and she noticed that the taller of the two was quite handsome with brown wavy hair and blue eyes and he did not have that exhausted look that seemed to cling to all the other men in the vicinity.

'How can we help, miss?' he asked, smiling and hastily wiping his hands on a rather grubby rag.

'You're an American!' Mae blurted out in surprise at his accent.

He smiled again broadly, revealing perfect teeth. 'I am indeed. Phillip 'Pip' Middlehurst from Boston, Miss . . . er?'

'Strickland. Mae Strickland. We've just arrived and have to report to the Gare de Boulogne and we haven't a clue where or what it is,' she informed him, wondering what on earth an American was doing here.

'I guess then that you're new recruits for the hospital trains?'

164

Mae nodded. 'Yes, we've to report to a Sister Allinson.'

'Then I'll be delighted to escort you there, ladies. Lenny here will stay with the ambulance, won't you, Len? Not that either of us has got a clue as to why it refuses to start.'

The other young man nodded amiably and turned back to inspect the engine as the little group moved off up the street.

'Is it far?' Mae asked her companion.

'Not really, only a couple of blocks. Boulogne isn't a very big town, you'll soon find your way around,' he replied. 'I did,' he added.

'Can I ask you a personal question, Mr Middlehurst?' Mae enquired a little hesitantly, although he seemed friendly enough.

He grinned down at her. 'Fire away, Miss Strickland, but I have a feeling I know what it is you're curious about. What is a boy from Boston doing here in France in the middle of a European war?'

Mae smiled up at him; she liked his direct manner. 'That's about it.'

He became serious. 'I'm a volunteer. Although my government's policy is that it's not America's war, there are many folk back home who think we can't just stand on the sidelines and watch, me included. So, being able to drive an automobile, I volunteered for the American Field Ambulance Service, which is a non-combatant group officially under the control of the Red Cross, and here I am. All the way from Back Bay to Boulogne.'

'It's very gallant and . . . brave of you,' Mae replied, feeling that both adjectives were somehow inadequate to describe the selflessness of his actions.

Pip Middlehurst shook his head. 'Nope. I'm not nearly as gallant or brave as the men and boys who are over here fighting,' he replied grimly. 'I just transport them from the clearing stations to the trains and the trains to the hospitals.' He glanced down at the girl beside him and thought of the two others following behind. None of them were any older than his own sister, he surmised, and wondered if they were prepared for the sights and experiences that awaited them. 'Where is "home" for you, Miss Strickland?' he asked to lighten the conversation. Even in the drab and rather severe uniform she was a pleasant and very pretty girl with that light blonde hair and blue eyes: a real 'English rose'.

'Liverpool, and this is the first time I've been more than ten miles outside it,' Mae answered candidly, holding up her long skirt to keep it out of the dirt.

'I know it. We docked there when I came over on the *Aquitania*. It sure is a fine city.'

Mae nodded, swallowing hard. Any mention of Cunard's remaining big transatlantic liners always reminded her of her da. 'It is but there are poor areas too,' she replied, thinking of the slums.

'We have some of those in Boston. I guess every city does. Well, here we are,' he announced as they reached the railway station and he ushered them inside. 'The main offices are just over there to the right; I'm sure your Sister Allinson will be pleased to see you all.'

Mae smiled at him. 'Thank you, Mr Middlehurst, we would have been wandering around the town for ages without your help.'

He laughed. 'I wouldn't bet on that, not three attractive

young ladies such as yourselves.' He held out his hand for Mae to shake. 'I'd better be getting back now and try to get that darned engine fixed, but I'm glad to have been of service. Good luck and as you'll be on one of the hospital trains and I'm always ferrying wounded from them I guess we'll see each other again.'

Mae shook his hand and smiled. 'Thank you and I . . . I'll look forward to seeing you.' She started to turn away but he touched her arm.

'Perhaps we could even have coffee when you get some time off and you can tell me how you're getting along? There's no shortage of cafés here where it's served but I'm afraid tea is something the French don't really go in for much.'

'I'd like that and I don't drink just tea,' Mae replied, wondering if and when she would get some time off but thinking that he was very nice and she would like to get to know him better.

'He was a very pleasant young man and he seemed to be quite taken with you, Mae,' Ethel remarked teasingly. Mae didn't have time to answer as they had reached Sister Allinson's office.

They knocked and entered rather hesitantly, not knowing quite what to expect. Mae had assumed that this woman would be very much like Sister Forshaw: brisk, efficient, indomitable, meticulous, her uniform starched and immaculate. She wasn't. She was tall and angular and her uniform would have given Sister Forshaw a fit of apoplexy. Her hair was confined under a simple, unstarched short veil gathered at the back, her apron and cuffs were also unstarched and her somewhat faded blue cotton dress was covered by an Army greatcoat; she had a permanently harassed look about her.

'Nurses Lawson and Rhodes, you are both to join number three train. Nurse Strickland, you're on number five train,' she informed them, ticking off their names on a list. 'There are six trains that run between here and the casualty clearing stations, which are approximately ten miles behind the front-line trenches so there is little personal danger to you, although artillery fire is almost constant. You'll get used to the noise. Each train carries two or three medical officers, four sisters, half a dozen nurses and about forty orderlies, and up to four hundred sick and wounded men. You have each been allocated a first-class compartment, which will be your billet, but don't think it will be luxurious. As well as it serving as your bedroom, office and bathroom it is also a storeroom for supplies both medical and practical. You will have one half-day off per fortnight – if you can be spared – and apart from that the train will be your "home". You will be responsible to a nursing sister and ultimately to the senior medical officer on board. Is all that clear?'

They all assented and were then directed to their respective trains. Mae was a little disappointed that she would not be with Lizzie and Ethel for they had trained together and had become friends but she squared her shoulders, picked up her bag and followed the orderly out on to the station concourse and then across the tracks to the rail head where number five train stood awaiting departure, the last of the wounded having been taken either to the hospitals in the town or directly to the waiting ships.

''Ere you are, miss. 'Ome from 'ome! They're bigger than our trains but they're a damned ruddy sight slower.' The orderly grinned as he passed over her bag and helped her up the rather high steps.

She thanked him and made her way along the narrow corridor, which was being washed down, to find yet another sister who would supervise her. When she was at last shown her billet she realised that Sister Allinson had been serious when she'd said the compartment wasn't luxurious.

'Get your things unpacked, Nurse, and then report back to me immediately,' Sister Chapman instructed briskly before leaving her.

Mae glanced around the cramped space. There was a bunk about six feet long and three feet wide, a folding canvas washbasin, a jug for water, a mirror attached to one wall and a small locker. Every other available bit of space was taken up with supplies. They were stacked floor to ceiling and there was hardly room to move. She sighed and began to try to make room for her clothes, toiletries, sewing and mending kit and the Army greatcoat that she had been issued with. Well, this was what she had volunteered for so she'd better get on with it, she told herself sternly. After all, it was far, far better than anything the lads in the trenches had. She would at least be warm and dry and had a bunk to sleep in. The train juddered suddenly into life, causing her to momentarily lose her balance, and she realised that they were on their way back to the clearing station to pick up more sick and wounded. She'd better get a move on, she thought; soon she'd have work to do: work for which she'd been trained but which in reality she had little experience of. She suddenly wished that Alice were with her.

Her inexperience hadn't lasted long, she thought wryly two weeks later as she wearily negotiated the long swaying corridor of the train on her way back to her billet. She'd lost count of the number of times she'd walked up and down this corridor today, her long skirt seeming to catch on every protruding corner. There were at least three rips she would now have to mend and she heartily wished skirts could be a more practical length. Not only did they catch but their hems became caked in mud and dirt as she scrambled down the steps on to the tracks at the wayside halts where the stretchers were laid out in rows. The orderly had been right, she thought. French trains were bigger but they were interminably and frustratingly slow.

She opened the door to her cramped compartment and, moving aside a box of bandages, sat down on the edge of the bunk. At least she had something to look forward to tomorrow, she thought. Her first afternoon off and she was going to meet Pip Middlehurst in the Rue Nationale for coffee.

She took off her short veil and removed the pins from her hair, letting it fall over her shoulders. She would fine comb and then wash it, she decided. The fine-combing was yet another daily chore for the wounded soldiers were all verminous, having come directly from the trenches, and it was inevitable that the nurses picked up both head and body lice. Combing her hair and searching her clothes every night was absolutely essential.

Rummaging amongst the boxes and packages she found her mending kit and, taking off her uniform dress, she hastily pulled on the flannel dressing gown Maggie had insisted she bring. First she'd have to brush the dried mud from the hem, then mend the rips, then she'd have to wash her apron, cuffs and veil in lukewarm water in her canvas folding bowl when all she wanted to do was lie down and sleep.

She'd seen Pip on three occasions since she'd joined the train and each time he'd come over to have a few words with her. But neither of them had been able to spare the time for long conversations, so she still knew very little about him – but no doubt she would remedy that tomorrow. They'd made the arrangements to meet in the Café Arc-en-ciel on the last occasion and she was looking forward to a few hours away from the endless work on the train. She was more than experienced now in tending the wounds of the men who were carried on on stretchers or who hobbled aboard. Those able to stand were seated eight to a compartment; those unable to do so were laid on their stretchers across the seats and on the floor. She could still remember how appalled she'd been that first day that their wounds had received only the very basic attention at the Field Dressing Stations. Men had been brought aboard with bandages caked in blood and dirt, some with only rifles acting as splints for shattered bones. As gently as she could she had picked out fragments of muddy uniform from gaping wounds and mangled flesh, cut away filthy uniform sleeves and trouser legs to reveal the horrific damage caused by shrapnel. Inevitably many of those wounds were already septic and suppurating. The men must have been enduring terrible pain and there was nothing to ease it save morphine for the worst cases, but few complained and she had felt desperately sorry for them. It had come as something of a surprise to realise that not all the men had sustained wounds; some were very ill with pneumonia, enteritis, dysentery or chronic rheumatics, but they all shared one thing: the need to sleep. She had never seen so many utterly exhausted men in her life.

She sighed heavily; it would be another hour yet before she herself could sleep, and she still had the letters to Alice and Aunty Maggie to finish for she wanted to post them tomorrow.

* * *

At least it wasn't raining, she thought thankfully as she left the train the following afternoon. The sky was grey and a blustery cold wind whipped at her skirts as she made her way along the Rue Faidherbe towards the Rue Nationale where the Café Arc-en-ciel was situated. For the first time in a fortnight she was not wearing her uniform and it felt somehow liberating to be dressed in her dark blue skirt, white blouse and warm black wool jacket, her hat firmly anchored by two long pins. She found the café without much trouble: the faded painted rainbow from which it took its name above the door helped. It was warm but rather dimly lit, she noted as she pushed open the door. Pip was sitting waiting for her but instantly got up to guide her to her seat.

'I'm so glad to see you,' he greeted her, courteously pulling the chair out and smiling.

'I'm so glad to be here. I seem to have been on that train for months on end. It's such a change to be away from it and to sit in a proper chair and at a table,' she replied, smiling.

'Shall I order? Will you have coffee and – if they have any – a pastry?' he asked. She looked even more attractive out of uniform, he thought.

'Please, that would be a real treat.' She felt quite relieved that she wouldn't have to do the ordering; so far she had only managed to pick up a few words of French from the soldiers and she wasn't sure just how accurate their pronunciation was.

'So, Miss Strickland, how are you finding nursing here?' he asked after the waiter had gone to fetch the coffee.

Mae managed a wry smile. 'I think I'm getting used to it although it certainly isn't what I expected.' She frowned and toyed with the edge of her serviette. 'No one prepared us for the terrible state these men and boys come to us in. I mean . . . the dirt, the lice, the wounds already infected, the sheer and utter exhaustion.'

He nodded gravely. 'I know. I feel great admiration and pity for them. The conditions in the trenches are appalling and if you'll excuse me, Miss Strickland, the whole damned affair is a mess!'

She wasn't in the least offended and concurred with him. 'That's very true and please, call me Mae.'

'Only if you'll call me Pip,' he countered and they both smiled.

The coffee and pastries arrived.

'So, Mae, you're glad to escape for a few hours?'

She nodded as she sipped the rather strong coffee. 'I've been looking forward to it and praying that my time off wouldn't be cancelled at the last minute. It sometimes is – one of the other nurses told me.'

'This must all be very strange for you. Have you been nursing long?'

'No. My training was crammed into a few months and I worked as well, I was a typist. Have you been over here long?'

'About a year now. I'd graduated from Harvard and wasn't sure what I wanted to do so . . . I decided to volunteer. Being here has certainly broadened my outlook and experience and given me a very different perspective on life. The family weren't too happy though; my mother in particular thinks I'm mad.'

Mae smiled. 'My Aunty Maggie thinks I'm mad too. My mother died when I was a few days old; my aunt brought me up,' she explained, cutting the pastry into small pieces.

'What about your father, does he think you're crazy too?'

Mae told him about her father's death.

'I'm so sorry, Mae. That was a cowardly attack on innocent people. Many Americans were outraged.' He meant it and felt sincerely sorry for her but he admired her courage for volunteering.

'Shall we talk about something else? Tell me more about your life in Boston, your family, what kinds of things you like to do.'

He proceeded to tell her of his life in the big Victorian brownstone house on Newbury Street in the prosperous Boston suburb of Back Bay with his parents and sister, and she told him of her cousins Alice and Eddie, the friends who were also here in France, her training and her life before she had joined hospital train number five.

All too soon she realised that it was time to get back and he offered to escort her.

'Would you like to have coffee again, Mae, next time you're off?' he asked, for he'd enjoyed her company.

'Yes, I would, Pip,' she agreed. She liked him. He was easy to talk to; he seemed far more mature than the boys she'd known at home. He was certainly more self-assured and . . . sophisticated than Harry, but then he'd travelled halfway across the world and had been more highly educated than them, and she realised that he came from a far more privileged background too.

'Then shall we make it the same place, same time?'

She nodded and smiled. 'In another two weeks, but I'll probably see you before that.'

'You're bound to. Our work doesn't stop, does it? Sadly

there will be more sick and wounded men needing our meagre skills. But at least we get the occasional afternoon off,' he finished on a more optimistic note and was pleased to see that she was looking happier.

Chapter Seventeen

———◆———

MAGGIE STARED AT the small buff-coloured envelope with dread. From the early days of the war telegrams had been used to convey the news of casualties and fatalities of serving soldiers or sailors to their relatives. So many had been delivered in the intervening months that they were now viewed as harbingers of tragedy.

'Mam, what's the matter? You've gone as white as a sheet,' Alice asked as her mother came back into the kitchen. It was Saturday lunchtime so she'd finished work and was preparing to set off for her shift at Walton Hospital.

'This!' Maggie replied, holding out the telegram, her hands shaking a little.

Alice's eyes widened. 'Oh, Lord! It . . . it must be about our Eddie. Open it, Mam.'

Maggie felt her throat go dry as she ripped open the envelope and scanned the lines.

'Oh, Mam, is he . . . is he . . . ?' Alice pleaded.

Maggie shook her head as she passed the telegram over to her daughter. 'No, thank God, but he's in Highfield Hospital in Southampton . . .'

Alice breathed a sigh of relief and then began to read it aloud. '"Regret to inform you Private E. MacEvoy dangerously ill in this hospital. If you wish to visit him and are unable to bear expenses take this telegram to the nearest police station."'

'It's still not good news, Alice. What do they mean "dangerously ill"? What's the matter with him? How serious is he?' Maggie said, biting her lip and sitting down heavily in the nearest chair.

'It doesn't say. Well, I think they might have told us a bit more. I'll put the kettle on,' Alice said firmly, thinking it wouldn't have cost that much more for a couple of extra words. 'At least he's not dead or even wounded,' she added.

Maggie nodded, still very worried. Eddie had never been 'dangerously ill' in his life. 'I'll have to go, Alice and as soon as I can.'

'Of course you will, but you're not going all that way on your own, Mam. I'm coming with you.'

'But . . . but your work and your training at the hospital?' Maggie queried.

'I'll tell Sister this afternoon and I'll send a note into work. Surely none of them will object to me having a bit of compassionate time off. He's my only brother and he's lying ill in a hospital in Southampton, for heaven's sake.' She looked perplexed as she handed her mother the cup of tea. 'Where exactly *is* Southampton?'

'Somewhere on the south coast, I think,' Maggie replied. She was feeling a bit calmer now.

'Will I take the telegram to the police station, like they suggest?' Alice enquired.

Maggie shook her head. 'No, I can afford to pay the expenses and he's my only son. There will be other poor souls who have more than one son and who can't afford to be traipsing all over the country who will need that money. But you can call in and ask them if we can get a train down there.'

'I just wish they'd brought him to a hospital a bit nearer,' Alice thought aloud but then wondered why whatever was wrong with Eddie hadn't been treated in a hospital in France. She also wondered if the long journey had made him worse and secretly hoped that his condition wouldn't deteriorate before they got to Southampton.

She was informed by the desk sergeant, after he'd expressed his sympathy, that they could get a train from Lime Street Station to Crewe and then one to Euston Station in London but would then have to get another train to Southampton – a large port on the coast in Hampshire, he'd added helpfully. He was becoming more and more accustomed to worried wives and mothers coming in bearing these telegrams and was now familiar with the procedure. 'Does your mother require financial assistance, miss?'

Alice replied. 'Thank you but no, we can pay.'

'But you'll need somewhere to stay when you get there.'

She paused, not having thought about that. 'We will, as we don't know how long we'll be there. They didn't say what's wrong with him.'

He nodded kindly. 'If he hasn't been wounded it's usually either pneumonia or dysentery or some such, but don't worry, miss, I'm sure he's in very good hands. If you call in tomorrow, I'll have sorted out a place for you to stay. The powers that be in the Army have issued lists of places – hostels and even private boarding houses – where relatives can stay.'

Alice thanked him and had resolved to call into the railway station on her way home to find out the train times. Mam would be so worried about Eddie that she'd want to go as soon as possible.

Sister Forshaw had been quite sympathetic, she'd thought as she tucked the timetables she'd been given at the station into a pocket in her bag. The January afternoon was bitterly cold with a freezing wind blowing down Lime Street and she shivered as she hurried towards the tram stop. After she'd explained that her mother had never travelled further from Liverpool than New Brighton in her life before and was quite obviously worrying herself sick about Eddie – her only son – Sister had said that it would be sensible for Alice to accompany her; she'd also said she was confident that her brother was receiving the best care and attention. Alice had posted the note she'd written to the office manager on her way out, so now all she had to do was sort out these train times and pack a few things.

Agnes was sitting with Maggie when she arrived home; Bertie was minding the shop, Agnes had informed her.

'Did everything go . . . all right?' Maggie asked.

Alice nodded as she took off her coat and hat and gratefully accepted the tea Agnes handed her. 'Yes. I've got the timetables and if I call into the police station they'll have found somewhere for us to stay.'

'I'd wondered about that,' Agnes mused. 'It's not as if you're going just a few miles away. Bertie said it's a long way to travel, and you will want to see that he's being properly looked after.' She felt sorry for her old friend but had impressed upon Maggie that it was a real blessing he wasn't wounded or worse. That was something they all lived in dread of, herself included.

They all pored over the timetables and had worked out the travel plans.

'It's going to take ages and ages, Mam!' Alice finally announced.

'Then we'd better go as soon as possible,' Maggie replied.

'I'd go first thing in the morning to the police station, Maggie, then straight on to the station,' Agnes advised, glad that Alice was accompanying her mother. She wished she could have gone with Maggie, but she had no idea how long her friend would be away and she had a shop to attend to, young Lucy and her mother, who was becoming increasingly frail.

'We'll do that, although heaven knows what time we'll get to Southampton,' Maggie replied.

'Well, one thing is for certain, Mam, it will be far too late for hospital visiting,' Alice said flatly, familiar with the strict hospital routine.

'When you do see him, Maggie, and if he's well enough, of course, would you do me a big favour?' Agnes asked anxiously.

'What?'

'Ask him how those lads of mine are doing. I mean, he'll be able to tell you more about how . . . things really are. Our Harry doesn't say much in his letters and I worry more about him than our Jimmy. He's always been the quieter of the two.'

Maggie nodded. It was understandable that Agnes would want to know more details than Harry supplied.

'It's just a pity that Mae wasn't sent over a bit earlier. She might have been able to see him before they shipped him back home and she'd have told us more than they did in that telegram,' Alice remarked.

Both women nodded although Agnes thought that probably Mae would have been sent straight to the hospital train as soon as she'd arrived. 'I'm sure she would have – but how would she have known Eddie was so ill?' she asked.

'I never thought of that,' Alice agreed and went to find a bag to pack for the journey.

Neither of them had slept very well that night and were up early. They set off straight away, having packed their few things into a carpet bag the night before. At the police station they were given an address and wished a good journey with good news at the end of it by the desk sergeant and they had duly caught the train for Crewe. Even though she was filled with anxiety about her brother, as the train travelled ever southwards Alice took in the passing countryside with great interest; she was looking forward to arriving in the capital city for, like Maggie, she had never been far from Liverpool before. They had to wait half an hour at Crewe for the London train and there was no time to marvel at the sights when they finally arrived for they had to find their way across the city to Waterloo Station to catch the train to Southampton. There they had to wait for over an hour for their connection and they both noticed that there seemed to be many other women making the same journey, all looking worried, harassed and a little bewildered. The sheer scale of the casualties began to dawn on Alice and she determined to work harder at her training and drop as many hints to both Sister Forshaw and Sister Tutor about how nurses were needed – no matter how young they were. Every pair of willing hands appeared to be desperately required.

It was very late when they finally reached their destination: a hostel in Eastleigh where they were assured that public transport to the hospital would be available the following day. They were both tired and irritable as they finally got to bed.

'Oh, I never thought we were going to get here! How they expect us poor folk from the North and Scotland to negotiate all these strange towns and cities when we're half out of our minds with worry, I don't know,' Maggie declared.

Alice mentally agreed, thinking that Mae's journey must have seemed even longer for she'd had to cross the Channel as well. 'Well, we're here now, Mam. Try and get some sleep. We'll see our Eddie tomorrow and hopefully he'll be much better, which will put your mind at rest,' she replied firmly, before closing her weary eyes.

The hospital reminded her very much of Walton, Alice thought as they entered. Same smell, same air of ordered routine. She was well aware that it wasn't visiting time but was prepared to stick determinedly to her guns if they were going to be officious about it. They'd travelled so far that the hospital could bend the rules for once.

'Yes? May I be of help?' a nurse sitting at the reception desk asked.

Maggie handed her the telegram. 'My son Private McEvoy is here.'

'We've travelled from Liverpool,' Alice added. At least the nurse didn't seem too stiff, she thought.

'Ah, yes. Would you please take a seat, Mrs McEvoy, while I fetch Sister.'

'What's the matter with him, Nurse, please? They didn't say,' Maggie asked a little fearfully, wondering why they were being asked to wait.

The woman smiled kindly. 'Sister will give you all the facts.'

They both sat at one end of a long bench as the nurse disappeared. 'At least she didn't tell us to come back at visiting time,' Alice said quietly, hoping they were not going to be left sitting here for long. She was relieved when the nurse came back down the corridor accompanied by a middle-aged sister. They both stood up, Maggie clutching her bag tightly and feeling sick with apprehension.

'How bad is he, Sister? What's wrong with him? Can we see him?' The questions tumbled out for she was so worried and tears pricked her eyes.

'Sit down, Mrs McEvoy, there's no need for you to upset yourself. The news is good, very good. He's over the worst now. He was brought in with severe pneumonia and for a while we were very concerned indeed about him, which is why you were notified, but he's young and appears to have a strong constitution . . .'

'Oh, thank God! Oh, thank you, Sister! I've been half out of my mind with worry.' Maggie's tears of concern had turned to those of joy and relief.

'Can we see him, please? I'm his sister,' Alice asked. She felt close to tears herself, she was so relieved.

'Of course. If you'll wait I'll get a student nurse to show you to the ward. I'm afraid I am rather busy at present.'

Maggie sat down again; her legs seemed to have become weak.

'Is the hospital full, Sister?' Alice asked.

Sister raised her eyes to the ceiling. 'To capacity, Miss McEvoy, believe me. I just wish we had more beds, more staff, more equipment, but we must make the best of it for the patients' sake.'

They were taken down a long corridor and then up a flight of stairs and along another corridor, which had wards leading off from each side and Alice noted that they were all full, the beds crammed in. Far more beds than were in the wards at Walton, she thought. There were so many questions she had wanted to ask the sister but hadn't had time. At last they were taken into a ward and followed the young nurse who finally stopped beside a bed near the middle.

'Here he is, Mrs McEvoy. He's asleep but I'm sure he won't mind you waking him.' She smiled before turning away.

Maggie looked down at her son and bit her lip. He was so thin and so pale and looked so . . . so worn out. He'd changed so much from the lad she'd watched marching to Lime Street Station that day; it seemed long ago now. His experiences had aged him. 'Shall we wake him?' she asked Alice in a whisper.

Alice nodded; she too was shocked by his appearance. 'He'll be delighted to see you, Mam. It's the best tonic he can have, I'm sure.' She bent over and gently patted his thin shoulder. 'Eddie. Eddie, Mam's here to see you,' she said quietly.

He stirred and slowly opened his eyes. 'Mam? Mam, is it really you? Alice? I'm not dreaming? I've not died?' he asked. His breathing was still a little laboured. He'd spent days – weeks it seemed – burning with fever, fighting for breath and not knowing if he was alive or dead. There had been brief moments when he'd realised he was on a train, then a ship, then a hospital ward, but they all seemed unreal.

'Well, it's the first time I've ever been confused with an angel,' Alice replied laughing, for Maggie was unable to speak, she was so overcome.

Eddie struggled to pull himself up and instantly Alice put her arms under his shoulders to assist him, the way she'd been taught. 'Mam, prop those pillows up behind him, he'll find it easier,' she instructed her mother.

Maggie did as Alice told her, pulling herself together. All that mattered now was that he get well. 'It's really me, Eddie, luv. They sent a telegram and we came at once. You've been very ill, luv, and we were worried sick about you.' Gently she stroked a wisp of hair from his forehead, thinking his skin still felt a little clammy.

'I know, Mam. When the lads got me to the clearing station I didn't think . . . I'd make it.'

'Thank God you have. They said you had pneumonia.' Relief was evident in Maggie's voice.

'I . . . I only began to feel better yesterday. Before that . . . I don't remember much.'

'You're in the best possible place, Eddie. You'll be up and about in no time now,' Alice said, smiling.

'And we're staying a few days to make sure,' Maggie added firmly.

'How are the other lads? Jimmy and Harry?' Alice asked him. She had glanced quickly down the ward and had seen the other men with arms, legs, heads swathed in bandages and she'd thought of the twins still in France and in danger.

'Not doing too bad when I last saw them, but that seems ages ago now. Jimmy, Harry and Tommy carried me out of the trenches to the clearing station. They wouldn't hang about waiting for a stretcher. They're good mates, the best.'

'Tommy Mitford was with you?' Alice remarked.

'Yes, we sort of took him under our wing because he only lives a few streets away,' Eddie replied. He was already beginning to feel tired again.

'I'll tell his mam that when I get home. I'll go and see Nelly, she'll appreciate it,' Maggie said determinedly.

'We're tiring you, Eddie, I can tell. You're still very weak. We'll go soon but we'll be back later at the official visiting time,' Alice promised.

Eddie nodded and closed his eyes. The effort and the emotion of seeing them seemed to have drained what little strength he had.

'Sleep is the best thing for him now, Mam,' Alice said quietly.

Maggie agreed. 'I think I'll go and have a word with the sister to see how she thinks he's doing and how long he'll be here,' she said, turning away and walking towards the desk in the centre of the ward where the sister sat writing.

Alice bent over her brother. 'I'll just make sure he's comfortable.' She gently eased him down against the pillows and as she did so he opened his eyes. 'Get some rest now, Eddie,' she urged.

'I'm glad you came too, Alice. Is Mae all right?'

'I couldn't let Mam make that journey on her own, Eddie. It was a bit of an ordeal, but she'll be happy now she's seen you and knows you're on the mend. Mae is nursing aboard a hospital train in France now. She writes when she can but as I'm sure you know, they're kept busy.'

He managed a nod. 'Alice, it . . . it's nothing like we . . . expected. It's worse than all your nightmares put together . . .'

'Hush now, Eddie, try not to think of all . . . that. At least you and the twins and Tommy have come through it all so far,' she replied, trying to sound optimistic. It was something Sister Forshaw impressed upon them, the need to be cheerful and optimistic, but despite herself she shuddered at his words. The horror of what lay out there seemed almost unspeakable. It was no wonder he'd ended up here in hospital, she thought, and it made her all the more determined to join Mae one day, hopefully in the not-too-distant future. After all, Mae would be eighteen this year and she was seventeen now and they'd let Tommy Mitford come over to fight.

As she found her mother she could see that Maggie was upset and that Sister was looking grim. 'What's the matter? Not bad news?' she asked, glancing from one to the other.

'That depends on how you consider it,' Maggie replied curtly.

Alice looked questioningly at the sister. 'Eddie is going to make a full recovery, isn't he? There won't be any permanent damage to his lungs?'

'None at all, and with care he should fully recover,' Sister answered confidently.

'Then what's the matter, Mam?'

It was Sister who spoke. 'I have informed your mother of all this, and that when he is fit enough he will be transferred to convalesce in a large country house on the edge of the New Forest, which has been converted for that purpose. It's standard procedure.'

'But then they'll send him back!' Maggie stated angrily. 'Back to those damned trenches so he can get pneumonia again or be killed or wounded. He's only twenty, Sister, for God's sake! Hasn't he been through enough?'

'Mrs McEvoy, please calm yourself! There are boys here who are even younger and some have been badly wounded, had legs and arms amputated, been blinded . . .'

Alice caught her mother's arm; she understood how her mam felt but surely she'd realised that he would be sent back when he was fit. She, too, felt it was grossly unfair but there was nothing they could do. What Sister was saying was that eventually Eddie would be able-bodied, not like a lot of the men and boys in the ward. 'Mam, I know it doesn't seem right but Sister doesn't make the rules and I'm sure she isn't very . . . satisfied . . . that they've worked so hard to nurse Eddie to health only to see him sent back again. But there is nothing any of us can do about that. It . . . it's war and it's horrible. Come on, we'll go back to the hostel and you can have a bit of a rest. I know you didn't sleep well last night. We'll come back later,' she urged.

Sister stood up and nodded. 'I think that is very wise, Miss McEvoy. Nerves get rather frayed at times like this. Visiting is between six and seven thirty.'

Alice thanked her and led a still distraught Maggie towards the door.

Sister gazed after them. What the girl had said was true. She didn't make the rules. As Miss McEvoy had said, it was war. She was a sensible, compassionate and spirited girl, she thought, especially for one so young.

Chapter Eighteen

M AE TURNED THE letter over in her hand, recognising
Harry's writing, despite the stains on the envelope.
They didn't write frequently now and in some ways she was
relieved. She felt they were slowly drifting apart although she
did worry about his safety, but then she worried about them
all. He was still up in the front-line trenches with Jimmy
and Tommy enduring the terrible conditions and the bitter
February weather, and she was kept more than busy for
although there had been no major battles or 'pushes' over
the weeks, the flow of casualties hadn't diminished. The
bombardment wasn't continuous but both sides kept up a steady
pace of shelling and the grey trains painted with red crosses
continued their slow and arduous progress between the town
and the clearing stations.

As usual she was exhausted at the end of another long and
trying day and there were the tediously routine chores to be
undertaken before she could hope to sleep. She decided she

would leave reading the letter until morning and try to find the energy to reply tomorrow night although she felt guilty about it. At least she was safe, warm, dry and had a bed – poor Harry and the other lads out there had none of those things and she knew the effort it must have cost him to write. Each night she prayed for them all, that they wouldn't be killed or wounded or succumb to illness, like Eddie. She'd been shocked when she'd heard from Maggie that Eddie had been shipped home with pneumonia just as she had arrived in France; thankfully he was recovering, but she was aware that as soon as he was fit again he would be sent back here. He'd been lucky to get over the pneumonia, she'd nursed lads suffering from it who hadn't even got to a hospital in Boulogne, but would his luck hold out? She placed the letter on top of the little locker and sighed. She knew that sooner or later she would have to tell Harry about her meetings with Pip for they were becoming increasingly friendly. She'd never considered herself to be Harry's 'girl' but she knew he still regarded her as such and so she kept putting off telling him about Pip, suspecting it would upset him and she was sufficiently fond of Harry not to wish to add to his problems.

She'd met Pip on every afternoon off she'd had and her feelings for him were growing stronger. He'd asked her was there anyone 'special' in her life and she'd told him about Harry. How they'd grown up together, how he'd asked her to 'walk out' just before war had been declared. She'd told him that she hadn't given Harry a definite answer as although she was fond of him it was affection similar to that she felt for her cousin Eddie. All she'd promised to do was to write to Harry. She still felt guilty she'd let Harry kiss her but that kiss had made her realise she didn't love him. Even before she'd met Pip she'd known that; 'fond' was the only word she could use to describe her feelings for Harry. A little shyly she'd asked Pip if there was a girl in Boston waiting for him. He'd smiled and said there were a couple he'd 'dated' but he hadn't heard from either of them since he'd been in France. He hadn't viewed either as anything serious, he'd added, and she'd felt relieved.

As she went about the routine tasks of combing out her hair, brushing and mending her dress, washing apron, cuffs and cap, she felt weighed down by her emotions. She was meeting Pip tomorrow and although she was looking forward to it she felt anxious and apprehensive. She'd seen him earlier that day for a few minutes and he'd said there was something important he had to tell her tomorrow, but he hadn't looked very happy at all. She wondered now if he was planning to tell her he was going home – she suddenly realised that if he were, she would be utterly miserable.

Pip was waiting for her as usual and Monsieur Clari, the café proprietor, nodded genially to her as she sat down. They met quite regularly and were an attractive couple, the pretty English nurse and the young American ambulance driver, he thought.

'Oh, it's freezing out there! I shouldn't be surprised if it snowed,' Mae commented as she took off her gloves.

'I know but a cup of coffee will soon warm you up,' Pip replied, smiling at her, wishing there was some easy way of breaking his news.

'What is the "important" news you mentioned yesterday?' she asked slowly when the coffee had been served.

Pip frowned. 'I'm afraid I'm being moved.'

Mae looked at him in dismay. 'Moved! Oh, Pip, when . . . where to?'

'Very soon, within a day or so. You've heard of Verdun?'

Mae nodded. 'It's a town in the mountains up in Lorraine.'

Pip looked grim. 'It's a citadel and permanently garrisoned, but the Germans have launched an attack and the French are determined to hold on to it at all costs, just as they did in nineteen fourteen, but this time the Boche have brought up massive long-range guns. They can fire shells that weigh a ton each. You can imagine the damage they're doing and you can imagine the casualties too.'

Mae shook her head in disbelief as she tried to picture what a shell that size even looked like, let alone the destruction and carnage it would cause.

'They desperately need ambulances and experienced drivers to take the wounded to hospital in Revigny, which I believe is about forty kilometres away from Verdun.' He didn't tell her that the winding mountain roads were dangerous, particularly in winter when ice and snow covered them, and now they were crowded with refugees, troops and supply vehicles.

'I don't suppose you've much choice,' Mae said dejectedly.

'None at all. Lenny and I are the most experienced drivers, so we've to go.'

Mae bit her lip. 'I don't suppose you know how long you'll be there?'

Pip took her hand. 'Do any of us know how long we're going to be anywhere? We go where we're needed most, Mae.'

She wanted to say that he didn't need to be here at all, this wasn't America's war, but she didn't; she miserably sipped her coffee, which now tasted bitter. 'I'll miss you terribly, Pip, I really will. Our little outings are the only bright moments I seem to have to look forward to.'

He looked at her earnestly. 'Do you mean that, Mae?'

'Of course I do. Without you, there's nothing . . . no . . . no joy,' she replied truthfully but bashfully.

He reached out across the table and took her hand. 'I'll miss you too, Mae. I've grown to like you . . . a great deal.'

She managed a little smile as his words brought some measure of comfort. 'I . . . like you a great deal too, Pip. I don't suppose there will be time to write?'

He shook his head. 'I don't think so. From what we've been told we'll barely have time to eat and sleep, things are so bad. But I'll try and get word to you somehow and I'll be back as soon as I possibly can, I promise.'

Mae felt the tears pricking her eyes as she nodded. 'I . . . I'll be here, Pip,' she replied. 'The casualties won't stop coming.'

They finished their coffee and reluctantly left the café. Usually he walked her back to the station and they made plans for their next meeting but today they walked in silence, although Pip took her hand and squeezed it and she smiled up at him.

They had to stop on the corner of the Rue Nationale for a column of soldiers was marching towards the station. They were obviously newly arrived for they looked healthy, their uniforms clean, their steps lively and they were merrily singing 'It's a Long Way to Tipperary'.

Mae watched them, wondering how long it would be before she was tending some of them on the hospital train.

'They always seem so darned cheerful,' Pip observed, raising a hand to wave to them as they passed.

Mae suddenly heard her name being called and saw a soldier step out of the line. It was Eddie.

'Mae! Mae! I hoped I'd see you,' he cried.

'Get back in line, lad!' the sergeant major roared and Eddie very reluctantly rejoined the column.

Mae went after him with Pip at her side. 'Eddie, Eddie! Are you all right? Have you fully recovered?' she asked, quickening her steps to keep up with him.

He grinned at her. 'I'm as right as rain now. Spent some weeks convalescing, living the life of Riley in Hampshire, but duty calls, so I'm back.'

Mae smiled at him, but despite his cheerful tone she had detected the note of unease in his voice and glimpsed the dread in his eyes.

'Will you write and tell Mam you saw me?'

'Of course,' Mae promised.

Eddie had noticed the tall, good-looking young man at her side and the fact that he was holding her hand. 'Who's your friend?' he asked suspiciously, knowing Harry considered Mae to be his girl.

'Oh, I'm sorry. This is Pip. Phillip Middlehurst of the American Field Ambulance Service.' She looked up at Pip and smiled. 'This is my cousin Eddie McEvoy – you remember I told you he'd been shipped back home?'

'Nice to meet you, Eddie, you take good care of yourself this time,' Pip replied pleasantly; then, realising their presence beside the marching column was being viewed with some animosity by the sergeant major, he drew Mae away to the side of the road.

'Eddie, take care of yourself! Write when you can, it'll find me at the Gare de Boulogne,' she called after him.

'I'll tell the lads I've seen you and that you're fine,' Eddie called back with a final wave and, Mae thought, a meaningful look.

Mae and Pip stood watching until the street was clear again, Pip wondering how many of those lads would survive in the coming months and Mae thinking that she really must write to Harry now and try to explain. Oh, she wished things were different. She didn't want to hurt Harry, but she had never felt for him the way she did about Pip, and now Pip was leaving for Verdun and all she could really think about was that she had no idea when she would see him again.

Later that evening and with a heavy heart she found writing paper and a pen and composed the letter.

My dear Harry,

I hope you are keeping well and that things are not too bad. I saw Eddie today in Boulogne and he seemed cheerful and completely recovered. By now I expect you will all have had a bit of a reunion. I'm finding this letter very difficult to write for a number of reasons: it's late and I still have many chores to complete but the most difficult thing of all is how to tell you that, although I am and have always been very fond of you, I think you know in your heart that I don't love you. I must be honest with you even though I know you will be desperately hurt by what I have to tell you. I have been walking out for a while now with a young American ambulance driver I met when I arrived in Boulogne and we have become very close. I can't tell you how very, very sorry I am, Harry, for I know this news will upset you terribly, but I never promised to be anything other than your friend. All I promised was that I'd write to you.

*My feelings for you are the same as my feelings for Eddie and
I'll always think of you with great affection but it's just not fair
or right for me to go on letting you think that there is anything
more serious between us.*

She paused and reread what she had written. Oh, it was so hard
but there was no way of dressing it up; she was sorry, she didn't
want to hurt him but she just had to tell him.

*I wish you well, Harry. Take care of yourself and I hope in time
you will understand and be able to forgive me.*
  Mae

She folded it and tucked it into an envelope feeling even more
dispirited.

Alice squared her shoulders as she fingered the letter in her
pocket. She'd asked Mae to write and describe in detail the
conditions and the casualties, for the letters Mae wrote to her
mother didn't give much information about either. Mae had
duly complied and now she intended to show that letter to Sister
Forshaw. Ever since she'd got back from Southampton she had
been dropping broad hints about how badly nurses were needed
but they had fallen on deaf ears. After reading Mae's letter she
was now determined to do everything in her power to follow
her cousin to France.

She knocked smartly on the door and waited until Sister
called for her to enter. She took a deep breath; this was her
chance.

Sister looked up, a slight frown of irritation on her face. 'You asked to see me, Nurse McEvoy? I hope it's not on a trivial matter, you know how busy I am.'

'No, Sister, it's nothing trivial. I'd like you to read this, please.' Alice held out the envelope. 'It's from my cousin Mae, Nurse Strickland.'

Sister took it but looked quizzically at the girl in front of her. She held Alice in some esteem for she was shaping up to be a very practical and competent nurse and she was fully aware of her desire to be transferred. 'Does it concern me?' she asked.

Alice nodded. 'I think it concerns us all, Sister.'

The older woman withdrew the pages of neat writing and began to read and Alice soon saw the expressions of shock, disbelief, pity and frustration that passed in rapid succession across the woman's face. They were the same feelings that had engulfed her when she'd first read what Mae was coping with. Now she understood the terrible conditions the soldiers were enduring, their horrific and often superficially treated wounds, the sheer scale of the casualties and the very basic medical and living conditions the nurses had to contend with.

'Is . . . is all this . . . true?' Sister asked when she'd folded the pages. Oh, she'd heard that things were bad but she'd never envisaged casualties on such a scale nor the appalling conditions both the soldiers and nurses were suffering for they'd had no official notification of the facts.

'Mae wouldn't exaggerate or lie about things like that, Sister. Please, please can I go too? We're all desperately needed. When things are really bad even the sisters and staff nurses have to go up the line to the clearing stations, leaving nurses like me in charge of the wards. I know I'm young, but surely I'm of more use there than I am here? Those poor lads are suffering dreadfully and if I can help . . .'

Sister looked at her in silence. She was right; if things were *that* bad then . . . 'You realise what you are asking me to do, Nurse?'

Alice thought at least she hadn't turned her plea down flat. 'I do, Sister. I know I'm really too young but surely in these circumstances age doesn't matter? Surely it's experience and training that count?'

At last Sister Forshaw nodded slowly. They wouldn't be the first to falsify records; Alice wasn't the first to lie about her age but at least she wouldn't be in any physical danger and she was right, every pair of hands was needed. 'All right, Nurse, but only on the condition that your mother approves and I will require her consent in writing.' She wasn't going to accept just Alice's word. She needed to know that her mother knew and approved.

Despite the feeling of elation that was surging through her Alice realised that obtaining her mam's consent was probably going to be as hard as getting Sister to agree to let her go to France. 'I'll have a serious talk to her, Sister. I think I can persuade her.'

Sister Forshaw raised an eyebrow. 'I hope you can, Nurse, otherwise no matter how much you are needed, you'll be staying here.'

All the way home Alice pondered the matter, trying to find the right words to persuade her mam. She had to impress on her how much she was needed, how much she wanted to go and help, despite how young she was. She finally but reluctantly decided that she would have to let Mam read Mae's letter.

When she arrived home she was relieved in a way to find that Agnes was sitting with Maggie; after all, Agnes had both her sons fighting in France.

'A hard day, Alice?' Agnes greeted her, thinking she looked tired.

'I'll get you a cup of tea, luv,' Maggie offered, getting to her feet.

'There's something I want to talk to you about first, Mam,' Alice said, taking off her hat and unbuttoning her coat.

Maggie looked at her suspiciously. 'Now what?'

'I had a talk with Sister Forshaw this afternoon, Mam. I . . . I asked her to let me go to nurse in France, like Mae.'

Maggie started to protest but Alice held out the letter. 'Mam, Aunty Agnes, please read this. It's from Mae and . . . and when you've read it you'll know why I want to go. Why I *have* to go.'

The two women looked anxiously at each other but Maggie took the letter and placed it down on the table between herself and Agnes. Alice held her breath. She hadn't really wanted to worry her mother any more than was necessary, she'd wanted to try to keep from her Mae's descriptions of the atrocious conditions in the trenches, the appalling wounds, the state in which the wounded were brought in, their terrible suffering and the hardships all the doctors and nurses endured, but she was certain it was the only way she could get her mam to give her consent.

When they'd finished there were tears in both women's eyes and Agnes was shaking her head in disbelief.

'Dear God, Maggie! What have we sent them to? Why didn't we stop them?'

Maggie was pressing her hands so tightly together that her

knuckles were white. 'We didn't know, Agnes, we just didn't *know*! And . . . and Eddie . . . They've just sent him back again.'

Alice saw her opportunity. 'And it's for Eddie and Jimmy and Harry that I want to go, Mam. If I can help, if I can do *anything* to help all those lads . . . Mam, can't you see that I just can't stay at home, not when . . . Please, Mam, I have to have your consent and in writing before Sister will do anything,' she begged.

'Oh, Alice, you're so young, luv,' Maggie replied hesitantly.

'I'm the same age as Tommy Mitford, Mam, and I'm not going to be in any danger – unlike him,' Alice reminded her quietly.

Finally Maggie nodded. She was shocked to the core by Mae's letter and was now desperately worried about Eddie and Agnes's boys and young Tommy Mitford. 'I won't stop you, Alice, not if that Sister Forshaw is willing to let you go. She must think you'll be able to cope.'

Inwardly Alice breathed a sigh of relief. 'I'll cope, Mam. If Mae can cope then so can I,' she replied determinedly as Maggie got to her feet to get a pen and some paper to write the letter that would send her daughter – only just seventeen years old – to France.

Chapter Nineteen

———◆———

LATER THAT WEEK Mae was summoned to Sister Allinson's office. She wondered why but she quickly found out.

'Nurse Strickland, I have to inform you that you are being transferred,' Sister announced.

Mae was surprised and prayed it wasn't going to be somewhere further away. 'Where to, Sister?'

'General Camp Hospital Number Twenty-four, one of the hospitals that have been erected on the coast behind the dunes and the railway line. You will be replaced on the train by a nurse coming over from England.'

Mae nodded. There was a terrible shortage of hospitals in France and as no one had envisaged or planned for the scale of the casualties things had become so desperate that new hospitals had had to be hastily erected. They consisted of bell tents and marquees which served as wards, operating theatres and accommodation for the medical staff. 'When do I go, please, Sister?'

'Tomorrow, Nurse Strickland, and Nurse Lawson is also being transferred.'

Again Mae nodded; it would be good to be working with Lizzie again, she thought as she was dismissed, but she wondered whether life would now be harder than on the hospital train.

Mae read Alice's letter as soon as it arrived. When her cousin had first written asking her for a brutally truthful description of conditions Alice had told her that she intended to use it to help persuade Sister Forshaw to let her come out to nurse. Mae had wondered about the advisability of it all at first but knowing of Alice's determination and the desperate need for nurses she had overcome her doubts. Now Alice was to join her, she thought, and that thought made her feel more cheerful than she had been since Pip had gone. She *did* miss him; out of habit when the ambulances arrived she found herself looking for him. They'd only ever exchanged a few words on those occasions but just to see him had somehow been the highlight of her day. She'd received one scribbled note, telling her he was fine but exhausted as there was barely time to sleep or eat, and she'd written back with her news, hoping that somehow in the confusion he would receive her letter.

She hoped Alice would be sent to one of the hospitals here in Boulogne; although the conditions were still very basic at least the air was fresh – if cold, as it came in off the sea. Of course there was no running water, it all had to be brought in in buckets, and the wards were lit by hurricane lamps. The tents, Mae had to admit, were always gloomy in these dark winter days for the beds were covered by red or brown blankets, white cotton counterpanes being out of the question. When a convoy of wounded arrived – which happened day and night – the bugle would sound for 'Fall In'; it was a sound she was becoming very familiar with. It was all very different from the hospital trains; only the suffering of the wounded remained the same. Alice would find it a world away from the wards of Walton Hospital, but she was glad her cousin was finally being allowed to make the journey.

The day Alice arrived was a typical blustery March day but at least spring appeared at last to be in the air, she thought, screwing her eyes up against the bright and unaccustomed sunlight. Just as Mae had been, she too was at first confused by all the people and traffic that surrounded her but she was quickly instructed to join the convoy of wounded that was being taken a little way down the coast to the General Camp Hospital where she was to live and work.

When she arrived there was little time to take in her surroundings; depositing her case quickly on a camp bed in one of the bell tents and donning her apron, cap and cuffs she followed the sister across the compound to a marquee where the wounded were being attended to.

'First of all, Nurse, cut away their uniform and wash the patient but be aware that they are all verminous. Then do whatever you can to make them comfortable until a medical officer can assess their wounds and decide upon treatment,' Sister instructed briskly. She then peered closely at Alice. 'I'm aware that you haven't had to cope with anything like this before but I don't want any hysterics or fainting fits. You look very young, Nurse McEvoy.'

Alice had scraped her hair back under her veil, hoping it

would make her look older. 'People always tell me that, Sister, but I'm not as young as I look. Don't worry about me, I won't be fainting or breaking down. I can cope,' she asserted firmly before turning to what appeared to be a bundle of filthy cloth, blood and bandages on a stretcher, which she realised with shock was in reality a lad of about twenty. Taking a deep breath, she got down to work.

She'd never worked so hard in her life before, she thought when at last she was relieved. There hadn't been time to dwell on the sights she'd seen or the tasks she'd had to perform; there were times when she'd felt faint and even nauseous but she'd gritted her teeth and the overwhelming emotion that filled her had been that of pity. Now it was dark and she had no idea of what time it was. Her back and shoulders were aching, she was hungry and thirsty and cold, and as she made her way across the compound towards the tent she began to shiver with a combination of weariness and distress. But she had coped, she thought; she'd given no outward sign of her inexperience and Sister had even grudgingly said, 'Well done, Nurse.'

The tent, which had been empty earlier, was now occupied by a dozen other nurses, all as tired as herself, their uniforms filthy and blood-spattered – and there was Mae sitting on the edge of the bed she'd been allocated earlier. Alice's face lit up in a smile. 'Mae! Oh, I'm so glad to see you! I hoped I would be sent to the same hospital but I had no idea when I arrived and . . .'

Mae hugged her. Throughout the day she'd asked everyone whether any new nurses had arrived, describing Alice, and found out that her cousin was indeed here – somewhere.

'Come and sit down, Alice. You look exhausted. We've brewed up so there's a hot drink for you. We're all done in and I feel too tired to eat but we'll have to go and get some supper; we've got to keep our strength up.'

Alice held the mug of hot tea gratefully between her hands, glad of the warmth now slowly seeping into her fingers. 'I just want to lie down and sleep.'

'Don't we all,' Lizzie said, adding, 'Hello again, Alice.'

'Lizzie! Oh, it's great to see you. Is Ethel here too?' Alice asked, delighted to see her companion from Walton Hospital.

Lizzie shook her head. 'No, she had to stay on the trains although I know she wanted to come with us.'

'Is it always like . . . this?' Alice asked Mae.

'Only when you hear the "Fall In". At other times it's mainly helping to dress wounds, give bed baths, take temperatures, general nursing in fact.'

Alice looked around, noting for the first time that the beds were set out in a circle around a small stove, there was a makeshift kitchen at one end, and empty sugar boxes were provided for their clothes; that was all there was in the way of comforts.

'Not very luxurious, is it?' Mae stated.

'I didn't expect it to be,' Alice answered, sipping the hot tea and beginning to feel a bit better.

'I'll help you get unpacked, we'll get something to eat and then we'll have to wash these filthy aprons and cuffs and go through everything – hair, underclothes, dresses – looking for flaming "greybacks". Then we can finally go to bed and get some sleep and you'll feel better tomorrow,' Mae said, trying to sound cheerful, despite her own weariness.

'Providing we don't get another convoy in during the night,' Lizzie added.

'Oh, I almost forgot to tell you, Alice. Jimmy Mercer was brought in today. I haven't had time to go and see him but apparently he's been shot in the arm. It's not too bad. The bullet's been removed and thankfully the wound was fairly clean – which is almost a miracle as you'll know by now. He's really fed up that he won't be getting a "Boat Sitting ticket" back to Blighty. He's in ward seven. I'm sure it would cheer him up no end to see you if you can get a minute tomorrow. I think he might be able to get up by then.'

Alice had at first felt a sense of shock that Jimmy had been wounded but Mae's words had been reassuring. She'd seen so many infected, suppurating wounds today and had witnessed the excruciating pain that cleaning them had caused that she realised Jimmy had been fortunate. 'I'll make time, Mae, and I'll write to Aunty Agnes tomorrow night,' she said determinedly.

Mae smiled at her. 'It's not what we expected, Alice, is it, but you do get used to it. There's not nearly as much scrubbing and cleaning as in hospitals at home and definitely no sink rooms. Remember how embarrassed we were about using tow?'

Alice managed a wry grin. 'If we'd known then what we know now . . .' She shrugged.

Mae nodded. 'I'm so glad you're here, Alice. I've been feeling a bit down since Pip left. I really do miss him.'

'Who's Pip?' Alice asked, surprised.

'He's a driver with the American Field Ambulance Service. I met him the day I arrived in Boulogne. He's very nice and we go for coffee in town whenever we can – or we did until he was sent to Verdun.'

'What about Harry Mercer? I thought you and he . . . ?'

Mae shook her head and bit her lip. 'I'm fond of Harry, you know that, just the way you are, Alice. But that's all and I never promised I'd walk out with him. I only promised to write.'

'Mam and Aunty Agnes think it's more than that and I'm sure Harry does too,' Alice put in sharply.

'It's not. I . . . I don't feel anything . . . special . . . for Harry.'

'And do you for this "Pip Middlehurst"? Do you love him?'

'I don't know if I love him, Alice. We haven't known each other very long but I know that what I feel for him is very different to what I feel – and have always felt – for Harry,' Mae answered truthfully.

'Does Harry know you've been "having coffee" with someone else? Have you written and told him?' Alice demanded. She didn't feel that Mae was treating Harry very fairly at all.

'I've written to him, but . . . but I haven't heard anything back from him. Truly I really didn't want to upset him, not when he's in the front-line trenches.'

'That's a bit underhanded of you, Mae,' Alice said flatly.

'I didn't mean to be. Oh, I hope this isn't going to cause trouble between us.'

'I just think you've not treated Harry very well.'

'I do feel guilty about it, Alice. I never meant to hurt him. He knows about Pip now anyway – though I think Eddie may have already told him. We saw Eddie in Boulogne. Pip was holding my hand, Eddie asked who he was and I introduced them. I suppose Eddie will have told Harry all that.'

'Knowing our Eddie, he probably has,' Alice said sharply. She felt very upset with Mae. 'Will this Pip Middlehurst be coming back?'

Mae shrugged. 'I really do hope so but as to when – who knows?' She stood up. 'Right, supper first, you must be starving.'

'I am,' Alice replied, wondering if food would give her the energy for the chores Mae had mentioned. As she wearily pulled on her greatcoat she hoped so.

They walked across to the mess tent together, Mae conscious that Alice's disapproval had changed things between them. It saddened her. 'At least that's your first day almost over,' she said.

Alice just nodded. It had been a shocking day in more ways than one. But tomorrow she would be able to visit Jimmy and see how he was: that was something to look forward to.

Thankfully they hadn't been disturbed during the night but Alice felt tired and stiff as she reluctantly dragged herself from under the army blankets early next morning. After breakfast she found herself walking across the compound with Lizzie and she was surprised when the older girl broached the subject of the coolness between her and her cousin.

'Have you had a falling out with Mae?'

Alice explained, 'I didn't know she was seeing this American ambulance driver. I . . . we thought she and Harry Mercer were . . . close.'

'I know he writes to her but Mae has said to me that she's only fond of him, nothing more.'

'That's not what he thinks and I really do feel that she's not treated the poor lad well at all, Lizzie. '

Lizzie frowned. 'I suppose it's not the easiest thing to do, to write and tell someone who's in the front line that you've begun seeing someone else. And things out here are very different to home, as you'll soon find out. For one thing, often at the end of the day you are so tired it's an effort to eat let alone write letters of any kind. And I also think that you begin to look at . . . relationships in a different light. You certainly view the future in a very different way. Don't be too hard on Mae and don't let it drive a wedge between you. You'll regret it if you do; we all value our personal friendships very highly. We need each other to get through each day and you and Mae have always been so close. She doesn't love Harry, Alice, and she can't help that. I don't know if she's falling in love with Pip but . . .' Lizzie shrugged.

'I just think that she hasn't been fair to Harry,' Alice persisted.

'Maybe she hasn't, but there are reasons. Just don't let that come between you, Alice,' Lizzie urged once more. 'I'm older than you both so maybe I see things differently.'

Alice nodded, thinking about everything Lizzie had said. Perhaps Lizzie was right – she *was* older and wiser; but that still didn't stop Alice feeling upset and annoyed with Mae.

When she reported for duty Sister Harper informed her that she was to work on wards four, five and six with Mae, except of course when there was a convoy in, when everyone was required.

One of their first tasks was to make up the hypochlorous acid solution which was used to wash out infected wounds.

'Eusol, we call it,' Mae told her cousin as the solution was funnelled into big glass demi-johns.

'It stinks!' Alice said, pulling a face. 'It's like . . . chlorate of lime.'

'You'll get used to it. What you never seem to get used to is the smell of gas gangrene.'

'Does this stuff work?' Alice enquired, still wrinkling her nose.

'Sometimes. Sometimes the gangrene has spread too far and then the limb has to be amputated, but it *does* help in a lot of cases,' Mae informed her as she wiped her hands. 'But only if the wound is washed out with it every three hours day and night.'

'Thank God Jimmy's wound was clean,' Alice remarked as she followed Mae out on to the ward to start work.

It wasn't until that evening that she managed to find a few spare minutes and after hastily swallowing a mug of tea and a sandwich she made her way to ward seven.

'I'm looking for a Private James Mercer. I grew up with him, Staff,' she informed the staff nurse on duty.

'Fourth bed on the right side, miss,' the woman replied curtly, pointing down the ward.

Alice peered down the gloomy interior of the tent and nodded. 'Thank you, Staff.' When her back was turned she raised her eyes skywards. 'Miss' indeed, she thought. Some of these Regular Army nurses flatly refused to call the VADs 'Nurse', so jealous were they of their own positions and titles and thinking that girls from her background and with only months' training were not really qualified. Maybe their attitude would change in time, she thought, but then again maybe not.

'I see you've managed to get yourself a nice cosy billet, Jimmy!' Alice greeted him, smiling. He was sitting up in bed, his right arm heavily bandaged and in a sling, and he looked pale and tired.

He looked at her blankly for a second and then he grinned

broadly, delighted to see a familiar face from home. 'Alice! Alice, what the hell are you doing here?'

'That's a nice way to greet anyone, Jimmy Mercer, I must say! I've given up my few minutes' break to come and see how you are.'

'When . . . how . . . ?' Jimmy stammered, completely fazed at seeing her here.

'I arrived yesterday and I'm working with Mae on wards four, five and six, and don't you go saying anything to that poker-faced one back there about me only being seventeen. She wasn't impressed that I'm only a VAD as it is. How did you manage to get wounded?'

Jimmy had regained his composure. 'Stupid really, I was passing Mills bombs – hand grenades – to our Harry and the others and got a Boche bullet in my arm. We were involved in a bit of a skirmish with them and were firing over the parapet,' he explained.

'At least you had it attended to before it got infected. I've seen the mess some of the lads are in when they finally get to us.'

He nodded, still trying to take in the fact that she was actually here. 'I never thought you'd be able to persuade your mam to let you come over. She *does* know, Alice?'

'Of course she knows! She had to give her written consent to the sister at Walton. I got really annoyed that I was stuck there when I wanted to be here, where I'm of more use – although there's some here that wouldn't agree,' she added caustically, glaring down the ward in the direction of the staff nurse.

Jimmy's admiration for her increased. Somehow she'd managed to get both her mam's and the authorities' consent to come out to nurse, he didn't know how, but he'd always known she had guts and determination.

'I'll write to your mam tonight and tell her I've seen you and not to worry, that you're doing fine. How are the rest of them? Our Eddie, your Harry and Tommy?' Alice asked to change the subject.

'As well as can be expected, I suppose.'

'Our Eddie isn't showing any signs of having a relapse, is he? I know what the conditions are like, Jimmy. Mae's told me.'

'No, he's all right and the weather has improved a bit lately. I thought your Mae was still on the hospital trains. Eddie said she was. He saw her in Boulogne.'

'She was transferred here two weeks ago.' She paused. 'How . . . how did your Harry take it about Mae and Pip Middlehurst?' she asked cautiously.

'Mae and *who*?' Jimmy asked, a look of complete mystification on his face.

Alice was surprised. 'Eddie didn't tell you?'

'Tell me what, for God's sake?'

Alice sighed, wishing she'd kept her mouth shut; she'd been as sure as Mae that Eddie would have told Harry. 'She's become quite . . . very friendly with an ambulance driver. His name is Phillip Middlehurst but everyone calls him Pip, apparently. He's American. I think you can say they are walking out – or they were, but he's been sent to Verdun. I only found out last night and I certainly don't approve of the way she's treated Harry and I told her so. She couldn't go up the line to see him, so she had to write to him.'

Jimmy silently digested this. Mae would have met this Pip when she was nursing on the trains. Everyone had great respect for the drivers of the American Field Ambulances. They'd travelled thousands of miles, leaving the safety and comfort of their homes to undertake the sometimes dangerous work of moving the wounded. He knew how his brother felt about Mae but he'd always thought that she really didn't reciprocate those feelings, and as far as he knew Mae hadn't agreed to walk out with his brother. Oh, she wrote to him and Harry wrote to her but then Alice wrote to *him*. 'Our Harry's been sweet on Mae for ages but . . . but I think she doesn't really . . .' He was struggling for words.

'She doesn't love him, Jimmy. Both Mae and Lizzie told me that. She likes him a lot, the way she likes you and our Eddie, of course, but I think she's fallen for this Pip Middlehurst.'

Jimmy frowned as he considered what Alice had just told him about Mae and Harry. His brother hadn't mentioned that he'd had a letter from Mae and he knew Harry would have been upset by this news, but then the mail might have arrived after he'd been wounded and brought here. 'I'm saying nothing about it, Alice, not until our Harry does. After all, none of us know what's going to happen to us tomorrow.'

Alice nodded her agreement; what he said made sense. No one knew when this terrible war would end or who would survive it. But she still couldn't help feeling upset with Mae.

The staff nurse had risen to her feet and was looking pointedly at her watch and Alice realised that she would have to go. 'I've got to get back now, Jimmy, she's giving me daggers.'

He looked disappointed. 'But you'll be able to come and see me again, Alice? Or maybe I could come to see you. I'll be up and about tomorrow.'

'Don't you go making an "instant" recovery, Jimmy, or

they'll have you back up the line before that arm is fully healed. No, I'll brave old frosty-features and I'll come and see you when I can,' Alice promised. She was relieved that he appeared to be well and in good spirits.

'I'll look forward to seeing you.' Jimmy grinned. He felt much more cheerful. He'd always liked Alice, and he liked her more now, he thought; she really seemed to have grown up. He wasn't even as fed up about not getting back to Blighty as he had been. It really wasn't so bad here: his arm didn't seem as painful and Alice – and probably Mae too – would visit him; Alice McEvoy would be a match for Staff Nurse Thomas any day, he mused happily. He wouldn't even have to write to his mam; Alice had promised to do that too. Yes, you could rely on Alice.

Chapter Twenty

———◆◆◆◆———

TRUE TO HER word Alice visited Jimmy whenever she could and as soon as he felt able they walked around the compound and even as far as the edge of the sand dunes, if time permitted. The weather was gradually improving and the sunlight sparkling on the waters of the Channel lifted their spirits, these moments a brief respite from the rather depressing atmosphere of the hospital where it was impossible to escape the effects of war.

'They might even let you come and take a dip in the sea in summer, Alice,' Jimmy had teased one day when the water had reflected the blueness of the sky.

'I wouldn't fancy it, I bet it's freezing. Whenever we went to New Brighton, no matter how hot and sunny the weather was the water was always cold,' Alice had replied, thinking back to the infrequent day trips she'd made to the seaside resort as a child. 'How is your arm today? Any pain or stiffness at all?'

Jimmy had shaken his head. 'Maybe the odd twinge if I try to lift anything heavy.'

She nodded. 'That sounds about right but in time you'll find it won't bother you.'

'You sound just like Sister.'

Alice had laughed but then Jimmy had become serious. 'They'll discharge me soon, Alice, and I'll have to go back.'

'I know. It doesn't seem right, but . . .'

'But I am in one piece and able to fight and it's my duty. I took the oath for King and Country, but I can't say I'm looking forward to going back up the line.'

Alice had felt as though a dark cloud had crossed the sun and involuntarily she had shivered. She'd miss the time she spent with him; she looked forward to it and she knew he did too. They'd always got on well together but since he'd been here they'd grown closer.

'It might not be for a few weeks yet,' she had thought aloud; then, trying to sound more cheerful, she'd added, 'Just don't go stopping any more Boche bullets. Now we'd better get back before they send out a search party and Sister Harper hauls me over the coals.'

She thought about that day now as she stood at the gate to the hospital compound, waiting to say goodbye to him as she'd promised. He'd only had another week before they'd told him he was being sent back to his battalion. She wished he didn't have to go for in her heart she was afraid for him. There was talk that when summer came there would be a concerted attempt to 'push' the enemy back and that would mean more fatalities and casualties. She only had a quarter of an hour break and he'd have to march off with the others who were now fit to rejoin their units, so she'd arranged to meet him here a few minutes before the men assembled.

At last she caught sight of him coming towards her, his heavy pack on his back, his tin helmet hanging from its strap over one arm, his rifle in the crook of the other. He looked well, she thought, he had colour in his cheeks now, he'd put some weight back on, his uniform was new, his boots polished.

'I'd almost forgotten how damned heavy this pack is,' he said, gratefully easing it from his shoulders on to the ground. There were a few minutes yet before the bugle would sound for assembly. He looked down at her and smiled, trying desperately to hide his feelings. He didn't want to go. He didn't want to have to face again the hardships and the danger, and fear was already gnawing at his guts, but most of all he didn't want to leave her.

'Well, off I go again. At least the lads will be glad to see me back and I've got some ciggies for them. I know you don't get much free time but will you write, Alice? When things quieten down they bring the mail up the line.'

'Of course I will and . . . and will you do something for me, Jimmy? Keep an eye on our Eddie. I dread him getting ill again.'

'We all watch out for each other, Alice, you know that, we're mates. I'll give you a detailed account of his health when I write, if that will help.'

Alice laughed. 'Oh, stop that. You know what I mean. I'll write with all the news from here – such as it is – and from home. Mam has more time to write than your mam does. She's always saying the house is so quiet now with us all over here.'

Jimmy nodded. 'Mam's got her hands full with the shop, our Lucy and Gran, who's getting very confused now.'

The first notes of a bugle rang out and Alice bit her lip, steeling herself. 'You'll have to go now, Jimmy. Please take care of yourself.'

'I will.' He hesitated for a second, then he bent and kissed her. 'I'll miss you, Alice. I'm very . . . fond of you, you know. You're a great girl.'

Alice felt her heart turn over and she reached out and gently touched his cheek. 'Look after yourself, Jimmy. I couldn't bear it if anything happened to you,' she said quietly.

The notes of the bugle became louder, the call more insistent, and Alice forced herself to be cheerful. It was something that Sister had instilled in her. Cheerfulness and optimism at all times. Men going back wanted to be sent off with smiles and waves, not tears and long faces. 'Off you go, Jimmy. I'll write but I don't want to see you back here ever again as a patient.'

He managed to grin back although desolation was sweeping over him. 'With a bit of luck you won't, Alice. Goodbye.'

'Goodbye, Jimmy. Give my love to Eddie,' she called, waving as he walked away towards the assembling ranks. Then she turned and surreptitiously wiped her eyes with the corner of her apron. Would she ever see him again? she wondered. She prayed she would – but not here, please God, not here.

Mae knew how her cousin was feeling for she'd watched Alice grow closer to Jimmy during the time he'd been at the hospital and knew that Alice was missing him. Alice's attitude towards her had gradually thawed during that time and she'd been very relieved for her cousin's disapproval had only added to her despondency. Alice had told her that Eddie hadn't in fact told Harry about Pip and that he wasn't going to tell his brother either so she still had that to worry about. She'd had the occasional note from Pip but she had no idea when he would return. The French were still holding out at Verdun although their losses were crippling.

The days had lengthened and grown warmer and a light summer breeze was wafting over the sand dunes as she stood staring out at the sea. The June evenings were long and despite the weariness she always felt at the end of the day she'd sought the solace and quiet of a walk by the sea. She wished they'd send Pip back. She knew she was being selfish for he was needed more at Verdun and Revigny, just as she was needed here, but she knew now that she loved him: life was so empty without him. It was also so hard to think that across those few miles of calm blue water there were no battles or skirmishes, but there were plenty of casualties. Every hospital in Britain was filled with them and still there was no end in sight at all. At the end of May there had been a huge naval battle off the Danish coast at Jutland. The expectation had been that the superior British fleet would blast that of the Kaiser out of the water, for hadn't Britannia Ruled the Waves for centuries? Wasn't the Royal Navy invincible? The great victory hadn't materialised, she thought dully, but there had been no outright defeat either. Even that confrontation appeared to have ended in stalemate. There had been terrible loss of life on both sides, dreadnoughts torn apart by exploding ammunition, battleships sinking in minutes, their crews drowned. The wounded had stood no chance in the cold waters of the North Sea, just as her poor da had stood no chance in the stokehold of the *Lusitania*. She shivered despite the warmth of the evening and turned her steps back towards the hospital compound. She'd thought that some time alone would make her feel better but it hadn't. It was almost impossible to escape the war although when she was with Pip they never talked about it; somehow it always receded into the background.

The flap of the tent was pinned back allowing the warm evening air to enter, and Alice was sitting at the rickety table finishing a letter to Jimmy; his letter, which had arrived that afternoon, lay on the table beside her.

'Has he anything interesting to say? Are they all well?' Mae asked, sitting on the edge of her bed and beginning to unpin her hair.

'They all seem to be fine but he's talking about there being "something big" coming up soon.'

Mae nodded. 'I've heard that too on the wards, and this morning Sister was going through all the notes and asking Dr Nicol how many patients did he think could possibly be sent back to Blighty. It looks as though they're trying to clear the place.'

Alice frowned. 'I suppose it had to come. They couldn't just spend the rest of the year stuck in those trenches; that doesn't seem to have achieved anything so far.'

Mae sighed. 'I suppose they'll tell us when they think we should know.'

'Mae, there's someone asking for you,' Lizzie announced as she entered the tent, just having come off duty.

'Who?'

Lizzie grinned. 'Tall, good-looking, American. I said I'd—'

Mae jumped up from the bed, her heart pounding. 'Pip! It's Pip!' she cried.

'He was standing outside ward four when I left him. You know no men are allowed near our billet, Sister would murder them with her bare hands . . .' Lizzie replied but her words fell into empty air for Mae had hitched up her long skirt and run out, heedless of the fact that her hair was falling down over her shoulders.

She was a little out of breath when she reached the tented ward and saw him waiting outside patiently. 'Pip! Oh, why didn't you let me know . . . ! I'm so glad to see you!' she gasped, the words tumbling out.

He laughed and caught her hands and held them tightly. 'There wasn't time, Mae. I only found out I was coming back this morning and I came out here as soon as I could. Lenny is covering for me so I can't stay long. The ambulance could well be needed.'

'Let's walk for a bit,' she urged. 'If Sister sees me here there'll be trouble.'

Still holding her hand Pip began to walk towards the gate. He'd been relieved at first when he'd found out he was coming back. He was exhausted and tired of the still-difficult driving conditions in the mountains. The weather had improved but the roads were constantly choked, which he'd found more and more frustrating, not to say infuriating. Men had died because the ambulance had been stuck for hours on the road to Bar-le-Duc where the mountain road to Verdun began and ended. New troops and ammunition carts seemed to take precedence over the wounded, the *déchets* as the French called them – the 'scrap', but then he'd found out he was being sent back because a massive offensive was imminent, on the Somme.

'Are you back permanently or is this just a bit of leave?' Mae asked, hoping it was the former, not the latter.

He smiled at her. He'd missed her, he'd almost forgotten how delightful she was. And pretty. Just now, with her long, blonde hair framing her face and her blue eyes alight with joy, she looked radiant. 'No, I'm back for good – or at least for the foreseeable future.'

'Oh, I'm so glad, Pip. I've really missed you.'

'When is your next afternoon off? Will you be able to get into town?'

'I'll ask Alice to swap with me, she's off tomorrow. I'll get a lift, there's always something in the way of transport going to and from town,' she assured him. She'd walk every single step of the way if she had to, just to spend some time with him, she thought.

'Then we'll meet at the café as usual. I'll be there at two. Don't worry if you're late, I'll wait. I've waited this long to see you, Mae, a bit longer won't matter.'

They'd reached the gate and she saw the ambulance parked there, reminding her that he had to get back. 'I'll be there as soon as I can, I promise. I'm so . . . so delighted you've come back, Pip.'

He raised her hand to his lips and kissed it, wishing he could take her in his arms and kiss her but he was aware that people were around and that such behaviour would be discussed and maybe reported and then she'd be in serious trouble with Sister. 'Goodnight, Mae. I'll see you tomorrow. Sweet dreams.'

She smiled up at him. 'They will be now, Pip.' She felt happier now than she'd been for months.

Chapter Twenty-One

———◆———

EDDIE DREW DEEPLY on what was left of his cigarette and then dropped the butt on to the floor of the trench; there was no need to extinguish it for the weather had broken yesterday and the mud had quickly seeped up from between the duck boards. For a week now the bombardment had gone on day and night and the air was thick with smoke and the stench of cordite, which stung his eyes and made his throat feel raw. His ears and his head ached from the incessant thundering; it had been impossible to get any sleep. Between them and the front-line German trenches was no man's land, a strip they called the 'racecourse' because apparently that's what it looked like from the air. Five hundred yards of untouched greensward but covered with thick, ugly, murderous coils of barbed wire. He thought again about the letter tucked into the inside pocket of his tunic. The letter addressed to Harry which he'd been handed with the mail for all of them. The letter he'd forgotten about when Jimmy had been wounded. After Jimmy had gone to the dressing station he'd remembered it and he'd recognised Mae's writing. He'd had a strong suspicion that she was writing to Harry to tell him about the American he'd seen her with in Boulogne and he'd decided, after much deliberation, not to give it to his mate. Things were bad enough for Harry – Jimmy wounded, conditions as bad as ever and knowing an offensive was in the offing – without getting news like that. He supposed he'd have to pass the letter over eventually, but not yet. Not today.

Dawn was now breaking but the rising sun of the July morning was obliterated by the thick smoke and they all knew that in an hour or so the bombardment would cease and then . . . then the flag would drop, whistles would sound and they would climb the scaling ladders and go over the top. He was dreading it – his guts were already knotted with fear – but at least he would be doing *something*; it was this interminable waiting that they all found so hard to endure. It had sent a couple of the lads mad: they'd been taken away shaking and gibbering or screaming; it had been very unnerving. They were dug into the assembly trenches east of Talus Boise, below the German-held village of Montauban and to the right of the depleted French force.

Jimmy and Harry Mercer stood beside him, Harry leaning his head on his arms against the trench wall, his eyes closed, trying to blot out the noise. Jimmy was gripping his rifle so tightly with fear that his knuckles were white. Tommy Mitford was passing equipment up the line.

'What the hell is all this?' Eddie yelled irritably.

'Waterproof sheet, iron rations, ammo, Mills bombs, entrenching tool, field dressings . . .' Tommy rattled off.

'Christ! We won't be able to move carrying this lot as well as a rifle and bayonet,' Jimmy shouted above the din.

'Stop bloody moaning!' Tommy bawled back, managing a pale imitation of his usual infectious grin.

'I wish this damned din would stop. It's as though every wretched shell is exploding in my head,' Harry muttered to himself, although he was fully aware of what would happen when it did stop. He thought of Mae: whatever happened to them all today at least she was safely behind the lines in Boulogne. He knew she would be kept busy today but he hoped she would think of him.

The odd ray of strong sunlight now penetrated the haze of smoke as they stowed the additional items of kit in their backpacks and shifted uncomfortably in the line.

'Remember what we all promised,' Jimmy reminded them and they nodded. They'd made a pact that so far as it was humanly possible they would look out for each other; it seemed the only chance they had to get through the next hours and days. 'And I just hope this bombardment has cut through that bloody wire,' he added to himself.

At twenty-five past six the guns ceased firing. The seconds of silence that followed were somehow eerie, Eddie thought, but there wasn't much time for further coherent thought as the scaling ladders were brought up, the flag fell and they jerked into action, following Captain Dixon up the ladder and over the top of the trench.

Gunsmoke still swirled around as they stumbled forward, weighed down by their packs.

Harry's stomach was churning with fear as he moved forward through the smoke but he kept going. He was almost blinded by the flash as the shell exploded but he didn't feel the shrapnel as it tore into his chest; he only felt himself falling slowly to the ground. It wasn't easy to breathe and then he heard his name being called and peered up through the darkness that seemed to be closing in on him. He could hear Jimmy's voice very faintly, telling him he was going to be all right, but he couldn't see his brother's face. He tried to reply but he was choking and the darkness was pressing down on him. He couldn't see and now he could hear nothing. He felt as if he was drifting away from the battlefield but before the darkness claimed him completely he thought for the last time of Mae.

All Eddie could see ahead of him were flashes and columns of smoke erupting like small volcanoes. There were smaller flashes and he knew that was machine-gun fire; lyddite shrapnel burst all around him but he had to go on, despite hearing the screams of men falling around him. He shook his head, trying to clear his vision, trying to see where the twins and Tommy were but it was impossible to make them out individually. He didn't even know where he was supposed to be going. He tripped and stumbled but as he got to his feet he recognised Captain Dixon over whose prostrate form he'd tripped; he'd been shot through the head. Who were they supposed to follow now? he thought frantically. Where should they be headed now? All he could do was stagger on and hope.

Within a few yards he tripped again, screaming as pain ripped through his left arm and he fell into a shell crater. He was shaking with terror and his arm was throbbing fiercely but after a few seconds he gingerly raised his head and peered over the edge of the crater. A figure lay sprawled in front of him: whoever it was had to be alive for he was moaning in pain. Eddie reached out and managed to drag the man into the hole beside him. It was Jimmy; the lower half of his right leg was mangled, the bone exposed and gleaming horribly white against the shredded flesh.

'Jimmy! Jimmy, mate, it's me, Eddie!'

Jimmy grasped his arm and Eddie yelped in pain. 'I think I've got shrapnel in my arm, but we've got to get some kind of tourniquet around that leg or you'll bleed to death. Where's your Harry and Tommy?' he asked, trying to extract his field dressings from his pack and also trying to ignore the agony this caused him.

Jimmy's face was drawn, he too was trembling violently and tears began to slide down his cheeks, making clean rivulets on his dirt- and smoke-streaked cheeks. 'Both . . . gone. I . . . I stayed with Harry until . . . Told him he'd be all right but his chest . . . ripped wide . . . open! Oh, Jesus Christ! What'll I tell Mam? Then . . . then I got hit in the leg.' He was sobbing now as Eddie was desperately trying to tighten the bandage he'd managed to wrap around Jimmy's leg but the effort was too great. 'Jimmy, pull this as tight as you can. Pull! Pull, for God's sake! I can't, not with this arm,' he yelled.

Jimmy did as he was instructed and when he had calmed down a little they both leaned back against the wall of the shell hole. 'Captain Dixon's dead too. What happened to Tommy?' Eddie asked dully.

Jimmy rubbed his hand across his eyes, trying to blot out the images of the past few terrible minutes, which were like a kaleidoscope of horror. 'I . . . I don't know but just before our Harry . . . fell, I saw Tommy go down, roll over and . . . and lie still, just staring up at . . . nothing.' It was all too much and Jimmy broke down again.

'Pull yourself together, Jimmy, lad! Don't think about it now! We've got to get the hell out of here, we've got to get to the dressing station.' Again he gingerly raised his head and yelled 'Stretcher!' until he was hoarse and he realised that either he couldn't be heard or there were no stretchers or bearers available. 'We're on our own, mate,' he informed Jimmy. 'Can you get up?'

Jimmy tried but it was obvious he was unable to even hobble.

'Right, there's nothing for it, I'll have to carry you.'

Jimmy was dizzy with pain and shock. 'How . . . how . . . with your arm?'

'There's nothing wrong with your arms, Jimmy. Hang on to my shoulders, I'll carry you on my back, my legs still work. We promised to look out for each other, remember? There's just the two of us now.'

Slowly and with some manoeuvring and groans and cries of agony from them both, they managed to drag themselves over the edge of the crater. Shells and bullets still burst around them and Eddie had no idea in which direction the field dressing station was but he staggered on determinedly. Harry and Tommy were past help now but Jimmy wasn't.

He had no idea just how long it had taken them but they were both close to collapse when at last and by good fortune they staggered into the pile of rubble which was all that was left of the village of Montauban, now in Allied hands, and found the crowded dressing station. It was chaotic so, propped up against the remains of a stone wall and utterly exhausted, all they could do was wait until someone came to attend to them.

It was growing dark when finally an orderly shook Eddie

gently. 'Name, rank, battalion, lad? I can see for myself it's your arm,' he said, looking at the torn and filthy blood-soaked uniform sleeve.

'See to my mate first, would you? His leg's in a mess, he's lost a lot of blood,' Eddie urged.

Jimmy was almost unconscious so Eddie gave his details, which were scribbled down on a card and placed in a waxed envelope and tied with string to Jimmy's tunic. A similar one was attached to him. 'Christ!! We're just like bloody parcels now,' Eddie muttered.

The orderly, clearly exhausted, ignored him; he dressed Jimmy's leg as best he could and then Eddie's arm. 'You'll be taken to the clearing station in due course,' he informed Eddie.

'How and when?' Eddie demanded. It was fully dark by now so he realised it must be after half past ten; they'd been wounded early that morning and Jimmy was in a bad way.

'He'll have to wait for a stretcher but I can't say when he'll get one. We've been inundated all damned day and many of the stretcher-bearers have been wounded too.'

'He'll be bloody dead by that time!' Eddie protested.

'I can't help it, lad. There are worse cases than him still waiting.'

Eddie dragged himself to his feet. 'How far is it? I've carried him this far, I'll carry him the rest of the damned way! I'm not leaving him here to die!'

'Half a mile down the road, that way. From there they'll take the pair of you by train to a hospital. It's the best we can do, lad.'

Eddie nodded and the orderly helped to hoist Jimmy on to Eddie's back again. 'Just hang on to me, Jimmy! We're going to make it, don't you worry. We'll both be going back to Blighty now so just hang on, mate.' He gritted his teeth as he staggered forward.

Both Mae and Alice had been told that there was to be an offensive along a fifteen-mile front and that casualties would be heavy. The hospital had been partly cleared, medical supplies increased and all medical staff from units not involved in the offensive had been drafted in. To add to their apprehension they learned from Sister Harper that all save two sisters were to be sent up the line to the clearing stations.

'But that'll leave just two sisters in charge of twenty wards!' Mae had replied, shocked.

'I'm fully aware of that, Nurse, but there are staff nurses here and you'll all just have to manage,' Sister had replied. 'The powers that be consider it absolutely necessary that experienced staff be at the clearing stations,' she'd added grimly. She was not looking forward to going herself.

'And God help us if they are all like that Staff Nurse Thomas,' Alice had muttered as they'd left the office. 'She thinks all we're fit for is skivvying.'

'Oh, just ignore her, Alice. We're experienced now, we're used to the convoys, but if it's as bad as Sister thinks, it's going to be the worst we've faced. But we'll all just have to cope,' Mae had replied.

On the morning of 1 July Pip drove into the hospital compound early, just as Mae was going on duty. 'I've brought you a patient, Mae.'

'He's not the first, is he, Pip? The battle hasn't started, has it?'

He shook his head. 'No. He fell awkwardly in one of the communication trenches, he's broken his leg, but I think he's relieved in a way. He told me that just before he fell the bombardment had stopped and the ladders were being brought up, so I guess that by now it's gotten under way.'

Mae nodded. Only occasionally and if the wind was in the right direction could the sound of gunfire be heard here – faintly. 'I think we're as prepared as we can be, Pip. How soon do you think it will be before the first casualties arrive?'

He shrugged. 'It all depends on how long it takes them to get from the field dressing stations to the casualty clearing stations, then the trains, then us and finally the hospitals – and that will all depend on just how many wounded men there are.'

'We're both in for a busy time, Pip.'

'Sadly yes, Mae. Let's hope it's all a success this time.'

'Right, we'd better get this lad in to see a doctor,' she urged as Staff Nurse Thomas appeared, frowning disapprovingly at them both.

'I'll take charge now. Go to your duties. You know the procedure. Start on your allotted tasks and don't dawdle,' she instructed curtly, her voice devoid of any emotion.

Mae nodded and smiled at Pip. No doubt she'd see him again during the day.

She and Alice worked in silence until almost ten o'clock and then the first casualties began to arrive and ward duties were abandoned. As the morning wore on it was becoming apparent that there were more wounded men than had been anticipated and stretchers were placed on the floor between beds in the wards.

Mae and Alice had stood beside doctors picking fragments of bone from gaping wounds, helped move men with mangled, mutilated limbs from stretchers, cut through shredded cloth to clean and dress deep wounds and hold the instruments for amputation. A couple of times Alice had felt faint but she'd concentrated hard on the bowl she'd been holding until the feeling passed, determined she would show no weakness before Staff Nurse Thomas.

By early evening the flow had increased and the hospital was packed to capacity and still the convoys arrived. Neither of them had had anything to eat or drink since early morning but neither had anyone else, Mae thought as she went to attend to a lad who was sitting on the ground, leaning against the side of a marquee. She bent down beside him and saw the small hole in his chest; quickly and carefully she cleaned it and covered it with a small pad of clean lint.

'You'll be fine, it's a small, clean wound and we'll find you somewhere more comfortable as soon as we possibly can, I promise,' she soothed, trying to sound cheerful.

He nodded but then she noticed that his breath was coming in short bubbling gasps and there were traces of blood on his lips. Something was very wrong and she wondered if she should call a staff nurse, but another convoy of ambulances was drawing in. Gently she turned him towards her. There was a gaping hole in his back that she could have fitted her fist into and the lungs were torn and collapsed. There was nothing she could do for him; clearly he was dying. She packed a long swab into the wound and then bandaged it as tightly as she could.

'That will make you feel more . . . comfortable,' she soothed, glancing briefly at the label tied to his tunic. 'Private Arthur

Pickavance. 18th King's Liverpool. Chest Wound', she read and then for the first time that long, chaotic day she thought of Eddie, Harry, Jimmy and Tommy. 'Oh, please God, let them be all right,' she prayed.

Long into the summer night the wounded continued to arrive until the only place to lay them was on the ground in the compound itself; there weren't even any more stretchers to place them upon and every available space inside the tented hospital was full. Every doctor, nurse, medic and orderly was exhausted but still frantically working and still the ambulances and even carts and lorries continued to arrive.

Mae was holding the shoulder of a man while the surgeon prepared to amputate the arm below the elbow when suddenly she began to see two doctors, two patients and started to sway.

'Nurse! You are no use to me if you pass out!' the exhausted surgeon snapped.

'I'll take over. Go and get something to eat, girl!' Staff Nurse Thomas commanded grimly. The girl had shown she was experienced; this was no sudden indication of a delicate constitution, it was the result of hunger and unrelenting work.

Mae groped her way outside and across to the mess tent which was also half full of wounded men. She felt too tired and too sick to eat but she accepted a bowl of soup and a slice of bread and slowly and automatically ate, knowing that shortly she would feel better. They'd long since passed the point where they could possibly hope to cope with the number of wounded; the sheer scale of the casualties was overwhelming, she thought, wondering how Alice was managing – she hadn't seen her for a few hours. And there was still no end in sight. She handed back the bowl to the harassed young girl who appeared to be the only person in charge of the kitchen. She had to get back; she was still needed.

Another line of ambulances had pulled up by the gate, the only space available for them now, and their drivers were helping to unload yet more casualties. Amongst them she saw Pip, his uniform as caked in blood and dirt as her own. She crossed towards him. Despite the fact that he must have been here dozens of times today she hadn't seen him since this morning.

He caught sight of her. 'Mae, you look done in!'

'I am, Pip, we . . . we all are. Please, please tell me these are the last?'

He shook his head, his face like hers grey and drawn with exhaustion.

Suddenly she felt hysteria rising in her. 'We can't cope with any more, Pip! We're overwhelmed! Men are lying on the bare earth and we're running out of everything and they're dying, Pip! We can't help them! We can't even clean their wounds properly before we ship them back home and they'll get gangrene and they'll . . . die!' She was shaking and crying and he took her in his arms and held her tightly. He'd asked himself time and again during this long and terrible day: would this tide of mangled and broken men and boys ever cease? They'd expected heavy casualties and he had seen more than his fair share in the time he'd been at Verdun but nothing . . . nothing on such a scale as this. 'Hush now, Mae. You're doing your best. Everyone is.'

Mae clung to him. 'Oh, Pip, I can't describe . . . there are no words! There are just *no words*!'

She was so right, he thought, there were in fact no words, no suitable adjectives to describe the sights, sounds, smells and sheer horror of this day. She was at her wits' end and all he wanted to do was take her away from it all because . . . because he loved her. But that was impossible. 'Mae, Mae, hush now, my darling. When this is all over will you come home with me, as my wife? I love you, Mae. I realised it when I was sent to Verdun and I was away from you.'

Mae sobbed into his shoulder. 'When will it be over, Pip?'

'I don't know, my dear love, but will you be my wife when it is?'

Mae fought down her sobs. She loved him – she'd known she was falling in love with him for months – but could she, amidst all this horrific chaos, look forward to what seemed a remote future? 'Pip, I love you too.'

'Then say "yes", Mae,' he begged. He hadn't intended to ask her like this or now in such terrible circumstances but suddenly it had become so very important.

'Yes, Pip,' she said, feeling a little calmer and wondering if she would feel more emotional – elated even – about this in time.

He bent and kissed her forehead, knowing that they would both have to go back to their duties. 'It's dark now, Mae, at least the fighting will have stopped for today. That's something to hang on to.'

She raised her head and nodded slowly. 'I . . . I'll try to think about that, Pip. I really will.'

He kissed her again before leaving her but as he walked wearily back towards the ambulance he knew that although the actual fighting had stopped the number of casualties still out there awaiting transportation were probably legion. Was there a single unwounded soldier in the whole front line? he wondered bitterly.

Chapter Twenty-Two

A T TWO O'CLOCK IN the morning Staff Nurse Thomas instructed three of her VADs to go and get a couple of hours' sleep; they would all rest on a rota basis, for everyone was on the point of dropping from exhaustion and mistakes were very likely to occur, mistakes which could prove fatal. Mae, Alice and Lizzie Lawson were the first to go.

'I've changed my opinion of her,' Alice said grudgingly as she dropped down on her camp bed. 'She's not that bad after all.'

'Dear Lord, was there ever such a day?' Lizzie groaned, dragging off her stained veil and apron and throwing them on the floor. There was no time to even think of washing them.

'But at least the fighting will have stopped now it's dark, so Pip told me,' Mae informed them both. 'I saw him after Staff told me to get something to eat. I nearly fainted I was so hungry.'

'That's what I mean about her; she chased me off too earlier

– although she still won't address any of us as "Nurse",' Alice added.

'Well, we can't work at that pace indefinitely without food or sleep,' Lizzie concurred.

'I could sleep for a week but a couple of hours will have to do, it will be light again soon,' Alice said, her eyes already closing.

Mae was too exhausted to contemplate what tomorrow would bring but before she fell into a deep sleep she remembered that she'd promised to marry Pip and a sense of contentment filled her.

It seemed as if they'd only been asleep for minutes when the next batch of grey-featured nurses arrived to wake them. Mae, struggling to lift her head from the pillow, wondered whether she had dreamed Pip's proposal. Had it been wishful thinking and the desire to be far away from all this? A figment of a mind pushed to the brink of hysteria? Well, there wasn't time to dwell on it now, she told herself as she pulled a clean apron, cuffs and veil from the sugar box beside her bed and joined Alice and Lizzie to cross to the mess tent for a mug of tea and hopefully a slice of bread.

The first streaks of dawn were spreading across the sky and the breeze coming off the sea was fresh and smelled of salt as they made their way towards the marquee where the wounded were taken initially. There were still vehicles at the gate, some stationary, some arriving, some departing, taking those men not considered too dangerously ill to be moved to the ships which would take them across the Channel to hospitals which could care for them properly and in better conditions.

Mae looked for Pip and with a sigh of relief she caught sight of him. 'Go on ahead, I'll catch you up,' she instructed Alice.

'Don't be long or she'll murder you, don't forget she's had no sleep at all,' Alice replied. She hadn't had the chance to meet Pip Middlehurst properly but he was a handsome enough lad she thought as she walked on, and she supposed the history between Mae and Harry wasn't his fault.

'How are you? Have you had any rest, Mae?' Pip asked with concern. All he'd managed was half an hour slumped over the steering wheel as they'd waited for the next train to arrive. She still looked drained but he noted the clean parts of her uniform.

'I got two hours' sleep and I'll be fine now but . . . but did I dream it, did I imagine . . . ?'

He grinned at her. 'No, Mae, you didn't imagine it; it wasn't a dream. You promised to marry me and despite everything, I've never felt happier in my life. I love you.'

Happiness surged through her as she smiled at him. She could cope with whatever the day might bring now. 'I love you too, Pip,' she said, blowing him a kiss as she turned to follow Alice.

'Will you two please start to attend to those men there who've just arrived,' Staff Nurse Thomas instructed Alice and Mae before turning to Lizzie. 'Will you come with me, please, we've patients to get ready to go down to the dockside.'

Mae bent down beside a man whose head was swathed in dirty bandages but feeling a tug on her skirt she turned. 'Oh, my God! Eddie!'

He tried to grin but was too weakened and exhausted. 'At least I made it here, Mae.'

She started to cut away the bandages around his arm. 'When did this happen, Eddie?'

'Yesterday, early morning, just . . . just after . . .' Eddie gripp-ed her arm with his other hand. 'Mae, see to Jimmy, please? He's over there . . .' he begged.

As she got to her feet Mae's heart began to beat in odd little jerks. Eddie and Jimmy . . . how many more of the lads were here and in what condition? She took one look at Jimmy's prostrate form and knew he was in a far worse state than Eddie. 'Alice! Alice, here!' she called. 'It's Jimmy, Jimmy Mercer!'

Alice's face drained of what little colour it had possessed as she crossed to Mae's side. 'Oh, dear God, Jimmy!' she cried, dropping to her knees beside him.

'They were wounded yesterday morning, just after the attack began. Eddie's here, wounded in the arm, but it doesn't seem too bad,' Mae informed her.

Alice was trying hard to push aside the feelings which threatened to overcome her and had slowly and gently started to remove the filthy bandages around Jimmy's leg. 'Oh, Mae, this is bad,' she groaned, looking up at her cousin.

'Then try to get a doctor to see him, Alice, as quickly as you can. I'm going back to Eddie. At least his arm doesn't appear to be broken but it will need cleaning with Eusol, it's already infected.'

Alice had risen to her feet, her expression stricken, her eyes full of fear. 'Mae, I could smell it . . . you can't mistake that smell.'

'Then *go*, Alice!' Mae urged and Alice turned and hastily went in search of a doctor.

Mae went back to Eddie. 'This is going to hurt, Eddie, but it's got to be done. Those bits of shrapnel have to come out and then I'll dress it and they'll probably take you straight down to a ship. We've not enough room here. Think about that, Eddie, while I see to your arm. Concentrate on all the . . . comforts you'll have when you get to Blighty.' She began to clean the yellow pus from the wound and Eddie groaned. 'Sorry, sorry, Eddie,' she said, gritting her own teeth as she worked. He must be in agony and she had nothing to give him to help ease the pain.

'Will Jimmy be going home too, Mae?'

'Not just yet but . . . but later on . . . probably,' she replied, hoping it would be true.

'Jimmy and me were lucky, Mae. Harry and Tommy . . . won't . . . won't be going home.'

Mae closed her eyes for an instant. She'd seen so much of death these past days, weeks and months that she should be used to it, but she'd grown up with Harry and she knew he'd loved her. 'Oh, poor Tommy and . . . Harry! I wish I'd never sent that letter, Eddie. I feel so guilty now. I never wanted him to die believing—'

'I . . . I've got something to tell you, Mae,' Eddie interrupted. 'Harry . . . he never got that letter. I've got it. I kept it from him. It . . . it's in my pocket.'

Mae looked at him in disbelief. Then she managed a bitter smile. 'So . . . so he never knew?'

Eddie shook his head.

'Thank you, Eddie. Will you destroy it for me?'

Eddie nodded and then winced as Mae resumed dressing his wound. She'd be overcome by the grief later, she knew, but at least poor Harry had died believing she still cared for him and that she was his 'girl'. She remembered too waving to Tommy as he'd marched past her that day on Lime Street. Seventeen years old and lying dead on some patch of shell-blasted earth. She shook her head and continued with her work. There was nothing else she could do now. She told herself working to help Eddie and the other men around her was what she should fix her mind on.

Alice finally found a doctor who wasn't too preoccupied to listen to her pleas. 'Where is the lad, Nurse?' he asked, turning from the patient he'd just finished attending.

'Over here, sir. I'm sure I could smell gas gangrene. He suffered the wound early yesterday morning; it's taken this long to get him here. I know it's wrong of me, sir, but . . . but I grew up with him. He's . . . special,' Alice confided.

There was no mistaking the affection in her tone, he thought. She wasn't being very professional but then she looked very young, far too young even to be here at all. He frowned. No younger than some of the lads he'd treated these last hours. 'Let's see what we can do for him then,' he replied firmly.

He too could smell it even before he gently examined the lad's leg. 'You were right, Nurse. I'll operate now.' He looked directly at Jimmy, whose face was a mask of pain and dirt but whose eyes were wide with fear. 'I'm sorry, lad, but I'm going to have to amputate it, otherwise you'll not survive.'

Alice bent and took his hand. 'You won't feel anything, Jimmy, I promise. We'll give you something to make you sleep. You . . . you can't die, Jimmy. Not after everything you've been through. You'll be all right.'

Through the haze of agony that seemed to have clogged his mind for days a sudden shaft of terror penetrated and he gripped her hand tightly. They were going to cut off his leg! 'Alice, Alice! Stay with me! Don't leave me!' he begged.

'Hush now, lad,' the doctor instructed firmly as he signalled for the orderlies to carry the lad to be operated on.

'I'm here, Jimmy. I'll look after you. You'll soon be going home,' Alice soothed, still holding his hand tightly and forcing back her tears. 'I'll look after you, Jimmy, I promise. I'll always look after you.'

She suddenly realised that Staff Nurse Thomas was beside them. 'I don't think it will be a very good idea for you to stay with him while the Surgeon Major amputates. You're too . . . involved.' She had come over to assist and had recognised the lad Alice had visited each day last time he'd been here.

Alice couldn't stop the tears now. 'But I promised him! I promised him! Please at least let me stay until the chloroform takes effect? He's terrified,' she pleaded.

The staff nurse looked pointedly at the medical officer, who nodded curtly. 'All right, but then there are other patients in urgent need of attention.'

Alice nodded and dashed her hand across her eyes. 'Will I be able to see him . . . after . . . and before he's sent home?'

Emily Thomas felt a grudging respect for the girl who, over these last frantic terrible hours, had shown a strength of character and a level of competence she'd not expected, for she was certain that the girl was a lot younger than she purported to be. 'Of course, now pass me the mask and the chloroform, Nurse.'

Alice was so thankful to be allowed to stay with Jimmy that it was a while before she realised that Staff Nurse Thomas had for the first time addressed her as 'Nurse'.

When Jimmy had succumbed to the anaesthetic Emily Thomas passed the instruments to the surgeon major for what seemed to her like the thousandth time in twenty-four hours. He took them and looked down at the mangled, gangrenous limb. 'This isn't surgery, Nurse. God help us, this is . . . butchery!' he said bitterly.

'But he'll live, sir,' she replied.

It was six hours before Mae saw her cousin again; they'd both been given ten minutes to get a drink and something to eat. Again, they were both weary, hungry and blood-spattered.

'How is Jimmy?' Mae asked, gulping down a mouthful of tea.

'They've taken his leg off above the knee. Surgeon Major Fawcett said he'll recover, thank God, and if he doesn't haemorrhage they're sending him back tonight. He'll be better off in a hospital at home. They let me stay until he went under the anaesthetic – poor lad, he was terrified. How is our Eddie?'

'He's going home in about an hour. If the wound is kept clean he should be all right – in time.'

Alice nodded thankfully, feeling guilty now that she hadn't even seen her brother let alone done anything to help him. Jimmy had been her only concern.

'Eddie carried him on his back all the way to the dressing station and then on to the clearing station because there were no stretchers.'

Alice shook her head and whispered, 'My God! He deserves a medal.'

'He probably saved his life, Alice. But . . . but he told me that Harry and Tommy Mitford were killed. He said Jimmy stayed with Harry until . . . he died. Poor, poor Harry.' Mae told her how Eddie had kept her letter from Harry.

'He really shouldn't have done that, Mae. I think it's probably an offence but maybe it was for the best. It's better that Harry died still thinking . . . Oh, Mae, how many more of the lads we knew are dead now?' Alice asked with a sob in her voice, understanding Mae's feelings of guilt and loss.

'I don't know, Alice. I don't think *anyone* knows *anything*, it all seems so . . . chaotic, but at least when Eddie gets home he'll be able to tell Aunty Agnes about . . . Harry.'

'I'll write to her, Mae, if we ever get any time off again. I can tell her I was with Jimmy. It's the least I can do,' Alice replied quietly, feeling the weight of sadness in her heart for all her childhood friends who would never walk the streets of Liverpool again.

The news from France had been good, according to the newspapers, Maggie thought as she tidied away the few dishes she'd used for her evening meal. She missed both the girls and Eddie; the house always seemed too quiet and far too tidy.

'FORWARD IN THE WEST', 'START OF A GREAT ATTACK', 'FIERCE BATTLES ON THE SOMME' the headlines in all the newspapers had proclaimed last week.

Both she and Agnes had prayed that at last there would be some hope of the war coming to an end – and soon. She'd go over to see Agnes, she thought; she was having a bit of a hard time with old Mrs Webster who was getting quarrelsome as well as forgetful now.

It was a lovely evening, she mused as she crossed to the shop. The street still held the warmth of the day but the fierce heat had gone with the slowly setting sun. It would be a good time to take a stroll on the waterfront, she thought. She might even suggest it, give her friend an hour or so away from the ever-present chores and concerns of daily life.

There was no sign of either Agnes's mother or young Lucy when she entered the kitchen. She assumed Bertie was closing up the shop for his wife for Agnes was sitting at the kitchen table just staring ahead. She hadn't even turned her head and Maggie realised instantly that something was wrong.

'Agnes, luv, is your mam all right? Where's Lucy?' she asked in concern. Then she saw them. Two small buff-coloured envelopes lying on the table. 'Oh, Agnes, no! No! Not . . . both . . .' She couldn't go on.

Slowly Agnes shook her head and turned towards Maggie, who gasped aloud at the pain in her friend's eyes. 'Just . . . just Harry. Jimmy . . .' She pushed the envelopes across the table.

The lettering was so stark, Maggie thought. 'REGRET INFORM YOU PRIVATE HENRY MERCER 18TH KINGS LIVERPOOL KILLED IN ACTION 1ST JULY'. Poor Harry, such a nice lad, and he'd been sweet on Mae; she'd known that and both she and Agnes had had hopes that one day they might have married, but those hopes had been dashed now. She opened the other telegram. Jimmy had been wounded but had been shipped home. She grasped at this straw. 'Agnes, luv, you'll be able to go to see Jimmy. He'll be in a hospital down south somewhere; they'll let you know and I'll come with you, luv.'

'Maggie, I can't . . . I can't take it in. My boys! My poor boys!'

Maggie gathered her in her arms and held her as the first of so many tears finally flowed. 'I know, Agnes, it's the shock. You let it all out, luv.'

* * *

Maggie stayed until it was dark and Bertie came in. She could see by his face that he was crushed by grief. He'd been walking, just walking, he told her, and it reminded her forcefully of the way her brother John had walked the city streets the night he'd learned that Beth had died. 'Everyone has to cope in their own way, Bertie. I'm . . . I'm heartbroken for you all, but Jimmy has survived and you'll be able to go to see him and then . . . then you'll have him home.' She was struggling to find something optimistic to say.

He nodded.

'Where's Lucy and Agnes's mam? Do they . . . know?' she asked hesitantly.

Again he nodded. 'Lucy's with my sister and Ma-in-law's upstairs – asleep. Agnes had some laudanum, I . . . I gave her a few drops. I . . . I don't think she really understands, Maggie, her mind . . .'

'Maybe that's a blessing in disguise, Bertie. Will I make a fresh pot of tea for you?' she asked, thinking that Agnes should take a few drops of the laudanum too; at least she would sleep and find a bit of respite from her grief for a few hours.

'I'll do it, Maggie. I have to do . . . something.'

She could understand that and so after yet another cup of tea, and feeling that she could do nothing more for them that night, she went home feeling heartsore and very weary.

When she saw it lying on the floor in the lobby she stared at it in horror. The lad must have delivered it while she was with Agnes. Vividly she recalled the last time she'd received a telegram. Alice had been with her when she'd opened it but now . . . now she was alone. She picked it up and leaned back against the door she had just closed.

247

Would she see those same stark disjointed words? She tore it open before she had time to dwell on it further and then she let out a sharp cry of pure relief. Eddie wasn't dead. He'd been wounded and shipped back. Over and over she thanked God for sparing him, for sparing her the grief that was tearing her friend apart. By now Eddie would be in one of those hospitals she had promised to accompany Agnes to; they hadn't said how badly he'd been wounded, of course, but they hadn't said 'seriously' or 'dangerously' or 'fatally' or any such words that would cause her to panic. No, she was fortunate. He'd survived for a second time and for that she'd go down on her knees every day of her life and thank God.

Chapter Twenty-Three

IN THE WEEKS AHEAD, as the offensive continued, slowly their workload had decreased and some semblance of normality had returned, Mae thought as she accompanied the medical officer and Sister Harper on the ward rounds. Once again they were getting their one afternoon off per fortnight, which allowed her to meet Pip. The relationship between them had changed; it was much stronger and closer now because of the shared bond of those first terrible days of the Somme, and she had at last written to Maggie telling her that she had agreed to become Pip's wife when the war was over. In reply she had received a rather cautiously worded letter, from which she had gathered that Maggie hadn't received the news joyfully, very probably because she'd assumed Mae's feelings for Harry had been deeper than they actually had been. When she'd shown it to Alice, her cousin had advised her not to take too much notice of her mam; she'd had rather a lot to contend with of late with the worry of Eddie and Jimmy being wounded and the shock and grief of Harry and Tommy being killed. Despite this she'd even made the effort to go and see Tommy's mam.

Alice had finally met Pip properly as the weeks had gone by. At first she had been a little cool and reserved with him but Lizzie had urged her not to let her feelings colour her judgement for Mae loved him and had agreed to marry him. She'd found that after the first few minutes she felt easier and acknowledged to herself that she liked him. Whatever Harry had felt for Mae had been buried with him and as Lizzie had said, no blame could be apportioned to Pip. She'd become close to Lizzie for she found her advice sound and sensible. Despite the difference in their backgrounds, they had much in common when it came to their outlook on life.

The doctor's round being complete for the morning Sister Harper announced that she wished to see both Mae and Alice in her office when they'd finished the dressings.

'I wonder what we've done now?' Alice pondered aloud as they began to remove the bandages from the first of their patients.

'Or what we haven't done,' Mae added.

'Oh, well, we'll find out soon enough,' Alice said laconically.

It was almost lunchtime before they could finally keep the appointment and they could see that Sister Harper was harassed and not in a particularly good mood, which didn't bode well.

'I'm sorry we are so late, Sister,' Mae apologised.

'That's infinitely preferable to rushing your duties, Nurse,' Sister replied, taking a sheet of paper from the top of a pile in front of her. 'You are both due for leave, I see. As you will both understand, it hasn't been possible to let anyone go on leave lately. However, Matron has agreed that we return to the rota and you are both to have two weeks to go home. She will arrange the travel warrants. You both deserve the time off – as do all my nurses – and unless there is an unexpected development, everyone will be allowed the leave due to them.'

This came as a complete surprise to them both. Mae had been aware that the nurses were allowed leave every nine or twelve months but she'd never contemplated being given the time off in the near future and she saw Pip in what free time she did have so she didn't mind too much. Alice hadn't expected leave at all for they were still very busy and at the end of the day they were in the middle of a war, for heaven's sake. 'Thank you, Sister, we didn't expect—' Mae began.

'When will we be able to go, Sister, please?' Alice interrupted, feeling a frisson of excitement run through her for the first time in months. Home! She'd be able to see Jimmy again – and Mam and Eddie, of course.

'Not for two more weeks, I'm afraid, but it will at least give you time to inform your families,' Sister told them.

When they left they hugged each other delightedly.

'I can't believe it, Mae! We're going home!' Alice cried, her cheeks flushed.

'Oh, a proper bed, decent meals, running water . . .'

'Tea that doesn't taste of chlorine, a hot bath! No having to wash aprons or cuffs every night,' Mae added, laughing.

'Or having to go through all our clothes and hair looking for lice. It will be heaven!'

Alice declared, 'And I'm going to shorten the damned skirts of my uniform dresses to ankle length. I'm sick to death of them catching on everything, tripping me up and getting caked in dirt. I don't care what *anyone* says or thinks, long skirts are just not practical for this kind of life.'

'I know that only too well, but are you sure it's a wise thing to do? I can't see either Matron or Sister Harper or even your mam being very understanding about it.'

Alice shrugged, and then smiled joyfully. 'But the very best thing will be being able to see how Jimmy is doing.'

Mae nodded. Alice received news regularly from Maggie on the progress of both Eddie and Jimmy's health for they were both at home now. Eddie had been taken to a hospital in Birmingham but Jimmy had been too ill to travel far and so he'd gone to one in Portsmouth, then on to a convalescent home and finally back to his family in Liverpool. He was invalided out now, but she knew there was a real possibility that Eddie would have to return in time. 'I'll have to tell Pip that I'm going, but I'm not off this week,' she said a little wistfully.

'I am, do you want me to try to see him and tell him, maybe give him a note?' Alice offered.

'Would you? I know I do see him a couple of times a week when he comes in the ambulance but we never have time to chat much then.'

'Scribble a few lines to him tonight and I'll make sure he gets it tomorrow,' Alice said firmly. She'd be writing to both her mam and Jimmy tonight with this great piece of news and would post the letters tomorrow.

The news that all the nurses were to go on leave, sooner or later, lifted the spirits of everyone. True to her word Alice, had given Mae's note to Pip so on Mae's next afternoon off he surprised her by producing a small box when they met at the Café Arc-en-ciel.

'What's this?' Mae asked, looking bemused. She hadn't expected a gift. 'A going-home present?'

He smiled. 'I guess you could call it that. When I got your note I was real pleased for you, Mae. After . . . after everything you've been through you deserve a rest, a vacation, and then I thought, Isn't it about time you got her a ring, Pip Middlehurst? You *are* my fiancée now, Mae.'

Mae opened the little box that was covered in rather faded dark blue velvet. Inside was a ring, a square-cut ruby in an antique gold setting. 'Oh, Pip, it's . . . beautiful!'

He took it out of the box and slid it on to her finger; then he reached across and kissed her. 'It's for the most beautiful nurse in France and it's the best I could find. I bought it from an acquaintance of our friend Monsieur Clari. It's antique. I didn't have much time so I enlisted his help,' he confided.

Mae studied the ring on her finger and felt the happiness well up inside her. She was indeed now his fiancée and this beautiful ring would pronounce that fact to the world.

'I've never had anything as beautiful or as expensive as this before, Pip,' she said, her eyes bright with tears of joy. 'The only jewellery I have is the watch Da brought me from New York, which I cherish, but I'll cherish this so much too.'

Before Pip could reply Monsieur Clari appeared with a bottle of his best wine. 'We make a *célébration, oui?* For the *fiançailles*.'

Mae beamed up at him. 'Oh, Monsieur, *merci, merci*! It is so . . . *aimable* . . . !'

He beamed back as he poured the wine, delighted to have been involved in the procurement of the ring. 'Much . . . happy . . . to you . . .' His command of English then failed so he handed them each a glass carefully.

'To *ma belle fiancée*!' Pip said, touching his glass to hers. 'I'll miss you while you're away.'

'I won't be away for very long and I'll think of you all the time. I wish you could come with me, Pip.'

'I do too, but one day, Mae, we'll be together – always.'

Monsieur Clari had lost the gist of the conversation but had informed his other customers of the importance of the occasion and now the happy couple were toasted loudly and enthusiastically by the clientele, urged on by the café proprietor, for after all there wasn't much to celebrate in life these days, he thought. Except perhaps that he was alive and still had his café and pleasant, friendly young customers like these two.

Alice exclaimed in open admiration at the ring when Mae returned to the hospital, but before returning to her duties Mae had reluctantly taken it off and replaced it in its box, knowing there would be very few occasions when she could wear it here.

'At least you'll be able to have it on all the time when we go home,' Alice had reminded her. Mae couldn't wait.

Maggie had been delighted when she'd heard the news and had given the house a thorough going-over – especially the girls' bedroom – for the occasion. She'd scoured the shops for the ingredients to bake a cake and for the meals she intended to cook for them – for the Lord alone knew what kind of food they had to manage on, she'd told the various shopkeepers – and she was at Lime Street Station eagerly and impatiently waiting when their train pulled in.

'Mam! Oh, Mam! It's great to be back!' Alice greeted her,

hugging her tightly. Everything looked just the same, she thought joyfully, delighted to be home.

Mae greeted her in a similar fashion and then Maggie looked at them closely.

'You've lost weight, both of you, and you look worn out,' she announced.

Alice laughed. 'I don't know about the weight but we're ready for a decent meal and a good night's sleep in a proper bed, Mam.'

Maggie tutted and shook her head as she ushered them towards the station exit. 'I've a good meal waiting and then you can tell me all your news.'

'How's Eddie?' Mae asked as they emerged into Lime Street in the warmth of the early September evening. The familiar sight of St George's Hall reminded her of the day the lads had marched to the station, a memory tinged now with sadness.

'Coming on fine. I hardly recognised him when I saw him in that hospital in Birmingham. He was so thin, pale, weak and exhausted but he's looking much better now.'

'And Jimmy?' Alice asked, wondering how soon she could go across to Agnes's to see him.

'Much better now that he's home. You can go and see for yourself later on. I know he and Agnes will be glad to see you. She . . . she's still in a bit of a state about Harry.'

'She must be,' Mae added sadly. 'We were all very upset. Did Eddie tell you . . . much?' she asked tentatively.

'Not a great deal. Neither of them will talk about it all, so I expect to get more details from you two,' Maggie replied firmly.

The two girls exchanged glances. 'We only know what Eddie told us about the battle, Mam. We were miles away,' Alice said.

'But did he tell you that he carried Jimmy on his back all the way to the dressing station? He almost certainly saved his life,' Mae informed her aunt.

'No, he didn't tell me that. All he said was they'd promised to look out for each other and they did, but that he was so relieved when he saw you both at the hospital.'

'I think he deserves a medal and I really do hope he gets one,' Alice added. 'But don't say anything to him about it if he hasn't mentioned it. Quick! Here's a tram. Let's get home. I'm starving,' she added, urging them hastily towards the tram stop.

They'd both declared it was the best meal they'd had since they'd left home and had almost gone into raptures over the first pot of tea Maggie had made.

'You've no idea what the tea tastes like, Mam. All the water has chlorine added to it for health reasons,' Alice had informed her mother, who had grimaced at the very thought.

They were both also relieved to see that Eddie was in much improved health and spirits.

'You certainly look a lot better than the last time I saw you both, much cleaner and tidier,' he'd greeted them, 'and out of those uniforms you look more . . . normal.'

'You always did have a nice way with words, Eddie, always ready with a compliment,' Alice had replied sarcastically, although her words were softened by her smile.

'You can go over with your sister to Agnes's,' Maggie instructed him as she cleared the table, for she could tell Alice was impatient to see Jimmy and she hadn't failed to notice the ring on Mae's finger and wanted to find out all about it.

'No, I'll go for a bit of a walk, Mam, it's a fine evening and our Alice won't want me playing gooseberry,' Eddie said to her. He hadn't seen Jimmy so animated or cheerful before, not until they'd learned that the girls were coming home on leave. He knew Jimmy was very fond of Alice. When he'd rejoined the battalion his pal hadn't stopped talking about her. How much she'd grown up, what a great nurse she was, how she'd visited him every day, how they'd walked by the sea; the lads had often ribbed him over it.

'Suit yourself, son,' Maggie replied, thinking that maybe Jimmy would open up more to Alice about his experiences than he had to either of his parents. The fact that he didn't worried them both.

When Alice and Eddie had gone Maggie sat down opposite her niece. 'So, I see he's bought you a very nice ring, Mae.'

Mae smiled at her; she'd had a good idea that this interrogation was coming. 'It's beautiful, isn't it? It's antique and French.'

Maggie nodded. 'And no doubt expensive, but are you sure about marrying him, Mae? It's a very big decision.'

'I'm sure, Aunty Maggie. I love him. I never loved poor Harry, even though I knew he was fond of me. I liked him a lot, of course, he was like a brother or a cousin, but I didn't give him any false hopes.'

'Both Agnes and I hoped, Mae, that you and Harry—'

'I couldn't have married Harry, Aunty Maggie,' Mae interrupted her. 'I just didn't love him. He was a thoroughly nice, kind, quiet lad. Alice was really angry with me when she found out I was seeing Pip.'

'Indeed?' Maggie hadn't known this. 'Doesn't she like him?'

'Yes, she does.'

'Well, at least your da would have been happy with your choice, Mae. He told me that although he had nothing against Harry, he wanted better for you. I think he'd be quite pleased with the son of a Boston lawyer, but are you sure it wasn't anything to do with being so far away from home or being caught up in the middle of all that . . . chaos and suffering?' She didn't want her niece to make the same mistake she'd made, she thought, remembering Billy McEvoy.

'No, I'd fallen in love with him long before that but sharing those . . . awful days brought us closer together. You'll like him, Aunty Maggie, I know you will. Of course he comes from a very different background, his family are quite well off and he went to one of the finest universities in America, but he's not a bit snobbish.'

'And you do realise, Mae, that when you marry him you'll be starting a new life on the other side of the Atlantic Ocean?'

Mae nodded and smiled. 'Yes, but it takes less than a week to cross now and Boston isn't too far from New York.'

Maggie had to concede this and in fact her doubts were receding for Mae wasn't impulsive or impetuous. 'Well, the lad did volunteer to come over and drive an ambulance even though his country isn't involved in the fighting – although there are a lot of people here who think they should be. That shows courage and decency.'

'I know it's selfish of me but for Pip's sake I hope they stay out of it. We don't intend to get married until all the fighting is over, Aunty Maggie, and who knows when that will be?'

'Soon, I pray, please God. I could weep every time I see Agnes and their poor Jimmy. Twenty years old and a cripple and his brother in his grave long before his time.'

'I know, Aunty Maggie. Alice and I have seen enough misery to last a lifetime,' Mae replied sadly. 'Which is why I don't want Pip to have to fight.' She decided that this train of thought was becoming too sombre and depressing so she smiled. 'Shall we have another cup of your wonderful tea? It tastes even better than the wine Monsieur Clari gave us when Pip gave me the ring. I'll tell you all about that day.'

Alice had embraced a tearful Agnes and Lucy and had smiled happily at Jimmy as she sat down beside him. 'I'm so glad to be home, Jimmy, even if it's not for very long. How are you getting on? Mam's written giving me a progress report on both you and our Eddie, who appears to be making a complete recovery.'

Jimmy had been filled with a sense of happiness when she'd come in. He'd been looking forward to seeing her again for there was a lot he had to say to her, but at the mention of Eddie's recovery he felt some of it fade. 'They'll send him back again, Alice.'

She nodded. 'I know, Jimmy. There's no end in sight but at least it's all over now for you,' she said quietly.

Agnes decided that it would be better to leave them to talk; they shared some of the experiences which Jimmy refused to discuss but which tormented his dreams – perhaps Alice could help him in that respect. 'Lucy, luv, will you take your gran up a cup of tea and then come and help me and your da to close up the shop,' she instructed.

Jimmy flashed a grateful glance at his mother; he knew she too wanted to speak to Alice for her grief was still raw and had been increased by the news that Mae was engaged to an

American. He knew his mam had hoped for Mae as a daughter-in-law.

'I've been looking forward so much to seeing you again, Alice—' he started tentatively.

'We don't have to talk about it if you don't want to, Jimmy,' she interrupted gently, placing a hand on his arm.

'I . . . I want to, Alice. I want to thank you for everything you did . . .'

'Our Eddie did far more than me, Jimmy.'

He nodded. 'I know. If it hadn't been for Eddie I'd have died and I've told him I can never repay him for that.'

'He knows that, but you would have done the same for him, Jimmy. I really didn't do much, it was Surgeon Major Fawcett's skill that saved you.'

'But you stayed with me, Alice.' He took her hand in his as he remembered how dark and terrifying his world had been that day.

She managed a wry smile. 'I nearly had a stand-up fight with Staff Nurse Thomas to stay, but I'd promised I'd look after you. I had to leave though when they . . . operated, even though I didn't want to. I'd seen a lot of cases like yours so I wasn't going to faint. But she was right, I was too involved, too close to you, and there were so many other men and boys needing help. You've no idea how many there were, Jimmy – thousands – and we just couldn't cope in the end. We couldn't even put clean dressings on their wounds before we had to ship them out.' She paused. 'But at least I managed to see you afterwards.'

He told her slowly, 'After . . . after you left me and they took me to the ship, everything was still confused . . . the pain . . . the shock . . . but we were packed like sardines on that ship, Alice.

There wasn't an empty space on the deck and I . . . I realised just how many . . .'

'I know, Jimmy. Don't dwell on it. It's all behind you now.'

'I can't help it, Alice. Often during the day . . . it all goes away, but at night . . . our Harry and Tommy and . . . the noise and the . . . agony . . .' He broke down despite himself.

Alice took him in her arms and held him tightly, tears stinging her own eyes, How she wished she could take away some of his grief and pain. 'It will get better, Jimmy. The memories won't seem as bad . . . in time. Just think how lucky you are. You'll be able to get around soon. They'll fit you with an artificial limb so you won't need the crutches and you'll never have to go back to face it all again.' Unlike her poor brother, she thought bitterly. Twice they'd sent Eddie back now. Would he survive a third time?

Jimmy seized on her words as a lifeline and began to calm down. 'I know, Alice. I'm . . . sorry. Damned fool blubbering like a baby.'

'You've nothing to apologise for, Jimmy. Those . . . experiences have driven some men mad. Oh, officially it's not supposed to exist, we're never to even utter the words, but we all know, even the medical officers, that it's a condition called "shell shock". You have nothing to be ashamed of! You served your King and Country to the best of your ability – and I'd say far beyond that.'

'But you'll have to go back, Alice,' he reminded her, wishing she could stay with him.

She nodded. 'I will, but we're not in any danger and I've got lots of time before then.'

261

'I'll be much better now, Alice. You being here will help me get over . . . things.'

She smiled at him. 'I'm glad, Jimmy, really I am. I'll come and see you every day,' she promised. 'I said I'd look after you – remember?'

'And you did,' he said, feeling cheered, for her words had made him realise that he wasn't a fool or a coward for breaking down in tears or waking screaming in the night.

Chapter Twenty-Four

———◆———

THE TIME HAD flown by, Mae thought as she packed her case. They were going back tomorrow. She'd enjoyed being with her family and friends and she'd definitely savoured the comforts of home that she'd always taken for granted before she'd gone to France but now appreciated so much more. Basic things such as being clean, knowing she hadn't picked up any unwelcome 'visitors', being able to appreciate unhurried meals at a proper table or sit and enjoy the luxury of reading because her day wasn't punctuated by bugle calls. But she'd missed Pip, even though he'd written to her. In his letter he told her he'd managed to get a few days' leave himself. He hadn't left Boulogne; he'd slept a great deal and enjoyed walking in the autumn sunshine by the sea. He'd caught up with his correspondence and written up his journal, which had been greatly neglected, in the relative comfort of the Café Arc-en-ciel, much to Monsieur Clari's amusement and curiosity. But he was looking forward to her return. Part of her was also looking forward to returning, but part of her wasn't.

Her musings were interrupted by the sound of Aunty Maggie's steps on the stairs.

'I've ironed these things, Mae, so try not to get them too creased,' her aunt instructed as she placed Mae's dresses and aprons on the bed.

'Thanks, I'll do my best, Aunty Maggie,' she promised.

Maggie sat down on the bed, shaking her head. 'God knows what that Sister Harper is going to say to our Alice about cutting three inches off the bottom of her dresses. Oh, I can see her reasoning about the dirt and dust and tripping over but I've a feeling there will be hell to pay. But you know our Alice, she's a self-willed little madam when she chooses to be and I told her so. "On your own head be it, miss!" I warned.'

Mae grinned. 'I don't think they'll send her home though. She'll get a dressing down – we both will – but I bet it won't be long before the other girls shorten theirs.'

Maggie tutted disapprovingly. 'You shouldn't have let her shorten yours as well, Mae.'

'I thought that if we showed a bit of solidarity it might help. Anyway, I agree with her, long skirts are nothing but a nuisance out there. Fine if you're working in a hospital that doesn't consist of tents with packed-earth floors and has lovely polished corridors instead of open compounds. And with winter coming we'll be back to contending with muddy boots.'

Maggie nodded. 'I wish there was some way I could keep our Eddie at home, Mae, I really do. I'll not have a minute's peace, I'll be worrying myself to death when they send him back and, as you say, with winter coming how will he cope in those trenches? Surely to God having to be shipped home twice is enough?'

'I know, Aunty Maggie. It's very hard on him, on all of them.'

'I never dreamed that we'd have to endure a third Christmas with them still fighting. No one did. Will you try to keep an eye on him, Mae, if you possibly can?'

'If he's sent to the front-line trenches, all I can do is write to him, Aunty Maggie. They do take the mail and parcels up the line. But I'll enquire regularly about what the battalion is doing and where it is. Has he said anything about going back?' She remembered very well the fear in his eyes when she'd seen him that day in Boulogne last time he'd been sent back.

'No, but I know he's dreading it. He goes very quiet whenever anything is mentioned,' Maggie confided. She didn't blame him. He'd lost a lot of his mates, he'd been wounded and had seen and endured God alone knew what horrors. She'd tried to imagine what he'd gone through the day Harry and Tommy Mitford had been killed and what he'd endured as he'd carried Jimmy all that way, but she knew that beside the actuality anything she could hope to imagine probably paled into insignificance.

Mae sighed. 'I suppose it's only to be expected. I can't say I fancy the journey back myself. I just hope there won't be much of a wind blowing across the Channel.'

Maggie got to her feet. 'Well, I'll be sending him back with plenty of socks and warm clothes. Come down when you've finished packing and we'll have a cup of tea. Our Alice should be back by then, she hasn't finished her packing yet.'

Mae grimaced. 'After tomorrow it's back to tea with chlorine!'

* * *

Alice hadn't been looking forward to saying goodbye to Jimmy and his family. Both Agnes and Bertie were still very down and upset and Mrs Webster's increasingly failing health only added to Agnes's burdens. But the old lady had had a long life, Alice thought, and at least she'd die in her bed, which was more than a lot of people did these days. Lucy was growing up and although she was obviously affected by her brother's death she seemed to be coping with it.

'Well, this time tomorrow Mae and I will be back to the luxury of General Camp Hospital Number Twenty-four, Jimmy,' Alice joked. 'I really can't say I've missed it much.'

'It'll be getting cold now, Alice. Do you have any kind of heating?' Jimmy asked. His stay there had been very brief; it had been summer and he'd been too ill to notice much.

'Stoves. They're not bad but it's not like being in a warm cosy house,' she replied, glancing around Agnes's comfortable, tidy kitchen. 'But we manage – it's a case of having to,' she added brightly, knowing they were far more fortunate than the men in the trenches.

'You will write to me, Alice?' Jimmy asked earnestly. He didn't want her to go; she'd brought hope and happiness into his life – and he loved her.

'Of course I will – and you let me know how you are managing and when you're getting your new leg. When I get home next time I expect to see you striding about –and without crutches, mind.'

Jimmy nodded. It had been decided that when he was able, he would take over in the shop from his mam. Agnes would help, of course, but he would be in charge. It wasn't the same as going out to work with his mates, the way he'd done before the war, but he had to do something, he'd told Alice. He couldn't sit here all day feeling sorry for himself. 'Do you think you'll get leave again soon?' he asked hopefully.

Alice shrugged. 'I doubt it will be soon. Even if there are no further battles it won't be for months – there are plenty of others who haven't had leave yet.'

'The brass don't seem to think there's anything to be gained by mounting any big pushes in winter, going by the last couple of years,' Jimmy mused.

'Then I hope they've informed the Boche,' Alice said rather cuttingly. 'It would make everyone's life a lot easier.' She sighed. 'I won't be home for Christmas, I know that. It'll be my first Christmas away from home but I'll have Mae and Lizzie and the others.' She got to her feet. 'I'd best be getting back, I haven't finished packing yet.'

Jimmy, with the aid of his crutches, got up too. Alice made no attempt to help him, knowing he would have to come to terms with and learn to cope with his disability.

'Take care of yourself, Alice, and come home . . . safe,' he said awkwardly.

She hugged his parents and sister and then turned to him. 'Come on then, you can see me to the door.'

She slowed her steps to match his and when she reached the door to the street she stopped. 'You'll get stronger each day, Jimmy, and you'll know that I'm thinking of you and worrying about you.'

He swallowed hard. He *had* to tell her before she went away. 'Alice . . . I want to say something. I . . . I know I'm a cripple now but I . . . I love you.'

She smiled, and reached her hand out to his. She'd been

longing to hear him say those words. 'I love you too, Jimmy, and I don't think of you as a cripple, I never will. I'm just so grateful that you're alive and not paralysed or blinded or gassed.'

He felt relief and happiness rush through him but then sadness that she was going. 'I don't want you to go, Alice, I don't want to lose you.'

'I have to go, Jimmy, to help other lads like you, and you won't lose me. I told you I'd always look after you and I meant "always". There won't be anyone else for me, Jimmy Mercer, and that's the truth.' She reached up and put her arms around his neck and kissed him. Someday she'd come back to him for good. When the war was over she'd come back and they'd be together and they'd be happy.

Jimmy smiled as he watched her cross the street. Life looked infinitely better now, he thought. She was the dearest, kindest and bravest girl he'd ever known even if she was only seventeen.

Next morning they were all up early and as a treat Maggie cooked them bacon and egg and fried bread. 'You've a long journey ahead of you, you need a good breakfast, and you still need building up, Eddie,' she said firmly as she placed the plates in front of them. 'And I've made sandwiches for you to take with you,' she added.

'Savour every mouthful, Alice, it's back to mess food and terrible tea tomorrow,' Mae said, grimacing.

'Aye, make the most of it,' Eddie added, forcing a grin. He only expected to be home for another couple of weeks now but having them both here had made him forget the war – sometimes. At least Alice's presence had cheered Jimmy up no end.

'As soon as you hear . . . anything, Eddie, will you let us

know?' Mae asked, remembering her promise to Maggie. 'You know where we will be but we'll have no idea where you'll be.'

Eddie agreed. He'd be going wherever the 18th Battalion was but there wouldn't be many of his mates left in it now. 'You give my regards to that feller of yours, Mae. Those lads do a great job.'

Mae smiled at him. 'I will, Eddie.'

'What will he be to us two when you get married, Mae?' Alice asked to lighten the conversation for she'd seen the worried look on her mam's face and she knew Eddie was doing his utmost to put a brave front on things.

Mae thought about this. 'Cousin-in-law, I suppose. I haven't really thought about it.'

Alice sighed as she finished her meal. 'At least you'll be able to spend some time with him at Christmas. All I'll be able to do is send Jimmy a card and some small gift.'

Mae nodded as she digested this. It would be the first Christmas she too would spend away from home but also the first she would spend with Pip, and she was so looking forward to seeing him again, although it probably wouldn't be for another couple of days.

Eddie said nothing. He didn't want to think about where he would be this Christmas. He was the only one left of their little group who would be in France for Christmas this year. Of course Harry and Tommy were there, in one of the military cemeteries that now lined the coast, ever-increasing fields of white crosses that faced the sea – and home. But they were never coming home.

* * *

They were both tired and travel-stained when they finally arrived in Boulogne at the end of a rough crossing, although neither of them had actually been sick, Mae thought thankfully as they disembarked from the Channel steamer. It was dark and there was a sharpness in the tangy air now which foretold of colder days ahead.

'I never thought I'd say it, but I'll actually be glad to get back to the hospital,' Alice announced as she struggled with her case and her hat, which she hadn't pinned securely enough and was now threatening to blow off in the stiff breeze.

'I'm just glad to get back on dry land. That was worse than the Mersey ferry in a gale in winter,' Mae added, pulling the collar of her jacket up around her neck as she followed Alice.

'Isn't that your Pip over there, Mae?' Alice cried, pointing and feeling greatly pleased as she spotted the ambulance and the tall figure now heading towards them.

'Welcome back, ladies! No need to try to hitch a ride. I managed to persuade them to let me have half an hour off. It's great to see you, Mae. I've missed you so much,' Pip greeted them both, putting his arm around Mae and kissing her cheek.

'Oh, I didn't expect to see you tonight, Pip, but I'm so glad you're here!' Mae was both delighted and relieved. 'I've missed you but I did enjoy being home.'

'What we didn't enjoy was the crossing on that flaming ship. You wouldn't think such a short stretch of water could be so rough!' Alice shuddered.

'Give me those cases and I'll put them in the back. At least you can ride the rest of the way in some comfort,' Pip instructed as he shepherded them towards the ambulance.

Mae felt utterly content as she sat next to him with Alice

squeezed in beside her on the front seat. It was as if she wasn't . . . complete without him.

'Our friend Monsieur Clari thinks you've left me,' Pip joked to Mae.

'You did explain that I'd only gone on leave?' she asked earnestly.

Pip laughed. 'Darling Mae, you are delightful! Of course I did. There's a good bottle of wine waiting for us on our next visit, to welcome you back.'

Mae smiled. 'He's very kind.'

'He certainly seems to have taken a liking to the pair of you,' Alice stated. 'Though personally I'd sooner have a decent cup of tea.'

Both Pip and Mae chuckled. In a strange way she really was glad she was back, Mae thought. Meanwhile, Alice was peering at what little of the road ahead she could see in the headlights and wondering what kind of reception awaited her tomorrow morning when she reported for duty in a dress that showed her ankles.

Chapter Twenty-Five

'**M**AE SAID WE were mad to go all that way for a decent afternoon tea,' Alice confided to Lizzie as they arrived back in Boulogne one afternoon in mid-October.

'But it certainly was worth it,' Lizzie said with satisfaction. They'd heard that the Pré Catelan further up the coast, actually served full English-style afternoon teas with unchlorinated water, cream and even jam for the scones and so they'd organised a lift there and back on their afternoon off.

'It was absolutely delicious!' Alice enthused. 'Although it was a bit pricy and I don't think we'd be as lucky with our lift in future, so we won't be doing it regularly.' The whole area was now a vast military zone so there was always the chance of a lift in some type of vehicle.

'I thought it was very good of Surgeon Major Fawcett to give us a lift in a staff car no less, even though Matron would kill us if she knew,' Lizzie added, for nurses were forbidden to be seen out in the company of any officer. The wounded officers had their own wards, separate from NCOs and other ranks, for the rigid class system even extended to the field hospitals.

'We did tell him it was a special treat as it was your birthday, Lizzie, and mine in a few weeks, and he was intending to drive up the coast anyway this afternoon to visit a Canadian doctor friend.'

'That wouldn't have cut any ice with Matron, Alice, and you know it. We're still in her very bad books over the length of our skirts.'

Alice nodded. Both she and Mae had been severely castigated by Sister and Matron over that – Matron had been furious and utterly scandalised and had actually called them 'immoral' – but it hadn't taken long before Lizzie and two other girls had shortened theirs. It was just so much easier to work. She grinned. 'But it was greatly appreciated by the patients, Lizzie.'

Lizzie laughed. Although she was six years older than Alice, Lizzie admired her tenacity.

'Well, if a glimpse of a couple of inches of black woollen stocking can make them feel better, after what they've been through, I don't see the harm in it. And we'll have to start thinking about what we can do to cheer them up for Christmas. It's not all that far away.' They'd reached the entrance to one of the big yards where the horses and mules used to transport supplies and ammunition up the lines of trenches were stabled, and Lizzie frowned, catching sight of a soldier waving frantically at them. 'Do you know that chap, Alice? I think he's coming over to us.'

Alice peered intently into the yard and then her eyes widened. 'It's our Eddie! What on earth is he doing in *there*?'

'Alice, I was going to get a note to you, to let you know I'm stationed here now.' Eddie pointed over his shoulder into the yard, grinning broadly.

'What are you doing?' Alice asked, still surprised at seeing him.

'I've been transferred. I'm not going back to the battalion – not yet anyway. They've been amalgamated into another division and they were very short-handed here, and maybe someone somewhere thought it was time I deserved a change.'

'But you don't know one end of a horse from the other!' Alice exclaimed.

'I'm learning,' Eddie shot back.

A sergeant wearing a leather farrier's apron over his uniform and looking decidedly grim appeared behind Eddie. 'Well, you won't learn very much standing there chatting up the girls, lad! I thought I told you when you'd finished cleaning harnesses you were to start to grease axles?'

'But this is my sister, sergeant,' Eddie explained. He was rather in awe of this Regular Army man who seemed to know everything possible about the animals he worked with.

'Oh, aye, I'm, sure!' came the frankly sceptical reply.

'I *am* his sister, sir! VAD Nurse Alice McEvoy, General Camp Hospital Twenty-four,' Alice retorted. 'And this is VAD Nurse Elizabeth Lawson, same hospital. It's our afternoon off.'

His attitude softened a little; he had the greatest respect for all the nursing staff. 'Sorry, ladies, but he's got work to do.'

'Can I just have a few more moments, Sergeant, please?' Eddie pleaded.

He nodded curtly. 'Five minutes, that's all. I want to see you hard at work after that, lad, no slacking,' he emphasised as he strode away.

Alice smiled at him, relieved. 'So they didn't send you back up the line, Eddie. Mam will be delighted to hear that.'

'I'm delighted myself, Alice. It's great here. I don't mind the work, the food isn't too bad, the other lads are showing me the ropes and best of all I've even found myself a spot up in a corner of the hayloft where it's warm and dry. It's all a damned sight better than being stuck in a dugout with nothing but bits of corrugated iron or wood to keep out the weather, especially now it's getting cold. Of course when there are supplies to be moved it's hard work, out in the rain and wind, and when the carts get bogged down in the mud, it can be tough on the animals and us, but . . .' He shrugged, thinking anything was better than being in the front-line trenches, exposed to the elements and living with the constant terror of being wounded again or . . . worse.

'And you really don't mind working with horses and mules? I'd be terrified being so close, they're so . . . unpredictable!' Lizzie confided.

Alice suddenly realised she was being remiss. 'Oh, sorry, Eddie, this is Lizzie. We've been out for afternoon tea.'

'Oh, get the pair of you!' Eddie replied but he was smiling at the dark-haired, attractive girl standing beside his sister. 'Nice to meet you, Lizzie.'

'And you, Eddie. I've heard a lot about you. Alice and Mae think you deserve a medal. I take it your arm has healed now?'

Eddie nodded, looking a bit embarrassed. 'Our Alice would think anyone who helped Jimmy Mercer deserves a medal.'

Alice ignored him. 'Knowing you, you won't have written to Mam yet so I will.'

'I've only been here a week, Alice,' Eddie protested.

Again Alice ignored him. 'And we'll be able to see you when we come into town – providing you're not moving supplies – so I can keep her informed, save her worrying.'

'I'll look forward to that, Alice,' Eddie replied, thinking he'd like to get to know Lizzie better. She looked very pleasant although she was obviously older than Alice, but then every nurse was older than his sister.

'Perhaps we can go and have coffee at that café Mae and Pip like so much,' Alice suggested.

Eddie was very doubtful. 'I don't know about that, Alice. I'm still a serving soldier and even though things are fairly quiet, the war hasn't stopped.'

'Well, there's Christmas to look forward to in the not-too-distant future. Wouldn't it be great if we could spend a bit of time together then – all of us? Mae and Pip included,' Lizzie added. Alice had never mentioned that her brother was such a handsome lad and she admired him; she thought he was very brave.

Reluctantly Eddie turned away. 'I'll have to go, I don't want to get on the wrong side of Sergeant Walker already. He might decide he can do without me.'

'You mind you stay out of the way of all those hooves,' Alice advised, smiling and waving her hand as she and Lizzie walked off.

Eddie returned to his duties, thinking himself very fortunate. It would indeed be great if at Christmas he could spend an hour with Alice and Mae and Pip and Lizzie: it would take his mind off the people who wouldn't be there this year; but even if it wasn't possible it was something to know that he'd be safe and reasonably comfortable this Christmas.

* * *

As December approached the weather worsened. Heavy frosts turned the ground iron hard and Eddie, huddled up in blankets, burrowed deeper into the hay and thanked God he was not freezing in a dugout. It was impossible for men to be kept out longer than forty-eight hours in weather such as this and in the hospitals the cases of frostbite, trench foot, severe, crippling rheumatism and bronchitis began to outnumber men wounded in the skirmishes which still took place.

Alice and Mae and the other nurses were suffering too as dense icy fogs swirled in from the Channel.

'We're all going to be exhausted again, there's so many coming in now, and I'm going down with a cold, I know.' Alice sniffed as she stood before the small stove in the tent, shivering. In addition to their duties they now had to massage their patients' badly affected feet for fifteen minutes twice every day.

'Here, put this on and then put your greatcoat over it,' Mae instructed, holding out a heavy knitted cardigan Maggie had sent.

'Thanks. This stove is useless. My front is warm but my back is frozen!' Alice complained, rubbing her chapped, numbed hands together.

'It's the men I feel so sorry for,' Mae mused, handing both her companions a mug of hot tea each. 'It doesn't seem to help much, rubbing their poor feet with oil and putting thick fishermen's socks on them, the damage has been done in the trenches. Standing for hours and hours in freezing mud, their feet soaking wet and numb with cold – and those puttees don't help, they're bound too tight and they get wet and then cut off what little circulation there is. Some of the men have lost toes with frostbite and there's one lad on ward six whose feet are just two enormous chilblains. He can't walk.'

'There's one on ward five who can't walk because he just can't feel his feet, they're totally numb, and he's not the only one,' Lizzie added.

'Oh, a fine Christmas this is going to be if it's going to stay as cold as this,' Alice said glumly.

'Come on, Alice, let's try to be cheerful,' Mae urged. 'We'll be able to decorate the wards – there's plenty of holly and stuff growing outside the villages – and there will be parcels from home.'

'I heard Sister saying that she read there's simply *tons* of stuff at the Channel ports that people at home have donated for the troops, just waiting to be shipped over,' Lizzie informed them, gratefully sipping her tea despite its taste.

'If the damned fog ever lifts,' Alice put in gloomily.

'So we should all have some home comforts. Aunty Maggie said she's sending more woollens and chocolate and shortbread. I think I'll take some of that into Monsieur Clari, I know he's very partial to it,' Mae said.

'Do you think Eddie will be able to get an hour off on Christmas Eve, Alice?' Lizzie enquired, for Mae and Pip had already asked Monsieur to save them a table and he had readily agreed. Lizzie had managed to exchange a few words with Eddie last time she and Alice had braved the weather and gone into town, and they were all looking forward to a festive couple of hours at the Café Arc-en-ciel. They'd already sought Sister's permission for the time off.

Alice forced a smile. 'I hope so. Part of me wishes Jimmy were still over here.' Then she frowned. 'On second thoughts

I'm glad he's not. He'd be stuck out there in this terrible weather. Thank God Eddie's not.'

As Christmas approached the fog lifted and the nurses, braving the severe cold, went out into the surrounding countryside to collect holly and ivy which they used to decorate the wards. The amount of food and comforts now being shipped across the Channel was staggering; crates were piled high on the dockside and everyone knew that there would be a lot more Christmas cheer this year for the troops. There was very little fighting because of the weather and the fact that the Germans had withdrawn to their heavily fortified Hindenburg Line, and apart from the discomfort the weather inflicted everyone was looking forward to the festive season.

On Christmas Eve, as the three girls set out for the town, heavily muffled against the cold, it started to snow. Pip had managed to come to pick them up and they were all thankful they wouldn't have to walk.

'Will we all fit in?' Mae asked as he kissed her on the bit of her cheek that wasn't shrouded by a thick muffler.

'I guess it will be a bit of a squeeze but we'll be okay. I just hope I can get you all back again; the snow's getting heavier and there's a strong wind behind it.'

'Oh, it shouldn't settle too much here by the coast, there's too much salt in the air,' Lizzie said airily, determined to enjoy the evening and not think about getting back or the fact that they might have to walk.

'Did you see Eddie?' Mae asked Pip, for he'd been detailed to find out if her brother had been granted leave.

'I did. He was just finishing bedding down the last of the

mules. He was going to get a wash and then walk down to the café. I think we're all looking forward to the evening. Lenny's meeting us there too; I couldn't leave him out, now could I?'

'So there will be quite a little party of us,' Lizzie said happily.

It was snowing heavily when they all trooped inside the café where Eddie and Pip's friend and companion Lenny were waiting. Mae passed over the shortbread biscuits that had come in Maggie's parcel to Monsieur and they were received with delight and effusive thanks by their host.

The café was crowded with local residents who all raised their glasses and wished them '*Joyeux Noël!*' and they reciprocated in fairly good French.

'As I might not get to see you tomorrow, Mae, I'd better give you this now,' Pip announced, taking a box from his pocket. 'Happy Christmas, darling.'

Mae smiled fondly at him while Alice and Lizzie impatiently urged her to open it. Inside the box was a gold brooch shaped as a bird with seed pearls for eyes.

'Oh, thank you, Pip! It will look lovely on the lapel of my coat,' Mae said shyly. 'I didn't know what to get you so . . . so I hope you like this.' She handed over a small packet wrapped in tissue paper. She'd racked her brains wondering what to get him but had finally found a cigarette case made of tortoiseshell, which she thought looked smart.

'Lizzie and Mae and I decided to wait until tomorrow to give each other our gifts,' Alice told Eddie as Pip thanked Mae, kissing her on the cheek. 'But I got you a good penknife; it's got a thing for taking stones out of hooves so I thought it would be very useful,' she added, passing Eddie the gift.

'And I bought you this, Eddie,' Lizzie said a little awkwardly, wondering if she wasn't being a bit too forward.

Eddie was surprised but pleased as he unwrapped Lizzie's gift. 'It's a Vesta case!' he exclaimed delightedly, examining the little carved box in which matches were kept.

'It's not ivory. The man I bought it from said he thought it's made from whalebone,' Lizzie told him.

'It's beautifully carved just the same, Lizzie, thanks. Thanks so much.' He delved into his pocket and passed her a little flat packet. 'Nothing nearly as . . . grand, but . . .'

Alice smiled at him. She knew what was in the packet: two fine lawn handkerchiefs edged with French lace – he'd asked her to buy them for him to give Lizzie. She had Jimmy's gift, which had arrived with their parcels earlier in the week, safely stored in the sugar box by her bed ready to open tomorrow morning.

'I didn't expect anything but they're beautiful, Eddie. I'll keep them for best, thanks,' Lizzie replied, thinking she wouldn't use them at all. They were far too delicate and rather special.

'And we'll be giving out a special gift to every wounded and sick man tomorrow, so Sister told me,' Alice informed them, lowering her voice a little for it wasn't supposed to be common knowledge yet. 'I've seen them. Little white cards inscribed with gold lettering – from the King himself! Saying that he and the Queen are thinking of them and are very grateful for their suffering and all the hardships, or something like that.' She intended to keep one back for Eddie. Oh, he wasn't wounded now but he had been – and after what he'd done for Jimmy, in her opinion he deserved one as a keepsake.

'Now it really does feel like Christmas!' Mae laughed, gazing around at all the happy faces. Pip had pinned the brooch to her dress and she fingered it fondly.

Pip ordered brandies for the men and wine for the girls and an old man sitting in a corner by the bar counter started to play carols on an accordion.

Pip raised his glass. 'This brandy should help keep the cold out. Cheers! Happy Christmas, everyone!'

'Let's hope that it will all be over by next Christmas,' Alice said, thinking of Jimmy.

'I'll drink to that,' Mae agreed, smiling at Pip and thinking if it was then she might well be Mrs Middlehurst next year and spending her first Christmas in Boston.

'I'll be honest, I wasn't looking forward to this Christmas at all, but, well, isn't it turning out . . . great?' Eddie said, smiling at Lizzie. 'And I've got a nice little collection of "special" things now too. My leather wallet that Uncle John brought from New York, my silver cap badge from Lord Derby, a first-class penknife and now a carved Vesta case. Aren't I a fortunate fella?' The brandy had warmed him up, the atmosphere was friendly and festive, even the snow outside added to the scene. He was amongst family and friends and Lizzie was smiling happily at him, plus he had a fairly warm and dry billet to return to. It all helped him to put aside the memory of last Christmas and of the mates he'd shared it with. He couldn't stay long but he was going to enjoy what time he did have.

The old accordion player had begun to play 'Silent Night' and they all joined in, English and French languages merging together as a beaming Monsieur refilled everyone's glasses. Looking around the room as she sang, Alice thought that if Jimmy could have been with her it would have been a really memorable Christmas Eve. Her gaze fell on her brother. Eddie would have another 'special' thing to add to his collection tomorrow – his card of thanks from King George V. She was very proud of her brother, who had proved his courage beyond doubt and definitely deserved the royal token.

Chapter Twenty-Six

A LL MEMORIES OF Christmas were long past now, Mae thought as she knelt rubbing the swollen feet of a soldier with olive oil before wrapping them in cotton wool and oiled silk to try to keep them warm and get the circulation going again. She looked up at him and smiled cheerfully but she felt so sorry for him, for them all, they bore all their sufferings with such uncomplaining fortitude. 'I'll stick a pin in and you tell me if you can feel it,' she said. It was part of the routine now.

He grinned back at her. 'If I can I'll yell so loud they'll hear me down at the harbour, Nurse. I'll know then that the feeling is coming back.'

She wiped her hands and extracted a needle from the little flannel case in her apron pocket and gently probed the white, swollen, dead flesh. There was no reaction at all.

'Well, you'll have to put up with my ministrations for a bit longer, Private Franks,' she joked to disguise the disappointment they both felt.

'I don't mind, Nurse, I'm better off here,' he replied quite cheerfully.

She supposed he was. After Christmas the weather had become really atrocious. The temperature seldom rose above freezing during the day; at night it was so cold that no one got much sleep. Thick snow and ice covered the countryside, even the beaches and sand dunes. Snow disguised the shell-pocked battlefields and lines of trenches; it covered dugouts and the hospital tents and compounds. It was the coldest winter that anyone could ever remember, so Monsieur Clari had informed them, shaking his head. The ice on the ponds and rivers was feet thick. Everyone was suffering.

It wouldn't be any warmer in their tent, she thought, for the supply of coal for the stove was now running low. Back home the miners were on strike and again, thick freezing fog had closed the Channel ports, limiting supplies of everything. Boulogne harbour was at present blocked by a ship which had sunk and that made matters worse. Rations had been reduced and comforts were very scarce: she wished they'd hoarded some of the sweets and biscuits they'd received at Christmas. Illnesses caused by exposure amongst the troops remained common and even the medical staff were falling ill. So far, luckily she, Alice and Lizzie had suffered nothing more serious than heavy colds.

'We'll try with the pin again tomorrow, Private Franks, but it will be Nurse McEvoy who'll be seeing to your feet. I've got some time off,' she informed him, preparing to move on to the next patient.

'What will you be doing, Nurse? Anything . . . interesting?'

She smiled. 'Yes, I'm going to wrap up and go for a walk with my fiancé. He's heard of an inn in the country where you can get an omelette made with fresh eggs.'

'I wish I could taste one of those, Nurse. I don't think I've ever had one,' he said.

'Neither have I, Private Franks. I'll let you know what it tastes like. Keep those feet warm,' she instructed. She was looking forward to the outing, despite the cold. It would be good to get away from the hospital for a few hours because they really didn't get much time together alone.

'I still think you are mad,' Alice said firmly as next day Mae pulled on her woollen mittens and wound a thick scarf around her neck. Under her coat she had four layers of clothes. 'Wouldn't you sooner spend your time in Monsieur Clari's café? At least it's warm and the coffee is hot,' Alice pressed.

'We'll be warm enough with a brisk walk and Pip says they have pretty severe winters in Boston, so I'd better get used to it. Besides, the inn will be cosy and it will be great to spend time with just Pip.'

Alice grinned. 'And everyone else who has heard about their omelettes.'

They both had rosy cheeks from the cold and their exertions, for Pip hadn't realised that it was quite so far out as they'd tramped across the snowy fields. 'I hope it's worth the walk, Mae. I'll be taking Lenny to task if it's not, you can be darned sure of that,' he said as at last they reached the tiny hamlet that boasted a couple of houses and the inn, aptly named 'Le Poulet Brun'.

'I won't care as long as it's warm!' Mae replied, laughing. 'My nose feels frozen. I'm glad you're here to order the food – your French is better than mine,' she added.

The inn consisted of one large low-ceilinged room with black smoke-stained beams but there was a roaring log fire burning in a fireplace at one end; Mae held out her hands to the glow thankfully while Pip spoke to the middle-aged Frenchman behind the small counter that served as a bar.

'I've asked for two omelettes, some bread and cheese and two bowls of coffee, if he would be so kind as to provide them. I told him we've walked from Boulogne,' Pip informed her as they settled themselves at a table near the fire. 'He shook his head and muttered, "*Fous! Fous!*" He thinks we're totally mad to walk miles through the snow for just coffee, an omelette and bread and cheese.'

'He hasn't tasted what we have to eat and drink these days,' Mae replied, smiling across at the proprietor.

Pip took her hand. 'It's worth it just to be able to spend some time alone with you – well, almost alone,' he amended. Apart from two ancient farmers sitting in a corner drinking and talking, they appeared to be the only patrons for now.

Mae nodded. 'I know, we always seem to be surrounded by people. Not that I mind but it's nice sometimes to have some privacy.'

'I keep thinking that we should be making some plans for the future but then I wonder . . .' Pip began.

Mae sighed. 'It's so difficult when we just don't know what the future holds. I suppose that when spring finally arrives the battles will start all over again. Oh, I wish there was an end in sight, Pip, I really do.'

He squeezed her hand. 'I know, and so do I. Sometimes I think it would be great if in summer we could sail away to Boston. No war, no hardships, no suffering.'

'I suppose . . . in reality we . . . could, Pip. America isn't at war and I know I'll never be called on to do anything other than nurse, but . . .'

He shook his head. 'We neither of us can leave, Mae. We can't escape it, our consciences won't let us.'

'I know,' she agreed, although there was a note of wistfulness in her voice. 'I'm needed and I'll go on being needed until it's over.'

'As I will. But, hey, we didn't come here to depress ourselves. Ah, here's the coffee,' he announced, trying to lighten their spirits. He loved her and he desperately wanted to take her back home to a life of peace, comfort and security but he couldn't – not yet – so these occasional outings would have to suffice until then.

Mae sniffed appreciatively at the steaming bowl of dark liquid placed in front of her. 'It smells good but isn't it a little . . . strange to have it served in a bowl instead of a cup?'

He laughed good-naturedly. 'To us yes but I guess it's the French way and "when in Rome ...", as the saying goes.'

They drank the coffee and chatted about Lizzie and Eddie's blossoming friendship and Lenny's current dalliance with a young French shop assistant until the food arrived. They both tucked in heartily and Pip declared it was the best omelette he'd ever had.

'We'll come again, Mae, if you don't mind the walk,' he said as he passed over the francs in payment, plus a fair-sized tip.

'It would be a very pleasant walk in spring or summer, Pip,' she mused as they walked out into the freezing air.

'It would,' he agreed but wondered if he would still be in Boulogne by then. American public opinion was becoming very hostile to the Kaiser and his forces; anti-German propaganda was increasing, his father had told him in his recent letters, as were the number of merchant ships being attacked by the U-boats. Americans were crossing the border into Canada to enlist to fight in France in what was being termed the American Legion, and President Wilson was becoming more and more unpopular for his policy of non-involvement in a European war. His father felt that the day would come when the President would have to capitulate and declare war – and when that day arrived, Pip knew he would leave the Field Ambulance Service and join the American Army.

They did return to the little inn in the countryside in early April, just before Easter. Winter had gradually and reluctantly released its Arctic stranglehold but its toll had been heavy and not only amongst the troops, although they had suffered terribly. The cases of frostbite and trench foot had reached such epic proportions that orders were issued to every man serving in the trenches that he was to remove his boots and socks and rub whale oil into his feet at least once a day, but as Alice had stated acidly, what fool was going to take much notice of an order like that in such freezing weather?

'Every officer is to be held responsible to see it's an order that's carried out, Nurse McEvoy,' Sister Harper had replied sharply, although she herself didn't hold out much hope of it being obeyed so no doubt they'd be treating the results of exposure for weeks to come.

In February Alice had received a letter from Jimmy telling her that his gran had died and one from her mother informing her that Esther Ziegler, who had always had a weak chest, had succumbed to pneumonia. Harold was heart-broken but winter was always a hard time for the very young, the old and those with delicate constitutions, Maggie had written sadly. It hadn't improved Alice's mood, which remained subdued as spring struggled to break through.

Both Pip and Mae knew possibly before Easter an offensive against the Hindenburg Line at Arras would begin for the British, Canadian and Australian troops, because the bombardment had been going on for twelve days now. When the fighting began they both knew casualties would be heavy so they'd made arrangements to take what would very likely be their last opportunity for a while to spend the afternoon in the countryside at Le Poulet Brun.

At lunchtime on that April day, as Mae had come off duty, Alice had come rushing into the tent, her cheeks flushed.

'Mae! Have you heard the news? It's spreading all over the hospital like wildfire!' she cried, clutching Mae's arm.

'What? What news?' Mae had demanded, praying that German U-boats hadn't sunk another hospital ship. Everyone had been outraged and horrified by the sinking of the *Asturias* at the end of March; her Red Cross signs had been brightly lit so it must have been a deliberate attack.

'America has declared war on Germany, Mae! Over ninety German ships have been seized in New York harbour! Men are flocking to join up!'

Mae's heart had sunk like a stone. She knew she shouldn't feel so dismayed, but all she could think about was how this would affect Pip. 'Oh, Alice!' was all she'd been able to say by way of a reply.

Now, as they walked hand in hand through the countryside

where fresh green shoots and buds were appearing on the trees and the birds sang in the hedgerows, she wished the snow was on the ground again and America's entry into the war still months away. It had been the first thing he'd said when he'd met her and she could see he was pleased about it.

'I guess you'll have heard the news, Mae. President Wilson finally gave in. He had to; the vote in the Senate was ninety for and six against and in the House three hundred and seventy-three for, just fifty against. Panama and Cuba have also declared war. Don't you see, Mae, with fresh troops and munitions the Boche could be pushed back to Berlin by Christmas.'

She nodded; what he said did make some sense. America's entry should shorten the war.

He'd talked about it almost all the way to Le Poulet Brun and she'd listened with an ever-increasing sense of despondency. When they entered the low-beamed room, the proprietor uttered a cry of delight and rushed towards Pip, embracing him as though he were a long-lost son and crying, '*Vive l'Amérique! Vive l'Amérique! Et bien, monsieur!*'

Pip looked both bemused and embarrassed as the innkeeper led them both to a table and then produced two small glasses of Calvados.

When toasts had been drunk and their host's enthusiasm had diminished slightly and he had departed to the kitchen, Mae tentatively asked Pip how the news would affect him. 'When will you have to leave Boulogne?'

'I'm not exactly sure, Mae. I'll transfer to an Army unit – when one arrives, that is – but no one seems to have much of an idea when that will be.'

'I know it's selfish of me, Pip, but I hope it won't be soon.'

He smiled and then frowned. 'I guess it will take some weeks to get the men and equipment organised. I know thousands are rushing to join up but they're raw recruits, they'll need training,' he replied, thinking aloud.

'And ships will be needed to bring them across, a lot of ships,' Mae added, thinking of the distance involved and the U-boat menace.

'And in the meantime the attack on Arras will go ahead . . .'

'And we'll be inundated with wounded,' she finished.

He could see she was upset. 'I know you don't want me to go to fight, Mae, that's understandable, but . . . but I have to. It's my duty, the way it's Eddie's duty.'

'I don't want you to get hurt, Pip, not like Eddie or Jimmy Mercer or . . .' She wouldn't even voice her fear of him being killed like Harry Mercer and Tommy Mitford.

'I don't particularly want to get hurt, Mae. Don't forget I've seen at first hand the results of shells and shrapnel, unlike the boys coming over from the States. I know what's ahead of me. But let's not talk about it any more, let's just enjoy this spring afternoon, the food and the apple brandy and hope that the war will be over soon.'

Mae managed to smile, determined to push all her fears to the back of her mind for now. 'What is spring like in Boston, Pip?'

'Oh, you'll just love it, Mae. The sunlight and the sail boats on the Charles River, the Swan Boats on the lake in the Boston Public Garden and then every May there is Lilac Sunday when all the lilac trees in the public parks and the Arnold Arboretum at Harvard are in full bloom and everyone picnics outdoors. The blossoms are gorgeous, every shade from white to purple, and their perfume just fills the air.'

'I'd love to see that, Pip,' she said wistfully.

He took her hand and squeezed it. 'Maybe next year we both will, Mae.'

Monsieur arrived bearing the food and as Mae cut into the freshly cooked omelette dusted with herbs she tried to think of Boston sunlight and lilacs, not the bombardment close to Arras or the fact that within days men would be dying and maybe within weeks she would have to watch Pip march away to fight.

Chapter Twenty-Seven

To MAE'S PROFOUND RELIEF it was June before the first American troops arrived in France. The attack on the German lines at Arras and at Ypres had commenced on Easter Monday in a freak snowstorm and casualties had been as heavy as they had been on the first day of the Somme, so Mae had little time to dwell on the fact that she would one day have to say goodbye to Pip. He was equally busy, as was Eddie, who was toiling through mud with a team of mules and a wagon, struggling to get supplies up to the front line. Eddie had soon realised that the cost to the animals was nearly as heavy as that to the troops as mules and horses plunged and strained to move heavy equipment through quagmires of mud and shell holes, often dropping dead from sheer exhaustion, or breaking legs which meant they had to be shot, or being hit by bullets, shrapnel and shell blasts. Their screams of agony haunted his dreams. But as the weather gradually improved and the offensive continued, the 1st Division of the American Expeditionary

Force arrived under the command of General John 'Black Jack' Pershing and Mae knew that Pip had little time left with the Field Ambulance Service.

The day he came to the hospital to say goodbye was one she would never forget. Sister Harper had relented under the circumstances and had allowed her to go to the gate to meet him, and as she crossed the compound and saw him standing there waiting she couldn't help but think how handsome he looked in his uniform, a uniform so different to those of the men she nursed. She hadn't realised that he would be an officer, and as the summer sunlight glinted on the buttons and braid on his jacket she felt so very proud of him. He'd already contributed so much to the war effort, his skilful driving had probably saved many lives, but now he was going to fight beside his own countrymen and she was holding back her tears.

'I hardly recognised you, you look so . . . splendid! Do I have to call you "sir" now?' she greeted him jokingly, determined she wasn't going to send him away with tears and words of despondency.

He laughed. 'Officially it's Lieutenant Middlehurst – thanks to my Harvard education – but I'm still "Pip" to my fiancée and friends.'

She wasn't going to let her mood of forced joviality slip. 'You know I'm not supposed to be seen "socially" in the company of an officer, but maybe that rule doesn't apply to American officers.'

'That's one of the rules we "Yanks" don't have, Mae. We don't have your British class system,' he reminded her gently.

'I know. You will write to me, Pip?'

'I've promised I will. No matter how hot things get I'll find the time,' he said seriously. Then he took her in his arms. 'I love you, Mae, and I'll come back for you.'

She clung to him, not caring if the whole hospital was watching. 'I . . . know you will, Pip. I love you so much. Take care of yourself, please?' Tears were threatening all her resolve. 'I'll be thinking of you every spare minute I have and I'll write regularly.'

He bent and kissed her and she felt as though her heart were breaking. What if this was the last time she would ever feel his lips on hers, the last time she would ever hold him? She knew something inside her would shrivel up and die if anything happened to him.

'Take care, Pip. Be safe, my love,' she whispered.

'I will, my darling Mae. I'll come back and we'll never be parted again and we'll walk in the Arboretum every Lilac Sunday, I swear.'

She couldn't hold back the tears as he walked away, nor did she try to, but she waved for the last time as he got into the staff car. She watched it pull away and then she stood there in the hot midday sun just staring down the empty dusty road until Alice came and put her arm around her and they walked back to the wards.

Alice knew how she felt. She'd had to say goodbye to Jimmy twice and the first time she had wondered if he would survive the journey home. 'He'll be back, Mae,' she said firmly.

Maggie folded her daughter's letter and put it back in the envelope then gazed unseeingly out of the kitchen window. Poor Mae was taking Pip's absence hard, Alice had written. She was very dispirited and worried even though she tried to put a brave face on it before the patients. Mae had had so much to contend with in her short life, Maggie thought: mother and father both dying tragically, then young Harry Mercer and many of her childhood companions; having to face daily the harrowing duties of nursing and all the attendant hardships; and now . . . She prayed that nothing would happen to Phillip Middlehurst, for even though she had never met him, Alice had told her that he adored Mae and she him. It would break the poor girl's heart if she were to lose him too. 'Oh, please God, keep him safe. Keep both him and Eddie safe,' she prayed.

Slowly she got to her feet. The kitchen was stuffy with the residue of the day's heat and as always was too quiet. She wondered would the girls get leave soon? It might do Mae good to come home for a visit, she thought as she filled the kettle.

She was interrupted by a knock on the front door and, tutting impatiently, she went to open it. Didn't people know her hours of business by now? She was muttering irritably to herself when she opened the door to a middle-aged man in a shabby suit, the right sleeve of the jacket empty and pinned up. She stared at him. He wasn't anyone she knew, not one of her regulars, and so she viewed him with some suspicion.

'Hello, Maggie,' he said quietly.

Her eyes widened and she gasped as she recognised the voice. 'My God! *Billy McEvoy!*'

He nodded. 'Aye, it's me.'

She quickly regained her composure. 'You've got a flaming nerve! What the hell do you want? All these years and not a word from you!'

He shifted awkwardly. 'I know. Sure, I know, Maggie and I'm sorry about . . . that. I'm sorry about . . . everything.'

Her eyes narrowed as rage and hurt welled up inside her. 'It's easy to just turn up and say "sorry", Billy. Clear off! Go to hell!'

'Maggie, I deserve that, I do, but I just want to talk to you, to try to explain . . .'

'There's nothing to say, not after all these years, not after the way you ran off without a word, leaving me with two children, not a penny to my name and not knowing if you were alive or dead!' She made to shut the door but he quickly put out his foot.

'Will you not even listen?' he asked. She was wrong; it wasn't easy, it had taken him weeks to pluck up the courage to come here.

She hesitated, acutely aware that curtains in the nearby houses were twitching. She didn't want to become the talk of the street. 'I'll give you five minutes, Billy McEvoy, no longer,' she snapped as she ushered him inside and closed the door. She'd never expected to see him again and it was a shock. As she followed him into the kitchen she realised that she was shaking.

'Well, what have you got to say?' she demanded, not attempting to sit or indicate that he should. She could see now that he had changed a great deal from the young man he'd been when last she'd seen him. His hair was almost entirely grey now, his face lined and weather-beaten, he was thinner and he'd obviously suffered.

Billy had been rehearsing. 'I was a young eejit then, Maggie. I didn't know when I was well off. I . . . I wanted . . . adventure, more excitement in life—'

'Not a wife and kids!' she interrupted bitterly.

'I was wrong. I got too fond of the drink. It made me think I could do better with my life, it gave me false expectations—'

'And that you weren't "fond" enough of me,' she interrupted again.

'Maggie, please?' he said wearily.

'So why have you come back now?' she wanted to know, still very wary of him.

'Because I've changed, because I'm not getting any younger, because I realised that I wanted to see my family and to see you again, Maggie. The world has changed . . .'

'So, now you've had all the "adventure" and "excitement" you want to come back?' Her tone was bitingly derisive.

'I *have* changed. I've been through . . . a lot, Maggie. I've seen things that made me think and look at life . . . differently.'

'We all have,' she replied curtly but then she relented a little. 'Sit down, Billy. What happened?' She nodded, indicating the empty jacket sleeve, the missing limb.

'I lost it at Jutland but I was one of the lucky ones, I survived,' he said flatly as he sat down.

That surprised her. 'You fought at Jutland? Surely you were too old?'

'No, I was Regular Navy, Maggie. I didn't just enlist when the war began, I was an NCO. A petty officer.'

She frowned, trying to take this in. 'But . . . but when you left . . . ?'

'I know. I was on the way to being a drunken bum and believe me, I *do* regret that.'

She stared at him hard, and then she got up. 'I was just going to make a pot of tea. I . . . I think you'd better begin at the beginning, Billy.'

'I didn't come to embarrass or upset you, Maggie. I didn't come looking for your pity, just your . . . understanding and maybe forgiveness.' He looked around the tidy, comfortable kitchen. 'I don't want to inconvenience you either. Does John still live here? Are you expecting him home?'

'No. John . . . John . . . went down with the *Lusitania*,' she informed him as she busied herself with the teapot. She was filled with conflicting emotions: all the old hurt, humiliation and anger but also curiosity, although she was determined not to show it. Nor did she have any intention of giving him any idea that he could just walk back into her life.

'I'm truly sorry about that, Maggie. I saw a lot of good men drown. Unlike the soldiers, we had two enemies to contend with at Jutland. The Boche Navy and the sea and there's not much to choose between the two when it comes to cruelty.'

'So, what happened?' she asked.

Billy told her with as little emotion as he could of his experiences at Jutland, of ships destroyed and sunk, men with horrific injuries drowning in that bitterly cold sea. She listened in silence until he'd finished. 'When you left all those years ago, what did you do?'

'I signed on an old tramp steamer looking for "excitement",' he said bitterly. 'There was precious little of that and I'd soon had enough of it, but at least it got me off the drink – months at sea with bad food, hard work, barely any money and no booze. But I grew to really love the sea, so when we finally got back that's when I joined the Navy.'

'You didn't . . . want to . . . come . . . back?' she stated. Oh, it was painful now to recall those years and of how she had suffered, feeling abandoned and worthless.

'I was still looking for an adventurous life, eejit that I was. Well, I certainly saw some of the world and I found that the life suited me, and as I got older it got harder to think about leaving it and then I was promoted and I had something I'd never had – respect – and I felt I'd actually achieved something worthwhile.'

Maggie said nothing. He *had* changed, she thought, but for all these years he'd ignored his family and his responsibilities, he'd just suited himself. 'And did you never think of . . . us?'

'Sometimes. I wondered . . . how you were managing, but I didn't feel as though I belonged, that I was still part of a family,' he admitted. 'I'm not proud of deserting you, Maggie.'

'I "managed", Billy. Thanks to Isaac Ziegler and our John we didn't end up on the streets. I brought Eddie and Alice and Mae up on my own.'

'So John stayed at sea? Well, I can understand that, it becomes a way of life.' He frowned, puzzled. 'But Isaac?'

'He lent me the money to start my own business. I'm a moneylender, Billy, and I'm not ashamed of it. I provide a service which many find essential and I don't charge exorbitant rates. It's kept a roof over our heads and food on the table.'

He nodded slowly. She'd always been good with figures and she was fair. And he'd left her almost destitute and unable to go out to work. 'Eddie will be . . .'

'Twenty-one and serving in the Army in France,' she answered curtly. 'He's been shipped home twice.'

Billy felt a surge of pride at his son's undoubted courage, and he hadn't failed to notice that the room was very tidy and devoid of the usual paraphernalia associated with two young girls. 'Mae and . . . Alice, did you say?'

'Yes. Your daughter and your niece are both nursing in a field hospital near Boulogne.'

That surprised him. 'My . . . Alice?'

'Is only eighteen, but she's a strong-willed, determined little madam if ever there was one. She browbeat us all to let her go but she's a good nurse and a brave girl, even if I say it myself. Both she and Mae gave up good jobs to go, office jobs, they were typists. John and I saw they got the proper training: we paid for it,' she said proudly. Then, feeling she'd given him enough of her time, she got to her feet. 'I think your five minutes are more than up, Billy.'

Reluctantly he rose. 'Thanks for not turning me away, Maggie, and for the tea. Can I . . . can I come to see you again?'

'I don't know. I don't want you to think that you can just walk back into my life, Billy.'

'I know, but I'd like to come, Maggie, occasionally.'

'Where are you staying?' she asked.

'In lodgings in Stanhope Street. I've been discharged from the Navy but I've a small pension because I lost my arm. I manage.'

She hesitated. 'Maybe occasionally but . . . but not for a while, Billy. '

He supposed he should be grateful that she'd seen him at all after the way he'd treated her, but he was determined that even if it took years he would win her round. He wanted to come home, he wanted to get to know his son and the daughter he'd never met, and he'd realised that he was still fond of his wife.

When he'd gone, Maggie sat down at the table and picked up Alice's letter. She'd never expected to see or hear from him again, but she'd agreed to let him visit her and now she wondered why. She'd have to write and tell both Eddie and Alice, and she didn't know how they would take it.

She felt so confused and restless that she decided she would go and talk it over with Agnes, but when she entered her friend's kitchen Bertie, Lucy and Jimmy were all in.

'Agnes, luv, will you come over and have a cup of tea with me? I've . . . well, I've had a bit of a shock.'

'Is it Eddie or the girls?' Agnes asked, looking concerned.

'No, I've had a letter from Alice and they're all fine.'

Agnes nodded and they went back across the road, Agnes wondering just what on earth would upset Maggie, apart from worries about her family.

As Maggie made the tea she told her friend of Billy's visit and of the troubled state of mind it had left her in. 'God knows why I said he could visit again, Agnes,' she finished.

Agnes drank her tea in silence, trying to digest this bolt from the blue. 'And you think he has changed, Maggie?' she at last asked. Maggie had been alone for so long and although financially she'd had few worries, her life hadn't been easy.

'Yes, I think he has. I think he finally grew up in the Navy. Learned the meaning of responsibility and self-discipline and duty, but in all that time he never tried to get in touch, Agnes, and I don't know if that's something I'll ever be able to understand.'

'Do you think he does want to come back . . . home?' Agnes asked tentatively. What would Maggie think of that? She knew only too well how hurt and humiliated her friend had been when he'd left.

'I think he does, but . . .' Maggie shook her head, feeling even more undecided.

'Could you forgive and forget, Maggie?'

'I might be able to forgive, Agnes, but I can never forget what he put me through or the way he's ignored his children.'

Agnes nodded; that was understandable. Yet the future was so uncertain for everyone, she thought, no one knew what worries or heartache lay ahead and neither of them were young women any more – maybe Maggie might find Billy a comfort and support in the years ahead. 'I can't tell you what to do, Maggie. You know that I never really thought much of him when you married him and I know what you went through when he left, how hard it's been for you all these years, but I suppose people can and do change, especially when they've been through such . . . experiences, but it's a decision you alone must make. Just don't cut off your nose to spite your face, luv. You might find that you've still got some . . . feelings for him.'

Maggie digested this in silence; she knew what Agnes was trying to tell her. 'But . . . but the kids?' she said, wondering if she could ever find it in her heart to take him back. He wasn't the person she'd known; they'd have to get to know each other all over again and it might not work out. Legally, however, she was still married to him.

'They're adults, well at least Eddie is, and maybe they'd want to get to know him. You'd have to let them make up their own minds, Maggie,' she advised.

Maggie said despairingly. 'Oh, Agnes, luv. I don't know what to do, I really don't.'

Agnes reached across and took her hand. 'Think long and

hard about it, Maggie, before you come to a final decision. Life hasn't been easy without him but you might come to think that the years ahead could possibly prove to be better for you all.'

Maggie smiled at her. She had a great deal to think about but now she at least felt as though she'd done the right thing in agreeing to let him visit her again. She'd just have to see how it all worked out.

As he walked home from work a few weeks later Bertie Mercer wasn't surprised when he caught sight of Billy McEvoy getting off a tram, for Agnes had told him of Billy's sudden return.

'Never thought I'd see you again, Billy. How are you?' he greeted him not unpleasantly for he'd also heard of his experiences at Jutland.

'Never thought I'd see you either, Bertie. And I'm grand but a lot of water's gone under the bridge since I last saw you.'

They had drawn level with the Albion pub on the corner and before either could comment further the door was thrown open and a figure was forcefully ejected with much abuse on the part of both the landlord and his unwelcome customer.

'Jaysus!' Billy uttered as the man, who was obviously more than worse the wear for drink, collapsed in a heap on the pavement.

'That's Fred Jackson – local drunk. You remember him; he lives in York Terrace. He's regularly thrown out of the pubs around here these days,' Bertie enlightened him.

Billy shook his head slowly as the man, still muttering curses, tried to get up but only managed to get on to all fours before collapsing again. 'Begod but isn't that a desperate sight? And there but for the grace of God goes meself, Bertie. '

Bertie nodded. 'I heard. So I can't tempt you into having a pint with me – for old times' sake?'

'I'd have a pint of lemonade or something like that with you but the pair of us would probably be laughed and jeered out of the place. No, my drinking days are well and truly over now, Bertie. I've no intention of going down the same road as himself back there,' Billy replied seriously.

'Where are you going?' Bertie asked, thinking that perhaps Maggie was right. Billy *had* changed. He'd certainly tell her about this encounter.

'To see Maggie. I know she told me to leave it for a while but I just want to make sure she's not getting into a state about me turning up again. I know it was a shock.'

'It will certainly take some getting used to, Billy, on all their parts. Well, I wish you luck,' Bertie replied as he crossed the road heading towards the corner shop.

Maggie was startled to see him again so soon. 'Billy, I thought we agreed . . .'

'We did and I've not come for a lengthy visit. I just wanted to make sure that you were, well . . . not . . .' He shrugged, feeling a bit awkward.

'Oh, come on in,' she replied. 'I've just made a pot of tea.'

'No, really I didn't expect . . .'

'I'm not going to stand here arguing with you, Billy.'

He nodded and followed her down the lobby.

'I've written to both Eddie and Alice,' she informed him as he sat down.

'That couldn't have been easy, Maggie.' He was watching

her closely for any sign that she was upset.

'It wasn't but it was something I had to do,' she answered, handing him a cup of tea. Her initial surprise was subsiding and she realised that she wasn't annoyed that he'd called and that she felt more at ease with him this time.

'It will come as a bit of a shock to them both, I don't wonder,' Billy mused aloud and wondered whether he should ask what she thought their response would be to the news. No, he couldn't do that. After all, she was still getting over the shock herself.

'God knows how they'll take it. All I can do is wait until I hear from them,' she supplied.

Billy drank his tea, wondering if Eddie and Alice would encourage or discourage her from having anything more to do with him. There was little he could do or say if they were dead set against him, he thought regretfully, although he hoped that with further visits, at least Maggie would learn to trust him.

Chapter Twenty-Eight

———◆———

To SAY ALICE WAS stunned was an understatement. She reread the lines her mother had written to make sure she had fully understood. Then she handed the letter to Mae, who had been watching her cousin's expression closely, a worried frown creasing her forehead.

'Read that. I just can't take it in. It's . . . unbelievable!'

'What's wrong? Is it Jimmy?' Mae asked, taking the letter from her.

'No, it's got nothing to do with Jimmy. Read it, Mae!' she urged.

As Mae read, her eyes widened and she looked across at Alice with confusion evident in their blue depths. 'I'm . . . stunned! He's been gone for . . .'

'Nineteen years! I never knew him, he was long gone by the time I was born.'

Mae sat down next to her and took her hand. It was news neither of them had ever expected to hear. 'I was only a few weeks old myself, Alice. We . . . Aunty Maggie never thought he'd come back. We all learned to manage without him. She never even *mentioned* him.'

Alice replied, 'But she says he's changed. That he wants to visit her again and she's agreed.'

Mae nodded. 'Maybe she thought about him, Alice, even though she didn't talk about him. Maybe she . . . well, maybe she is still fond of him.'

'How can she be, Mae? How can you still have feelings for someone who walked out and left you the way he did?'

Mae shrugged. 'I don't know. We don't know exactly how she feels about him or has felt over the years. How do *you* feel about it – apart from the shock?'

Alice considered this. She was astounded and confused. During the years when she'd been growing up she hadn't really given him much thought; there had been no photographs of him and his name was never mentioned. She'd looked on her Uncle John as a surrogate father and she'd been almost as devastated as Mae had been when he'd been drowned – she still missed him. But because of him she'd never felt the lack of a father in her life. Now she was grown up and she'd matured so much in this last year. She was curious to know why he'd deserted her mam and herself and Eddie, for her mam would never talk about it. What had driven him to take such a drastic step? Mam said he'd changed so much, he was older and wiser now, he'd been a petty officer in the Navy and he'd fought and lost his arm at Jutland. 'I . . . I think I'd like to meet him, Mae,' she finally announced. 'Maybe he can explain why he left us and why he's never got in touch. I feel that maybe I can . . . try to understand more now. Because I know that one day I'm going to marry Jimmy and have a family of my own, I can try to understand Mam's position. Look at things in a different light.'

Mae nodded. 'One day we'll both leave to be married, Alice, and I think it's only right that Aunty Maggie thinks about her own future.'

'She's not had things easy, Mae. She's worked hard and she must have been very lonely at times. Maybe it would be a good thing if she did take him back – she says she is still legally married to him.'

Mae smiled. 'All that is not going to be simple to put into words in a letter, Alice.'

Alice grimaced. 'I know, but I'll have to try. She'll be expecting a reply soon and she wants to know how I feel about it.'

'Maybe it's a good thing we're going on leave next month. We'll both get to meet him, if she hasn't already sent him packing.'

Alice sighed. The fact that she might actually meet the father she had never even seen would be hard to come to terms with. Would she like him, let alone be able to accept him? She just didn't know.

'I take it she's written to Eddie as well?' Mae asked.

Alice replied, 'She says she has.'

Mae reflected. 'I wonder how he's taken it? He might remember him, even if only vaguely. Maybe when you next go into town you'd better go and see him. After all, he's got no chance of getting leave so it will be up to you to tell him how things are . . . progressing at home, if indeed they are.'

'I think you're right, Mae. I'd better go and see how he feels about all this. I'll think about it all for another day or so before

I write to Mam.' She stuffed the letter into her pocket. 'Now, we'd better get back to work or Sister might reconsider about us going on leave.'

She'd made three attempts to reply to her mam's letter; the other two were now just crumpled balls of paper. She frowned as she reread what she'd finally decided to write.

> *Dear Mam,*
>
> *This is the third time I've started to write this letter and I've decided to be brief and to the point. There's no use me rambling on – that would just confuse us both. It was a shock, I can't deny that, but I've thought long and hard about it and I've talked to Mae and Lizzie about it too and I've decided that it's your decision. You are his wife, you are the only one who really knows how you feel about him, but I'll support you whatever you decide to do. I'm not going to try to influence you one way or the other. Just don't go getting yourself into a state about it. Write and let me know, that's if you've made up your mind before I get home on leave,*
>
> *Your loving daughter,*
> *Alice*

She tried to concentrate fully on her work but she found it difficult. Questions kept bubbling up in her mind, questions to which she had no answers. Why did he go? Why did he now want to come back into their lives? What did he look like? What would he think of her? Did either she or Eddie resemble him? How would she feel when she saw him? It was very strange to think that after all this time she would have a father in her life. Her overwhelming feeling was of curiosity but she reminded herself of her promise that whatever her mother decided to do, she would support her.

On her next afternoon off she walked purposefully to the yard where Eddie was stationed and sought out Sergeant Walker. 'Sir, could I have some time to speak to my brother, please. It is important. We've had some very . . . unexpected news from home.'

'Nothing bad I hope, miss,' he said with concern. He'd noticed a change in the lad over the past few days. He'd become quieter as though totally absorbed in his own thoughts, his usual good humour seeming to have deserted him. It hadn't affected his work so he'd not commented on it.

'It depends on how you look at it, but no one has died or has been taken ill.'

He nodded. 'You wait here, miss. I'll go and find him: the yard is in a bit of a mess after those showers we had this morning.'

Alice waited, leaning against the edge of a stone water trough until at last she saw her brother heading towards her, his sleeves rolled up and a pitchfork still in his hand. Obviously he'd been engaged in mucking out.

'I take it you got a letter from Mam too,' he greeted her, and she could see by his expression that he was far from happy.

'I did. This is the first opportunity I've had to come and see you. Quite a surprise, wasn't it?'

Eddie frowned. 'It was a bloody shock, Alice, that's what it was! Him turning up bold as brass after all these years! He's got some nerve. I'm surprised Mam gave him the time of day.'

'I gather you don't think Mam should even entertain the thought of seeing him again?'

'No, I damned well don't. He ran off, Alice, like a bloody thief in the night, leaving her with us and no means of supporting herself. What kind of a man does that?'

'Don't swear at me, Eddie,' Alice said quietly.

'Sorry, but I just can't get over the cheek of him wanting to worm his way back, now that he's lost his arm and his job.'

'He did fight, Eddie, unlike a lot of men his age. He was Regular Navy.'

Eddie laughed bitterly. 'Then he had no choice, did he, Alice? And why did he never attempt to get in touch? He never wanted to know anything about *us* – that's why. He didn't damned well care!'

'I know it's hard to understand, Eddie, but I think we should at least give him the chance to explain . . . all that.'

'Try to fob us off with a load of lame excuses, you mean,' Eddie sneered.

'Mam's made a decision to see him again. She's not saying she's welcoming him back with open arms but, Eddie, we have to respect her decision. She's not getting any younger and we . . . well, we'll both get married eventually and have our own lives. Is it fair of us to demand that she has nothing more to do with him?'

Eddie hadn't thought of this, he'd been so incensed that all he'd thought about was the fact that Billy had deserted them and had wanted nothing to do with them – until now.

'All he wants now that he's getting old and he's disabled and can't work, Alice, is a comfortable home and an easy life. He probably knows Mam's got a few bob. He's still being a self-centred, selfish bastard.'

'Don't call him that, Eddie! Whatever else he is, he isn't *that*!' she snapped for it was the most demeaning and insulting term imaginable. Illegitimacy carried a terrible social stigma. 'Well, I can see that you've made up your mind about it all but I think you're wrong. We should at least give him a chance.'

'Why? He doesn't deserve it. He never gave us one!' Eddie shot back furiously.

'For Mam's sake. If she decides to have him back, it's *her* decision. We're due leave next month, you know that, so I'll be able to judge for myself just what kind of a man he is.'

'Please your bloody self, Alice, but don't expect me to welcome him back with open arms. Too many years, too much hurt and bitterness have been suffered for that.' Eddie turned and stormed off.

Alice sighed. She hoped this wasn't going to drive a wedge between them; surely they all had enough to contend with at present. The war was still being fought and they didn't need another war to break out at home. She turned away and walked slowly out on to the road. Maybe Lizzie could talk some sense into him for they seemed to be quite close these days.

They were both quite apprehensive when in September they arrived back in Liverpool. Maggie was waiting at Lime Street and Alice was delighted to find that Jimmy had accompanied her.

'Oh, look at you!' she cried, hugging him. 'You look great, you really do.'

Jimmy laughed. 'And so do you, Alice. A bit tired but after

that journey it's only to be expected. And I'm getting around like a two-year-old now with my new leg.'

'I should hope you are, you've had it for months now,' Alice replied but her eyes were shining with pride. He looked so much better and he was far more cheerful too.

'Right, let's get home. Agnes is standing in for Jimmy in the shop but I know she's got some shopping herself to do,' Maggie informed them, guiding them towards the station exit.

No mention was made of Billy until they were home, the girls had unpacked and Maggie had made a cup of tea. Then Alice broached the subject.

'So, Mam, have you seen anything of . . . him, my da?' The word sounded so strange to her.

Maggie nodded as she poured the tea. 'Yes, he's called a few times and stayed a couple of hours.' She sat down opposite the girls. 'I . . . I haven't heard a word from Eddie. I know he doesn't write regularly but I thought . . .'

'He's not happy, Mam. Not happy at all.' Alice stirred her tea slowly. 'I went to see him and he doesn't think you should encourage Billy. He feels very bitter towards him.'

Maggie had assumed this, given Eddie's lengthy silence. 'And you, Alice?'

'You know how I feel, Mam. It took me hours to compose that letter, didn't it, Mae?'

Mae nodded her agreement, remembering how Alice had struggled to articulate her thoughts and feelings.

'It's your life and your decision, Mam. Only you know exactly how you feel about him.'

Maggie sighed as she sipped her tea. Her emotions were still turbulent, but as he'd talked about the years he'd spent away, she had begun to realise that Billy had changed a great deal. He appeared to be far more serious, more reserved and considerate. There was little now of the brash, irresponsible young man everyone had said was a 'waster', interested only in enjoying himself. There was none of the blarney, although he still had a sense of humour. She was coming to the conclusion that she actually liked this man far more than she had the young Billy McEvoy. 'We had a long talk, Alice, but I haven't given him any indication of what I'm going to do because I haven't made my mind up properly yet. Oh, he's changed – even Agnes and Bertie think so – but so have I and a lot of time has passed and there are things I can't forget. He did say he would like to meet you . . . both. That's if you wished to see him, of course. He said he would understand if you didn't.'

'I'd like to meet him, Mam,' Alice said quietly.

'And so would I, Aunty Maggie,' Mae added.

'I thought you would. I said I'd get word to him so I'll invite him for supper on Sunday evening. He looks as though he could do with a decent meal – the Lord alone knows what he eats in those lodgings of his,' she added.

Alice smiled at this; so her mam was obviously thinking of his welfare. 'Good, that will give me some time to spend with Jimmy first. Does Aunty Agnes know about him coming to visit?'

Maggie said, 'Yes. She was the first to know. I went straight over as soon as he'd gone. You know Agnes and I have been friends for years, there's no secrets between us.'

'And what did she say?' Alice asked.

'Much the same as you: that it's my decision. But she also told me not to cut off my nose to spite my face.'

Alice replied, 'I'm sure you won't, Mam, and don't take too much notice of our Eddie. I think he'll come round in time. At least Lizzie thinks he will.'

Maggie refilled their cups, smiling as Mae commented on the chlorine-free taste. 'Do you think he's serious about this Lizzie? He mentioned her often – before he stopped writing, that is.'

Both Mae and Alice grinned. 'Well, Lizzie is, I know that, even though she's from a middle-class family. The war seems to have changed a lot of people's attitudes,' Alice remarked.

'And knowing Lizzie Lawson, she's a very determined young woman who usually gets her own way,' Mae added.

'She's really nice, Mam, I get on great with her even though she's a lot older than me. She's a bit older than Eddie too. She lives in Aintree, in a big house near the racecourse, and until the beginning of the war they had a maid, but she's not a bit snobbish,' Alice informed her mother.

'Really? She sounds like a sensible girl who knows what she wants and that might do our Eddie good,' Maggie pronounced, wondering how Lizzie's family would feel about having a son-in-law from the working class. 'Have you heard from Pip, Mae?' she asked, to change the rather intense subject.

'He writes regularly. Thank goodness he's not yet been sent to the front but he thinks that by next month he will be. The unit he's with are regular American Army so they don't need training; they'll be supporting the French or the Canadians. He says the main body of those who enlisted probably won't be over for some months yet as President Wilson is insisting that they be properly trained and armed first.'

'It's a pity our politicians and generals didn't take that

attitude instead of sending the lads into conditions they were unprepared for.' She sighed heavily. 'And it looks as if we'll have another Christmas of it too.'

'Don't be downhearted, Mam. When the Americans come over in force it's bound to make a difference. Everyone is hoping and praying it will soon end,' Alice reminded her.

'I'll say "Amen" to that,' Maggie replied.

Mae echoed her aunt's word, the awful prospect of Pip facing the German forces in the near future filling her mind. The thought haunted her day and night.

Chapter Twenty-Nine

MAGGIE AND ALICE were both very apprehensive as Sunday approached. Mae was less so for she wasn't as deeply involved, although she did wonder just what her Uncle Billy would have to say for himself.

Maggie had made a cottage pie and there was an apple tart to follow, and the kitchen table had been set with a crisp white cloth and her best dishes.

'You're putting on quite a spread for him, Mam,' Alice remarked as she placed the cranberry-glass cruet set in the centre of the table.

'Well, it's not often I have anyone for supper and with you two being home as well, it's a bit of an occasion,' Maggie replied as nonchalantly as she could. If the truth were told she was a little nervous as to how he and Alice would get on. She'd seen Billy a couple of times now but for Alice it might prove to be an ordeal.

He arrived punctually at six o'clock, and as her mother

opened the front door Alice glanced at Mae. 'I still don't know what to say to him. To start with, what do I call him?' she whispered.

'Just be your usual self, Alice,' Mae whispered back, giving her an encouraging smile.

As Maggie ushered him into the kitchen Alice was surprised. He wasn't what she had imagined at all and it was something of a shock to realise that she resembled him, although his once dark curly hair was now grey.

'Billy, this is your daughter Alice and this is Mae, John's girl,' Maggie announced rather formally.

To cover the sense of guilt and embarrassment that washed over him as he met the child he'd never before seen, Billy smiled and spoke first to Mae. 'You're the image of your mam, Mae. Sure, a bit taller perhaps, but anyone who knew Beth would have no doubts as to whose child you are and John must have been very proud of you.'

'He was, Uncle Billy,' Mae answered quietly, thinking how strange the name sounded on her tongue.

He didn't miss the note of pain in her voice. 'I'm sorry that he's . . . gone. War is a terrible thing as I'm sure you know only too well.' He turned to Alice at last. He'd spent the last few days and nights wondering what he could possibly say to her. 'Alice, I'm very glad you agreed to see me. I would have understood if you'd felt you didn't want to. I'm sorry for . . . everything, for not even knowing I had a daughter. I can see for myself that you're a fine girl and I know from what your mam has told me that you're a good nurse too.'

Alice felt the tears prick her eyes. He was just a quietly spoken, ageing man who'd lost his arm in the service of his country. 'I . . . I think Mam has been exaggerating.'

'Ah, not a bit of it, Alice. It's brave of you both to go over there to nurse,' Billy replied, relieved that she hadn't greeted him with hostility or resentment.

'Right, well, if you'll all sit down I'll get that pie out of the oven,' Maggie instructed, feeling relieved herself that the atmosphere wasn't nearly as tense as she'd anticipated.

During the meal Alice, Aunty Maggie and her new-found Uncle Billy all seemed to be watching what they said, Mae thought. She found him quiet, good-humoured and, when he spoke of his time in the Navy, quite knowledgeable. She'd told Maggie earlier that she thought it might be helpful if Alice could spend some time alone with him and Maggie had agreed. Mae helped her aunt to clear the dishes when the meal was over and then announced that she was going across to see how Jimmy was getting on.

'I'll pop over with you for a few minutes. I want to ask Agnes a favour,' Maggie added, ignoring the searching look Alice gave her. 'I won't be long, Billy.'

As they left Billy smiled at Alice, who sat opposite him at the table. 'They weren't very subtle about that, were they?'

Alice shook her head. 'I think it was Mae's idea. I . . . I told her I wanted to see you and to ask you . . .'

'Why I deserted you all,' Billy finished for her.

Alice nodded, her hands clenched tightly in front of her, anxious to hear what he had to say and wishing now that Jimmy was with her for support.

Billy took a deep breath; he'd anticipated this. 'It was a long time ago, Alice, and I was a different person then. I was not much older than Eddie is now and I felt that life wasn't working out the way I wanted it to. I'd come from Belfast in the hope of a better life but I . . . I could get no steady work and we were always hard up. I was young, restless, craving adventure and excitement, but I was tied down with your mam and Eddie. I started to drink far too much and that only made my situation seem worse. Then when Beth died your mam told me she'd promised her she would bring Mae up too. I knew John would carry on going away to sea – he had little choice, it was a steady job – and I resented the fact that your mam had saddled me with John's child. It added to my sense of . . . desperation.'

'And . . . me? Did I add to it as well?' Alice asked quietly, trying to imagine the person he had been all those years ago.

Billy nodded sadly. 'I'll speak plainly, Alice, there's no use wrapping it up. I'm sorry to say that when I found out your mam was expecting again I felt I couldn't take any more. I had to get away. I felt I was trapped in a tunnel and there was no light, no hope at the end of it. I'm sorry, girl, I was a fool, an eejit. I was selfish and irresponsible. I didn't even know if your mam and Eddie and you would be all right. I thought of no one but myself and I have no excuses for that.' He leaned forward and placed his hands gently over hers. 'I'm so very, very sorry, Alice. I can't undo the past but believe me, I feel that I'm the one who has lost the most by what I did. I don't know my children and I can never regain those years.'

Alice nodded slowly. He had been brutally honest with her. 'Why did you never try to get in touch?'

Billy sighed heavily; he'd known she would ask this too. 'By the time I came to my senses I was in the Navy, I had been for many years and it had become my . . . home. I didn't feel as if I belonged to a family. I didn't know if any of you would want to hear from me or wish me to come back into your lives after so long an absence and then . . .'

'Jutland,' Alice said flatly.

Billy nodded. 'Jutland. It changed everything.'

'What happened to you?' she asked. 'Don't be afraid to tell me, I'm used to seeing what guns and shells do to men.'

'I was in charge of the for'ard gun battery on HMS *Indefatigable*. She took a direct hit and the explosion blew me off my feet and hurled me against the shattered bulkhead. A piece of jagged iron plating ripped through my arm and I really don't remember much after that but I realised that all my lads on that battery had been killed. It all happened so quickly. There was thick black smoke everywhere, more explosions and then I was in the water. I can still remember the shock as that freezing cold water closed over me, but they said in the hospital that it was probably the intense cold that saved me from bleeding to death. Somehow I managed to grab hold of a piece of wreckage and hang on until I was picked up, but I lost the arm. It was too badly mangled to save. But I was lucky, I survived. Hundreds didn't.'

Alice thought of all the hideous wounds she'd seen. 'I was with Jimmy Mercer, my young man, when they put him under to take off his leg. He'd been so long getting to hospital that gangrene had set in. He was terrified even though he was in terrible pain but he was one of the lucky ones too. I've lost count of the times I've stood and held the instruments for amputation, picked shrapnel and fragments of cloth from wounds, seen mangled, shredded limbs, awful stomach and chest wounds, and have closed dying eyes.'

His hands tightened on hers. 'Things no girl of your age

should ever have had to do or see, Alice.'

'I never told Mam just how . . . bad things were or how atrocious the conditions the lads had to contend with. The Somme was really terrible, like a nightmare. We worked until we were ready to drop but we couldn't cope, there were just too many wounded men coming in. That's when Jimmy lost his leg and Eddie was wounded too, but despite that he carried Jimmy on his back all the way to the clearing station. He saved his life. But Jimmy's brother Harry and his mate were killed.'

Billy couldn't speak; there was a lump in his throat and his memories of *Indefatigable* and the battle and the pain he'd suffered faded before the overwhelming pride and admiration he now felt for his son and daughter.

'I . . . I couldn't tell Mam things like that, she'd get upset and worried.' Alice managed a wry smile. 'And she'd put her foot down and not let either of us girls go back. Both Mae and I are too young to be officially out there but we had to do something to help.'

Billy understood. 'I'm glad you felt you could tell me, Alice. You're very brave – all three of you.'

'Do you want to come . . . home?' she asked bluntly to hide her emotions.

'I do, if your mam can find it in her heart to take me back. I want to get to know my family. Would you be agreeable, Alice?'

Slowly she nodded. 'I think so, but it's Mam's decision. I know Jimmy and I will get married one day and so, please God, will Mae – but I have to tell you that Eddie isn't going to like it. He's very bitter.'

'That's only to be expected and it's no more than I deserve,' Billy said with resignation.

Alice smiled. 'But he might come round, given time. No one knows when the war will end and he won't get leave until it does.'

'Unless he gets shipped home again.'

'No, I don't think there will be a third time. He's with a supply unit now, he's behind the front lines.'

'Sure, that must be a relief to your mam. She's been through so much over the years, Alice. I can only try and make up for all the pain and hardship I've caused her: I sincerely mean that.'

Alice smiled at him again. 'I know you do . . . Da.'

Billy now felt the tears prick his eyes. 'I never thought I'd hear you say that, Alice.'

'I wondered myself if I'd ever say it,' she replied, thinking that when she'd first met him she'd had no intention of calling him Da or Dad, but now she felt that there was the beginning of a bond between them. A bond forged by their experiences of war and suffering.

The intimate conversation ended as Maggie and Mae came into the room but Maggie was relieved to see that they seemed to be getting on well. It was a hopeful sign, she thought, although she still hadn't reached a decision about Billy coming back to live with her.

When he'd gone, having been invited for supper again before the girls returned to France, Mae looked questioningly at her cousin. 'Well, did you ask him?'

'I did and I think I can understand how he felt . . . then, but it's still hard to accept that he just walked out and never really thought about us for years. That hurts, but maybe in time I'll be able to forget, he's so different now.' Alice was struggling to put her feelings into words. 'If . . . if he weren't my father and I'd met him for the first time tonight I would think he was a really nice man.'

'But because he is your father you don't think he's nice?' Mae asked.

'No, I did like him and I think he really is sorry and wants to try to make it up to Mam and me and our Eddie, but I think what I'm trying to say is that what he did all those years ago wasn't *nice*.'

'It certainly wasn't,' Mae agreed.

'But I could talk to him, Mae, about the war, the way I can't talk to Mam. He told me what happened to him at Jutland, how he lost his arm and is lucky to be alive and that's what made him want to come home, want to get to know us, and I hope Mam gives him another chance.'

Mae smiled at her. 'If she does then I'd say you are lucky, Alice. Oh, I know the circumstances are very different but I wish I'd been able to get to know my mother and I wish Da had survived.'

Alice bit her lip. She supposed that despite everything she was fortunate to be given this chance to get to know her father. 'I know, Mae, and I'm glad he's coming again before we have to leave.'

'Will you go and see Eddie when you get back?' Mae asked.

Alice frowned. 'I don't know. He was really mad with me and I think he's being very unfair. I'll have a talk to Lizzie about it, see what she thinks.'

'Did you tell your da how Eddie feels?'

'I did. There was no use trying to hide it. I think I'll discuss it all with Jimmy, he's more detached from it all and one day he'll be part of this family, as will Pip.'

Mae looked unhappy. 'I hope there will be a letter tomorrow, Alice. His letters have always been so regular.'

'Don't forget they have further to come now, Mae,' Alice reminded her, although she desperately hoped that nothing awful had happened to Pip Middlehurst whilst they'd been away. If there was no letter this week Mae would be frantic to get back to find out why.

Chapter Thirty

———◆◆◆———

To EVERYONE'S RELIEF there was a letter from Pip in the afternoon post the following day but the news it contained wasn't what Mae wanted to hear.

'What's wrong?' Alice demanded, seeing the expression on Mae's face change from profound relief to fear.

'He's being sent to the front next week. Oh, Alice, it's what I dreaded.'

'I know, but you knew he would be sent sooner or later. They all have to go,' Alice reminded her gently.

'I'd just hoped it would be later – much later, perhaps when the next American troops arrived, but they're going to join the Canadians.'

'Try not to worry too much, Mae. He's not a fool, he won't go doing anything . . . rash.'

Mae nodded but she'd seen so much of the aftermath and consequences of battle that Alice's words didn't do much to allay her fears. Bullets and shells didn't discriminate between the rash and the cautious.

'I just want to get back now, Alice. At least if I'm there and anything . . . happens to him, I can get to Passchendaele Ridge – well, close enough anyway.'

Alice could understand that but she herself had no wish to rush back. She was reluctant to leave Jimmy and her mam, especially as Maggie had indicated that she still wasn't sure what to do about Billy.

'I just wish she would make up her mind one way or the other, Jimmy,' she confided the night before they were due to leave.

Jimmy looked perturbed. He didn't want Alice to go back but knew she must, but this business of her mam and Billy McEvoy was confusing and unsettling her and she'd fallen out with her brother over it. 'Don't go getting too upset about it, Alice. How did they seem to be getting on when he came yesterday?'

'Fine. I thought she was a lot happier than when he came for supper last time.'

'Probably because she wasn't so worried about how you and he would get on,' Jimmy deduced aloud. 'Was it any easier for you?'

'Yes, of course, and I said I'd write to him when I get time. He can't write back because he says all he can manage with his left hand is his signature but he said he'd ask Mam to include any news he has. I'd just feel easier in my mind, Jimmy, if I knew where we all stand.'

'We seem to know exactly where your Eddie stands on the matter,' Jimmy reminded her. He could see Eddie's point; he

329

wasn't at all sure how he'd feel if the father who'd deserted him as a baby suddenly turned up again.

'Well, I'm not going to go and see our Eddie and tell him that I got on well with our da and that I think I can forgive and forget, and that I hope Mam gives him a second chance. I'm going to have a chat with Lizzie first to see what she says about it.'

Jimmy nodded his agreement. He'd never met this Lizzie and it was so long since he'd seen Eddie that he didn't know if he'd changed much, but he was glad his best mate had met someone special. 'You think she can talk him round?'

Alice shrugged. 'If anyone can, it's Lizzie. Oh, Jimmy, I just wish there was some end to this war in sight. Haven't enough lads been killed and wounded? What have either side gained in three years? A few miles of useless mud and towns and villages in utter ruins! And now Mae is worried sick that something will happen to Pip and if – God forbid – it does, it will destroy her.'

'I don't know when it will all end, Alice. I don't know why they go on fighting. Do any of us know now exactly what we're fighting *for*?' Jimmy said sombrely. 'But it will have to finish one day and there *will* be peace again.'

'Let's hope that we're all still here to enjoy it, Jimmy.'

Jimmy put his arms around her. 'I will be, Alice, luv. One day you'll come home to me and we'll get married.'

'Oh, I wish I didn't have to go, Jimmy, I really do, but there will be lads who need to be cared for.'

'I know, and I hope you and Eddie can sort things out. You shouldn't be arguing – not at a time like this.'

Alice kissed him. 'Maybe everything can be worked out, once

Mam's made up her mind. I'd better get back now; we've an early start in the morning. It won't be until after Christmas that we'll get leave again, I'm afraid.'

'Maybe it will be over by then,' Jimmy said with far more optimism than he felt.

'That's what we've said for the past three years,' Alice replied.

Even though they were both cold and tired after the journey Alice decided she would take the bull by the horns and discuss the matter with Lizzie straight away. Clasping a mug of hot tea between her cold hands she sat down on the edge of the bed beside her friend while Mae started to unpack.

'So, how did it go, Alice? Did you see your father?' Lizzie asked.

'Yes, and I liked him, Lizzie. I didn't really know how I'd feel when I saw him but I found I could talk to him. I felt I could ask him anything and I did, and he answered all my questions honestly. He tried his best to explain. Of course, I really don't know or can't imagine what he was like when he was a young man, although he tried to tell me, but now he's quiet and thoughtful and I think he's still fond of Mam.'

'And is she going to take him back?' Lizzie probed, watching Alice's expression closely. She had something she had to tell her friend and she was not very happy about it.

Alice shrugged. 'I just don't know. She seems to be having trouble making up her mind.'

'You certainly can't blame her for that, Alice. It's a big decision, a real leap of faith, trust and hope that this time it won't end in tears.'

'Has our Eddie said anything more about it?' Alice asked tentatively.

'He's said a great deal, I can tell you. But I'm afraid it's not what you want to hear, Alice.'

Alice sipped her tea and grimaced at the taste. 'He's still angry about it then?'

'He is. I've tried hard to put your point of view over but he's adamant. He wants nothing to do with him and he says he can't for the life of him understand your attitude or your mam's. He keeps saying you should both have more self-respect, more pride and dignity than to let someone who treated you so badly just walk back into your lives.' Lizzie sighed and took a sip of her drink. 'He doesn't believe Billy's sorry for what he did, he's convinced that the real reason why he now wants to come home is because he's lost his arm and been invalided out of the Navy. He just wants someone to look after him. I've tried to point out that all your lives have changed because of the war, that maybe it really is the time to forgive but . . . Well, I'm not going to go harping on about it, Alice, it won't do any good and I don't want to drive a wedge between us. I care about him too much. I know he's got his faults but he's been through a lot. I'm really sorry, Alice.'

'You tried, Lizzie,' Alice replied gloomily.

Mae smiled at Lizzie. 'It won't resolve anything if you and Eddie fall out over it.'

'It won't. Would you like me to write to your mam and try to explain how he feels and how I feel about him?' Lizzie asked Alice.

'I don't know, is the honest answer.'

'I think I owe it to her anyway to let her know that Eddie and

I intend to get married when this damned war is over and I know Eddie isn't going to write to her,' Lizzie informed them both.

'He's asked you?' Mae enquired.

Lizzie nodded and smiled. 'He's even been talking about saving for a ring but I've told him to keep the money, we'll need it one day. An engagement ring would be a bit of a waste as I can't wear it very often – as you know from experience, Mae.'

Mae nodded, glancing at the ring on her finger, which she would soon have to replace in its box. Her thoughts inevitably turned to Pip, wondering where he was and if he was safe.

'I suppose all we can do is see how things work out,' Alice said but then she brightened. 'But I'm delighted that you'll be my sister-in-law one day, Lizzie.'

'And my cousin-in-law,' Mae added.

Lizzie stood up and collected the now empty mugs. 'The Lord alone knows when that day will come, none of us do, and Sister informed us that our troops now hold two of the three ridges around Ypres but that the Canadians are having a hard time of it at Passchendaele Ridge. But at least there isn't much likelihood of another big offensive before Christmas.'

'I suppose we should be thankful for that,' Alice replied.

Mae said nothing but cold fingers of fear were closing around her heart, for Pip's division was with the Canadians.

Life settled back into the routine of ward duties and the steady admission of wounded men from the front lines, and to Mae's intense relief Pip's letters, although far more infrequent, kept arriving. He always seemed to be cheerful and played down the hardships and the dangers but Mae knew full well that the casualties were heavy, although few came to their hospital, for the Canadians and Americans had their own. It was a blessed relief when they heard that on 10 November Passchendaele Ridge had at last been captured.

'Maybe we can start to look forward to Christmas now, Mae,' Lizzie said when she heard the news.

'It's great, Lizzie, to know that the fighting has stopped for now, but I wish I could see him. I wish we could have as good a Christmas as we did last year.'

Lizzie nodded, remembering that evening at Monsieur Clari's café when Eddie had given her the lace-edged handkerchiefs and they'd realised that there was something more than just friendship between them.

'You'll be the only one of us who will be able to spend it with your fiancé, Lizzie. Jimmy's at home in Liverpool and Pip is up at the front,' Alice reminded her friend.

'Yes, I'm lucky that they've kept Eddie at that supply depot, and he thinks so too; the last thing he wants is to be sent back to his battalion. I know it won't be like last year but we should try and make the best of it,' Lizzie urged.

'How?' Alice demanded. 'Our Eddie and I are not on speaking terms.'

Lizzie frowned, that was one situation that didn't look like being resolved any time soon. 'Perhaps it would be best if just the three of us went out in the afternoon on Christmas Eve, providing Sister lets us off. Then I'll see Eddie on my own. I'll ask him to find out when he thinks he'll get time off,' she suggested tactfully.

It was a far from ideal situation but there was little they could do to change it, Mae thought regretfully. It wasn't going to be a 'season of goodwill' between Alice and Eddie and she wondered sadly how Aunty Maggie was feeling about Eddie's refusal to write to his mother. She wondered too just when her aunt would come to a decision about Billy.

As Christmas approached Maggie felt she couldn't put off her decision much longer. She was deeply unhappy that Eddie was taking it all very badly and refusing to write, but she'd had a long and lovely letter from Lizzie explaining how he felt and asking for her blessing on their engagement, although she'd said there was no hope of them setting a date yet for a wedding. Even though she had never met her future daughter-in-law Maggie had warmed to her and realised that the girl was in a very difficult position, caught between love and loyalty to Eddie and her friendship with Alice. Perhaps if she herself stopped dithering and made a decision – even if in Eddie's eyes it was the wrong one – it would help . . . somehow.

She poured herself another cup of tea and thought back over the past months. She had become accustomed to Billy's visits, she'd become accustomed to the man he was now, she'd even admitted to Agnes that she was fond of him, but still at the very back of her mind the doubts niggled. What if it was all an act? What if when she took him back he reverted to his former ways? What if he was only looking for someone to look after him in his advancing years? She sighed heavily; this was getting her nowhere at all and she knew her indecision was helping no one. Not Alice, not herself, not Billy and certainly not Eddie. If she had any hope of trying to reconcile her son to his father, even if it took years, she had to make up her mind.

At last she stood up and went the drawer in the dresser where she kept a writing pad and envelopes. She had three letters to write before she could hope to get some sleep. One to Alice, a very difficult one to Eddie and Lizzie, and the note to Billy telling him he could come back home.

She hadn't expected him to arrive quite as soon as he did. He must have packed his things and left the day after he'd got her note, she thought as she ushered him into the house. He carried one small suitcase; he obviously hadn't had much to pack.

'I'll put the kettle on and then we'll get you settled in, Billy,' she said.

Billy put the case down and took a small box from the pocket of his jacket. 'I want you to have this, Maggie, as a token of my thanks for letting me come back home and of the affection I still feel for you. I know it's been a hard decision for you to make.'

Maggie was surprised but took the box and opened it. Inside was a gold brooch shaped as an anchor set with tiny rubies. 'I didn't expect anything, Billy, but it's beautiful and . . . thoughtful of you.'

'I bought it years ago in India. It took my fancy and the Indian chap who sold it to me said it would be a lucky charm for a sailor. He didn't get that right though!'

'It was in a way, Billy. You survived. Thank you.'

'You still haven't heard from Eddie?' he asked as he sat down at the table, feeling a sense of relief that at last he was able to call this house 'home' again. His lodgings had been decidedly bleak and impersonal and he'd come to hate them.

Maggie shook her head sadly. 'No, but I had a lovely letter from the girl he's courting, Lizzie. It appears that she's going to be our daughter-in-law, Billy, one day. She's a nurse, a friend of

Mae's and Alice's, and she's tried hard to explain how Eddie feels. I've never met her of course but she sounds a sensible and caring girl.'

'Maggie, I never wanted to cause a rift between Eddie and Alice. When I came to see you the first time, that was the last thing I envisaged would happen. I don't want to be the cause of bad feeling between them and heartache for you.'

'I know that. Well, the decision was mine so I suppose some of the blame must be laid at my door. All we can hope is that he'll change his mind one day. This war will have to end sometime and then he'll come home and we'll just have to see how things work out. I've written to them both and I've "made my bed". And, talking of beds . . .' Maggie placed the teapot on the table and sat down opposite him. 'I . . . there hasn't been . . . a man in my life since you left, Billy, and well, I don't feel as if . . .' She was struggling, becoming embarrassed.

He nodded. 'I understand, Maggie. It's going to take time for you to get used to having me here again and it's too soon for anything . . . intimate, although I do have feelings for you.'

She was very relieved for this had been causing her some concern. Yes, she was fond of him but he was right, it was just too soon to think that they could share a bed again. Perhaps in time but not now. 'Then you won't mind having the room Eddie shared with John?'

'Not at all. And I'll be able to do a bit around the house: the Navy made me self-reliant. I'll contribute to the expenses too, Maggie. I've got my pension and a little saved. I don't drink or gamble any more, all I'll need is a few coppers for my tobacco.'

She smiled at him. 'You certainly have changed, Billy. What money you earned before always burned a hole in your pocket until it was gone. Now that we've sorted all that out we'll get your case unpacked and then I thought we'd have a fish supper as a bit of a treat.'

He reached across and took her hand. 'I won't let you down again, Maggie, I promise. We'll be grand together from now on, sure we will.' He smiled, and looking at him Maggie was sure he was telling the truth.

'I hope so, I really do. Welcome home, Billy,' she said quietly. She was happy now the decision was made, and happier still that she felt she could trust him.

Chapter Thirty-One

EVERYONE KNEW THAT the offensive was coming, for the Bolshevik Revolution the previous October and the resultant collapse of the Russian Army had released thousands of German troops from the Eastern Front.

Christmas had passed quietly without much in the way of either festive spirit or fare, even though the countryside had been scoured for chickens or pigs to provide a meal. They had decorated the wards with greenery but there were fewer comforts coming from home, for things were getting expensive and scarcer as U-boat activity had forced the merchant ships to sail in convoys now with naval escorts, a slow and often costly means of bringing in supplies.

The early months of 1918 had been bitterly cold with heavy snow and frost, and again the troops in the trenches had suffered terribly, but now spring was on the way and the war was into its fourth year. The girls knew the fighting was about to start again for the hospital had been cleared of as many patients as possible to make room for new casualties.

'Oh, I'm so glad Jimmy is out of it,' Alice had remarked wearily as they'd bade farewell to the last of the 'Boat Sitting' patients, en route to the hospital ship.

'I just wish Pip was,' Mae added. In the last letter she'd had from him two weeks ago he'd written that they were being moved up to Arras, which she knew was closer to the front line, and she lived in fear of him being so exposed to danger.

Lizzie said nothing. She was thankful that Eddie was still stationed at the supply depot and therefore relatively safe, but to say it aloud she felt was tempting fate, particularly as the offensive was expected to start at any time now. It upset her that Eddie and Alice were still not speaking. His attitude had hardened after he'd received his mother's letter telling him Billy had moved back in, and his views on his father had become even more bitterly entrenched, but Alice and Mae had seemed to take the news well.

'Are you going to see Eddie on your next afternoon off?' Mae enquired as they walked together to the mess tent.

'Of course. It might be the last time for quite a while. There will be no time off when the hospital trains start to arrive. You know that, Mae,' Lizzie reminded her.

'See if he knows anything more than we do. They take supplies up the line so he might have more news. At least then we'll be a bit more prepared.'

Lizzie nodded. 'Has Pip heard when the next lot of American troops are expected to arrive? The weather on the Atlantic won't be as bad as in the winter months and surely they've had enough time to train them and organise ships to bring them across. It's almost a year now since they declared war. Their doctors and nurses have been here for ages – they've had time to set up their hospitals.'

'He seems to think it will be sometime this month – I hope it will be soon. At least when they finally do come over they'll all be fresh and fit, not like our lads who are getting weary of the conditions and the fighting. We could certainly do with their extra support now.'

'I think it's going to be a big offensive this time. I heard Surgeon Major Harris telling Sister Harper that deeper defences were being dug and new trenches and strongholds were being fortified. Trench raiding has been forbidden and artillery barrages curtailed.'

Mae frowned. 'That means the hospitals will be even more overcrowded.'

'And it will double our workload but I don't see them sending any more nurses over to help,' Lizzie added.

'With the amount of men we've already sent back I'm sure the hospitals can't spare any more staff and Aunty Maggie said in her last letter that things are getting bad at home too. Coal is still expensive owing to the continuing disputes over pay by the miners and so is the cost of living – and they are bringing in rationing because so much is having to be shipped in.'

Lizzie sighed. 'I know we say this a dozen times a day but I wish to God it was all over and we could go home.'

Mae nodded her silent agreement followed by her usual prayer. *Keep them all safe, God, please. Keep them all safe.*

To her consternation Lizzie found Eddie in a very depressed mood. Sergeant Walker, equally grim-faced, instructed Eddie to take his young lady for a short walk by the harbour. It was a chilly early March afternoon with a brisk wind blowing in off the sea and the waterfront was crowded with the usual activities of unloading supplies and embarking the last of the wounded, but as they walked towards the sand dunes it became quieter.

'Eddie, luv, what's wrong? I can see by your face that something's upset you and you've hardly said a word while I've been chattering on. Has the offensive already started? Is that it?'

Eddie shook his head. 'No, but it will start any day now, Lizzie. I've got to go back. I got the order yesterday to rejoin the battalion.'

Lizzie stared at him in horror as fear surged through her. 'Oh, no! Oh, Eddie, no! Can't Sergeant Walker do anything? Can't he say he needs you here?'

'I asked him the same thing, Lizzie. There's nothing he can do. I know he's not happy about it but it's an order. There are three of us going back, the other two are in the Gloucestershire Regiment. After he'd told us, he said he was sorry to lose us as we were all good lads and then he walked away but we heard him muttering "short of bloody cannon fodder". And that's what we are, Lizzie. The Boche have got all those troops from the Russian front now. I don't want to go. I don't want to have to face it all again. Every hour of every day wondering when I'll be hit. I'm not a coward, Lizzie, I just . . .'

Lizzie put her arms around him. 'Of course you're not a coward, Eddie! You've proved that. Twice they've sent you back to the front and anyone who says they're not afraid to face it all again is a damned fool!' She was more in control of her emotions now. 'When will you have to leave?'

'Tomorrow, first thing,' Eddie replied dully. Oh, he'd

become so used to life here and its relative safety and comforts. Of course going up the line to the front held its dangers; there was always the chance that a stray shell or burst of machine-gun fire would catch you, and in the dire winter conditions the animals would often stumble or slip and that could cause the cart or gun carriage to overturn, but it had never happened to him. He'd been spared the atrocious winter conditions in the trenches, he'd been decently fed and he'd been able to sleep at night, but now . . .

'Will I see you again before you go?' Lizzie asked, feeling utterly dejected but also thinking of Alice. She couldn't let them part with so much animosity still between them.

Eddie didn't reply.

'Ask if you can come to the hospital tonight for half an hour, after you've finished your duties, of course. I'll ask Sergeant Walker, if you like. Eddie, you can't leave without seeing Alice and Mae, you just can't!'

Still he didn't reply.

'Eddie, if you go without seeing your sister and . . . if anything happened to you, I'd never be able to forgive myself and I don't think Alice would either. Please, Eddie?' she begged.

At last he nodded. 'I'll ask him, Lizzie, but you'll have to understand that if he refuses there's nothing I can do about it.'

Thankful that he had agreed, Lizzie clung tightly to his arm as they retraced their steps, determined that she would wait to see what the sergeant had to say. At least if he refused she could go back and see if perhaps Alice could be spared for half an hour to make her peace with Eddie before he left.

* * *

343

Both Mae and Alice received the news with stunned disbelief but it was Alice who found her voice first. 'They can't! They can't send him back again, Lizzie! This is the *third* time!'

'I know, Alice, but they are. Even Sergeant Walker can't do anything about it. I'm just as upset and angry as you are. It simply doesn't seem fair. But he's coming to see us tonight.'

Mae was as worried as the other two but she realised that if they were sending men back to their regiments then it looked as if things were bad, that they expected the Germans to break through the line this time. But she didn't voice her thoughts for now Lizzie would know the terrible anxiety and anguish she suffered every day over Pip.

Sister Harper, having heard the circumstances from Lizzie, gave her permission for Eddie to be allowed to say his farewells in the comparative privacy of the billet her three nurses shared.

'It's extremely irregular, Nurse, but under such circumstances I will allow it. There will be the other nurses present but at least it's better than having to stand at the gate of the compound.'

Lizzie thanked her and as the girl left, Sister felt a frisson of resentment run through her. She knew he wasn't the only one – but was it absolutely necessary to send the lad back? she thought. Hadn't he been through enough already? There was only so much stress the mind could endure. Surely he was better deployed in the supply lines where he was familiar with the work and routine? But then, like Mae, she knew that the brass were expecting a major offensive and very soon.

By scrounging and begging from both the other nurses and some of their patients they'd managed to scrape together a few things for Eddie to take with him. A small bar of chocolate, five cigarettes and some matches, half a dozen humbugs wrapped in a twist of greaseproof paper, an extra pair of woollen gloves and a very small flask of brandy, donated – surreptitiously – by Sister Harper herself, with the instruction that if a single word was said about it they would all find themselves in dire trouble.

Lizzie and Mae had carefully packed the items into a small canvas bag, Mae hoping they would help lift Eddie's spirits a little and Lizzie praying silently that they would be a reminder of the love and affection they had for him.

Alice paced restlessly up and down, wondering how she was going to tell her mam that they'd sent him back again, and feeling apprehensive and miserable that their last meeting had ended in such harsh, angry words.

A middle-aged orderly escorted Eddie to their tent, remarking tersely that this was usually strictly forbidden and advising him not to take advantage of Sister's generosity. 'I've to come back for you in half an hour,' was his parting comment.

He'd hardly changed since she'd last seen him seven months ago, Alice thought as he entered. But then what had she expected? she asked herself. Had she expected him to have put on weight, to look healthier and stronger? They all had to put up with far from comfortable conditions but at least he was clean and tidy, his uniform looked smart and his boots polished.

'Eddie, come on in and sit down, luv. We've had a bit of a whip-round and managed to get you a few comforts to take with you,' Lizzie informed him, trying her best to inject a note of cheer into the occasion although she felt her heart was breaking.

'Everyone was very generous,' Mae added, handing him the

canvas bag and lowering her voice to a whisper, 'even Sister Harper.'

Eddie smiled at them both as he delved into the bag. 'Tell everyone thanks. You know I appreciate it.'

'Eddie, I'll . . . let Mam know . . .' Alice said quietly. 'And I'm sorry we . . . don't agree.'

Eddie nodded grimly. 'I don't think we'll ever agree on that subject, Alice,' he said coldly.

'But *we* don't have to fall out over it, Eddie, do we?'

Eddie looked away. He didn't answer.

Mae realised that the situation was deteriorating fast and could see that Lizzie was getting upset. 'Let's not spend what time we have dwelling on past . . . differences. Let's all have a cup of tea – I begged a few biscuits to have with it. Eddie, did you manage to get a lift back too? It's bitterly cold tonight.'

'I did, Mae. There were some supplies to be delivered here so I'll go back with the driver,' Eddie replied, gratefully taking the mug Mae offered.

The precious minutes seemed to fly past, Lizzie thought as they drank their tea and Eddie exclaimed over the generosity of the comforts, particularly the brandy. The tea tasted even more bitter than usual and it was as if a lump of lead had settled in her stomach. She was very grateful to Mae and the other two nurses who were off duty as they tried to keep the atmosphere light and cheerful. Mae would know exactly how she was feeling, wondering when she would see Eddie again, praying nothing would happen to him. Pip had been away so long and all Mae had to depend on were his letters. She'd made Eddie promise faithfully he would write.

All too soon the orderly poked his head through the flap and Eddie stood up.

'I'll walk to the gate with you,' Lizzie said firmly, grabbing her cape from the bed where she'd placed it, determined to stay with him until the very last minute.

'Thanks for the tea and biscuits and everything else,' Eddie said, glancing round. 'Mae, you look after yourself.'

Mae hugged him. 'I will. Good luck, Eddie.'

Alice bit her lip, wondering what to do, for his attitude towards her still seemed chilly and formal. 'Try and write, Eddie, please? You know how worried we all will be about you,' she said.

Eddie nodded and turned to leave but then turned back, his expression changing. 'Alice . . . I'm sorry . . .'

Alice hurled herself at him, tears trickling down her cheeks. 'Oh, take care, Eddie! We can sort it all out. Just . . . just come back safely.'

Eddie felt a lump come into his throat as the memory of the day he'd brought Jimmy into this hospital to her returned; the old terrors were closing in on him. 'If . . . if I don't come back, Alice, tell Mam . . . tell her . . . I'm sorry,' he choked.

And then Lizzie was beside him, her hand firmly on his arm, her eyes full of love and a quiet determination. 'You'll come back, Eddie. I'm convinced this is third time lucky for you. Now, we'd better go before we're all reported to Sister.'

Mae put her arms around Alice as they left. 'I think Lizzie is right, Alice. He'll come through it safely this time.'

'I hope you're both right, Mae, but at least he didn't go with bad feelings still between us. I'll write and tell Mam that.'

Chapter Thirty-Two

———◆———

THE BOMBARDMENT HAD started on 18 March, the day after he'd rejoined the 18th Battalion, Eddie remembered now as he searched his pockets for a cigarette, but it was a battalion of strangers, all Liverpool men but none whose faces were remotely familiar. The lads he'd joined with, trained with and fought with were gone, just memories. He'd stoically endured the constant thundering of the guns and the explosions of bursting shells; even though the dugout was thirty feet deep the blasts had shaken the ground, cracked the wooden support posts and sent earth trickling down on their heads. And then after forty-eight hours, as suddenly as it had started, it had ceased and he'd felt the familiar twisting of his guts as he knew what they faced.

Dawn of the twenty-first had been chilly with a thick, swirling fog, a mixture of smoke, gas and low cloud, but none of them had been prepared for what had faced them: the sheer speed and ferocity of the German advance. By mid-morning the crack troops from the Russian front had smashed through the front lines. The men in those lines had died to buy time for those who followed them but still they'd been forced to retreat, and from then on the nightmare had begun in earnest. He'd estimated that the enemy was a bare half an hour behind them and those who hadn't been wounded had had to run until they were gasping for breath and forced to slow their pace. Field dressing stations and casualty clearing stations had been overrun; most had managed to get their nurses away safely but doctors, orderlies and wounded alike had been taken prisoner. For fifteen chaotic and terrifying days it had been retreat, retreat, retreat, he thought bitterly, finding at last a butt end of a cigarette. The roads had been clogged with lines of withdrawing men and equipment, ambulances, refugees and reinforcements being rushed forward to try to stop the German advance. At times they'd been ordered to stop and fight but had suffered such heavy casualties that they'd inevitably had to fall back. Roiglise, Rouvrel, Roupy, Ham and now they were entrenched at Elverdinghe on the Ypres Salient.

He looked dully around at the group of lads he was with – those that were left, he thought bitterly. They were all filthy, exhausted, hungry and thirsty; nearly all had flesh wounds. He couldn't remember when he'd eaten the last of his bread ration or taken a swig of water from his canteen, which he knew was now virtually empty, but what was far worse than any of these privations was the terrible sense of defeat and despair that enveloped everyone. All the ground gained in the past years of fighting, ground paid for dearly in blood and loss of life, was now in enemy hands. He was so tired and utterly demoralised that he no longer cared what happened to him; he couldn't think straight and he didn't even feel fear any more. His hands were shaking with fatigue as he attempted to strike the match.

''Ere, mate. I'll do it. Yer shaking that much yer'll set yerself alight.' A match was struck and he drew deeply on the butt end. He nodded his thanks to the lad beside him, whose name, he thought, was Evans.

'Eh, up! Here comes trouble,' the lad muttered, digging Eddie in the ribs as Captain Pitman appeared. He at least wasn't as filthy as the rest of them, Eddie thought vaguely, in fact he looked almost clean and tidy, but then he hadn't been with them for very long.

'At ease, men,' the captain started and then cleared his throat. 'We've been ordered to join the eighty-ninth brigade tomorrow. Regretfully, there are so few of us left from all the Pals Battalions that it's the only sensible option. We'll be moving into the front line between the towns of Hazebrouck and Bailleul. The enemy has commenced an offensive in the Lys Valley and another towards Ypres and we have to stop them.' Again he cleared his throat. 'And I have received an Order of the Day from General Headquarters, issued this morning by Field Marshal Haig to all military personnel.'

This news was received in silence. You could see and feel their lack of interest, he thought, their hopelessness and despair, and although it unsettled him he could understand in part how they felt; however, it was up to him to rally them, for the situation was now desperate. He had no intention of reading it all, it definitely wouldn't raise morale for them to know that over 150,000 men had been killed, wounded or taken prisoner in the past three weeks or that all the reserves had been exhausted and the German line now stretched beyond Bapaume and Albert in the south and Armentières here in the north, putting the Channel ports in imminent danger.

'I will now read the concluding paragraph of that order. "There is no other cause open to us but to fight it out. Every position must be held to the last man. There must be no retirement. With our backs to the wall and believing in the justice of our cause, each one must fight on to the end. The safety of our homes and the freedom of mankind alike depend on the conduct of each one of us at this critical moment." Signed, Field Marshal Haig. That's it, lads. No more retreating. We stand and fight to the last man.'

No one broke the silence but you could feel the change in the atmosphere, he thought with some relief as he turned away. He'd leave them to digest Haig's orders, just as he'd taken the time to contemplate their dire meaning.

Eddie felt his mood shift; it was as if everything had suddenly become crystal clear to him. They were fighting not for some vague concept loosely defined by the words 'King and Country'. He realised now that what that really meant, and had in fact always meant, was they were fighting for their homes and their freedom. He was fighting now for Lizzie and their life together, their children as yet unborn and future generations. For Alice and Jimmy, Mae and Pip Middlehurst, Mam and even his father: the man who had walked out on them, but in the end hadn't he fought for them all at Jutland? Eddie's opinion of him was gradually changing: yes, he was fighting for Billy too. He was fighting for Harry and Tommy Mitford and all the other lads who had made the ultimate sacrifice. As Haig had said, their backs were to the wall, there was no other option open to them if they were to save their homes and families. If they were to stop the Channel ports from being overrun, leaving only that narrow stretch of water as the last bastion between oppression and freedom, they would fight to the last. He felt the weariness and the hopelessness of defeat fall away. Tomorrow he knew he would experience again the gut-twisting fear before the battle, but he also knew it wouldn't overwhelm him or stop him. This time it would be different because now he knew what he was really fighting for.

The first indication the girls had had that the offensive was under way was the steady stream of ambulances moving slowly down the road towards the hospital. Rumours had surged through the hospital all morning, terrible tales of the German advances, of medical staff and wounded being taken prisoner, but it appeared that no one actually knew *what* was happening or exactly *where* the enemy were.

There had then been no time to dwell on the situation as the wounded and dying were brought in.

They should all have been stretcher cases, Alice heard Sister Harper declare bitterly as she helped a man from the first ambulance who was using his rifle as a crutch for a mangled foot. They were all ragged and filthy, some with wounds that had not even been dressed, their faces grey and haggard with fatigue, eyes dull and glassy from lack of sleep, shock and despair. They hobbled on feet swollen and black from advanced trench foot, some crying openly and pitifully from the pain of gaping wounds and shattered bones.

'There are five hundred in this convoy and more on the way, God help us all!' Sister Harper informed them as she quickly and curtly issued orders. 'Nurses Strickland, McEvoy and Lawson to the dressing lines. Platt, Livesey and Stanford to the surgical assessment. The rest of you stay here to help these men.'

Alice, Mae and Lizzie ran across to the tent where tables stood piled with bandages, swabs, splints, sponges, boric ointment, gentian violet and two basins full of Dakin's solution for wet dressings. A medical officer followed them and took up his position at a small table, orderlies with stretchers awaiting his instructions.

'Nurse, let them in half a dozen at a time, please. Do whatever you can with their wounds, those you deem more serious pass on to me.'

Grabbing a pair of scissors each, Lizzie, Mae and Alice went to help the first of the walking casualties. Within minutes they were overwhelmed, surrounded by men and boys with bloody bandages that had dried and were stuck to their wounds.

'There's no easy way to do this, I'm really very sorry,' Lizzie apologised to a ragged corporal as she cut away his tunic to reveal a deep jagged shoulder wound covered with a filthy lint pad. He screamed in agony as she quickly ripped off the pad and then directed him on to the medical officer.

It was the Somme all over again, Alice thought, but she thanked God that she had not seen Eddie amongst the wounded – yet. They worked on all through the day, the evening and into the early hours of the morning, until they were on the point of dropping from exhaustion. During the late afternoon they'd been joined by staff nurses and sisters, equally as exhausted as themselves, who'd escaped from the clearing stations – now behind enemy lines – and whose experiences had at first sent shivers of terror running through them until tiredness had overcome the fear.

It was almost dawn before the hospital was declared totally unable to take any further casualties and the Chief Medical Officer sent orders that subsequent convoys were to be shipped straight across the Channel.

'I can hardly put one foot in front of the other I'm so tired,' Mae sighed as they finally made their way to their billet.

'I feel awful. I'm filthy, I'm sure I've picked up some greybacks and my head is throbbing,' Alice said, pulling her grubby short veil off in a weary gesture of exasperation.

'We'll have to share our billet and beds too. Those poor nurses who escaped have nowhere to go, they had to leave everything behind,' Mae reminded her.

'It must have been terrifying. I do feel so sorry for them but all I want to do is sleep,' Lizzie yawned.

'Look, it's dawn!' Mae exclaimed and they stopped and stood gazing at the sky, which was gradually lightening from the east. Slowly the first fingers of light crept over the horizon and spread in ribbons of gold across the pale misty-blue and pink-tinged sky, giving promise of a beautiful spring morning after a night filled with darkness, pain and death.

Lizzie watched the dawn with mixed emotions. Thankfulness that the long, exhausting and traumatic night was over. Relief that although for days to come they would have to work long hours, there would be no more convoys of wounded brought to the hospital. The gnawing fear and anxiety for Eddie's safety and the knowledge that in the east where the sun was now rising was the battle line. Suddenly she shivered; it wasn't all that far away, she realised, and no one knew if that line could be held.

Exhausted though she was, Mae could still marvel at the

sunrise. 'It's beautiful and it makes you feel that somewhere there's peace, that somewhere the dawn is breaking on a place where there's no suffering and death. Let's hope it's an omen – a good omen,' she said quietly.

'And judging by what we've seen and heard we desperately need a good omen and some good luck,' Alice added as they resumed picking their way carefully between the stretchers laid in rows across the compound, which was now bathed in glorious sunlight.

That sunlight fell on Pip, warming the back of his neck as he lay at the top of a small hill overlooking the village of Cantigny on the German front line, the field telephone on the ground beside him. Below him to the south of the village he could see the American front line and he smiled grimly. His countrymen were about to go into action for the first time as a wholly American unit. They were full of enthusiasm, eager at last to have a pop at the Hun, despite the fact that their old Springfield rifles and Hotchkiss machine guns had been virtually worn out in training. He'd been both astounded and somewhat appalled when he'd learned that the United States Army was short of weapons, for they hadn't been engaged in conflict since the Spanish-American War twenty years ago and before that the Civil War over fifty years ago – and what weapons they did have were old-fashioned compared to those of the French, British and Germans. It hadn't even been considered worthwhile to ship the four hundred or so field guns across the Atlantic, they were so antiquated, and until new artillery pieces and munitions could be manufactured in America their weaponry had to be supplied by the British and the French. But none of that mattered to them today, he thought. They had a saying: 'Heaven, Hell or Hoboken by Christmas'. He wondered how many of them would still believe that by the end of today.

As he scanned the lines of eager but restless troops through his binoculars, he reflected that his job on this occasion was important for he had been ordered to observe the assault and to report the troop movements to the French gun batteries supporting the American infantry who were to attack and hold the village, an objective which required artillery support. For once he wouldn't be in the thick of it, he thought thankfully. So far he'd been lucky; he'd come through with only cuts and bruises, although at Passchendaele a machine-gun bullet, mercifully deflected by his helmet, had grazed his forehead and he'd suffered a mild concussion.

He shifted his position and then shuddered, a purely reflex reaction now, as the German field artillery opened up; he reached for the field telephone to instruct the French gunnery officer. He watched all afternoon as the 'Doughboys' attacked, supported by the French guns, feeling alternately anxious and then proud, as although he saw many of them fall, they kept on advancing doggedly. For men and boys going into battle for the first time and on foreign soil they were proving their mettle.

Eventually, as the sun began to sink lower in the sky, he realised that they'd achieved their objective; the Kaiser's troops were falling back from the now half-demolished village and he picked up the field telephone and yelled, '*Cessez le feu! Cessez le feu!*'

In the silence that followed he watched the stretcher-bearers and medical orderlies as they worked taking the casualties to waiting ambulances, remembering the years he'd spent in the

Field Ambulance Service; inevitably his thoughts turned to Mae. They'd all had a hard time of it since 21 March; he knew of the British retreat and its terrible cost and he'd wondered how they had all coped. Had Eddie survived? He hoped he had for he liked Eddie and all being well he'd become family. But at least now more American troops were on their way, he reflected as he prepared to leave his vantage point. By 1 May there would be over four hundred thousand of them and with all their fresh vigour and enthusiasm they would surely bolster the morale of the battle-weary British Tommies and French *poilus*, for the German advance appeared to have stalled. Had they reached a turning point? He prayed that they had.

Chapter Thirty-Three

MAGGIE WAS FRANTIC with worry. She'd heard nothing from any of the girls for weeks now. The last letter she'd had from Alice had informed her that Eddie had been sent back to his battalion as an offensive was imminent but that they'd patched up their quarrel before he'd gone. That at least was a relief, she'd told Billy, but the news that Eddie would once again be in the front line was something she had never wished to hear. And now the newspaper headlines added to her fears.

Billy tried to calm her although he too was very concerned. 'You know what they're like, Maggie, luv. They often exaggerate things.'

Maggie shook her head. 'I don't think they'd be allowed to print stuff like that if it wasn't true. "British Retreat, Terrible Casualties, Germans Advance on Channel Ports". It must be very bad, Billy. And what about Field Marshal Haig's orders? They printed them in all the newspapers too. Oh, God knows what's happening over there! We don't know if they are alive, dead or taken prisoner!' Her voice broke in a sob and Billy put his arm around her.

'All we can do is hope, Maggie. We'll find out for certain soon, I'm sure of it. The girls are probably so busy with the wounded that there's been no time to write. I know from experience what the hospitals are like, how hard all those girls work. One of them will send word soon, luv.'

Maggie raised an anxious, tear-blotched face. 'And Eddie?'

Billy sighed. 'We'll just have to have faith, luv, that he's not been wounded or captured. Now, dry your eyes and I'll make us a cup of tea.'

Maggie dabbed at her eyes with the corner of her apron. At least she had him to share her worries with now. He was a comfort; over these last tense weeks when each day her fears had increased he'd given her strength.

'Oh, the world is a terrible place now, Billy. There doesn't seem to be any *brightness* in it at all.'

'It's hard to find any, luv, I'll give you that,' Billy agreed as he handed her the cup of tea.

'This terrible news and everything costing so much more than it did last year and now we've got to contend with rationing because things have to come in by sea and the convoys have been suffering such heavy losses. Coal is so expensive and scarce that we'll all freeze this winter and what's this new Act of Parliament Agnes was talking about? It's got her worried sick.'

Billy looked sombre. 'It's a law that means men up to the age of fifty-one can now be conscripted into the Army.'

Maggie was horrified. '*Fifty-one!* They'll make men of that age go and fight?'

'Things are pretty desperate, Maggie. The losses have been catastrophic. They wouldn't pass such a law unless it was absolutely necessary.'

'But . . . but that will include you and Bertie Mercer. No wonder Agnes is worried.'

Billy shook his head. 'Not me, Maggie, I'm no use to them with only one arm, but Bertie . . . yes.'

'Oh, dear God, hasn't Agnes suffered enough? One lad killed, the other losing his leg and now . . .'

'It might not come to that, Maggie. It takes time to conscript and train men and by then . . . who knows? The Yanks are coming over now in their thousands; there always seem to be troop ships arriving at the Pier Head. They'll surely make a difference.'

'They haven't done up to now, Billy!' Maggie retorted. 'They haven't been able to stop the Hun advancing almost to the Channel ports.'

'Give them time, luv, and don't forget they are fresh, they haven't been fighting for four years like our lads. Bertie might not be called on to fight.'

'I hope he isn't, for poor Agnes's sake. I thought things were really bad with all the shortages and so many girls and women doing war work, but when you hear things like that it sort of puts everything into perspective.'

'It does, luv, but don't go making yourself ill with worry. We'll hear from the girls soon, I'm sure, and then we'll have more of an idea just how things stand.'

'I hope you're right, Billy, I really do,' Maggie replied, thinking that she should try to make an effort not to worry about what were trivial things. They had a roof over their heads, food on the table and money in their pockets even if it didn't seem to go as far these days. And Billy would not be called on to fight again. She should be thankful for all those things. She would just feel much better if she knew that the girls and Eddie were safe.

By the middle of May the situation at No. 24 General Camp Hospital had eased and the girls were once again allowed time off duty – although as Alice commented tartly, that time wouldn't exactly be 'free'. It would have to be spent in catching up on all the things that had been neglected. 'Like writing proper letters to Mam and Jimmy, not just "Don't worry we're all still safe and well" on the back of a postcard.'

'I was delighted to receive just those few words from Eddie,' Lizzie replied, remembering how she'd burst into tears of pure relief when she'd finally heard from him when the remaining men of the 89th Brigade had been moved back to St Lawrence Camp at Brandhoek, as there were only 27 officers and 750 men fit for duty from the three Pals Battalions. Although there had been fierce fighting, the German advances had stalled. Haig's orders had been carried out to the letter. 'I won't mind catching up, it will be quite pleasant just to sit and write letters or do some mending,' she added.

Mae nodded her silent agreement. She'd had a short note from Pip too, saying he was well and now with the 137th US Infantry at Woincourt where he was training the new arrivals.

'I think we all deserve a bit of a treat, especially after the last awful weeks,' Alice announced firmly. 'Why don't we go and visit Monsieur Clari? We haven't been for months and at least his coffee is better than the tea we get here.'

Mae brightened up. 'We can tell him all our news and I'll have something more interesting to tell Pip when I write, other than what often seems like a list of complaints. And it is a beautiful sunny afternoon.'

Lizzie looked doubtful. 'We really *should* write home and give them a full account of things. They must all have been terribly worried.'

'We can do that this evening, after we've finished our ward duties. Come on, Lizzie, we'll take a walk along the waterfront too. We've not been outside this hospital for nearly a month now,' Alice urged, beginning to feel the stirrings of something she'd not felt for weeks: hope. The enemy wasn't advancing – in fact in places they were even falling back – Jimmy was safely at home, both Eddie and Pip were out of the front line and Mam *did* know that they weren't in any danger.

Lizzie was persuaded and they all did enjoy the afternoon. They were greeted with cries of delight at the Café Arc-en-ciel, coffee and even pastries were brought and in French and English news was exchanged. Then Monsieur Clari raised his arms to heaven and invoked what they assumed was a blessing that Eddie and Pip had survived, followed by the rousing cry: '*Vive la France! Vive la Grande Bretagne! Vive l'Amérique!*' after which they'd all cheered and laughed.

As they'd walked along the harbour front in the sunlight and with a pleasantly warm breeze wafting in from the sea, Mae remarked that she had thoroughly enjoyed herself and would now be able to pass on to Pip Monsieur Clari's regards.

'I'll write and tell Eddie too although I don't think I'll mention anything about the pastries. That wouldn't be very kind, not when he's on field rations,' Lizzie joked.

'What we get isn't very much better. The pastry was a real treat. I told you we'd enjoy our time off more coming out,' Alice laughed. 'Sometimes a change is better than a rest,' she added as they headed back, thinking that perhaps one day life might become brighter.

It was with a profound sense of relief that Eddie learned that they were being taken out of the line, for they'd suffered heavy casualties.

'Do we know where we're going, sir, and for how long?' he asked Captain Pitman.

The young officer smiled. 'As you are all so experienced now, you are going to help train the newly arrived men of the American infantry in the best ways to defeat the Hun. You're going to Woincourt where they're stationed. As for how long you'll be there – I don't know.'

This was met with a murmur of both relief and interest.

'What about you, sir? Are you coming with us?' Eddie asked. He'd come to like and respect the young man, who'd proved to be both courageous and fair.

'I'm afraid not, Private McEvoy. I'm being transferred. I haven't heard where to yet.'

'That's a shame, sir,' Corporal Wynne piped up, and the others nodded their agreement.

Captain Pitman looked a little embarrassed. 'I understand that you will be taking your orders from an American officer, and I also understand that facilities and rations are far better than we are used to, so in that respect I'm sorry I'm not coming with you. Now, I'll leave you to organise your kit.'

When he'd gone there was a lot of discussion about how

relieved they were to be out of the front line, just what kind of facilities and rations they could expect and how they would get on with the 'Doughboys', as they were known. Eddie thought of Pip, wondering where he was, for he wasn't a raw recruit. 'My cousin's engaged to an American lieutenant and he's a really decent bloke. I got to know him through Mae. He came over and joined the Field Ambulance Service in the first year of the war. He was here doing his bit even before I arrived,' he informed Corporal Wynne.

'Maybe you'll get to see him again.'

Eddie shrugged. 'I hope so but I doubt it. As soon as America declared war he joined their Army. He was at Passchendaele but I don't know where he is now although probably our Mae does – that's my cousin.'

'Well, I for one am looking forward to having a decent billet and by the sounds of it something better than bully beef and dry bread,' Corporal Wynne said, winking at Eddie who grinned back. They all felt much more cheerful now.

Pip scanned the lines of men who marched into the camp looking weary, battle-scarred and decidedly unkempt. He'd been told they were all that was left of three British battalions, and having experienced the hardships, terrors and dangers of the trenches and Cantigny he knew what they'd been through. At least here they would be away from all that, he thought. They would have decent food, washing facilities and a dry billet with a bunk to sleep in. It went without saying that there would be comforts too. Chocolate, gum, cigarettes, magazines: things they'd not had for months. They were all very experienced and would hopefully pass on that know-how to the newly arrived American boys.

After being addressed by the commander they were ordered to 'fall out' and they were then surrounded by American soldiers all eager to hear their tales of battles hard fought and won or lost. All the weary Tommies were interested in was getting a meal, a smoke and a rest, but they were delighted when cigarettes, chewing gum, chocolate and Hershey Bars were pressed on them.

Pip smiled as he watched a group of young, fresh-faced Doughboys escorting three bemused-looking Tommies towards a row of long wooden huts, which would be their billets. Then he peered at the group more closely and began to walk quickly towards them. 'Eddie! Private Eddie McEvoy!' he shouted.

Eddie turned towards him, confusion, then astonishment, amazement and finally relief and happy amusement registering in his eyes. 'Pip! Pip! My God! It's really you!'

Regardless of the grins of the other men, Pip grasped Eddie heartily by the shoulder and vigorously shook his hand.

'Shouldn't I salute you or something?' Eddie asked when they'd both stopped laughing at this totally unexpected meeting.

'We'll dispense with the formalities for now. Let's get you settled in, and then we'll have a great catch-up.'

Eddie nodded. He hadn't expected to see Pip Middlehurst again, not for a long time. 'Wait until Mae and our Alice know that I'm stationed here with you.'

'That should make them both very happy and relieved too,' Pip replied.

'I have to say I'm rather glad about it myself, Pip. From what we've heard, to start with your lot certainly get better food.'

Pip laughed. 'It's a lot better here than in the trenches, Eddie, I can tell you.'

'Then I just hope they'll leave us both here for the duration,' Eddie answered, drawing deeply on the cigarette Pip lit for him. It was the first he'd had in days and he recognised the tortoiseshell case Mae had bought for Pip at Christmas two years ago. He remembered that somewhere at the bottom of his kitbag was the carved Vesta case Lizzie had given him. He hadn't dared use it since he'd been sent back to the front: it was too precious to him to risk losing it. He might actually get to use it again now, he mused.

Chapter Thirty-Four

L IFE HAD TAKEN on a sort of pattern over the years, Mae thought as she slowly sipped her coffee in the Café Arc-en-ciel one afternoon in late October. A pattern formed by the ebb and flow of the tide of war. Periods of chaotic, frantic work as the wounded had flooded in after the Somme, the Ypres Salient, Arras and Lys, followed by calmer, steadier periods of work when the casualties had not been so overwhelming. A pattern too to the periods of gnawing anxiety and fear for Pip's safety. Verdun, Passchendaele, Cantigny, and weeks of relief when he'd been in Boulogne and then knowing he'd been safely at Woincourt and that Eddie was there too.

She glanced out of the window at the banks of low iron-grey clouds that were being driven across the sky by the strong wind – the first of the autumn gales heralding the approach of winter – and felt the knot of fear and worry grow in her chest. Eddie was still there, Lizzie received fairly regular letters from him, but Pip had left with the now trained 137th Infantry.

At first he'd written that what they lacked in experience they made up for with an enthusiasm which bordered on a reckless disregard for their lives, and she knew that many had paid dearly for it. The American hospitals were now as overcrowded as theirs.

Throughout July, August and September American troops had arrived in their hundreds of thousands and they were fresh, well armed and equipped now, for the mighty US munitions industry was working at full production, and they'd advanced rapidly. They had turned the tide of war. Freed now from the trench warfare which had proved so futile, this 'war of movement', as it was being called, had seen the Kaiser's exhausted, battle-weary troops – some of whom on being taken prisoner were found to be as young as fourteen – driven back at Cambrai and pursued through L'Épinette and Le Cateau. Then the Hindenburg Line had been breached in the Bony region and the Allies had pressed onwards deep into Belgium. The war news was good but she'd had no word from Pip for over six weeks.

The knot seemed to expand and became a pain and the coffee now tasted as bitter as gall.

'You have not the ... *lettre*, no ... *billet*, Mademoiselle Mae?'

She looked up to find Monsieur Clari standing beside her, holding a small glass of Calvados. She shook her head, feeling the tears prick her eyes as she twisted her engagement ring nervously round on her finger.

He placed the glass on the table in front of her. '*Boisson*. Drink!'

She took a sip and murmured, '*Merci*,' and then she felt his hand on her shoulder.

'*Courage, ma petite! Courage!*'

She nodded as she took another sip, remembering how another kind Frenchman had given both her and Pip a glass of Calvados on the day America had declared war.

She finished the brandy and with a huge effort pulled herself together. She could not break down now and she would have to get back soon. Their time off was once again being strictly limited, for in the last weeks another enemy had emerged: one that was proving as deadly as any shell or bullet. It attacked both the fit and wounded and did not discriminate between Allied soldiers and civilians and those of Germany, Austria, Hungary or Bulgaria: a virulent form of influenza called 'Spanish flu'. It was claiming more lives than all the battles had done and there seemed to be nothing that could be done to help those affected. They either recovered or they died – and they were dying in their hundreds by the day.

She stood up and bade a fond farewell to Monsieur Clari, who escorted her to the door and stood, shaking his head sadly as he watched her bend her head against the wind and walk up the Rue Nationale.

As always, when she returned she hoped against hope that there would be a letter or a note but Lizzie shook her head before she even had time to speak.

'Don't give up, Mae. Things must be chaotic for them, they are moving so quickly now. They're not stuck in trenches with all the back-up of supply lines. You know he'll get word to you as soon as he can.'

'But what if . . . he's been badly wounded and is lying in some American hospital unable to speak or has gone down with this flu?'

'They'd have got word to you, Mae. You know he insisted on putting you as his next of kin, as well as his parents,' Lizzie reminded her, her heart going out to her friend. It was the waiting, the not knowing that was so hard to bear.

'Have there been any more cases this afternoon, Lizzie?' Mae asked dejectedly, taking off her cape.

'About a dozen and there have been another three deaths. Oh, it's so hard to bear, Mae. They've come through so much and now the Hun is retreating and they go down with this . . . this plague! I wish there was more we could do for them.'

Mae nodded as she tied on a clean apron.

'I did hear of what is being called a remedy of sorts although I can't see how it will work when nothing else does. One of the lads on ward six who so far hasn't succumbed says he puts black pepper in his tea.'

'Pepper?'

Lizzie nodded. 'I know, it sounds crazy to me but he swears by it. Might be worth a try though. We're just as vulnerable.'

'The tea already tastes bad enough!'

'Then it can't get much worse, Mae, can it? We should give it a try.'

Mae managed a grim smile as she left to resume her ward duties.

When she came off duty it was to find that Alice wasn't well. She was sitting on the edge of her bed and looked flushed and feverish.

'I feel terrible, Mae. My throat is sore, my head is thumping, I'm aching all over and I feel hot and yet shivery.'

Instantly Mae was alarmed. 'Get into that bed and I'll take your temperature,' she instructed. Meekly Alice did as she was told, praying it was just a heavy cold and not the deadly flu.

Mae was even more alarmed when she realised her cousin's temperature was 105 degrees. She passed the thermometer to Lizzie and they looked at each other in horror. Alice almost certainly had the virus.

'I'll go and inform Sister,' Lizzie whispered and Mae nodded. She bent over Alice, tucking the grey blankets tightly around her. 'I think I've still got some aspirin, Alice. It might help ease your headache.'

Alice tried to nod but the effort caused her to groan.

Mae found the aspirins and got a cup of water and helped Alice to take them but she knew they would have little or no effect.

Sister Harper arrived with Lizzie, both looking very concerned.

'How is she, Nurse Strickland? I hear she has a raging temperature.'

'She's got all the symptoms, Sister. I've given her two aspirins but . . .'

Sister Harper nodded grimly. There didn't seem to be any medication that had any effect. 'All you can do is try and get her temperature down, get her to take plenty of fluids and . . . and hope.'

'Sister, I'll stay up with her,' Mae said.

'We'll take it in turns, Mae,' Lizzie added.

Sister Harper replied, 'I think I can spare you tomorrow morning, Nurse Strickland, but not you too, Nurse Lawson. Maybe for a couple of hours tomorrow afternoon.'

'Thank you, Sister,' Mae replied, praying that Alice wouldn't be worse by then.

As the night wore on Alice's condition did become worse. Despite the fact that Mae and Lizzie sponged her down repeatedly her temperature remained dangerously high. She became delirious, not knowing who they were or where she was but calling repeatedly for her mam and then crying out, 'Don't be afraid, Jimmy! I'm here! I'm here!'

'Oh, God, Lizzie, what can we do?' Mae begged frantically. 'She can't die! She *can't*! Not now!'

'There isn't anything more we can do, Mae,' Lizzie replied, on the verge of tears herself. They continued to sponge Alice down.

At two o'clock Sister Harper appeared. 'Is there any change?'

'She's delirious, Sister. We're at our wits' end,' Lizzie fretted.

Sister bent over Alice, placing a hand on her forehead. 'Still burning up with fever, but at least there isn't any sign that it's affecting her chest and she's young and reasonably fit.' She straightened up, her eyes full of compassion. She prayed young Alice McEvoy would recover; she was a good nurse, even though she was so young, and she liked her and knew how close these girls were. 'You're excused duties, Nurse Strickland, until . . . until further notice.'

Or until poor Alice dies, Lizzie thought in desperation.

By morning Alice's condition didn't seem to have worsened although it hadn't improved, Mae thought. She was exhausted from lack of sleep and worry but throughout those long hours she'd held Alice's hand. 'Alice, please, please don't give up! You can't give up, Alice, Jimmy's waiting for you and he loves you so much. You promised him you'd look after him and he just wants you to come home to him. Don't give up, Alice!' she'd repeated over and over just in case her cousin could hear her but she wasn't convinced that she could.

When Lizzie came off duty she brought Mae a cup of tea and a sandwich. 'Get some rest, Mae. I'll sit with her now. You'll make yourself ill if you go on like this,' she urged.

'She hasn't improved, Lizzie,' Mae told her friend.

'It's too soon to expect any change but at least she hasn't deteriorated and it hasn't turned to pneumonia, thank God. Get some rest. I've got two hours off, then I've got to go back on duty.' Lizzie didn't tell her that she really couldn't be spared for there had been more cases overnight. In fact, now in ward seven there wasn't a single man who didn't have this flu and Sister was seriously concerned for her nursing staff.

Mae curled up on her bunk, cold and trembling with fatigue, but she realised that since Alice had taken ill she hadn't thought about Pip. Before her eyes closed she prayed that wherever he was, he hadn't succumbed to this terrible disease.

By the following morning it was clear that Alice was over the worst. Her temperature was still high but she was no longer delirious and seemed to be sleeping normally – although her breathing was shallow, Mae thought as she replaced the thermometer in its holder. Sister Harper had paid regular visits to check on both Alice and herself and had informed her, with evident relief in her voice, that for weeks now two American doctors at the No. 5 Base Hospital in Boulogne (which had formerly been the casino), had been studying the virus day and night in a laboratory and had finally produced what everyone hoped was an emergency vaccine. It had been hastily tested and they'd had some success and now all hospital personnel were to be vaccinated.

'Just a pity we didn't have it before Nurse McEvoy went down with it,' she finished, 'although it looks as if she will pull through.'

'I'll stay with her, Sister, if that's all right, just in case . . .' Mae sincerely hoped Alice would not have a relapse.

Sister Harper had agreed and left and Mae had sat beside her cousin, dozing intermittently until Lizzie again brought her tea.

'Have you heard, Mae, we're all to be vaccinated. Thank God they've finally found *something* that might help. Is she sleeping normally?'

Mae nodded, gratefully sipping the tea, oblivious now to its taste. 'Her temperature was almost back to normal last time I took it. Oh, Lizzie, I can't tell you how relieved I am. I don't think any of us could have stood it if anything had happened to her. She's worked so hard, she's been so brave and . . . she's only eighteen.'

'She'll be all right now, Mae, and there's more good news. Lille has been captured, the casino in town is covered in flags, Mons will be next, then Liège and that's not far from the border with Germany itself. The end can't be far off now, everyone is hoping it will be all over by next week.'

Mae smiled tiredly. 'And thank God Alice will be able to celebrate with us.'

* * *

Alice was still very weak when she finally got up three days later.

'I feel a bit light-headed, sort of . . . dizzy,' she said to Mae as she sat on the edge of her bed.

'You're bound to, you've been very ill. We were terrified you would die, Alice.'

Alice was chastened. 'Was I really that bad?'

'You were, believe me,' Lizzie replied grimly. 'We've lost count of the poor lads who haven't recovered. You were very, very lucky, Alice.'

'What if I . . . I get it again?' Alice asked timidly. Her apparent brush with death had made her feel very apprehensive of her future.

'You won't. You've probably developed an immunity to it now and besides, we've all been vaccinated. When you're stronger, you can be vaccinated too. Now, all you've got to do is rest and get your strength back,' Lizzie said firmly, 'so I'm going over to the mess tent to see what they can rustle up in the way of beef tea or *bouillon*, as Monsieur Clari calls it.'

Alice pulled a face although she knew Lizzie was only thinking of her welfare.

'And while you've been ill the news has been good. Everyone is saying the war will be over in a few days now,' Mae informed her.

'Really? Oh, Mae, I can't believe that after all this time the end is actually in sight. Have you heard from Pip?'

Mae's expression changed; all the joy of Alice's recovery drained away. 'No, still nothing.'

Alice took her hand. 'He'll come back, Mae. I know he will.'

Mae managed to nod but a terrible feeling of dread hung

over her. An awful sense of despair that she would never see him again. That they would never walk together under the lilac trees in the Boston Public Garden.

Chapter Thirty-Five

———•——•——

A T THE ELEVENTH HOUR of the eleventh day of the eleventh month of 1918 the guns fell silent. The Armistice was signed and the war was over. After four long years of bitter fighting and enormous loss of life it was at an end. The news was received in Boulogne with rapture. The Allied flags from the casino were taken down and paraded through the streets of the town by jubilant soldiers, medical personnel and civilians, Monsieur Claude Clari amongst them. A large Tricolour now adorned the entrance of the Café Arc-en-ciel.

The atmosphere in No. 24 General Camp Hospital wasn't as exuberant as in many of the wards, only the nursing staff were in a state to realise that it was all over. Their patients were unconscious or delirious.

Lizzie brought the news to Alice, who was still unfit for duty although feeling much better.

'It's over, Alice! The war's over! Sister Harper told us a few minutes ago and I came straight to tell you.'

Alice threw her arms around her. 'Oh, Lizzie! We can go home! We can all go home! I can go home to Jimmy and Mam and Billy. Eddie won't have to risk his life again and you can get married. We'll both get married!'

Lizzie hugged her but her happiness was tempered with sadness. 'We'll all go home – eventually, Alice, but I know many people are wondering was any of it worth it? So many dead, so many young lives blighted forever, so much . . . destruction. Towns, villages and hamlets in ruins, farmland turned into a wasteland of mud and shell craters, ships sunk and their crews lost, and now thousands dying of flu. And Mae . . .'

Alice's euphoric mood disappeared at Lizzie's words. In her initial excitement she had forgotten that no one knew if Pip Middlehurst was alive or dead. 'Oh, Lizzie, poor Mae! Where is she? Does she know about the Armistice?'

Lizzie nodded. 'She was with the rest of us but she's stayed on the ward.'

Without uttering another word Alice wrapped her cape around her thin shoulders and, followed by Lizzie, went in search of her cousin.

As they both entered ward six Sister Harper looked up from her tiny work station. 'Nurse McEvoy, you should be resting, you are far from well yet,' she admonished her.

'Where is she, Sister, please? She'll be so . . . upset. She hasn't heard anything from him.'

'Attending to a young private who thankfully seems to be recovering. But don't stay too long. Although the war is officially ended, our work here isn't. I'll need every one of my nurses as this epidemic is far from over and I've just received word that there is a convoy of sick and wounded men on its way.

Three hundred stretcher cases and they are expected this afternoon.'

Alice found Mae settling the young lad back against the pillows of a bed she had just changed. He looked far from well, Alice thought, but at least he wasn't going to die. 'Let me help you, Mae,' she offered.

'I . . . I didn't know what else to do, Alice. I . . . had to keep on working, I can't feel . . .' She broke down and Alice put her arms around her.

'Oh, Mae, don't give up. Things will get more organised now. If he's been wounded or is ill you'll soon hear – and now that the fighting has stopped you'll be able to travel to see him.'

'But what if . . . if he's . . . dead, Alice?' Mae sobbed. Now that she'd uttered the word that had haunted her for weeks it was as if the floodgates had been opened.

'Don't say that! Don't even *think* it! You would have been notified, you know you would,' Alice said emphatically. 'Don't give up on him, Mae,' she begged.

Sister Harper had been watching closely and now she quickly took the situation in hand. 'Nurse McEvoy, take Nurse Strickland back to your billet and both of you get a cup of tea and calm yourselves,' she instructed. 'This has been a very emotional and upsetting morning for everyone but I will need you, Nurse Strickland, to help with the convoy when it arrives.'

Her words had the effect she intended on both Mae and Alice, and as they went across to the mess tent Mae became calmer. 'She's right, Alice. It *is* a very emotional day and not everyone can celebrate.'

Alice nodded her agreement, thankful that at least Mae would have little time to dwell on the situation when the convoy arrived.

The line of ambulances arrived just after two o'clock with only six fit, able-bodied officers and six enlisted men accompanying it. The men on the stretchers were either suffering from the flu virus or had been wounded in the previous days. The medical officers and nursing staff and orderlies were waiting and the job of assessing the patients began.

'What regiment are you from?' Lizzie asked a young man with a bullet wound in his thigh as she removed the field dressing that covered it.

'Ninety-first Division, ma'am, and I sure am glad it's all over,' he replied quite cheerfully despite obviously being in pain.

Lizzie was surprised. 'You're American!'

'I sure am, ma'am, but there was no room for us at the casino. Besides, they're all out celebrating, painting the town red.'

'Are there many other Americans with you in this convoy?' she asked, her heart beginning to beat rapidly.

'There's an officer and a few men from the one hundred and thirty-seventh. Mostly down with this Spanish flu.'

Lizzie looked quickly around, searching for Mae, but in the press of wounded she couldn't see her. The 137th was Pip's division. 'We'll soon make you more comfortable now, soldier,' she said to him as the orderlies moved him on to the medical officer and she turned to the next patient.

Mae too had just realised that there were American troops

amongst the convoy and hope, then fear and desperation chased each other through her in rapid succession as she'd realised that so many of them were very ill with the flu. She knew she couldn't be spared, she knew she couldn't just leave this patient to go and search for him. She hastily dashed the tears of frustration away with the back of her hand and had bent down to the next stretcher when she felt a hand on her shoulder and she turned.

'I promised you I'd come back, Mae.'

A wave of pure joy enveloped her as she flung her arms around him, oblivious to the dust and dirt that streaked his face and covered his uniform. He was here! He was safe! He wasn't wounded or dying from the virus! 'Oh, Pip! Pip!' she sobbed with relief.

He held her tightly. 'It's over, Mae, at last it's over. We can go home. Soon we can go home.'

She gazed up at him, her eyes swimming with tears. 'I love you so much, Pip, and I thought . . .'

He smiled and gently wiped a tear from her cheek with his finger. 'I'm sorry I couldn't get word to you – there wasn't time. But surely you knew I wouldn't break my promise, Mae? We'll see next Lilac Sunday together, a world away from . . . all this. It's over and we'll never be parted again.'

Mae leaned her forehead against his shoulder as happiness enveloped her. In her short life she'd lost her mother, her father, her childhood friends, she'd feared for Alice's life and for a time she'd thought she'd lost him too, but now the war was over and the future looked so bright. After the years of darkness, death and suffering there was now hope and joy and love. She remembered that beautiful dawn morning last spring. It had indeed been an omen, an omen heralding a new life in a new land.

Maggie and Billy were rather taken aback when early on Monday morning they opened the front door and were confronted by Bertie Mercer, who was waving an edition of the morning paper. 'Look! Look, Maggie! Billy! Mr Lloyd George has announced that the Armistice was signed at five o'clock this morning. The Press Bureau got the information to the newspapers. Fighting will cease on all fronts at eleven o'clock. It's over! The war is over!'

Maggie's initial reaction was of profound relief and she felt tears prick her eyelids. 'Oh, Bertie, that's great news! Thanks for coming to let us know.'

He nodded, handing the paper to Billy. 'Agnes wanted you to know as soon as possible, before it's all over the city. I'll get back to her now, she's still feeling a bit . . . stunned by it all. We'll see you both later on.'

'It's over, Maggie. It's finally over, luv,' Billy said quietly as he scanned the lines of newsprint.

'I thought I'd feel sort of . . . overwhelmed with joy and happiness but all I can feel is relief. Relief that I can stop worrying now, that there won't be one of those damned telegrams arriving with terrible news about Eddie. We'll be able to read a newspaper without feeling sick with apprehension and fear.'

Billy nodded sadly. 'Sure, I'm relieved myself that it's all over and there will be thousands who feel the same, but there will be thousands of homes where there isn't much to celebrate.'

'And poor Agnes's is one of them, and Nelly Mitford's,'

Maggie replied, wondering how they were taking the news. No wonder Agnes was stunned, she thought. Would they too be thinking of the day when the lads had all marched away? Jimmy, Harry, Eddie and Tommy, all of them so young, fit, full of patriotic enthusiasm and pride. Now only Eddie was coming back uninjured, although he had suffered and bore the scars. 'What was it all for, Billy? Was it worth it? *Any* of it?'

Billy knew she was thinking of John Strickland and he remembered too the lads and men he'd served with at Jutland, all of whom had no graves but the sea. 'I suppose there will be those who think it was. We have our homes, our freedom and our way of life, Maggie, but to my mind it was all bought at a terrible price. But at least now those who've been spared will be coming home – Eddie amongst them, and the girls too.'

Maggie brightened at his words. 'Eddie has been so lucky, Billy, and our Alice can go back to her office job. I think she'll have had enough of nursing.'

Billy smiled. 'She did her bit for the war effort. They both did. But I suppose Mae will be going off to Boston.'

'I know that Jimmy will be glad to have our Alice home and I think they've got a future planned together and I'm happy for them.'

'And we may finally get to meet Lizzie,' Billy added, thinking that he would see his son for the first time in years. Eddie was a man now, an impressionable boy no longer, not after what he'd been through, and he was proud of him. At least they had the shared experiences of battle and wounds if nothing else to build a relationship on. 'But they won't be coming home immediately, Maggie, the girls still have patients to attend to.

It will be a while before they can organise the wounded and the troops and get them home.'

'I know, but at least now we can all look to the future with some . . . hope, and we can look forward to a new daughter-in-law. I just hope her parents will be happy with her choice, but as our Alice said; the world is different now – people and their attitudes have changed.'

Billy put his arm around her. 'They have, luv, and the best thing to come out of all the fear, misery and hardship – for me at least – is that I've got my wife, my family and my home back and they're things I hold very dear.'

Maggie smiled up at him. All the long bitter years when she'd struggled on alone were in the past and now they could put the four years of war behind them and build a future together. 'I know, Billy. We've got a lot to be thankful for now.'

It was a month later when they at last had the time to venture into the town. Mae and Alice and Lizzie had been kept busy, but the epidemic, although still claiming many lives, seemed to be losing momentum. Pip had been billeted in Boulogne helping to organise the first stage of repatriation of those American troops now deemed fit to travel, and to Lizzie's delight Eddie had returned to the supply depot to aid Sergeant Walker, for animals and equipment had to be shipped back too.

The Tricolour was still above the door of the café but hanging limply now in the cold, damp December air. The appearance of the little group in the doorway was greeted with a cry of delight from Claude Clari and they were all embraced and kissed in turn, both Pip and Eddie looking a little embarrassed by this typical Gallic greeting and Eddie muttering something to the effect that he didn't hold with being kissed on both cheeks by a chap. Of course Pip had visited the café as soon as he'd come back to the town but it was Eddie's first visit since his return.

'*Champagne!* It . . . you . . . have only *champagne!*' Monsieur declared, still beaming as he disappeared to fetch it.

'We'll be in trouble if we go back tipsy!' Alice laughed as they seated themselves around a table.

'She'll kill us. She's stretching her generosity in letting us all out together as it is,' Lizzie added, smiling at Eddie.

'Still, it is a bit of a special occasion. We've none of us had time to celebrate properly and we haven't been here together since Christmas of nineteen sixteen,' Mae reminded them.

Alice shook her head in disbelief. 'I can't believe it's *that* long ago.'

'And so much has happened to us all in that time,' Pip added, glancing meaningfully at Eddie, who nodded sombrely, both returning in their minds to all the dangers and horrors of battle, the hardships of the trenches and the friends they'd lost.

A silence descended on them all as Alice remembered the day Jimmy had been brought into the hospital and of how ill she'd been last month. They'd both come close to death. Mae thought sadly of her poor da and Harry and Tommy Mitford. Eddie wondered how he would get on with Billy when he finally got home but was resolved to at least give his father the benefit of the doubt. And then Monsieur returned with tall flutes and two bottles and corks popped, champagne fizzed and Monsieur Clari toasted them all. '*Vive la victoire!*'

'And a toast to the future – all our futures!' Pip added. '*Vive l'avenir!*' he added for Monsieur's benefit. 'And to going home,' he added, taking Mae's hand.

She smiled happily. 'And to Lilac Sunday in Boston.'

Author's Note

———◆◆◆———

Although *Liverpool Angels* is a work of fiction, using the events, battles and offensives of World War One has required a degree of accuracy and therefore some historical research, and I am indebted to Graham Maddocks, author of *Liverpool Pals: 17th, 18th, 19th & 20th (Service) Battalions, The King's Liverpool Regiment* and Lyn Macdonald, author of *1915: The Death of Innocence* and *The Roses of No Man's Land*, whose works use the documentation (i.e. correspondence, diary entries and reports) of the soldiers, nurses, doctors, medics and drivers who served throughout that conflict and give us such an accurate insight into the conditions endured throughout those four terrible and tragic years. For any mistakes I sincerely apologise.

Lyn Andrews
Isle of Man

Q&A with Lyn Andrews

WARNING: SPOILERS
If you don't want to find out what happens to some of the characters in the novel, don't read this interview before you've read the novel!

Q: How tough was it to write about the Great War, with its shocking casualty rate and terrible conditions at the Front? How do you as a writer keep your emotional distance from the dark subjects you're writing about?

A: Very hard indeed for although this is a work of fiction I had to do a great deal of research, particularly appertaining to Liverpool during these years and how the very real events of the war affected its citizens. The casualties amongst the four Battalions of the 'Liverpool Pals' were enormous, as was the suffering of both soldiers, medical personnel and the families left at home and I'm not ashamed to admit that there were times when writing when I could barely see for tears at the sheer waste, horror and pity of it all. Then I'd have to get up and have a cup of tea to calm myself down but I don't think you can put your characters through such traumas without experiencing some of their emotions yourself.

Q: Early in the novel Beth dies of childbed fever. How common was this in the early 20th century, and what were the different ways the motherless children were dealt with?

A: Standards of hygiene were not very good in the early 20th century and nearly all women had their babies at home, sometimes in far from ideal conditions, so sadly the mortality rates for both mother and baby were high. If the child survived and if at all possible it was usually cared for and brought up by the family – as Mae was – but if this was just not feasible then there was no other option but an orphanage or the workhouse.

Q: It's devastating for the family when Billy does a runner. Did you come across real-life examples of this happening when you did your research? Would you have accepted Billy back, as Maggie does, if he'd been your husband?

A: This idea was actually based on the experience of a neighbour of my mother's whose husband just upped and disappeared one day with no explanation at all and, unlike Billy, he was never seen again – leaving the poor woman with three children. It was assumed he'd just boarded a ship at the docks and sailed away to freedom, they didn't bother with such formalities as passports in those days. After the mandatory seven years he was declared dead and she married his brother, which was even more of a disaster as he turned out to be a wife beater. My redoubtable mother stood up to him to protect her on many occasions – no one got the better of my mother! If I'd been married to Billy McEvoy I don't really think I would have accepted him back. I'd always wonder if he really had changed and after spending years bringing up a family and being independent I wouldn't want to give that up. But maybe that's too modern a view, Maggie lived in the early 1900s and values, social attitudes and expectations were different then.

Q: It's fascinating to see Maggie setting up her own successful business at a time when female suffrage was still just a dream. What examples have you found of women entrepreneurs at this time?

A: There were many instances of women founding their own little businesses during these years, but they did it for different reasons to women entrepreneurs of today. It was usually out of the sheer necessity to keep a roof over their heads and earn a living to support themselves and their families, for there was no Welfare State to look after widows or deserted wives. It was also usually something they could run from home – it was very much looked down on for married women to go 'out' to work – and there are instances of women who turned their front rooms into little cafés serving homemade pies to workmen, making and selling toffee and sweets, taking in laundry, becoming seamstresses and, like Maggie, moneylending. In fact a great aunt of my husband – Aunt Babsey – was a moneylender. I met her once and she was a great character, very capable – like Maggie!

Q: We see the siblings and cousins growing up through the early part of the novel. You are a mother of triplets – have you used some of their behaviour as children to help bring your young characters to life? Tell us what it was like with so many children of the same age growing up together!

A: I think all mothers of small children will identify with Maggie's brood's behaviour at times and having triplets certainly gave me plenty of experience. Life could be chaotic, especially when they were toddlers – you had to have eyes in the back of your head! The boys were real 'climbers' and into everything and of course my little girl had to learn to stand up for herself in the rough and tumble and give as good as she got. Life was never dull but often exhausting.

Q: One of the most evocative scenes in the novel is when Liverpool celebrates its 700th anniversary as a city, with river floats, public events and fireworks. Can you tell us about some of the activities when the city celebrated its 800th anniversary earlier this century?

A: When Liverpool celebrated its 800th anniversary in 2007 the events rather eclipsed those of 1907. There were concerts, exhibitions, parties, Magical Mystery Tours linked to the Beatles and Magical History Tours at the Maritime Museum and other venues. The new Museum of Slavery was opened and on St George's Day (23 April) our magnificent St George's Hall was re-opened after a £23 million refurbishment. In June the Festival of Tall Ships and Naval Vessels was held on the river, in August there was the Mathew Street Music Festival and on Liverpool Day (28 August) one of the world's largest firework displays. In September we had the official opening of the River Mersey Cruise Liner Facility with the QE2 sailing in for her last visit before she ended her forty years of service with Cunard, a ship that I have fond memories of, having sailed on her many times as a guest lecturer. And then of course the 2007 events merged with those of 2008, when Liverpool became the European Capital of Culture and the party went on!

Q: When war is declared, many of the young men are so keen to do their bit that they lie about their age to get into the army. Did your research show you how many boys did this, and how many under-age soldiers were killed?

A: In the early days of the war the country was gripped by a patriotic fever and official records show that 250,000 boys under eighteen enlisted, determined not to miss out on the adventure because of their age. The youngest of which, a certain Sidney Lewis, was only thirteen and they did send him home when they found out. My father-in-law's youngest brother was just sixteen when he was killed.

I'm not sure if there are any official records of just how many of them were killed but you only have to read the names and ages on the thousands of headstones in the war cemeteries in France and Belgium to realise there were far *too* many, and many were young German boys conscripted in the latter days of the conflict.

Q: Many people are aware that food rationing was a problem for people on the Home Front in the Second World War and afterwards. Was there rationing in the Great War? If so, what impact did it have? Were particular items badly hit?

A: There was rationing in the Great War during the latter years but not on the same scale or for as long as in the Second World War. By 1916–17 the German U-boats were becoming a serious threat to shipping so all items that were imported became scarce. I can remember my grandmother telling me how my grandfather managed to smuggle some meat home (he was in the Navy and served at Jutland) and they had a slap-up meal. She then had to go through it all again in the Second World War, he was on the Arctic convoys in that one. They were tough times.

Q: Mae talks very movingly in Chapter 14 about the fact that she never knew her father. Very sadly, your own father was killed in the Second World War, when you were just a baby. Could you tell us about how that affected your life as you grew up?

A: Losing Joe (as we always refer to him) on D-Day obviously didn't affect me a great deal as a young child, although I was told how, when and why he died and I have photos of him as a handsome young man in uniform – he will always remain that way to me. Growing up, I looked on Frank as my father and I loved my 'Dad' dearly and at that stage in my life I had three grandmothers – talk about spoiled! But as I grew older I always felt that Joe was still with me in some respects. I resemble him, apparently I have his nature, and I think that my creativity comes from him because no one else in the family either writes or paints. He was a talented artist and I have a few of his pictures. In fact for most of the war years he remained in England, engaged in making detailed maps of enemy coastline for all three military services but of course on D-Day everyone had to go. In my spare time I 'dabble' in watercolours, I'm not terribly good and I find it so frustrating when my 'efforts' fail miserably beside his and I wonder would I have been any better as an artist if he had lived? Maybe, maybe not! He was twenty-seven when he was killed – a sacrifice that ensured that my family and I live in peace and freedom. We owe them all a great debt.

Q: It's fascinating to read in the novel about the hospital trains that ran between the Front and the hospitals in France. How did you first hear about them?

A: It was only when I started doing the research for the novel that I found out about the hospital trains as I'd never heard them mentioned before. Unlike the Second World War, the Front Lines in the Great War were close enough for the wounded to be sent back to hospitals in England to be treated. Large but rather slow moving French trains, manned by doctors, medics and nurses, were used to get them from the Field Dressing Stations to the hospitals at the Channel ports, so that those deemed fit to travel on could do so by ferry. Not the best conditions for patients and medical staff but the only way to transport them reasonably quickly.